# A VIEW TO A KILL

Harper pulled wrapping apart under the skylight, and sunlight glinted on a blue-tinged rifle barrel. Steel, not the high-carbon iron of the local foundry, though the design appeared contemporary.

The Algheran time-traveler set the gun to his shoulder and took aim at a window, stroking the front trigger slowly till it clicked on the empty chamber.

Match-rifle accuracy, calibrated loads, half-inch slugs... Perfect for punching watermelon-sized holes in anyone's head.

When Mlart tra'Nornst appeared, Harper would be ready.

By Mike Shupp
*Published by Ballantine Books:*

THE DESTINY MAKERS

*Forthcoming

# Mike Shupp

# Soldier Of Another Fortune

### Book Three of **The Destiny Makers**

A Del Rey Book

BALLANTINE BOOKS • NEW YORK

A Del Rey Book
Published by Ballantine Books

Library of Congress Catalog Card Number: 87-91877

ISBN 0-345-32551-6

Manufactured in the United States of America

First Edition: August 1988

Cover art by David Schleinkofer

For
Dr. James Cargal, Ph. D.

*Now you owe me one, Jim.*

## The First Compact

To end eternal war, it is agreed by the telepaths and normal men that never again shall telepaths establish a separate state and exercise their dominion over men.

This Compact shall be preserved by the thoughts and actions of both human races and witnessed by the ti-Mantha lu Duois.

The penalty for violation, in thought or action, shall be death.


## The Second Compact

To end the Second Eternal War, the Great Compact is reaffirmed by the Teeps and the Normals. It is also agreed by the Teeps and the Normals that never again shall Teeps employ their abilities in the service of national states and thus exercise their dominion over men.

This Compact shall be preserved by the thoughts and actions of both human races and witnessed by the spirit of the tiMantha lu Duois.

The penalty for violation, in thought or action, shall be death.

## Hemmendur's Solution

"We have observed that neither Compact prohibits the employment of the Teeps, in whole or in part, in any role whatsoever, by a single all-encompassing world state. I suggest to you that such a state must ultimately arise. By its nature, it will be everlasting and unopposable.

"I suggest as well that given that inevitability, we attempt ourselves to give birth to that state and shape its growth. If our intentions are worthy, our actions honorable, and our ambitions steadfast, we shall be successful, for we shall gain strong allies.

"Not the least of these will be the Teeps, who are entitled to a role in human affairs, and for whom I propose a most sacred responsibility—which is to ensure that men exercise no dominion over men . . ."

# CHAPTER ONE

"**We'd** go sledding," *Tim Harper said. "Most kids then* had a *sled*—little wood thing, low down, which was just long enough to lie on if you lifted your feet up, with a pair of metal runners. You steered by pushing on a handle at front, and that twisted the runners enough so it would change direction." He raised his hands, using gestures to supplement his deep baritone.

Outside the levcraft, tree-covered hillsides crept across the low window, alternately white, then green as the years advanced. A twilight sky showed through two ceiling panels. In the cabin gloom, his red-brown hair was dark, his green and black uniform almost invisible within the embracing cube chair. A jagged scar showed on his left temple; above it, silver glinted.

The raven-haired woman to his left stirred uneasily in her chair, one hand toying with the strap over her waist as she stared at the front viewscreens. She wore a green blouse and trousers made from stiff blue cloth; her feet were bare. Dimly superimposed on the hills beneath the shuttle was a face: narrow, wan, tight-lipped. The too-large eyes were almond shaped, upward sloping under thin brows; with more light or in a mirror they would show a green color, and the face would be freckle-strewn and high-cheeked.

Overhead, numbers flickered seemingly in midair. At the

top, 45414.002.25000 appeared in brown: a date from centuries in the past, belonging to the cabin she and Harper had left a fraction of a day ago. 47346.001.00000 showed in red: a destination. The blue numbers in between, showing their current position in time, changed too quickly for her to read more than the initial digits. Long Count years, Kylene Waterfall chi'Edgart remembered with a start. They were not measured from the beginning of time.

It was a calendar that had begun four hundred centuries after her birth; she still thought of herself as seventeen, but only legends remained from her world. *A.D. 5000*, she told herself, using dates the man had taught her. *5000, and I've come ninety thousand years more.*

To a "Fifth Era"—the concept was incomprehensible. The fifth portion of human existence in which men built cities.

She had never seen a city.

Kylene's world of A.D. 5000 had been a barbarian one. No records of a global civilization remained; even the cities had vanished. The First Era—Tim Harper's time—was over in Kylene's day; the Second had not yet been born.

Fohima Alghera had been founded in 47,036 L.C. That marked the beginning of the Fifth Era.

The city had been—would be—conquered by the Chelmmysian Alliance in 47,930 L.C. The Algherans she had dwelt with called that date the "true Present." Time travelers, refugees from their city's fall, they could not reach its future and hid from detection in its ancient past, ineffectually trying to postpone or divert its defeat.

She had never seen a war.

Ninety thousand years. Even the numbers were alien.

*We did not count that far in my world.*

*We did not give numbers to our years.*

Her eyes lowered, seeking familiarity. Viewscreens, bright in the unlit cabin; the tinted instrument displays before her; the drably painted shelves and cabinets on the interior walls; the too-warm air, thick with alien odors, ducted from invisible outlets . . . By now this was all commonplace, almost comfortable despite its differences from the world of her birth.

Harper smiled reminiscently, leaning back while displaced chair material plumped the arms and headrest of his seat. The calf of his right leg rested on his left knee; a booted foot swung aimlessly. "Sometimes you'd sit on it and steer with your feet, but lying down, you'd go faster. And you could brake with your feet or steer by dragging a foot. Of course, you got more snow in your face."

He was another captive of the time-traveling Algherans, but he was reconciled to his fate and had joined wholeheartedly in their history-changing "Project." A man who fought for them, who would slay for them. A soldier.

She had never known a soldier before.

An assassin. A killer. A kidnapper.

The man the Algherans feared, even as they used him to save them from their mistakes.

She had hated him once.

*Ninety thousand years,* Kylene thought again. And he was older still. *Ninety-three thousand years.* To bear memories from ages so distant, to recount childhood stories as if from yesterday—it seemed somehow wrong.

"Snow in the area where I grew up would get knee deep at times, but a handbreadth would do. You had to find the right hill—not too steep, not too rocky, with a good long straight stretch to build up speed. Pull your sled to the top, run to get a good start, and belly flop and go sailing . . .

"I remember once, I was ten and visiting someone in the country. They were on a road that was all up and down and must have been two miles—couple of thousand man-heights —off from a state highway, and the county hadn't plowed it yet. They had a spare sled, so . . ."

He exhaled at last. "Like finding heaven." His smile flashed. "Guess that's easy enough for kids."

"We wrapped bark around—" She stopped.

Harper murmured encouragingly. "Go on."

"The dogs would pull us." She stopped again, staring beyond her reflection in the viewscreen. In memory, a small girl on a slab of bark bounced shriekingly down a hillside trail, her face flushed, her fists bloodlessly tight on stout ropes, seesawing them frantically as dogs larger than she ran yapping . . . *I didn't realize I was alone.*

"Yeah?"

"Just . . . the dogs would pull . . . the children . . . on pieces of bark. When it snowed." She sighed softly, unwilling to face the man. "That was all, Tayem."

"Hmm." The redhead toyed with the steering ball of the pillar beside his chair. "Sounds nice, Kylene. Anything else?"

*We were poor!* her thoughts shouted. *We didn't have special toys and the wealth you did, and we never dreamed of it.*

*Machines that fly, that prepare meals, that talk, that show pictures from afar—we thought only wizards had ever had such powers. We were poor and ignorant and barbaric, and we did not know it.* "No, Tayem. It just . . . wasn't very interesting."

"Oh." The big man pursed his lips without argument. "We also had something called *skiing*. That was sliding down a hill with special boards on your feet. *Ice skating*. You wore a type of boot with a runner underneath, and there were *rinks* in some places so you could do that even in the summer. There was a game called *hockey* you played on skates, but I never tried that. And we had snowball fights. There was a big lawn in front of the orphanage, and we'd make up teams and— Did you have those too?"

Kylene was used to his habit of sprinkling his speech with words she did not recognize. She nodded solemnly. "No. We might throw snow, but—"

*It wasn't fair. It wasn't fair. It wasn't fair.*

"We didn't play, Tayem. We didn't have any play. I was alone. I didn't have other children to play with, and nobody else did when they were children. There weren't enough of us. We didn't have any of the things you had, Tayem." She twisted in her seat, pushing away trays of controls and instrument displays so she could pull her knees up. Black plastic from the chair folded over her legs and pushed against her back. She sniffed, foolishly near tears, and bit at a thumbnail for restraint. "There wasn't even anyone else near my age."

Harper mumbled a response, a sound without thought that she ignored. She blinked unhappily, letting her eyes rest on the lockers that covered the nearer wall. Her boots were there, other clothing was there, the flowers Tayem had given her earlier in the day were there. His partner, he called her, but he did not love her. For all his words, she was no more than a passenger.

*Mlart—the man he wants to kill. He thinks about him more than me.*

A giant's hand patted her thin shoulder, then came to rest with a thumb stroking her hair over her clavicle. "Don't get a cramp in there, kid, or it'll take a corkscrew to get you out." His voice was light; his face could not be seen from her vantage, but she sensed from his touch that he was smiling and that he wished to reassure her.

Creases showed across his forehead at such moments; tiny

cracks appeared at the corners of his eyes. Close to him, one could see scattered strands of white in his hair and eyebrows. He was still very strong, he was still fast-moving, but she knew that for an illusion. Tim Harper was thirty-five and already aging. In two decades, he would be deliberate in his motion; in two more, weak. He would die before other men entered maturity.

And no one would fear him then; no one would remember him.

Kylene tipped her head back so it touched his arm. "Tayem?"

The man moved his hand so she could clasp it, then put his other hand on her forehead. "Sure." It was a gesture of trust, the contact baring his mind to her examination despite the metallic mesh—the Teepblind he always wore—on his head. His motions were smooth, unaffected by pain, showing no sign of the wounds he had suffered a season before.

Affection, patience, touches of amusement, unsuspected respect for abilities he lacked himself, even a flattering but easily restrained lust . . . All showed clearly as Tayem caressed her, and none gave her cause for hope. Kylene closed her eyes, deepening her awareness of the coarse hairs on the back of Tayem's hand, the soft and hard places on his too-warm palm, the faint musky smell of his body, the firm muscles of his forearm. She breathed shallowly, trying to make the moment last despite its sadness.

*If only he were a telepath*, she wished silently. *To know what I know and feel what I feel.*

Loneliness, love denied, a stranger's fears, a wandering without end in this wilderness of alien years—he did feel those, she knew. Those were bonds that tied them together as firmly as the shared memories of lives taken and saved.

*Take me*, she urged his mind. *Forget your dead Onnul. Hold me. Make love to me. Feel despair and let me heal you. Please, Tayem.*

But madness lay in such thoughts. She was not season-taken. Her time of fertility was year tenths away, and even in that brief period of hormone-induced insatiability Tayem would withstand her.

*He knows what I feel. He knows everything I know.*

"I'm all right," she grumbled suddenly, pushing his hands away and standing stiffly. "Just tired."

"Sure." Something of Tayem's attitude showed that he did

not believe her, but he did not argue. He glanced upward at the changing digits on the central panel, then touched places on the front console, adding a prestorm darkness to the gray skies. "No need to rush. Get some shut-eye while you can, if that'll make things better."

His hands dangled helplessly as Kylene withdrew her faded wildflowers from a locker and shuffled from the cabin.

She did not sleep.

Alone in the tiny room that served her as a sleeping cabin, Kylene stared blankly at the numbers repeated on a small screen on the wall, then threw herself on the padded bed shelf and wept.

Alone in the cabin, Tim Harper moved stiffly, reseating himself in his command chair and mechanically inspecting the displays that reported the big levcraft's weapons and flight systems status. His slightest gestures would activate laser-pointed cannons, cast the vehicle through the sky at ten times the speed of sound, and transform the outside centuries to minutes within the vehicle. The power to destroy cities and rebuild history lay beneath his fingertips.

What he thought, she could not see.

*I love you, Tayem. I wanted you to love me.*

After a long while she heard footsteps.

"Kylene?" Harper rapped gently on the door.

She held her breath, but he did not go away.

"Kylene. We're about there. Kylene?"

She sniffed, then wiped her face on the bedding. "Not ready."

"Well, couple minutes. You can get decent."

Clothed, he meant. But she had not undressed. "All right."

"See you up front." The footsteps went away.

She sniffed again, then rolled to her feet.

When she reached the cabin, the sky was pink. The numbers on the overhead panels were not moving.

They were in stoptime. The levcraft was moving through time more slowly than the outside world, rather than more quickly.

Kylene flinched. She had no good memories of stoptime.

*"Persistent little girl, aren't you?" the man had said.*

*Inhumanly tall, he wore green and black. His hair was red; an old scar showed on his temple. His lips were tight with pain; blood from an unseen wound dripped down his sleeve, over his* hand, and onto the snow. Suspended in midleap, white-furred animals leered hungrily toward her. Yellow-rimmed, leaf-nude black bushes grew above green and scarlet soil. Flame shimmered among the bright boulders beyond the confines of normality. The rose-hued air sparkled.

Snow crunched beneath the man's boots. She stared upward, mouth open but silent as the weapon he pointed at her came nearer. She writhed, senselessly trying to rise, but her feet could find no purchase, her numbed legs would not obey. Beneath the blanketing snow, her bare hands scratched the rock-strewn path frantically, tearing uselessly at stones that could not be freed. Snow beaded her eyelashes, flowed like frozen sand over her arms.

Tower high, the man stood above her, alien emotion on his face, the scar on his temple livid. Behind his legs a silver triangle floated over the ground. His mouth opened, but she heard only her own gasping breaths and heartbeats.

Agony filled her, then inward-falling darknesses.

Dying, Kylene gazed unseeing at the mountain that held Kh'taal Minzaer.

"You feeling okay?" her captor asked. He faced her from a black cube chair, the seat strap raised in his hand. His hair was longer now; she could no longer see his forehead scar. In the cabin gloom his familiar green and black clothing seemed worn and drab. "Bad dreams?"

Bad memories? his attitude suggested. Warily. Guiltily.

"Just stumbled," she muttered, holding tight to the high back of her chair and finding anger. "Something rough! You need to fix your stupid floor, Tayem."

"What's wrong with—" His eyes moved, scanning the rubbery-surfaced deck and finding nothing to justify complaint. "Sure. When I get the time, Kylene."

She hated it when he did that.

Sullenly, she scuffed around her chair, making sure he witnessed her conquest of the treacherous footing, and fastened the restraints with additional caution. Plastic flowed about her body; the black chair enfolded her, unpleasantly warm. It was a seat made for clamminess without becoming clammy, and Kylene found herself resenting its failure to annoy her.

Trays protruded from the console, surrounding her at waist level. Pastel images rose in their depths: instrument readings, some of them duplicated on the overhead screens. Kylene shoved outward, forcing the colors to fade and the trays to retreat to their hiding place. *Stupid, stupid machines.* "I'm ready."

Harper's fingers, resting on a ball on a pillar at his side, trembled. Earth reared up; plastic pushed at Kylene's front.

"Bloodrill River." Harper gestured toward a narrow black chasm, which rotated clockwise as the vehicle maneuvered. "Shieldboss Mountain." That was a towering green flame, hayrick-shaped, surrounded by smaller fires of the same color, yellow-tinged, lighter and more translucent than the green of his uniform. "Road." A crimson line stretched across the green plains. Clustered about it, metallic blue and aquamarine structures billowed like carelessly handled sails. "And there's the town. Midpassage."

The horizon neared as he spoke. The crimson line took on width. Perhaps the pink of the sky darkened. Harper murmured, a satisfied sound without meaning.

Did he feel fear now, or excitement? Kylene looked sideways, but his face was expressionless. When she turned back to the viewscreen, the road was still expanding, seemingly flowing beneath too rapidly for features to be seen. Here and there flickers of green touched the crimson, alternately lapping over it and retreating. Tangled lines of chrome yellow blossomed among the green—skeletons of trees and bushes. The river could not be seen.

Under the vehicle, crimson spread as if spilled from a pan. Gold and white sparkled in its depths. A *ping* sounded inside the levcraft cabin, then another. Harper slapped at his console; the sound stopped. Yellow lines exploded before her eyes. Before she could react, the road threw itself skyward.

She slumped as momentum forced her downward, and then the sensation was gone. Harper moved his hands across his consoles without concern. The overhead images of meters and dials winked off. Motors whirred briefly; screens folded themselves flat against the cabin ceiling.

"How's it look?" Harper was unfastening his seat straps.

"Ugly." She saw no reason to please him.

"Well." He tapped at his console. For an instant the sky was blue, white-dappled. A black surface wide enough for five levcrafts ran straight to the horizon. What might be a house roof reflected sunlight from beneath distant trees on a hillside. Yellow and green grass wavered at the side of the road. Bushes were nearby. Her eyes moved, looking for flowers.

Then the jarring colors of stoptime came back.

"Looks okay," Harper said. "Probably worse places to live."

She said nothing. Undeterred by silence, he moved about the cabin, opening lockers and collecting possessions.

"You'll be all right." It was not a question.

She shook her head, then remembered and nodded as he did to show agreement. "Can't I go with you?"

"Soon enough. Let me look at the lay of the land first." Her question was not new, but he answered again without rancor.

"What's to be afraid of?" That also was not new.

He hunched his shoulders up, then released them. "Ignorance. Also that isn't the Station. Not much civilization yet in this part of the world."

She sniffed, not sharing his opinion. What she had seen of the Algheran time travelers in their underground home had convinced her that they were no different from other Normals: brutal, unthinking, thieves by nature, restrained only by mutual fear. Whatever they had was taken from the telepaths, or from their precious Plates, which amounted to the same thing.

What Tayem called civilization, with its arts and specialized occupations, political structures and ritualized behavior, was not possible for beings who could not see into minds and acted without knowledge of their own motives. She suspected that if it ever arrived, even he would find civilization dull.

Of course, what he really admired was struggle, she knew. A long difficult fight with uncertain outcome—like the war against the Present that the Algheran time travelers had created for themselves with their Project. It was the war that had made him return to the Fifth Era years ago, after running away. The war, not the fading but still cherished memories of his insipid Onnul Nyjuc, the Algheran woman he thought he had loved, the woman who had spurned him—the woman whose existence had been wiped out of history and whom, Kylene knew, he still dreamed of saving from a death that had already happened.

*"Penny for your thoughts."* He had noticed her attention. The words, in a trade tongue used in her era and unknown to everyone else, were a tug into comradeship that she rejected.

"I was wondering why the road was so wide."

"Military road," he said. His hands moved inside a tall locker, shifting about various objects that clanked as he replaced them.

"Won't need this." He grimaced briefly, holding an out-sized sword with one hand on its sheath and one on its hilt so she could see two handbreadths of bright metal. He grunted, then brought up the sheath and stowed the sword back in the locker.

"A road to where?" Tayem's unreasoning awe for weaponry was one of the peculiar male foibles he sometimes displayed. Ironically, and endearingly, he did not recognize it in himself but thought she was vulnerable to it.

"Fourth Era." He paused, his fingers caressing the firing mechanism of one of his handmade rifles. His face was pensive. "It drained this part of the country."

He looked outward at the road, and for a time she thought he would say nothing more. Then he went on. "They built it for peak capacity. There'd be long stretches—years—where only regular travelers used the road. Other times . . . From here to the horizon and farther, there were marching men. And machines, like this one, but much larger and unable to fly. They'd go by like blurs in the night, all night and all day.

"Sounded like a hive of wet bees." His lips quirked, then his face was neutral again, his voice even. "The men were quieter. Some talking, but not much. They always seemed to be tired, even the ones that must have been new. They kept good order, even in bivouac. I sometimes wondered if they were bred to be soldiers, but I never found out.

"There was a city on the coast to handle the shipping. It'd be inland by now, and lost, but it used to be a huge port—good-sized even in my time. And others, in the Gulf coast, to take them in, but those changed from time to time. Every peacetime they had to tear 'em up, so every time war got hot they had to rebuild a port and the roads. But this one they built to last, as if they knew from the start they'd always need it.

"At the start, when this was just a normal road where the pavement wears out, the men had rifles not much different looking from what I have here, almost man high. Later on, the guns got smaller, just big enough to need two hands, and they were strapped to the packs rather than carried over the shoulder. The uniforms seemed skimpier also, tighter.

"Progress." His lips quirked again. "They were running out of materials by then, I suppose. Always seemed to be plenty of men, though. And this road was here. Synthetic diamond, I guess—it doesn't wear out.

"Of course, I saw it backward." He sighed. "It was a Cimon-taken long war, Kylene."

The Second Eternal War against the Teeps—his people against hers.

His back straightened. Harper reached upward, placing the palm of his hand on the cabin roof; his elbow remained bent. "I think men got a lot shorter."

From inside the cabin, without standards of reference, Tayem seemed smaller. Vulnerable.

Senselessly, Kylene worried for him.

Harper stood at the edge of a circle. Within it, yellow grass, waist high, bordered a scrap of black pavement. Beyond, red and green flame waited. He had removed his pack and rifle before clambering up the side of the road. As she watched, he slipped his arms through pack straps and fastened the belt clips. His movements were slow, carefully precise, and she wondered if he was concealing his exertion because she was watching. Or was that simply an Ironwearer's behavior, a man's unwillingness to admit human limits when wearing the crossed sword insignia?

Metal glinted from Tayem's collar as he raised a hand.

That was his signal. Standing, Kylene pushed at unmoving plastic on her console, watching without surprise as the stop-time effect vanished. Overhead, the colored numbers began to move again. The world looked as it should for an early summer morning, and Harper stepped forward on the dark pavement without haste.

He turned, looking back even though inside the levcraft she was invisible to him. She stared back, matching his gaze until she read irritation on his face.

Reminded then, she touched the console again. Evening gloom fell at once. Night showed on the central viewscreen. The numbers flickered, digits changing too rapidly to be deciphered. Harper was gone.

# CHAPTER TWO

One winter day when Kalm was six years old, his visiting Uncle Sict, the tra'Ruijac, took the boy and his cousin Tagin for a sleigh ride. While the Sept Master asked about their schooling and drove over fields magically transformed into unfamiliarity by ice and snow, Kalm squinted against the sun's glare through beaded lashes, looking past farmland sleeping under its white blanket toward his future. The great city of Fohima Alghera and its famous Institute, the Settlement, the other Ruijac holdings, distant lands, strange peoples, unguessed wonders—this was all his world, he understood joyously, its riches created for him and Tagin, to be taken into their hands even as their eyes possessed it now. Realizing that, listening with little attention to the creak of harness and his uncle's soft words about the rebirth of man's history and science, somehow feeling both certainty and Tagin's excited giggles as she bounced on the seat beside him with the same crisp immediacy with which he felt the cold slapping gusts of air, he could remember that this understanding had been his the year before but that the thoughts had slipped from his immature memory as hastily as the glistening trails that spilled now from beneath the runners. He had become older, and mature, and he saw the one world with wisdom that his five-year-old mind would not have comprehended. He would never forget this moment.

## 47,913 L.C.

He was twelve when the headaches began.

"Sera samples look all right." The physician spoke over Kalm's head as his parents rose from the couch in the waiting room, then nodded fractionally as he threw his discarded laboratory gloves into a small sink. "Whatever the cause for your little boy's headaches, it isn't a disease." His voice was bleak.

Behind him, another man backed through the triangular doorway from the laboratory, pulling a cart decked with electronic apparatus. One hand reached out to cushion the falling plastic panel as he turned about; the other spun the cart on a back wheel and pushed it into the room so it stopped not far from Kalm. The newcomer was taller than the doctor, broader, and unmistakably younger, but after this display of energy he lingered at the doorway, acting with an older man's reserve. As he glanced toward the boy's parents, his eyes were dark, deep-set, narrowed slightly with private calculation. A decoration of some sort was fastened on his forehead, not jewelry or cosmetic paints such as Kalm had occasionally seen on his father but a blank piece of green plastic of which he seemed unaware. His hair was sandy and unruly.

He smiled suddenly at Kalm for no reason. It was the first warm gesture the boy had met in Fohima Alghera, and he smiled back reflexively, despite his sore shoulders, while shrugging to ward off his mother's grip.

"Additional tests," the physician muttered uneasily after a glance at the cart. "Best conducted by—" He stopped, then turned to look at the gloves disintegrating in the sink. "My assistant. If you'll agree, of course. Only indicative, you'll understand, but essential if . . . you'd want to know early if confirmation . . . should discuss the situation. Perhaps while the boy . . . my office next door." For some reason, Kalm heard the voice as a plea rather than the normal diffidence of the Septless when dealing with members of the great families.

"Dear," his mother said. It might have been addressed to anyone, but she pulled Kalm to her as she spoke so his head was imprisoned between her breasts and he could feel her heart beating. She squeezed tightly, adding pain to the bruises the physician's instruments had left.

She was afraid, he realized, and he tried to understand why; but he failed to penetrate her emotion. Nevertheless, she should leave now, he sensed—he wanted her to leave—so he moaned softly as she pulled at him and rubbed a hand across his forehead, saying nothing lest Lord Cimon see him lying but hoping that Lady Nicole would bless his stratagem with success.

"Sonol," his father said, reaching to pull his wife away, while he stared first at Kalm, then at the assistant. "Nothing's certain yet. We have to know if— Would it take long?"

"No," the doctor answered sadly. "Not long at all. But we'll know."

"Then do it," Kalm's father said, and his mother gasped softly and hugged him. "Sonol, let's discuss the evidence with the doctor." Then, after she had reluctantly left with the physician, he tipped the boy's chin up and ordered, "Son, do what you're told." And when Kalm shook his head gravely, his father grinned insincerely. "Good boy. You're still a Ruijac, aren't you? Don't forget it."

"I won't." Kalm stared into his father's eyes, seeing him not as a parent at this moment but as a stranger and an adult with concerns he was not yet ready to comprehend. "I won't, Daddy," he whispered.

"Good, son." His father's voice was no louder.

As his father went through the front door, Kalm saw his mother crying.

For an instant he had been between the two men, feeling a hand from each on his shoulders as if they were linked together. Now Kalm was alone with the man with the forehead decoration, and shyness overcame him. He waited without words.

"Niculponoc Banifnim," the man said finally.

"Sir?"

"My name, Kalm. If you have to say one, it's Niculponoc Banifnim. Come back to my office." It was a gruff voice, poorly modulated, harsher than Kalm had expected.

"Right here." A hand steered him, pushing gently on his shoulders so he was turned away from the smells and tubing before him toward an open doorway, then down a short corridor past several closed doors.

"This is it." The voice behind him had softened slightly, as if the man were out of practice with speech and were relearning it for his benefit. An arm reached past to raise the door. "Find you something to sit on." Kalm sensed that the man was smiling. Had he not seen other people in the city streets with the same emblem on their foreheads?

"Any seat you want." The man gestured comfortably.

Kalm looked about curiously. This might have been a winter living room in a private house. There were no windows. The walls were red-stained wood, crisscrossed by fine lines of wire, much like the decoration in the room he had occupied last night at Justice's Redoubt. Lights glowed at the edges of the white ceiling; more wires were visible overhead through the translucent plastic. The floor was carpeted. A bookcase loomed in one corner, stuffed high with unlabeled books. Near it was a small wooden desk topped by a reading lamp. There were two chairs—not the bulky plastic cube chairs reserved for company at home but old-fashioned leather ones that did not mold themselves to their occupants. Air entered from unseen vents, warm and delicately scented with an aroma like that of a purple flower Kalm had noticed in one of the city's gardens.

"Lilac," the man said. "You wondered about the odor, didn't you?"

Kalm shook his head in agreement, finding that the easiest response. "Have—have you been a doctor a long time, sir?"

"I'm not one yet. I work with them, and someday I may be a surgeon. Like my grandfather—it does run in the family." The man waved toward the bookcase. "But I have to memorize all those first, or find someone to memorize them for me. Have a seat." As if to set an example, he dropped into the farther chair and pulled a low table forward. "How do you like Fohima Alghera so far?"

"It's big! The people—"

"That's true." The man seemed amused. "But there are also fifty million people who don't live here. This is only a small part of the one world, Kalm."

Kalm hesitated, wanting to say more but afraid that someone who lived year-round in the city would find his observations a cause for humor. He stared at books and compromised his impulses politely. "Do you study at the Institute, sir?"

"No." The man seemed faintly surprised. "Why did you ask?"

"I will! My Uncle Sict said someday it's going to snow and snow and the snow will turn to ice and not go away. He says it'll be so high it'll cover Alghera and even the highest buildings in the whole city and we're going to need everyone we can get with real 'telligence to get ready for it, so if I studied hard and behaved myself, he could get me into the Institute and when I grow up I can help him!"

"'Real intelligence,'" the man repeated softly. "Sure. Well, that's a way off, isn't it, your uncle's ice age? One or two thousand years? So if you didn't—but if you're going to attend the Institute, you'll be living here in the city then, won't you? Would you like that? You would, I see."

He gestured toward the unoccupied chair. "Sit down, Kalm. Tell me, would you like to live in the city even if you didn't attend the Institute?"

"I—" Kalm stopped, feeling confusion. The two ideas had always been linked in his mind.

"It doesn't matter." The man pointed again. "Sit down."

Kalm sat nervously on the edge of the other chair and looked back toward the laboratory. "Will this hurt much?"

The man chuckled, resting his feet on the table with one ankle over the other. "No—no more samples. Right now we'll just talk. The instruments back there . . . Would you understand if I explained that those were to satisfy your parents? They would both prefer to believe a machine's truths than mine, so . . ." He raised his hands over his head, stretching as he arched his back, then grinned as if he were a small boy intending mischief. "We won't tell them, will we?"

Kalm frowned, forcing himself not to stare at the man's forehead. "They'll know, won't they?" He squirmed, dragging his left foot across the carpet.

"Yes. Never underestimate Normals, boy. They'll know, but they won't admit the truth to themselves unless it's necessary. Or is that what you mean?"

Kalm shook his head, searching for clearer thoughts. "You can tell, can't you, when someone is fibbing? I mean, they say something and they think something else, and if it's a big difference, so Cimon notices it, you can see it also. If you're looking at them just right, I mean?"

"Uh . . ." The man touched his tongue to his upper lip as he inspected the ceiling. "As a rule, I can. But not everyone can, Kalm. Why don't you tell me about 'looking just right.'"

Kalm stared at him, bewildered. It was not a thing that could be explained. It just happened. "It's—"

Inspiration came, a feeling of certainty. He closed his eyes and concentrated, pushing himself out somehow, reaching . . .

. . . and nothing happened. For an instant he had seen

images, lights, thoughts, as if he were in the head of another person, but a curtain had dropped and he was alone in blackness.

Disappointed, he opened his eyes. "You're a stranger," he grumbled. "I bet if I knew you before, I could—"

"Never mind." The man looked at him evenly, and Kalm saw no trace of small boy in him now, no air of foppishness despite his strange decoration. "How long have you been doing that?"

Kalm thought about it. "About a year, maybe. Since I was eleven, almost twelve. It doesn't always work, but I'm getting better."

"Umm huh." The man made one of the noncommittal sounds adults used in front of children. "So this started about the time your headaches became a problem, didn't it?"

"I—I guess so. Why?"

"Umm huh. Do you have a headache now, by the way? No. When do you most often have headaches? Bedtime—that's usually when they come, Kalm. Do you have dreams about— uh huh! Have you told your parents about this 'looking just right' business? They didn't believe you, huh? Or said they didn't. Umm huh! Did you tell your uncle?"

"I told Tagin."

"Tagin? Oh."

"She's my girlfriend." Kalm smiled at the man, telling him a secret he had never confided to anyone else. "She's almost my age, just two years older, so we're going to be hearthsharers someday." Then he fidgeted with remembered guilt.

"Umm huh." The man seemed pensive, as if not listening. "Your headaches aren't as bad now as they used to be, are they? You're a very healthy boy despite your parents' worries, Kalm, and you're developing quite naturally. It'll probably take another season, but soon your problems will go away. It'll just take some patience."

"All right."

"Do what your uncle told you and study hard. Marry well."

Typical adult advice, Kalm recognized. "Yes, sir."

"It never hurts! Also, young fellow, our Lord Cimon and Lady Nicole were hearthsharers themselves according to the Chronicles. They had a child. That means they probably kissed and surely did other things. They probably *are* watching when you and your cousin play show-and-touch in the barn, even with the hay bales stacked over you—but that's not evil, and Cimon isn't going to weigh it against you in his scales."

Kalm blushed.

"Think of it this way: Having a girlfriend at your age is a gift from Nicole. Nothing in it for you to be ashamed of. A warning, though: it will come to an end. Women outgrow that kind of interest in men except for a couple of days each year, but that won't be your fault."

Kalm considered the alien thoughts, then stored them in his memory for future examination. Practicality returned. "But you won't have to tell anyone, will you?"

The man chuckled "It's under iron." When the boy frowned, the man tossed his hand up as if displaying the ceiling to one who had not noticed it. "Nothing said here is heard or noticed outside. We have a Teepblind around us, and our thoughts can't escape. Or other thoughts come in. You'll learn all that."

A long silence followed. Finally Kalm asked the question he had contained, already knowing the answer but compelled regardless. "Are you . . . a Teep, sir?"

"'Telepath' is the polite word, Kalm."

"Does that mean—"

*Yes.*

The voice inside his mind was not his own. Kalm stared, filled with certainty and surmise, terror and wonder. All were incompatible with speech; he rose woodenly as the Teep gestured and followed like a poorly handled puppet.

"Normal experience of emergence," the Teep explained to Kalm's parents. "Physically he's a bit precocious, which explains the early onset. He's a year or two ahead of his cohort in development." The Teep's hand rested comfortably on Kalm's shoulder.

The words meant nothing to the boy. Nor did those that followed as his parents pushed objections and halfhearted interjections at the Teep and the physician. The physician's anxiety and embarrassment, his mother's fears, his father's restrained sense of loss—those were only backdrops for the world he suddenly saw within himself.

The hand on his shoulder squeezed him affectionately, protectively, already possessively. Kalm stared without feeling at his parents, watching them as the physician's words finally struck home, making them dwindle in some fashion, making them shrink away from him and even from each other.

He was already parting from them.

The waiting area outside the Inter-Sept Council chamber was gloomy and cool despite the late summer heat. The walls were great chunks of black- and brown-flecked granite, crudely dressed and mortared into place. The floors were slate, dull black, unfinished but worn smooth along a line from the chamber doors to the exits to the bailey. There were two doors, rectangular, like those on old buildings at the Settlement, but without handles, side by side and taller than his father could reach. They were of wood, light-colored once but darkened to dirty yellow under ancient coats of varnish.

Vertical slits made windows in the exterior walls. Light spilled from those in the top rows, thick, slanted beams of dust-flecked yellow. Traces of cloud and sky could be seen in the lower windows; narrow balconies ran beneath each row all around the inside of the Unifier's Castle. At the far end of the floor Kalm saw unrailed steps leading to the lower walkway; the others were reached by ladders that could not be seen.

A soldier passed by on the second walkway, pausing to glance through a slit at the empty courtyard, then continued his round, his footsteps clear but without echoes. At even intervals he slapped silently at the wall, switching on lamps. His shadow stretched above him on the granite, inhumanly distorted, its passage marked by the growing line of gleaming circles cast upon the floor far below.

The boy squirmed, uncomfortably confined by his new clothing and his parents' bodies on the wooden bench, trying to watch the stiff man in the black uniform who stood nearby without being noticed in return. There was a real gun hanging from his shoulder and a knife in a sheath on his hip. Metal insignia were pinned to his lapels: pairs of tiny crossed swords. He was an officer—an Ironwearer.

"Kalm!" His mother tugged at his forearm and reached to hold his hands together. He struggled weakly, impatient with the restraint but also reluctant to hurt her by disobeying. On the other side, his father rocked back and forth erratically as if to block his son's view. The man stared straight ahead, apparently unaware of anyone but himself.

Kalm was a captive in his mind as well, his concentration disrupted by the wound on his forehead. The woman who had placed the green plaque on him had said the punctures would heal in days as new bone formed, but for the moment his forehead was bruised and a bee-stinglike swelling made the plaque pinch unmercifully. The plaque seemed palm-sized and heavy enough to fall from place despite its prongs, but it was always small when he touched it, no larger than his thumbnail, and solidly rooted. It was just above his eyebrows, invisible even when he crossed his eyes to look, but he still tried to see it despite the headache the effort brought.

Someone inside rapped on the doors. The soldier turned to open one of the doors. Kalm heard meaningless whispers.

"In we go," the soldier said, then looked away discreetly as Kalm's mother dabbed at her eyes and his father rose with an old man's awkwardness. There was time for each parent to give him a hug, and then both doors were open.

One glance was enough to reveal globular lights hanging from chains, stone walls lined with shining mesh, a broad C-shaped table, and seated men. Then his eyes focused on two men in red uniforms, armed with long spears, standing just inside, waiting.

"Hujsuon stands on guard, and the authority of the Warder within these chambers is denied." The words were loud but so fast that the sentence might have been one word. Kalm could not determine which of the guards had spoken.

"Where order is maintained, the armed force of the Realm is never required." That was another composite word, politely spoken by Kalm's own soldier.

"Depart and inform your Master the Septs are lawfully assembled."

"I am required to witness this affair. The Warder wants a report." It was a departure from what Kalm already recognized as ritual.

"Your right?" asked the nearer of the men in red.

"I am of Sept Minursil."

"You are admitted." The guards stepped backward and stamped their spear butts on the floor. Kalm's father nudged him forward.

Kalm's feet scuffled, making a sound that had to be out of place. He concentrated on lifting his new boots from the floor as he walked. Then the soldier put an arm out to stop him.

"The next matter is the boy Rispar Kallimur ha'Ruijac," the man at the center of the curved table said. Amplified, his voice rang metallically inside the chamber, and Kalm wondered why he had not heard it outside. "All the parties are present now."

The Council chamber was small, but the ceiling was far above. Kalm, his parents, and the soldier stood along one wall; two men in formal clothing watched from the opposite side of the room. Green plaques were on their foreheads.

Kalm stared expectantly, but their minds were inaccessible and they did not look toward him. Impatient, he turned away, then focused his attention to the hanging lights. The glittering chains that supported them were silver-tinted. Were they of genuine metal? Did they reach all the way to the dark ceiling?

His attention returned to Earth as his father cuffed his shoulder. The blow was not hard, but it was unexpected. Kalm opened his mouth to protest, then stopped, sensing the man's mood even without mind-seeing.

His father, he suddenly realized. His mother. He had spent his life with them, taking them for granted, even resenting them at times, and it was too late to undo a moment of his neglect, too late to prevent what the changes in him had ordained. Too late. He blinked rapidly, hoping no one would notice, and sniffed as silently as he could.

"Ruijac, do you renounce the boy?" The man presiding over the Council spoke deliberately, untouched by emotion.

"We do. Definitely not ours. Must have been a mistake in the records somehow." Kalm never identified the man at the table who said those words, never ceased to wonder at the cool decisive tones so at war with the man's private thoughts. "Ruijac does not recognize him."

"Nyjuc?"

"We are prepared—" That was one of the men with a forehead plaque. Another man, seated at the table, spoke when he stopped. "Nyjuc will be pleased to accept him."

"So. Will any other Sept speak?"

There was silence. The Council chairman continued without surprise. "Rispar Sonol Ruijac, is this your son?"

Kalm's mother stood frozen; then her head lowered. She took three tiny steps toward the table, shaking without words.

"Is this your son?" The man repeated the question softly.

"No." It was a whisper. Kalm heard sighs from around the table.

"Rispar Siccentur ha'Ruijac, is this your son?"

"It is not." Kalm's father stepped beside his mother. There was no other sound in the chamber as he turned and held her,

no other motion as he stroked her back and stared at the men
who had taken his son from him.

And now Kalm was alone.

The soldier's gentle grip on his shoulder was unnecessary.
He held back his tears and kept his head high as his father
had, unwilling to disgrace those who had raised him, as the
red-uniformed men escorted his parents to the exit doors.
They did not look back.

## 47,917 L.C.

He could go no farther up the hill, Kalm admitted. The dirt
path had narrowed to little more than the width of his levcraft,
and there were branches not far ahead at the level of the pilot's
bubble. In a farm wagon, passenger-jostling brushes against
boulders and tree limbs were insignificant, but this thin-
skinned levcraft, bright in crimson paint and free of dents,
was an adult's vehicle, intended for hazard-free city boule-
vards.

The levcraft was new, one of two recently purchased by
Sept Nyjuc after much debate in the kennel about the expense.
A more experienced pilot, or a more daring one, might ma-
neuver it up the lane without difficulty and land it in the courtyard for envious inspection by luxury-starved admirers. Kalm
could only anticipate such pleasures; this was his first unsu-
pervised flight, and pride would not let him return a damaged
vehicle to Nyjuc House.

He had only a thousand man-heights to walk, after all, and
that was not a long distance here even though it would carry
him far in the city. He had already passed the outlying buildings of the Settlement, the sturdy storage sheds for implements and grain that could survive the winter with minimal
care. Fragments of the central complex—the steep-roofed
barns and habitats linked by their covered passages and
glazed-earth pathways—could be seen through the trees,
brown and black walls hiding behind the red and yellow late
summer leaves.

The walk up would be a warm one, he judged as he jockeyed the levcraft to the side and lowered the landing skids.
Coming back, there might be a nip in the air. He had not
brought a jacket, and he would have nothing to guide him but
the vehicle's lights until he reentered the city, so his stay
should not be a long one.

He would make that clear at once, he decided with a seventeen-year-old's foresight. This was his first trip home in two years and the first he had made unaccompanied by his adopted parents. If he or his parents became uncomfortable as they had on his last visit, an excuse for ending the visit had much value. He probed gently as he stepped from the vehicle, focusing idly on surface thoughts to locate people without attention to their private concerns.

*Unexpected. Of course.* There were only Normals ahead of him, no Teeps to predict his coming. Kalm closed the levcraft door with a strange reluctance, feeling as if the action were shutting him away from the world he knew.

There were people close by, he noticed as he unfolded the gauzy power wings on the top of the vehicle and pulled them out for the sun to shine on. He sensed three minds, two men and a woman, young, to his left, not far beyond the other side of the road and the curtain of corn that marked the edge of a field.

*Cousins.* Virtually all of the seventy people at the Settlement were Ruijacs; perhaps half of them were cousins by birth or in marriage. Four years ago he could have named them all.

And he had seen none of them for two years.

Kalm slapped at gray slacks, eliminating a dimpled hint of cling above one knee, and straightened his shoulders automatically inside a red shirt-jacket. He had fleshed out in two years and grown taller, to become a man, a truth belied only by the touch of acne upon his jawline and above his forehead plaque. He was leaving adolescence behind, as he had left the Settlement behind four years ago when he had entered Sept Nyjuc. What changes had two years made in those who had stayed and who had once been relatives?

It was reaping time now, he estimated, standing on the road's short-cut grass and sniffing the dust-heavy air. The cornstalks were more tan than green, if not yet the ripened golden brown of the wheat he had seen earlier; the ears inside their faded sheaths looked plump and sturdy, ready for picking.

The corn first, the wheat, and then threshing. Within a pair of ten-day periods the fields would be ready for stubbling and plowing, the dull but necessary task of returning the nitrogen-rich roots and stalks to the soil. That was always a race with the weather, he remembered, for the job became nearly impossible after frosts hardened the ground, but it would be done

before autumn's arrival was acknowledged. The last chore of
summer at the Settlement . . .

The levbarges would arrive days after that, bulky high-
sided vehicles that transferred the crops to the city and storage
depots along the river for sale to foreigners. As a child,
watching the fast-speaking men from Fohima Alghera with
their shiny clothing and easy profanity as they loaded the tall
barges, then stood in the open doorways of their cabs carelessly steering with one hand as they backed across the Settlement courtyards, Kalm had always known amazement that
these were Septlings also. It could not be believed that the
same men would return from year to year, praising the same
rabbit litter pies, smoked ox loin, and fruit pastries they had
feasted upon the year before, slapping the bottoms of the same
always unsuspecting single women, and laughing raucously
without change. But so it always was at summer's end. So it
would always be.

As if to reinforce the point, a broad V formation of birds
passed far overhead, their wings moving rhythmically, dark
against the pale blue sky, engaged in their own annual ritual.
Other animal minds were on all sides of him, instinct-driven,
hibernation-bound, too alien to be understood clearly but as
purposeful in their traditions as any Normal or Teep.

Winter would bring no rest to humans, though the days
were shorter. The farm vehicles were repainted then, and the
heavy engines lifted from them one by one for maintenance
and deferred repairs. There were oxen and ill-tempered giant
rabbits for the children to feed, hidden crevices and cracks in
the buildings to find and chink up before snow and wind discovered them, and schoolbooks that must be studied or opened
to conceal daydreams. The one world seemed shrunken to the
bounds of the Settlement then, a cold and dark environment
that promised to last unchanged for all eternity. Winter wore
away speech and the urge to speak, tightly compressing something deep within everyone that sprang free only after snow
had become a memory and the ground was soft enough for
plowing.

And yet it had been a good life, he recognized now—a life
with rewards and accomplishments for all its lack of city pleasures and sophistication. Almost, he could envy his Normal
relatives who had remained at the Settlement, even those who
had once dreamed of a life beyond its limits and would never
be so covered by the Lady's cloak.

He smiled fondly, looking back at the red levcraft under its dragonfly wings as he reached the edge of the field. The affluence of the urban Septs was also not to be rejected. Neither of the telepath Septs was as old as the traditional great families —R'sihuc in particular had been established less than half a century ago—and Nyjuc House actually had few more luxuries than the Settlement dormitories, despite the envious insistence of country folk, but there was no livestock to be watered at the kennel, no courtyards to be cleaned of manure, no slaughtering bloodreek and pandemonium, no curfew at darkness, no handed-down and repatched clothing. The Lady had been kind to him, and he twisted a hand in homage to her, as if pouring water on the earth to ease her thirst.

He stepped lightly, cautious lest the dirt discolor his soft leather boots, as he slipped through the green and brown stalks. The corn had done well, he judged, feeling the long solid ears inside their papery sheaths and inspecting the thick stalks and thick matted roots that plumbed the earth. The harvest would be rich. He smiled again, pleased with possessing such powers of observation and an understanding of nature so superior to that of the city folk in Nyjuc House.

Then he was at the edge of the corn. The field before him had been harvested, and broken stalks and leaves littered the ground. At intervals, pyramid piles of shelled ears, pale white and gray, were starkly distinct on the rolling black earth.

Fifty man-heights away a tractor and shelling machine had settled to the ground. The wagon resting behind them was only half-filled, a small hill of yellow particles at its front virtually rising to the sheller's hopper spout, while the back part of the bed appeared empty.

*Evening out the load*, Kalm thought, remembering as if from yesterday the hard kernels' weight in his hands and the pressure on his fingertips as he dog-paddled grain between his bowed legs, the corn before him hollowing out like sandpile excavations, then falling in a rush to wipe out the depressions he had carved.

His cousins would be in the wagon.

Four years in the city had not softened him, not yet made him scornful of those who sweated in the sunlight. Adult dignity was incompatible with running to the wagon, but he unfastened the seams of his shirtsleeves as he walked, intending to surprise his cousins with his presence, then help for a while despite what they would regard as city finery. It would be a pleasure to see them again, to help with a simple chore he could now avoid, to hear of their lives and changes in the Settlement before he answered their envious questions about affairs in the metropolis and life in a Sept lodge.

Grinning happily, listening familiarly to burrowing sounds within the wagon, enjoying his retained skills, he stepped onto the unused wagon tongue at the back of the carriage, reached for the top of the gate, pushed himself up from the protruding tongue, swung an arm and shoulder over the top, and—

—froze there, half over the gate, the wood hard against the inside of his biceps, his side dangling flat against the back of the wagon, his words of greeting only gurgles in his throat.

Teep reflexes were not enough. Before he knew how to react, a foot kicked out, smashed against his fingers, and hammered again upon them until he released his grip.

He fell painfully, scraping his knee against the tongue, then falling back on his right buttock, sprawling backward even before he understood that he no longer held on to the wagon.

*Get away!* his mind told him. *It wasn't— Get away!*

But it had been. *Tagin.*

Lying on the ground, he remembered as if it had been his own sensation the yielding diamond hardness of grain beneath him and upon his limbs, the pleasurable excitement of air upon his nude body, the warmth of flesh against his side, lips upon his nipples, moist and insistent, hands dancing without hindrance along the inside of his thighs, nibbling at his jaw as his head pushed backward into his couch of grain, rubber-textured flesh and hair damp inside his tight palms. He pulsated again with the thrill Tagin felt as the men pawed at her, the cold-filling intoxication of her power, the luxurious knowledge that each motion and each of her gestures dominated the foolish minds of the men who embraced her, understanding completely how they could be brought to moments of passionate Tagin-obsessed slavery, joyfully concealing from them the soon to be revealed coyness and withdrawal that would bind them to her more strongly than surrender. And knowing also the hating anger that filled her as her pleasure was interrupted and the awkward, bumptious men turned from her . . .

*Tagin!* The realization filled his mind, dismay masking any thoughts from inside the wagon. He stared at the levmotor casing at the bottom of the wagon carriage, wishing he could crawl and hide under it or burrow into the shame-concealing earth, knowing even as his eyes squeezed shut that he could not hide from the one world or those who ruled in it. A whimper formed in his throat as acid-dip pain burned below his torn fingernails.

"Asshole." The voice was even despite the rage he found in it. "Kalm the Teep. What are you doing back here, asshole?"

It was one of his cousins.

"The fucking Teep." That was another cousin, the naked body glaringly obvious to Kalm's mind despite the wooden gate that concealed all but his head. "Snooping fucking Teep."

Kalm shouted names, then protests, knowing that they recognized him, but sounds refused to come from his mouth. Only drool came out, a thin line of saliva that carried slime down his cheek. "Ta-Tagin," he croaked. It was both prayer and denial. "Please."

"Shut him up," he heard.

"Teach him."

"Yeah."

He did not give meaning to those words yet, but cowed, half curling into a fetal position as a man wearing only pants jumped beside him. He was too surprised to resist, too unprepared, too ill, as a bare foot slammed into his belly.

That was the first kick. He was unable to count those that followed.

He *tried* to resist, tried to reach out with fumbling fingers for the feet that whirled about him, stabbed at him, and slammed weight upon his side; he tried to wrap his hands about the pulsing calves that punished him.

He tried not to fear, tried not to notice the triumphant, dominating face of Tagin Ruijac as it rose above the wagon gate, tried not to understand the ecstasy that flooded her groin as she touched herself and watched him writhing in sacrifice before her.

Kalm vomited, his body limp, aching, aflame where dirt rubbed against raw cuts and abrasions, shamefacedly aware of the mud that had ruined his clothing and caked upon his skin, barely remembering the meaningless blows he had suffered, uncomprehending, unresisting as hands pushed at him, yanked at him, and hit at him as he lay in the field.

He did not fight as his cousins tugged his pants down and wrenched his arms backward, then pulled his shirt away from him. He did not understand that additional resistance was possible. Dimly, he sensed that the worst of the battering had ended, and he tried to wipe the slime and shame from his face upon the unconcerned black earth.

"Fucking Teep." It meant nothing to him now. Nor did the trickling sounds and humorless laughter that followed, or the sopping fabric that fell at last upon his naked chest. "Untie that, freak."

Kalm's hands went out without thought. He was grateful that the kicks had stopped, that the hands that had torn at him had stopped, that his clothes had been returned. He did not understand yet the contorted, complicated feel of the fabric. He did not realize that his clothes were dripping with the hot liquid that streaked across his body, did not recognize the reek of ammonia that hovered over him.

He hugged the clothing to his chest, feeling a strange pleasure.

"Shoes."

"Shoes?"

"His boots. I want them."

"Yes, give her the shoes."

The words were only a backdrop to his body's pains. He was not going to be hurt anymore, Kalm sensed, and he arched his feet cooperatively as his cousins tugged his new boots away from him, then almost smiled fondly as Tagin carried them away into the unharvested corn.

She was dressed now, he knew, though the back of her blouse had not been tucked in, and he remembered that in a corner of his mind, even as his cousins beat him, he had been with her as she had pulled clothing on and scrambled over the side of the wagon. His mind had greedily fastened on the feel of rough linen against her nipples and the clammy embrace of her pants as she pulled them tight and slapped the seams shut, the welcome hand-clutching sensation of fabric on flesh she felt as she walked.

His mind had fastened also on her other feelings: rage and frustration, an all-absorbing hatred of the wretched, mindless thing from her past that had interrupted her amusement and taken the men away from her. With Tagin, he understood the painless blows struck against the cruel person who had interfered with the moist, soothing lips on taut nipples, the feather touches of callused fingers setting cold fires aflame upon her skin, the hard-muscled flesh of men pressed against her body, the necessary and pleasurable control Tagin had been given over men blinded by unreasoning needs.

Kalm tried to sob, sharing Tagin's knowledge of his guilt, despising himself for his weakness and his unimportant pride as he scratched at the unforgiving soil and choked foul air into his gullet, so conscious of his bruises and his sin that nothing else on the one Earth mattered.

"Put these on him." It was not a girl's voice, it was a judgment—a joyous, stern demand—to which he acquiesced. He put his feet out to help even before the two men could reach for them, knowing somehow that he was obeying the dictates of fate.

He felt something warm, soft, thick, but liquid-yielding. His toes twitched as best they could, accepting this environment, rejoicing at this contact with something Tagin-touched.

"Out of here."

"Get."

"Let's."

The words rested on his consciousness like the damp weights on his body, without order or significance. "Yeah," he grunted back, not seeing any relevance to himself, speaking blearily only because relatives had spoken in his presence. "Out . . . here."

A slapping sound followed, in triplicate. Steps.

His cousins had left him. His mind reached out toward them despairingly as he crawled behind them, denying his aches and nausea, knowing but not admitting kinship to the writhing man that was himself, lying amid the dead corn-stalks.

Something squished under his feet and oozed greasily between his toes after he struggled upright and waddled after his cousins. Something soft and rancid, once at body warmth but now cooling rapidly.

Kalm stopped as recognition and reason flowed back into him, and fell full length onto the field, still clutching his urine-soaked clothing as his lips brushed a fallen cornstalk. He heard laughter in the distance, then a rustling sound as the tractor penetrated the grain.

The laughter remained with him as he tugged off his ruined boots. The stench remained after he heaved them away, as he scoured his foul clothing on the soft earth, even as he stumbled barefoot through the corn to Sept Nyjuc's levcraft.

**47,919 L.C.**

On the landing they escaped the full force of the wind, though powder swirls of snow from the building's gabled roof fell upon them as they waited by an old-fashioned rectangular door. In the distance, canvas fluttered over bales of cargo waiting beside the docks. The white-blanketed streets were empty, and the depressions their boots had made were invisible.

*Uncle Sict's snow,* Kalm thought as he looked past the varnished railing at the moonlit streets below, seeing into the distant future when snow would fall onto the darkened city without melting, without end . . . onto all the darkened, deserted cities and fallow fields, on Normals and Teeps alike. *Uncle Sict's end.*

But he could claim the tra'Ruijac as a relative no longer. If he had kin now, it must include the silent, often incomprehensible men standing before him.

"They'll have to hear the bell soon," his adopted father said, not looking around, pretending a familiarity with the building that his mind denied. His voice was soft, high-pitched, quite unlike the tones of Kalm's real father.

"Someone needs to get a jacket on," one of his adopted cousins said, speaking aloud to force an illusion of normality. "Or other clothes." He smiled quickly and humorlessly as he pulled back the hood of his parka. He was perhaps two years older than Kalm, but the difference had always seemed greater.

The remaining cousin said nothing, standing stolidly by Kalm, holding in a private mood he had not communicated to the others. As Kalm turned to look along the deserted streets, their parkas brushed; the cousin stepped away.

Kalm pushed a gloved finger along the railing, sweeping snow onto the steps below, killing time. *My treat,* he thought again. *He said this was a surprise just for me, a present. So why have they come too?* But the question would not receive an answer unless he asked it: Teeps explained themselves only to children.

He did not want a present from his pretend father, anyhow. He did not even want to be here.

He did not want to wear the new coveralls and underclothing his adopted mother had given him.

*One more day,* Kalm promised himself. *Less than that, and I'll be living with normal people again. Normals. And I'll be a man and not a child, and I'll be Rispar Kallimur and not Kalm ha'Nyjuc. Rispar Kallimur-once-ha'Ruijac, yes, and not once-ha'Nyjuc. No, not ha'Nyjuc. Never again, ha'Nyjuc.*

He wondered if his cousins knew that resolve. Or his meek Nyjuc pretend father and pretend mother. Had they ever felt as he did? Or was that feeling something unique to him, another part of the difference between him and other Teeps, another proof of his basic Normality?

"Sounds like someone's coming," his adopted father said unnecessarily, and his cousins straightened themselves, brushing imaginary snow from their clothing as if preparing for an inspection. They were all taller than Kalm, all fairer and thinner, all dismayingly not his kin, and for an instant he wanted to run down the stairs and around the corner before the door opened and escape the pretense.

But he had been promised a treat, whatever it was. Small-boy curiosity—or the surer knowledge that someday he would feel curiosity about this occasion—kept him in place.

*Yes?* It was only a thought. A Normal's thought. The man in the open doorway did not speak. He stood silently, haughtily, his muscular arms bare and gleaming in the yellow light of the antechamber. He did not wear a jacket for the cold. He did not move aside to let them enter.

The man was just a servant, Kalm realized, despite his attitude. The lace fronting on his shirt and the ruffled pants legs were only the uniform that the waiting man wore on duty, for all that it mimicked the attire of aristocrats. But his air was that of an in-family attendant at the lodge of one of the wealthier Septs, not a doorman in the dilapidated private house in a run-down section of F'a Alghera.

He probed, but the doorman's mental images were alien, tied to a language he had never encountered. A foreigner. Was this connected with his present?

"Pothius. The Pothius party," his Nyjuc father murmured. "We had an appointment."

"One appointment." The doorman spoke crisply, his eyes narrowing as he watched them. He did not move from the doorway.

"One appointment," the older man agreed, pointing with an outstretched hand. "My son, Kalm. The rest of us will wait."

His cousins moved away, exposing him. For an instant Kalm met the doorman's eyes. His head dropped involuntarily, and he looked away, pretending boredom.

"Certainly," the doorman said politely, seemingly impassive though his voice implied that Kalm had been graded and rejected. "You'll follow me, please." He said nothing else in the antechamber, though when Kalm turned from placing his parka on a peg by the interior door, he saw the doorman staring at him once more. For a few seconds their eyes locked, then Kalm looked away again, understanding that the doorman would soon permit himself to show an expression and knowing he could not bear to see it.

It was only a stupid game, he told himself, grateful that his cousins and Nyjuc father, busy with removing their boots, had not noticed the interchange. The doorman would cheat to win such a contest. The emotion he might show if Kalm provoked him would be feigned. It would mean nothing. *Only a servant.* The silly staring contest had nothing to do with his gift, whatever it was.

*Not a gift,* he remembered, correcting himself. A surprise, his pretend father had said. Something like a present, but not necessarily the same. A farewell dinner? Gambling? What?

But he found no answer revealed in his Nyjuc father's mind or in his cousins' thoughts, and the house itself was immune to his probe. Tracing a finger along the cloth-covered walls as he waited for the doorman to open the inner door, he discovered that they were lined with metal mesh.

There was more metal inside, concealed within the stuccoed walls of the winter living room. *To keep Teeps out—us out,* Kalm realized, conscious of the green plastic on his forehead and wondering if he should feel embarrassment. The room was dim, with only tables and a pair of cube couches as furniture, and no fireplace, though he had noticed a smoke spume while waiting outside. The couches were expensive, he knew, and it had taken much effort to build the gloss on the wooden floor. Yet the air was stale, unvented. There was luxury here, neglected, which Nyjuc House could not afford for its residents.

What went on here? The doorman had gone, and neither the thoughts nor the actions of the other Teeps offered guidance.

"Mr. Pothius." A man had appeared at a door at the back of the room. His clothing was dark and formal. A Teepblind rested on his blond hair. For a moment Kalm fantasized that only his face was there. Then the man beckoned with a hand.

"Why don't you look around, son," his Nyjuc father said, carefully gazing at the featureless walls.

*My treat.* He moved to the door awkwardly, his steps loud on the wood floor, uneasily aware that he was being watched by everyone. *This is illegal, isn't it? Will we share something when I'm through?*

*It's all right, son,* his Nyjuc father told him as he went past, gently touching his shoulder, smiling foolishly at him. *The worst penalty for this is probably something like being put in the Falltroop.*

The man in the doorway also smiled and held his hand out. "Kalm—good to see you again." His voice was soft and serene.

A lie. He had never met the man before; everyone present realized it. But the words accomplished the magic that was intended. "Good to be back," Kalm said easily, his shoulders high.

"We'll go through here." The man slid a door across the entrance, shutting Kalm away from the other Teeps and revealing a second doorway into a narrow passage. There was a kitchen, smaller than the one in Nyjuc House but no more exotic, then another door. He passed by jackets, a scattering of snow, touch-darkened walls—another entrance chamber, used more often than the one he had come through, with another hinged door to the outside at the far end. Nearer, a closed door waited behind a mesh curtain. "This is actually your first time, Mr. Pothius?"

"My first time here, yes," Kalm said, not certain to what he had agreed.

"Your first time." The man smiled at him. Close at hand, his clothing was elegant, made from fine-textured fabrics that no Teep would ever afford, neatly cupped and flared about his body as if tailored just for it. To his surprise, Kalm did not feel embarrassed by the simpleness of his coveralls. The clothing his Nyjuc mother had given him was clean and honest in its utilitarianism. The garments he had wanted more would only have mimicked this finery and left him shamed.

Preoccupied by that discovery, he listened blankly as the elegant man repeated his question, then shook his head. "Yes. I'm sorry—what is your name?"

"Sict will do, Mr. Pothius. You can always call me that." The man smiled comfortably, genuinely, his eyes moving with his lips, and Kalm realized suddenly that centuries hence the man would still address him as Mr. Pothius and still remember that Kalm had called him Sict. His question had only been a courtesy.

To a Teep, that talent seemed marvelous. With a sinking feeling, he understood now that his treat was even more expensive than it was illegal. What had his Nyjuc father purchased for him?

He swallowed. Why had the older Teep done this? He knew he had not been the child his adopted parents had sought.

"Your father said you were entering the armed forces." Perhaps it was offered as a hint. He had been told that some Normals read faces and gestures almost as well as Teeps read thoughts.

"The Falltroop, tomorrow. I was at the end of my education and—" *The Institute does not take Teeps, and I didn't have the skill to be in medicine. There was nothing for me to become in Nyjuc.* Deliberately, he attempted to erase his expression. It was an old wound by now, part of another person's existence. It seemed impossible that his Nyjuc father, already part of his past, was still only man-heights distant. *I could never do anything he would be proud of.* "I felt—I decided to leave."

"Ah-hh. A good choice. So you like excitement, even more than most young men. Surprises. Unusual things. Very strong pleasures."

Kalm swallowed. "This is a surprise from my father."

"Of course. I know you'll enjoy this." He stared at Kalm openly, his expression unreadable. "It's normal to like unusual things, Mr. Pothius. It's even normal to need them."

It was a test, Kalm sensed. He swallowed again, half fearing, half hoping despite the uncertainty that pressed upon him. "Yes. I know."

"Of course." The man smiled again and put his fingers to a plate on the corridor wall. Behind the hanging mesh, the triangular doorway dilated.

There was less furniture here than in the first room, Kalm discovered when he passed through the mesh: a small table, a cube chair, a couch arranged at one end, a cabinet of some sort at the other. He could not make out details, for the room was unlit, dark-paneled rather than stuccoed, without even the customary window onto the summer living room, though it had a modern brick fireplace with a flame rising from stout logs. The air was musty, warm, overused.

A man with a poker knelt before the pit, shoving embers to the back. Middle-aged, Kalm judged when he saw his face, but his body had preserved a youthful trimness and he seemed well muscled. Like Kalm, he wore coveralls, of better quality, perhaps, but not new.

"Tregweln, this is our newest guest, Mr. Pothius," the elegant man said, and the man with the poker rose. He nodded respectfully at Kalm, then spoke to the other man.

Common, Kalm guessed, listening to the meaningless words of their conversation. The lingua franca of the Alliance, an artificial tongue derived from the Fourth Era Plates. Like most educated Algherans, he could decipher short sentences written in that language; he had never heard it spoken until now, and its pronunciation had little connection with what he had expected.

*Several languages.* Another accomplishment he had not mastered.

His eyes wandered. The cabinet at the back of the room was reversed, he decided. Beyond it dark draperies concealed the entrance to the summer living room. Strangers' minds touched the edges of his consciousness; they were unaware of him, and he raised his mind shield, deliberately prolonging the mystery of his surprise.

The elegant man laughed. "We're being rude, Tregweln," he said in Speech. "In front of our guest we should use his speech."

"It's all right," Kalm said politely.

"No, in Chelmmys, dance Chelmmysian style," the man said. "And in Alghera, we should use Speech. Even for complaining about the cook, like Tregweln here."

"It's all right," Kalm repeated, but the man turned away.

"You'll see to Mr. Pothius's comfort, won't you, Tregweln? I'll complete the arrangements with his father."

Arrangements? While Kalm deciphered that, the elegant man vanished.

Tregweln waved him into the cube chair and poured a glass full of purple-black liquid. It was sour and left a variety of tastes on his tongue, so after a polite sip, Kalm left it before him on the table. "How is the cooking here?" he asked, looking for conversation.

"Eh?" Tregweln's voice had a Northerner's monotone twang.

"You were complaining about the cooking?"

"Eh? It's all right here, I guess." Tregweln contemplated the back of the cabinet for a moment, then grabbed recessed handles and began pulling it across the floor. "Could use more spice, maybe. Why? Are you hungry?"

"Uh-h, no. Can I help?"

"Heh!" It might have been a cough. "Don't need help from a customer. Just stay put, boy."

"Well . . ." Kalm stood.

"Now, I'll do this." Tregweln had maneuvered the cabinet to the side of the cube couch. Its back was still facing Kalm. "What you can do, you want to be a gentleman, is go to the lights over there and turn 'em on when I say."

Feeling foolish, Kalm obeyed, keeping his face to the wall and the light switch while rustling and couch-creaking sounds emerged from behind him. "Ready?"

"Give 'em a minute." Tregweln pushed the cabinet away. It rumbled emptily, and Kalm understood it was on wheels. His help had really not been needed.

"Okay," Tregweln said. As the ceiling lights came on, Kalm turned. "Aren't they the beauties, now?"

"Uh," Kalm said. "Uh." His mouth remained opened.

The whispered stories that had gone through the men's dormitory were true.

"Like to introduce. Ladies, this is Mr. Pothius Kallimur. Mr. Pothius, like to introduce. This is Sonol, this is Einulko, this is Hubau, this is Onaulo." Tregweln smiled pridefully, uxoriously. "Well, Mr. Pothius, you come close now and take your choice. But any one of these little ladies is going to give you a wonderful night."

"Hello, Mr. Pothius."

"Hello, Mr. Pothius."

"Hello, Kallimur. Have me tonight."

"Me, Mr. Pothius. Do things with me."

He could not assign the voices to faces.

They spoke. They were alive. Horrified, Kalm stepped toward them as if walking a tightrope, afraid of stumbling and disgracing himself forever.

"Take me, take me," one of the things was chanting. It was a woman's voice, coming from a woman's face. Kalm halted, feeling fear, conscious of his fear.

"No, me, me. Take me," another called.

"Me-me-me-me-me!"

For an instant he had the illusion that they were all chanting, all dancing before him, all holding their arms to him, each demanding that he select her for the night.

But it was illusion.

They had no arms. No shoulders.

They had no legs, no hips.

They had heads and bodies, but not even the stumps of limbs to mar their perfect symmetry. Side by side on the couch, half-supported, half sinking in the soft plastic, they seemed like eggs bobbing in a black sea.

"Me, me, me, me!" they chanted in unison.

Then they stopped and laughed. Together. At him.

## 47,924 L.C.

"So. Kalm ha'Nyjuc," the woman said. "Sit down, Kalm."

He hesitated. "I don't use that name now."

"Rispar Kalm, then. You prefer that?"

"Yes."

"Not even an Association name?"

"No." He was unmarried, but he did not explain that.

*Don't tell them lies, but don't volunteer information. Make them dig for it.* The words had been part of a long-ago lecture. It had all been theory then.

The reality had been landscapes pulled apart by violence, fragments of flesh in blood-slimed soil, stumbling men afraid to look before them, dying men weeping as children do and screaming in pain. Confusion and exhaustion. Orders that could not be trusted. Fears that could not be obeyed. Practicalities.

He had raised his hands when he saw *two* men pointing weapons at him. *One man I could have killed, not two.* He had decided to surrender to two men during the drop, even before he reached the ground, and he had repeated the promise to himself through all the following day till it became instinct. *If I'd taken time to think, I'd be dead now. Not here.*

*I don't have any information to give them, anyhow.*

*This isn't going to be important.*

The woman snapped her fingers. "Sit down, Rispar Kalm, of no status."

She leaned back in her black cube chair, watching him

coolly from behind a crystal desk. Her skirt and blouse were off-white, a color he had come to associate with his jailers rather than the brown of ChelmForceLand, but military insignia were on her shoulders. A tag on her desk read SANDIBECK; he did not know if it was a name or a rank. One of her bare feet rested on a small white rug; the other was fitted under her right knee. Her eyes were dark. Her hair was brown, almost black. It had been pulled back to leave cheeks and ears bare; a thick braid fell to her right shoulder. A window behind her showed a dark blue sky and the mountains of the lower Cordillera.

*This isn't going to be important.*

But less than two watches had passed since his surrender, and they had already brought him a thousand thousand man-heights from the Southern Peninsula. Why?

He let his gaze rove about the room freely but uncovered no answers. It held a desk, two drab cube chairs at either end, door, window, rug, and nothing else. The room was small, wider at the back than at the woman's desk, and shaped to emphasize the impression of length. The walls were without decoration, as if to focus attention on the room's occupant.

Stocky, the woman had a face pleasant rather than beautiful, olive-shaded, with red-touched cheeks showing sunburn. Her figure was broad-boned and full-breasted. The flesh promised softnesses, vulnerabilities. Kalm probed, reading curiosity mixed with indecision despite the attitude she had chosen to display. Below that he found traces of fear, aimed less at him than at the blue uniform he wore. Rape, violence . . . half hopes of delicious male terror bubbled through her mind.

Deeper pink touched the olive cheeks now. Her facial muscles stiffened, and he knew that she had followed his thoughts and saw herself for an instant as he did. A Teep, then—a Chelmmysian Teep.

*Only a child.* Kalm smiled, then gave an instant to exploring the surface of her personality. Sex: the annual fit of season-taken lust, periods of stress and unhappiness that had wakened the same short-lived unfocused passion . . .

In his mind—and hers—an adolescent girl lay sobbing with hatred and ecstasy upon a hillside while faceless Algheran soldiers pressed their hard bodies against her, forced her trembling traitorous flesh into painful joyous contortions, brutally fed the greedy demanding awakened needs . . . A parental figure shouting meaningless words in the background, fears and darknesses and bursts of light and energy mixed with scraps of memory . . . He fed her images back to her. *So this is what you want? Why keep so many soldiers between yourself and the Falltroop?*

"Very primitive," she said aloud, more evenly than he had expected. Her shields formed, shutting him away from the vistas of her mind. "I feel less sorry about what we intend for you."

Kalm snapped his fingers, disdaining the wounded little girl threat. So she had remembered that she was the jailer and he the prisoner. But words were only words.

Of course, he was a prisoner. *A point for me, game to her.*

Further insolence would not be productive. He took the seat she had initially offered and let his eyes roam around the small room as the chair shaped itself to his contours. Moments passed in silence.

"We've separated you from the others," she began anew.

*Because I was the only Teep?*

She read a different question in his face. "There were twelve other survivors in your drop unit. One is expected to die today." A piece of paper was in her hand. "Do you wish names?"

Twelve. Thirteen with him. From three hundred sixty.

"There were more when we surrendered." He did not ask for names.

"It *is* a war," she said, and Kalm was left to think about the implications of the words and about her acceptance of them.

"Algheran telepaths haven't played much part, have they?" She hesitated. "We've been waiting for you."

He waited for more words.

"For someone like you. The Algherans aren't using many telepaths as soldiers, are they, Kalm?"

"I don't know." He spoke only to fill the silence.

"Their telepaths aren't volunteering, are they?"

"I don't know."

"Why do you think that is, Kalm?"

"I don't know."

"Aren't their telepaths good soldiers?"

"I don't know." *I was.*

"Weren't they willing to fight?"

"I don't know." What was this aimed at?

She sighed. "How many telepath officers have you had, Kalm?"

"I don't know." *None*.

Her eyebrows rose. "None?"

"'Never again shall Teeps employ their abilities in the service of national states.'" He swallowed self-consciously, half-embarrassed by quoting those words before her. "I guess it's because of that."

"'The penalty for violation, in thought or action, shall be death.'" She finished the quotation somberly, then lifted her shield about her inner thoughts. "We have a different Compact in the Alliance."

Hemmendur, she meant. A single, all-encompassing world state, unalterable, everlasting. Appalled, he waited silently.

The one world was hostile. When the next Great Winter came, in several thousand years, civilization would fall, as it had twice before. Four-fifths of humanity would die according to the records in the Plates. Nature's winnowing would leave survival to individuals. The rulers of Hemmendur's state, having absolute power, would use it to protect themselves and those who protected them—the Teeps. Inevitably, tyranny would be reborn, as it had twice before in the times of the First and Second Eternal Wars.

"Algheran fantasy." Yet she hid her thoughts from view before speaking again. "Even in Chelmmys, it's understood that telepaths will never be allowed to rule again."

"They will want to rule!" Kalm stopped, listening to his words. Were they true? Did he himself wish . . .

He pushed the thoughts away.

She smiled at his confusion. "Tyranny requires force. And telepaths aren't much good at killing, are they, Kalm?"

"I managed it." She had not expected that, he saw, as his memories eroded her skepticism. Perhaps he should enjoy this victory. "If you have to kill to avoid being killed . . . it can be done."

"I see." She focused on the words, not liking the information but evidently wishing to remember it. Her shield remained in place, leaving him only her silence to consider.

The next question came as a total surprise. "How long do you expect to take before you join the Alliance's side?"

Kalm did not quite choke.

"When Cimon hangs up his scales," he said at last. "I'm with the *Falltroop*, lady." He did not say "Algheran."

"Without much cause," she said evenly, and he could see that she was older than he had believed, harder, more in control of herself. She rested her elbows on the desk and propped her chin on joined hands. "We have a need for knowledgeable paratroop instructors."

"Fight us on equal terms. We'll teach your soldiers plenty."

"How long before you join us?"

"Never." *I thought I explained.*

She smiled tightly. "Your views will change."

"I will not change my views," he said carefully. "I've been an Algheran soldier for five years, and I expect to stay one. See my mind if you doubt."

"I have seen enough of your mind, Rispar Kallimur ha'Nyjuc." The last name was stressed, irony-tainted. "Five years of peace, but we're at war now. Do you wish to be on the victorious side? Yes. Do you wish to avoid years of captivity? Yes. Would you like to receive a promotion to officer? Yes. Do you have reason to dislike life under Algheran rule? Yes. Can the Alliance offer you a better life? Yes. Can you find justification for serving with us? Yes."

The angry chant stopped abruptly. She leaned back in her chair and stared at him silently. "You will change your views," she said softly. "Of your own free will. We've examined you, and we're quite sure of it. You realize already there is justice on both sides of this conflict; you must also realize the Alliance is sure to win. At some point you must come to terms with our victory. Is that not so?"

"I'll wait for it to happen first."

"It will." There was no zealot's hysteria in her voice, only a simple statement of fact. "Alghera will be overwhelmed."

"It hasn't happened yet, lady."

"Oh? Aren't you a prisoner?"

Kalm hesitated. "We—the Battle Masters may have miscalculated. But I bet we hit you hard yesterday."

"Examine this." She held out a scroll.

Unrolling the paper, Kalm found a map of the Earth. The northern portion of the double continent was shown in swollen form so that it seemed to contain half the area of the one world. A jagged red line traced the boundaries of Alghera; a hollow bead the same color rested at the junction of the Southern Peninsula with the mainland. Cross-hatching bordered the inside of the lines and filled the bead.

He tore the map in half, then into quarters and eighths, and dropped the scraps on the floor before resuming his seat. "So?"

"Your country has lost the marked portion of that map in the first half year of the war. It has gained no territory."

"So?"

"So," she mocked. "So. Five year tenths from now Alghera will be even smaller. A year after that, smaller yet. And what is lost, Algheran, will not be regained." She pinched thumb and forefinger together slowly, satisfaction plain upon her face. "Shaddur, Loprit, Innings. There will be no Alghera between them, not even a city that bears that name." *And in the Sixth Era, not even a memory.*

Kalm felt sick. "You can't—" But the words belied his knowledge. *Even in the Plates?*

*We will write the next set of Plates our way. If we decide to leave such records.* "A battle to the end was the Algheran choice. Not ours."

He swallowed. "What if—" He could not continue.

"Surrender? What is left would remain a nation. We do not need to be vindictive." She leaned back in her chair, watching him carefully, her toes moving sinuously through the pile of the white carpet. "Pick up the paper, Kalm."

Shame stopped his movement. "No."

For half a minute she crossed eyes with him, then he turned away deliberately, fighting to keep his breath even. "No."

"Do you think this matters?" She snapped her fingers in dismissal. "It is nothing, ha'Nyjuc. Think of preserving your nation instead. Help us and bring the war to an end. End the killing and the waste. End the pain and injuries. End the second-class existence of your Septlings. Join us now and save what you can of your world, Kalm."

"No!"

She shook her head slightly, her eyes fixed on some vision hidden behind her mind shield. "Ultimately, you will be one of us. The only question is how long it will take."

Abruptly, her voice softened. "You want to join us, Kalm, don't you? It will hurt some of the people who hurt you, Kalm. You'd like that, wouldn't you?"

For the first time since he had surrendered, Kalm was touched by true fear, by shame. Something unseemly, which must be denied, crawled in the dark recesses of his mind.

"What are you offering?" He forced a sneer to follow.

"An education, perhaps. A ChelmForce commission, if you qualify. Hard work." She waited quietly.

"That's not much." It was half question, half complaint.

"Only what any Teep is entitled to in the Alliance. Any Normal."

Kalm considered that. "Why?" he asked. "Why me?"

"Pick up the paper, Kalm." Her voice was soft.

Red-faced, he obeyed and placed the scraps on her desk. "Here."

"Thank you, Kalm." She touched the paper idly with a finger, stirring the pieces around as if searching for a pattern. "You may sit down again if you like." Her eyes closed.

He wanted to sit, he found suddenly. "Why me?" he asked again, feeling the cube chair remold itself to him. The room was overwarm, he noticed; the chair's embrace was uncomfortably tight and clammy.

She waved a hand, her eyes still closed. "The war will not be truly won until the Alliance has the loyalty of the Algheran telepaths. Someone must be the first. You are a captive and you are a telepath. One of the few in the Algheran forces."

"You're wrong, lady. Even if—" Kalm sighed, wishing he could explain matters to her. "The Teeps are loyal."

"Most telepaths are, but do the Normals know that, Kalm? Aren't they afraid of you? Aren't they watching for some resistance to their war? Isn't it fear of revolt that keeps them from forming telepath units?"

"Custom," Kalm lied. "They trust us."

She did not listen. "And do the telepaths know as much about their state as you? Have they seen as many sides of it as you? Do they have cause to dislike it as much as you? Will they help us as much as you?"

He stood. "It won't be me, lady. You try somebody else."

She laughed curtly. "We have you, Kalm. You're already thinking of the rewards, aren't you? Think what the news will do in your Alghera, ha'Nyjuc—the very first telepath captured during the war defecting to the Alliance!" Her lips curled gloatingly as she leaned forward. "We were so pleased to find you, Kalm."

Kalm choked, feeling drenched in the contempt and hatred she was projecting at him. "No."

*Yes!* Her mind blanketed his, despite his screen, forcing him to see himself as he would be—proud, bitter, scornful, dominating, guiltless. *A hero, Kalm! Women, wealth, fame—*

*all you wish from life, all you wish to be, we will make that of
you!*

"No." He almost wept. "I don't want that."

An image formed clearly in his mind: Onaulo, sweat-
drenched on satin-smooth bedclothes, useless muscles throb-
bing above the tops of her breasts as Kalm thrust himself into
her body. A year ago. His last leave. Not yet lubricated, she
had wept and cursed at him. There had been blood. It had
been wonderful.

The image changed. Now it was Einulko writhing mind-
lessly as he used her body. Then a transformed Tagin. Then
Sandibeck herself, and finally a large weeping woman he
could not identify.

Then the memories and fantasies faded. He was millions of
man-heights distant from F'a Alghera and a prisoner. Sandibeck stared at him coldly, her face flushed.

He shifted position uneasily, waiting for her reaction.

"You're ashamed of yourself," she said finally, evenly, and
he knew she had created the images in his mind and waited to
expose them to him. "Of this need for control."

He nodded silently.

She ignored that. "You think we wouldn't dare use you."

That was true. He shook his head.

"We can find another telepath if you won't cooperate,
Kalm. And we'll cure you instead. Would you like that?"

"Yes." He said it softly.

"Four knife cuts and you'll never need to control another
person again." Her eyes flicked toward his groin. "Maybe five
knife cuts. They wouldn't have to be big."

Seconds passed before he understood—before he went
mad.

"No!" Blackness surrounded him. Kalm hammered at the
woman's mind with his own, pushing at it, trying to force the
emotions away from him, to dam them inside her own skull.

Without success. Without control.

He stumbled toward her, intending to strike or to leave, not
caring which so long as he could act. But after two steps, his
muscles would not work. His hands, his feet—nothing
moved, nothing responded to his will. The only sound he
could form was a muffled gurgle.

"Behave yourself," she said coldly. "I'll let you speak."

Pent-up air, released, made him gurgle again, but he managed to put words together. "No. No, please—don't do that.

Send me off to a prison camp, with the others. All I want is to be exchanged, just like anyone else."

Her eyebrows rose. "Do you really believe the Algherans will exchange for you, Kalm? A twenty-three-year-old telepath with no skills, little education, no noticeable talents? A private with a scrap of combat experience, forbidden promotion because of your precious Compacts? An ordinary killer who turned traitor to avoid his captivity? A Teep! You've no value to anyone, ha'Nyjuc, except the Alliance. No one else wants you or even cares about you."

*You are only a thing, Kalm. It's you that is helpless now.*
*You will do for us everything we wish.*
*Teep.*

Kalm fought a need to swallow again. "Not, not a traitor."

She snapped her fingers and let the sound hang in the air. "You will be. And you don't go to an exchange camp unless I say so. And I won't—traitor."

She sprawled backward, her arms spread comfortably on the sides of her cube chair, a foot resting on a corner of her desk top. Deliberately, maddeningly, clearly visible through the crystal, she spread her legs, then pulled her skirt back over both knees and slowly touched the insides of her thighs, miming knife strokes as Kalm stared.

She laughed without humor, her mouth open and devouring. "Or you might find a way to kill yourself. If not—we'll speak again when you've had time to think, Algheran pervert."

Guards appeared and forced a Teepblind over Kalm's hair, then led him to solitary confinement.

# CHAPTER THREE

*R*ain had begun to fall, and through iron mesh Kalm ha'Nyjuc looked down on a pair of unwary picnickers who hastily gathered their belongings and rushed across the suddenly deserted grounds of the Institute. Hand in hand, they darted into a hedge-lined path and vanished from his sight over the edge of the hill.

*Probably in love*, Kalm recognized wistfully. *Good luck to them*. Ceiling lights flickered on behind him automatically, brightening the storm-cast gloom and making a dark mirror of the glass wall. Against ghost images of demon-twisted towers, a cobweb-shrouded specter floated. Kalm stared at his own face.

Oval-shaped and swarthy, at thirty it pointed already to the mold of middle age it would bear for the next three centuries. Long creases were etched across his forehead and above his lips asymmetrically; the lopsided face itself was also asymmetrical with its rounder and higher left cheek. His hair was brown-black, cut short in current Chelmmysian fashion so its natural curl could not be seen. His eyebrows were dark, thick, curved bars. As he grimaced, his jaw moved sideways so that the lines of his closed lips and eyebrows slanted toward each other.

It was a medium kind of face, Kalm had often thought: neither handsome nor ugly, saved from total anonymity only by the pale lozenge of skin on his forehead and the tiny pit in its center. A medium face, and to go along with it he had medium height and a medium weight.

*A medium person.* He grimaced briefly. *Ordinary.* Suited to an ordinary existence.

But not to City Year 893, not to times like these. Reflected before him he could see the jumble of papers on the desk he had had brought in, the discarded combat gear strewn over the cobalt-blue floor of his commandeered office, the mesh hastily fastened over walls and ceiling, the open triangular doorway filled now by the tall SubLegate in the white uniform of ChelmForceOccupation.

The room behind the guardsman was empty, as was the rest of the floor; Kalm allowed himself a moment to worry about rebuilding an administrative staff.

"No trace of them," he said, repeating the SubLegate's message but not troubling to look directly at the man. And now he saw with two sets of eyes, focusing both on the lead-clouded sky behind the mirroring glass and on the paunchy red-garbed man who stood before the window. "Probably should have expected that."

"Chieftain?"

Listening with two sets of ears, Kalm felt the word arise within the SubLegate's mind, then heard him speak. He settled deeper into the other's thoughts, seeking direct knowledge.

"You're absolutely sure?" he said. Memories of conversations moved past his consciousness, houses visited and doors knocked on, records examined in the offices of the Institute and sought for amid the ashes in the still smoldering files of the late Warder, interviews with puzzled secretaries and grieving parents . . . The man had been thorough. "Yes, I believe you."

"Chieftain." The SubLegate was contented; he had carried out his orders well, and it was known. Perhaps he would be dismissed soon for reassignment to other responsible tasks, perhaps he would earn his release shortly and return to his wife and child.

*So simple it seems to him*, Kalm thought resentfully. *Seven thousand of ChelmForceDrop dead in one day, and then Occupation darts in like hummingbirds at flowers. Public order . . . Yes, they are needed, but it does not make them the equals of eagles.*

"Return to your barracks," he ordered. "Report back to me tomorrow at the end of the first day tenth."

"Chieftain!" The SubLegate made an across-the-chest salute and left the room. His thoughts vanished outside the curtain of mesh, but his footsteps were loud in the empty building.

When echoes told him the man had left the rampway, Kalm reopened his eyes and watched as the tall, dim figure walked without concern into the rain and away. Long after the SubLegate vanished, Kalm was still staring at the nearly invisible grounds of the Institute.

He was getting nothing done, he finally realized. Angry, he slapped at the switches that drew shutters upward to cover the glass and went to the brown cube chair at the table. A writing block lay before him; as the chair molded itself to his body, Kalm slipped a stylus onto his writing finger and began to list the facts he knew:

> Missing—Borictar ha'Dicovys, deputy administrator
> Tolipim ha'Ruijac, aide to deputy
> Siccentur tra'Ruijac, science faculty
> Verrict ha'Hujsuon, science faculty
> others, Normals—science faculty and students
>     Teeps—medical, administrative staff
>
> Not at Institute
> Not at homes or Sept lodges
> Not prisoners
> Not reported as leaving city
>
> Laboratory—deserted
> fire damage in an untouched building
> some kind of sled (?)

Two puzzles. Could they be linked together? He rapped absently on the table as he gazed blindly across the office, wishing a lightning flash of inspiration would illuminate, if only for an instant, his dark mysteries.

Insight did not come.

He sighed inwardly. Where were the missing men?

Not in the army. Not killed in the fighting. That would have become known by now.

An accident? Unfortunate if true but— *No!* He banged his fist on the table. Once, yes, but not twenty times. Coincidence

was ruled out by that. Besides, scholars, savants, doctors . . .
people such as his onetime uncle and cousin led protected
lives. *I'll bet they went away together.*

Hiding, then. Plotting. Doing something in secret.

He scowled. It was not possible; with one person in fifty on
the one Earth a telepath, only children believed that secrets
could be kept.

But he saw no alternatives. It was a secret, and neither
Algheran Teeps nor the telepaths of the Alliance had heard of
it. Even now, with the war over.

*It is not possible*, he told himself again. *The war is over.*

The war was over. There was no reason now to keep secrets hidden, even if—

But a government could keep a secret. The Alliance had.
The Algherans had never expected the assault that had captured their capital; even soldiers of ChelmForce had not shared
their High Command's plans until the very end.

His cheek twitched involuntarily. For an instant, it was
morning once more in the still high air and he was crowded by
other men against thin rails, seeing men in crimson sliding
downward to Earth through the darting blue-painted levcraft
of Alghera, while in the distance a great metallic tray rocked
upon emptiness like a tempest-tossed ship, sloshing against its
walls scarlet drops that were soldiers. In his memory, the tray
tipped slowly upward again, to hang vertically in one forever-
frozen moment while red pooled in a corner and poured like
fluid out upon the city beneath and the gnat screams of men
spilling without parachutes into the cold air were louder than
all the voices and commotion about him . . .

Had two days already passed? Yes.

*A government can keep a secret.*

What secret had the Algherans kept? What unimaginable
thing had they attempted? They had left no records, no proof
of anything.

But only two days had passed. Half the city's people were
homeless and unfed, and those miseries properly occupied the
Alliance's attention. No one but he was searching for the vanished faculty members. No one else wondered about valueless
Algheran schemes for resistance. No one else worried.

And what sort of evidence would a searcher find? he asked
himself wrathfully. Whom would he talk to? The Warder of
Alghera dead by his own hand, the Gathering Hall of the
Muster a gutted wreck and the delegates scattered, the Battle

Masters and their staffs dead in futile last-ditch combats . . .

*No government left here now, no authority. Even the Septs* . . . Swordthrust Castle, Gallant Home, Justice's Redoubt, Resolution Stronghold—all were ruins now, targets Chelm-Force had singled out for particular punishment. Even Nyjuc House, which no lunatic could have considered a military objective, had been demolished during the fighting. The lack of records proved exactly nothing.

*But the war is over!* There was nothing now left but mopping up. Another ten days and the tiny provincial garrisons that had not surrendered would be straggling in just to get fed.

Would the missing scholars be with them?

He did not think so.

Suddenly he tired of being pent up in his too-silent, too-lifeless, thought-shielded office. He was not ready for desk work, he recognized. It would be pleasant—it was necessary —to move around on his feet again and look at things through his own eyes.

*And it does the troops good to see their commander from time to time*, he added sardonically. *I'll wear my full kit.*

Practiced fingers stripped the sheath from the tiny Killing Right knife on his helmet and smoothed the flaps on his bandolier, then strapped his gleaming Wand of Persuasion to his belt. The grace knife in his boot, the neuroshocker at his side —they were never removed and needed no checking.

Moving briskly now that he had a clear goal, Chieftain Second Rispar Kallimur ha'Nyjuc-once-ha'Ruijac of Chelm-ForceDrop's Combat Interrogation Group, acting director of the Algheran Institute for the Study of Land Reclamation Issues, passed the door of his office and jogged down the five ramps that brought him to the ground floor.

The rain had stopped, and the sun was emerging from behind the clouds again. The air was clean for the moment, free of saltwater tang, free of smoke from burning buildings. The grass and trees about him were water-beaded, summer green. Kalm breathed deeply of the cool air, enjoying his sensations as he leapt the small puddles that made an obstacle course of the pathways that crisscrossed the Institute. The world and its promise had been reborn, and with peace arrived, there was time again to recognize its beauty.

The campus grounds were once more littered with people, many of the men wearing green and black uniforms stripped of insignia. *We should be importing some clothing*, Kalm thought. *Get these people back in civvies, if only to keep them acting like civilians. When High Command gets an inspector here, I'll bring it up.*

Meanwhile he ran deliberately at people on the pathway, awkward from his lack of exercise but determined, making them step into flower beds or onto the wet grass to avoid him. This was necessary, he told himself; Alghera had been defeated and occupied. Teeps were among its overlords now, and its citizens needed to have the fact smeared into their hair.

He might be accomplishing that; people grew silent as he approached them, and when he had passed, their conversations were louder and more voluble. He made no attempt to read their minds—he already knew what they thought of him and, consciously at least, was not troubled by it.

*Just be polite and don't spit till I'm out of sight*, he thought as he ran. But there was no one present to see into his mind.

A babble of voices grew louder as he moved. The building he sought was on the far side of the Institute grounds, and Kalm had elected to run around the perimeter. Now he detoured, breathing heavily and grateful for a respite as he walked down a graveled trail that led from the hilltop to a shabby side street.

*Mass confusion* was his first thought. Then he spotted the field whites of a ChelmForceOccupation guardsman. His consciousness split as he entered the mind of the guardsman.

Orders were orders, and his orders specified that these battle-damaged tenements were to be razed. On the invasion day they had housed two Falltroop companies that had not been flushed until ChelmForceLand seized the high ground of the Institute and outflanked them. The buildings had been shaken by LongPushers during the fighting and were structurally unsound. They had to be demolished and removed now, no matter how unhappy these upset Algherans became. Already a labor draft was at work, Land Watch parolees directed by engineers from the Mother Continent, slicing through the rose-colored walls of the nearest building with narrow-focused pushsticks and dumping the pastel rubble into a pair of waiting levtrucks.

The telepaths had certified the ex-soldiers as reliable, and the civilians seemed more frustrated than threatening. Even so, he was glad to look up the street and see the officer; the sight of a red uniform and weapons would have more impact on these people than any amount of moral authority.

Kalm understood the situation now; he returned to his own mind and accepted the guardsman's salute with a nod.

The crowd had also noticed him. Men retreated as he moved. A mother pulled a sullen-faced child to her. Silence spread.

Kalm unholstered the Wand of Persuasion from his belt and plugged its base cord into the power storage pack in his bandolier, then actuated the Wand and held it erect as he advanced.

A brush against a Wand would cause shocked nerves to tingle; a firmer touch would create pain. Even those who had never seen a Wand knew of them, and the open space between Kalm and the guardsman grew wider at once. Kalm smiled grimly at that and tucked his helmet into the crook of his arm, holding his head high so the Algherans could see the pale skin on his forehead and know him.

"A Teep!" someone exclaimed. Other voices completed the ritual: "The Teep! It's him—the traitor!"

Kalm smiled again, without mirth, at the recognition and turned to the confused guardsman. TRANSMONTANE KINGDOMS he read upon the shoulder patch; the man was from the northern part of the Mother Continent, his nation a mainstay of the Alliance for three centuries. And he was a priest of Cimon as well, by the sword and scythe on his collar—overburdened by a sense of duty and compassion.

"Having some problems with this pack?" Kalm asked. He spoke in Chelmmysian rather than Common, knowing that the patois of the Kingdoms was close enough to that language to be understood by the guardsman, deliberately stamping his alienage upon the crowd. "My once-fellow citizens are generally a docile lot—after you've knocked them on their butts a few times."

Someone understood that remark. Kalm quelled the resulting murmurs by turning toward the bystanders and raising the Wand.

"We're tearing down their homes," the guardsman said. He stopped, as if that explained everything.

In a way, it did. How many people lived in Fohima Alghera? Kalm wondered. Forty thousand? Fifty? No matter—it was a fantastic sum. No other city in the world was half so large, not even Chelmmys. He doubted if ever there had been a city with so many people—nearly one in every thousand of all the people in the world, Normal or telepath.

Say fifty thousand in Fohima Alghera and ten times that number who claimed her citizenship outside the city limits . . .

*Now begins the Fifth Era*, Kalm found himself thinking. *Now!*

Twelve thousand years to conquer Kh'taal Minzaer in the Second Era, four millennia to defeat the Teeps of the Fourth Era . . . *And now the one world is unified again. This was our war.*

There would never be another one. It had taken seven years for the Alliance to subdue Alghera, and even those now holding victory remained sickened at the cost. No other city, no other state would ever grow to this size again. Such a risk would never be allowed.

But necessity did not have to be cruel. When he spoke now to the guardsman, his tones were softer and he used Common so that most of the crowd could understand him.

"Tell them we are building new homes for them," he said. "Better ones than the hovels they've put up with because of the war. Tell them we'll be transporting them there in another few days. Tell them they'll be fed and given medical care if they need it. Tell them we'll reunite families and clothe their children. And then tell them we and they have a great deal of rebuilding to do—together—and that for anyone who seeks it there will be high-paying work. Tell them they are part of the Alliance now and we look after our own.

"Tell them the time for fear is past—and the time for hatred—and the time for hunger. Tell them defeat is hard but victory sweet, and that they are entitled to share our common victory. Tell them their honor remains. And tell them the day will come when each will know himself a member of the Alliance first and Algheran second—and have no regret."

"Sir." The guardsman saluted.

*They'll be obedient now.* Kalm frowned at the uncomprehending eyes, then deactivated his Wand and replaced it in his belt. He donned his helmet. He walked away without another word, and the crowd parted before him like waters beneath the prow of a ship.

The "new homes" would be a concentration camp, he admitted to himself bitterly as he leaned into the hillside trail going back to the Institute grounds. Until supply lines could be established for the occupation forces, the food would be half-ripened grain taken from Algheran fields. The clothing would come from ChelmForce stocks, made surplus as the Alliance's military shrank back to peacetime strength. And while the promised jobs existed, most were on the Mother Continent; Alghera would be a place where careers ended rather than began.

For an instant he remembered being Kallimur ha'Ruijac in a world where all men were kind and brave, being twelve years old and eager to attend the Institute and study under his oft-honored Septlings . . .

It seemed another's childhood.

*Getting sentimental in my old age*, he jibed as he pushed through shrubbery near the top of the hill. Those had been Association members back there, not the Septed. Losing the war would not hurt them, and while the Alliance kept them under control, the Septs would be powerless. Coercion would not be necessary, just the promise of a better existence. The Alliance would deliver what it promised; refocusing Algheran patriotism would be no great task.

A *pfftt!* escaped from between his teeth. There went Alghera. He tapped the butt of his Wand once more, drawing reassurance. *Take that, Alghera.*

He was at level ground again, on the paved trail that rimmed the Institute, and the shrubbery had given way to young trees. He followed the path around a corner and into a small clearing, then stopped suddenly. He had been noticed.

"Excuse me," he said dryly. "I thought I had the trail to myself."

The youngsters in the clearing looked up with confusion from their blankets. They appeared considerably distressed—and guilty.

Their conduct seemed innocent enough, Kalm thought with amusement. Some kissing, coupled with gentle fondling, all done with rather more passion than experience if he was any judge. He doubted if even a real director of the Institute would have been upset.

For a moment he watched them with one set of eyes, then watched himself from other eyes, knowing himself with a shock as ancient and alien and threatening. Then he withdrew to his own mind, alone again.

They were very young, he realized. A life span of centuries left much time for love and the search for love, and the loves of one's youth were not always the more meaningful or the more intense, to judge from the experiences of those about him. But there was something innocent and fresh about those newly in love and young in the still young world.

He smiled as genuinely as he could. *Cimon gift you, children*, he thought at them. But they were Normals, of course, and did not notice.

The boy heaved himself to his feet and stepped toward Kalm. "What do you want?" he asked threateningly.

"Through," Kalm said gently, hearing hollowness in the bravado. *Yes, I am dangerous, boy. But the war is over.* "I have work to do."

"Tlad, it's the director! See his insignia," the girl said, sitting up. She tugged at her companion's hand. Golden hair cascaded over her shoulders; seeing it, Kalm suddenly realized that this was the couple he had watched a tenth day before from the vantage of his office. So this was how their picnic had turned out.

"Sorry, sir," the boy said, holding himself back. "I didn't recognize you."

"No need for you to," Kalm said, restraining himself in the same fashion. "You thought to defend your companion, and that is estimable."

That was stiff and pompous, he sensed even as he spoke the words, and he wished he could call them back. But it was too late, and an awkward pause ensued while Kalm damned himself for always being stiff and pompous when confronted with people who were in love.

The girl broke the silence. "We're new students, sir, and—"

*Tagin*, Kalm thought suddenly. Tagin Ruijac might have looked like this at twenty, from his memories of her at seventeen. But those memories were two decades old. Tagin would be a woman now, perhaps with children of her own who would someday attend the Institute.

He grimaced involuntarily, his breath caught within his throat. *Children, a hearthsharer*... The barriers that time might have placed between Tagin and himself, should he ever meet her again, would not be surmountable. She the captive now, himself the victor, and yet Tagin had triumphed in a contest he had never realized. She would never be for him.

"I'm sorry," he said abruptly, breathing once more. "I was distracted. Repeat your question."

The girl looked at him with irritation, frown lines pointing down between her eyebrows. That, at least, was not like

Tagin. "Will there be classes?" she asked. "I have to tell my parents."

*The concerns of youth,* Kalm recognized with bitter amusement. *I'm seeking several hundred people who just might keep the world at war the rest of her lifetime, and she's worried about an allowance.*

*You wouldn't go home now even if your parents ordered,* he thought. But that lacked relevance to the words she had spoken.

"There is a certain amount of confusion at the moment," he answered instead, silently admiring his smooth understatement. "But we are trying to pull all the staff back together and get the buildings in shape. I think we'll have things running normally in less than a year tenth, at least on the academic end of the Institute. So your parents should leave you enrolled— and send you your allowance."

"Good." She smiled prettily at him.

Kalm did not allow himself to be charmed. "You should know—and tell them—the authorities will make some changes. There will soon be an exchange program with schools within the Alliance which are the equals of the Institute. So you may have a few students in your classes, or even a few instructors, who are not from Alghera."

"That will be all right," she said innocently. "Just as long as there are not too many of them."

Kalm made himself continue. "It is possible that you will be offered a chance yourself to attend another school for a year, if you desire, and if places are available. It would not be required of you, of course, but it may be recommended for some students." *For any of those who hope to become leaders.*

She frowned. "I— It would depend—on what sort of people, I mean." Then she stopped in evident confusion. Kalm steeled his heart.

"Finally," he said in metallic tones, "telepaths will be admitted to the Institute as students and staff. In proportion to their numbers within the Realm."

She stared at him with open dismay. "But there will be dozens of them!" she wailed. "That'll be awful!"

"It's going to be perfectly delightful," Kalm growled. "Now, I have work to do. Please excuse me." His voice had been clear and not elevated, but the rumble of an earthquake had been in it. When he stepped past, neither boy nor girl moved a muscle.

Ten minutes of trotting at a medium pace brought Kalm to a nondescript two-story laboratory building.

*Shabby*, he observed critically while collecting his breath. *This is supposed to be new. And it looked good when I saw it pictured in Algheran minds.* The building was settling unevenly, and cracks marred its brown-glazed exterior. The walkway had a washboard surface; in one spot, buckled pavement exposed the soil underlying the thin layer of red concrete. Shoddy construction, skimped maintenance, decay . . . the Algherans had noticed none of it.

*Seven years of living on ironberry skins*, Kalm thought grimly. The Institute was one of the glories of their state; the Algherans should have preserved it in gemlike condition. *One good thing about Occupation*, he vowed. *We'll fix up this dump.*

Then he was through the triangular doorway. "The new director is here," he heard from an open office. And the thoughts came: *The Teep. The telepath. The traitor.*

A sprinkling of clerical workers were already straggling through the halls; the fifth day tenth was coming to a close, and people were leaving for their homes. *Shabby attire*, Kalm noted as well, but he kept the thought from showing on his face. *No fear. No one's worried because I'm here.*

*Dicovys, a pair from Cuhyon . . . but mostly the Septless.*

*Victims, even if the Algherans had won.*

Meanwhile he sent his consciousness throughout the building. Only the basement floor was metaled, he had been told, so unless he missed people wearing Teepblinds, he would soon have the place to himself.

A sign forbidding telepaths from going farther had been mounted above a rampway on his right. Ignoring glances from the onlookers, he pressed past them wordlessly and went down to the underground floor.

One of the men assigned to him was there, a ChelmForce-Land soldier seated on a black cube chair outside the locked entrance to the laboratories. A neuroshocker was in his hand. He did not salute but stood when Kalm came into sight, then holstered the weapon when he recognized the officer.

"How goes it?" Kalm asked comfortably.

"Well enough, Chieftain," the man said. "A couple of curiosity seekers came down in the morning, but I chased them, and they went easily enough when they saw there weren't anything here but me."

"Any Teeps?" The question had to be asked, even if Kalm knew the answer already. Surely Algherans would not violate their own taboos.

The man nodded. "None of theirs, Chieftain. No forehead badges on them, and begging your pardon, no spot on their head to show where a badge might have been removed."

Kalm snapped his fingers. "Don't count on seeing those emblems much longer. We've got surgical teams flying in from the Mother Continent to remove them. With another ten-day period and some sunlight, it will take you a close look to tell Algheran telepaths from any others."

The soldier snapped his own fingers in return. The man was not interested, Kalm realized, or perhaps even hostile to the idea. He had to remember that possibility. The Teeps had made the Alliance feasible, and perhaps inevitable, but that had not made them loved. Hemmendur's Solution allowed Normals and telepaths to live together; it could not wipe out fifty thousand years of enmity.

So he gazed quietly at the soldier before proceeding, and the man shifted awkwardly under his glance.

"I'm going in," Kalm said at last. "When your relief shows, have him report to me, if I'm still here. And before you go, get a rock and knock down that Cimon-taken sign over the ramp."

"Yes, sir."

Kalm shook his head grimly, then fished a cylindrical key from a pocket of his bandolier and opened the triangular door-way. As it closed, he could see the soldier taking his seat once more.

*Dark* was his first thought. And the space remained dim, with only a soft glow coming from a few ceiling panels, even after he called out experimentally for more light. Power failure, he decided; ghost fluid had been cut off from the over-head panels. He would get a technician to check out the circuits tomorrow; now, he closed his eyes for several seconds to make his pupils dilate.

*Maze* was his next impression. However, exploration made the layout sensible. The basement was one large laboratory, concrete floored and split into sections by movable partitions. Iron mesh lined the outer walls and the ceiling, draped over nails and hooks rather than cemented into place as was customary. The mesh was not of uniform size; inspecting it by touch in the gloom, Kalm found roughly soldered joins and irregular gaps patched with scraps. Algheran workmanship normally was more fastidious; this suggested haste or carelessness.

The green ceramic walls were cratered and cracked; dust and glassy chips made small mounds beneath the broken places. Was that untidiness or battle damage? Kalm recalled the Institute's dilapidated condition and decided to reserve judgment.

He soon came to the site he had sought. Along one wall mesh drooped abjectly, the links elongated and warped. The surface beneath was flame-scorched, smoke-stained, and puckered. Ash lay over the floor in small piles, brown and gray in the dim light from the damaged ceiling. Kalm prodded them with a foot, making dust float in the air and streaking his boots. Nothing seemed to have survived the fire. He stamped his feet to clean them and continued his explorations.

Office cubicles ran along one long wall, carrels separated from one another by chest-high partitions of tan plastic. Others had done this before him, Kalm knew, but he searched the tables and files regardless. There was no sign of use to be found—not a piece of paper, or a holographic book or teaching reel, or even scraps of trash.

There was settled ash but no dust. The space had been used. For some secret purpose?

There was no answer to that. And meanwhile, the part of him that was the acting director of the Institute worried, *Where am I going to get people to replace my missing staff?*

Soon he left the office area to enter the work bays. There were four of those, and the dim light showed that two of them had been extensively damaged by arson. The Algherans' cleverness had caught them out here, he noticed with satisfaction; if the fires they had started had been intended to gut the entire laboratory, their removal of compromising material had not left sufficient fuel for the flames to spread. As a result, one bay had suffered little more than paint damage; another had escaped completely.

He saw no dust. That suggested recent use. Had they been too rushed by the city's fall to arrange the laboratory's destruction properly?

He abandoned that thought as he entered the fourth work

bay. Here was the "sled" that had so puzzled his investigators. What kind of technical background did they have? Able interrogators, he decided as he moved about; patient and experienced with people, to be sure—but none of them had been scholars or even engineers.

Nor was he, he admitted with ancient bitterness. Chelm-Force had given him an education; he could read the records left by the Fourth Era and use mathematical tables, but that was not enough to make a faculty savant. Circumstances had made him a soldier and at last a symbol; he could never be a true scholar. Only accident had brought a soldier to the directorship of the Earth's most prestigious university.

In the winter, when routine had returned to the Institute, a proper replacement would be found to administer it, and Kalm would be released from this duty. He could return to Nyjuc House then—empty, smashed Nyjuc House—if his fellow Teeps chose to accept him. Or to the Settlement for a brief while, despite every protest from Ruijac.

To do nothing.

His life was ending now, he realized—had ended with Fohima Alghera's surrender, despite the surprise of his survival. Another four centuries might well pass before he rose to Cimon, and he would spend that time eating, walking, dreaming, breathing, pretending to be alive. He could return to a soldier's occupation or find another. But he would not live, in spite of all pretense.

*The traitor Teep.* He would never become anything else.

The choice had been his own. The Chelmmysians had asked, but he had agreed, and no blame could be placed on them for that.

Centuries hence, Algheran citizens of the Alliance, smug and secure in their loyalty, never doubting that justice had been done by their nation's defeat, would remember him with scorn.

The sled's presence was a puzzle. Perhaps there was a shaft to the surface he had not discovered; otherwise he could not understand why the vehicle had been constructed here. Perhaps it was simply for testing, a prototype. But no—there were stalls here to house four sleds. He had to assume that the Algherans had done so—and that three sleds were missing.

He wandered around the laboratory, glancing once more into the offices and the storage rooms that ringed the work

area, but he found no exits other than the triangular doorway
that he had come through originally. The sled would not fit
through that. Grimacing unconsciously, he returned to the vehicle.

*Patchwork*, he thought, looking at the scaffolding around
the sled. Here was something else that the Algherans had
thrown together at the last moment, little more than scraps of
gray plastic tubing, bent at the tops and poorly straightened,
sloppily heat-welded to provide a supporting framework. The
sled was no more elaborate, a plywood box a man-height high
and wide. Twice that dimension in length, it rested, off balance but for the scaffold, on a pair of runners. Within it,
visible through the missing floor, he saw internal partitions
and supports for a levmotor and its power pack. The coils and
guiding vanes beneath were still exposed. Rectangular openings were unfilled at the front and on both sides. Had the other
sleds been just as flimsy and ungainly as this? He suspected
they were.

It was some sort of a carrier, he decided, clambering up the
scaffolding. *Lay down plastic sheeting over these rails and
you can move as much as you can with a medium-sized levtruck.* But if that was its purpose, why not use a levtruck?

*The real vehicles went to soldiers,* he speculated. *They
made these when they were out of resources.* What gamble
had people so impoverished made?

He grabbed the plank that formed a hatchway top and
swung himself in to balance awkwardly on two of the interior
crossbars, then moved forward slowly, clutching from upright
to upright to keep his balance till he had reached the motor. A
cube formed from six superconducting plates, correctly or-
iented, to judge by the symbols inscribed on them; the bundle
of power conduits for ghost fluid; fluid shunts and other control circuits . . . Those were normal enough, as were the battery packs.

But he counted six batteries rather than the normal two,
and all were fresh, without the bubbles that would show normally in the inspection tubes. The additional ones were not
wired in parallel with the others, and the conduits from those
did not lead to the levmotor but appeared to hang downward
through the floor rails.

Kalm cursed the poor lighting mechanically and removed
his bandolier and helmet. He put his combat gear on the levmotor housing and crouched as he moved along the cross-

beams, searching for terminals for the extra conduits.

*Camera mounting here*, he decided after a while. *Or maybe a very small gun will fit through this opening. Standard power plugs on the receptacle, so I can't guess what equipment might have been connected. Keep looking . . . two conduits explained, eight to go.*

There was space to stand at the front of the vehicle, forward of the wood partition, but there were no controls. A box rested at the center of the partition, mounted between two plastic rails adjacent to the opening. It was small—not quite large enough to hold two writing blocks. But the box cover had clips for receiving four power conduits.

Inside were wires, coils, metal clamps—and a ghost fluid circuit. It resembled nothing he could remember from the Plates, and he could make no sense of it. Kalm snapped his fingers in irritation. He was not one of the missing scholars; he had no part in creating this device; he was foolish for wasting his time this way.

There were scholars working for him now. He would report his observations, and within days a technical crew would unravel the Algheran secret. But it would be their discovery, not his. He would learn what it did; he would not understand it—because the acting director of the Institute could not spare the time necessary to learn technical details.

*No!* Kalm snapped his fingers again. Later he would report this, as he must. But he had come this far in his reasoning without help; he would continue as long as possible before he admitted defeat. He knelt to inspect the circuit more closely.

Was this complete? No. Ends of interior wires were visible, insulation stripped from them. Unless the device had intentional short circuits, some components were missing. But without clues, how could he—or anyone—finish the construction?

Frustrated again, he sat on the crossbeams, his legs dangling into space as he rapped irritably on the pipes. *Think more about this mess*, he ordered himself. *Think better.*

Was the circuit complete? Obviously not. But what type of elements would go into it? It had been built here. The pieces had to be here . . . if he could recognize them.

The equipment he had seen in the shops and storage areas had been ordinary laboratory instrumentation. Parts of the circuit had obviously been made especially for it—the strange glass tube fastened around several exposed wires, for instance. But for the most part he had seen standard wiring and normal ghost-fluid-handling devices: sluices and gates and dams that could be found in any parts catalog. The missing elements, if he could find them, would probably be equally conventional and innocent, unrecognizable as portions of a secret weapon.

*Probably lying around here someplace. But I don't see how to fit the pieces together*, Kalm admitted.

*Fit the pieces together . . .*

The pieces would have to fit together.

Kalm looked once more into the box.

He lost all track of time, knowing only that one electrical shock and three barked knuckles later he had finished. He still did not understand the circuit, but by treating it as a jigsaw puzzle he had managed to put together something.

Seated uncomfortably on the piping near the front of the vehicle, he held his hand over a knurled control lever. "Here goes nothing." His hand moved backward slowly . . .

. . . and nothing happened.

He pushed the lever forward, and again nothing happened. Did the vehicle shudder slightly? But that was his own shifting weight. The great Algheran secret weapon was a bust.

But there simply had been no other way to complete the circuit. The machine had to do something; of that Kalm was certain.

Perhaps he had to be in the air. That would explain the levmotor he had not thought to use. It was a silly idea, but reason gave nothing better to try.

Steering would not be possible, but hovering was. He could fasten wires to the levmotor leads and connect them to a variable sluice . . .

Five minutes later he was done. He had even located a pair of planks on which to sit in comparative comfort. He readied himself for another experiment.

Fortunately the levmotor was silent; Kalm had no desire to explain to the guard outside why his chieftain was tinkering with equipment awaiting explanation by legitimate investigators. But there was a risk, he suddenly realized, and while he could trust his life to the folds of Nicole's cloak, he could not make that decision for the man outside the laboratory.

Fatigue was ruining his judgment, he admitted. All the more reason to act with haste, then. He yawned, shook his head to clear it, left the makeshift vehicle, and returned to the triangular doorway, blinking as he emerged into the bright light.

There was a new guard outside, sitting half-asleep on the cube chair. He started as Kalm loomed over him, fumbling for his neuroshocker with unsteady fingers, nearly dropping the weapon.

"Try not to shoot yourself. Or me," Kalm said dryly.

"Eh-hooomfff," the trooper mumbled. "Er . . . Chieftain! Ooooom . . ." He pitched himself forward from the chair to stand unsteadily before the officer. "Er-umm . . . ready for orders, sir."

The soldier clearly had not been expecting an inspection. His red-brown tunic was partially unbuttoned at both collar and belly; his bandolier flapped loosely, as if he had been scratching under it; his fingers were food-streaked, and he was clandestinely attempting to wipe them clean.

*Not a Teep*, Kalm discovered by probing. The trooper had simply counted on blind luck to escape observation. Unsoldierly appearance, unsoldierly conduct—both called for a reprimand.

*If he were one of mine, now* . . . But ChelmForceLand's discipline was not the concern of ChelmForceDrop. Perhaps the fright he had just received would be punishment enough. Also—Kalm suddenly realized that he was ravenously hungry.

"Report the time," he demanded.

"Ninth tenth, Chieftain. The ninth tenth. Almost half more."

The man had begun in placating tones; he was calmer now, Kalm noticed. Evidently he had realized that he would not be shouted at. Surreptitiously, he tugged at his bandolier, attempting to tighten it and pull it into place.

A half tenth till dawn. Mess wagons would be just beyond the Institute gates. Kalm wondered if the trooper had left his post to get an early breakfast. *Probably*. It could be checked, but he would pretend the idea had not occurred to him.

"Er . . . is there something I may do for you, Chieftain?" The trooper tapped at his throat as he spoke, somehow managing to fasten the top clasp of his tunic.

Kalm grimaced. *Am I hearthmate to this lout that I must watch him dress in the morning? Yes, I will see him covered by the Lady's cloak, but I will make him pay for the good fortune.*

He smiled then, managing to upset the trooper more than he had with the grimace. "Yes," he said with satisfaction. "I want breakfast. Several breakfasts—I missed my supper."

The trooper gave him a hasty and unnecessary salute, carelessly snagging a thumb in a tunic loop. That left him with an idiot's expression upon his face and a hand awkwardly pushing upon his own shoulder. Kalm said nothing but gazed disdainfully at the sight.

The trooper's look changed to horror. Extra duty for the next tenth year; Kalm could read that without mind-seeing.

He smiled again. "I imagine you're hungry as well from your eagerness. No need to wait till you are off duty today."

The man managed to fasten one more clasp. "Er, yes, Chieftain."

"Good! We can eat together then, and get a good look at a beautiful sunrise. Excellent, Trooper!" *And the disarray of your uniform will be impossible to overlook,* he noted silently.

Evidently the trooper had reached the same conclusion. "Uh-emm . . . I'm really not hungry, Chieftain. I certainly thank you for—"

"Nonsense, I insist upon it," Kalm said. He probed quickly. "A good sturdy breakfast of fruit juice and five or six eggs does anyone a world of good. I positively order you to have breakfast, soldier. And I'm going to insist that you bring it back here so I can see that you are taking proper care of yourself. I want my men in top shape!"

"Very well, Chieftain," the man said resignedly. He hated eggs.

"Well, indeed!" Kalm exclaimed with satisfaction. "Five or six eggs! Go, then! Run to it, Trooper!"

Left to himself once more, Kalm returned to the laboratory and pushed aside the scaffolding around the vehicle. Seated again before the front partition, he twisted the top of the variable sluice, releasing ghost fluid to the levmotor, and raised the craft till its top was within a handbreadth of the ceiling. If he stood, he would be able to put his palms on the dead lighting panels.

"Here goes nothing for the second time," he muttered. One hand remained on the sluice for safety's sake. With the other, he pulled back on the lever that controlled the Algherans' alien machine.

Darkness surrounded him. He released the lever instinctively so that it sprang back to a neutral position.

The darkness remained a brief while, then sensors noted his presence. A wan white light began to glow from the ceiling. "Brighter," he called experimentally, and the lighting increased. Soon the illumination was at useful levels.

*Fast repairs*, Kalm noticed uneasily. But he was still in the laboratory. Nothing had changed. Was switching on lights the only function of the Algheran machine?

*I didn't put it together right.* He blew out his breath unhappily, feeling like a child who had not received an expected toy. Well, no child got all the toys he desired. He would live with this.

There was an explosion. The basement rocked about him. Equipment on the laboratory benches tottered, and small components clattered off them and onto the floor. Glass shattered upon the floor, unheard against the ringing in Kalm's ears. The loosely fastened metal mesh slapped at the walls.

The explosion was repeated. And now Kalm felt the building shuddering about him. Other sounds could be heard—the loud *crrumpff!* of artillery, the whip-crack snapping of air being split asunder by solid projectiles. Then another explosion. And another.

The walls of the laboratory were shaking, breaking. Cracks were spreading across their glazed coating, and rivulets of dust and mortar poured through them and onto the floor. The sound hammered at him, the very air pounding against his body like a solid thing.

*Bombardment!* he realized. *The Algherans have restarted the war!*

It seemed perversely unfair.

Nicole's cloak had been over him, Kalm had time to think; it had kept him from being on the ground and pelted with falling objects. Then he hunched himself forward to lock his arms about the framework of the sled and pressed his index fingers into his ears to protect them. Like a wounded animal, he waited without thought for the bombardment to end.

At last the clamor died as shelling moved to another sector. Now he could hear the muted crack of small arms, the *zing!* of ricochets. The ground itself creaked; armor moved nearby.

*The Institute!* he remembered. *The Institute— Cimon! What are they doing to my Institute?* He had to get out of this cellar! He had to see what was going on! He had to know!

He should not have been unprepared for this. And he hated

himself suddenly for playing all night long with the Algheran machine when he should have been at his post and defending the Institute.

*Get back as fast as I can!* He braced for impact, damming up the flow of ghost fluid to the levmotor so the sled would drop to the ground. The sled moved down a finger's length, perhaps two. Then it stopped and rocked alarmingly. From underneath it came splintering sounds. It was resting on something.

Another sled, Kalm saw, looking downward. Another sled —in rebuilt scaffolding, as if that which he had pushed over had been reerected in the darkness. He shook his head with bemusement.

A distant explosion sounded, recalling him to the present and the renewed fighting. He had no time to waste on speculation; he restarted the levmotor and stood to push at the lighting panels. When the sled had been crabbed across the ceiling to the adjacent work bay, he landed without further ado.

As he ran for the door, he fumbled into his combat attire.

*I'm in time*, he thought with relief as he came to the entrance of the building. The sun was coming over the horizon, and he could see men moving over the dew-sparkled grounds of the Institute. Crouched and cautious, as in combat—but they were steadily advancing in his direction. And they wore ChelmForceLand's brown uniforms, not Algheran green and black. The attack had been repulsed.

*Second wave forces*, he noticed. Assault troops needed shock weapons; they would carry projectile throwers and portable LongPushers; the men before him were armed with neuroshockers. He turned about, seeing soldiers on all sides rushing past him and into the Institute buildings. *Looking for armed Algherans to flush—if any but the dead are left here*.

But no resistance was left. The situation was in hand again.

Except— Where had the attackers come from?

He would find out. He looked up at the ChelmForceLand SquadChief moving toward him—and saw with two sets of eyes, thought from within two minds.

"It's all right," he heard the stocky officer before him saying. "This building is clear of the bastards." The voice was deeper and harsher than the one Kalm associated with himself, and he wondered for an instant if he normally sounded that way to others or if it was only an effect of his sleeplessness.

*An officer—this far ahead?* he found himself thinking, weighing the evidence of shoulder stripes and collar flashes. A chieftain second should not be here but at regimental headquarters, directing his forces. Was this one lost or mind-weakened by battle stress? *Hold him here,* he was deciding, *I'll get someone to escort him off the line to safety.*

"Special duty," the officer said quickly, showing irritation. He slapped at the Intelligence insignia on his chest. "I wanted to see the progress of the—"

Kalm broke off suddenly. He had been about to say "counterattack." But the words that lay in the Trooper's mind, anticipating the end of his sentence, were "flanking movement."

"I'm a little confused," he heard himself say carefully, and watched himself as he reached a hand cautiously to the side of the triangular doorway, as if he were ill and needed to support himself. "Must have got too close to a shell burst. What is the date, anyhow?"

"Day 72, Chieftain."

"Day 72," Kalm repeated flatly. The SquadChief was sure of that. And so this was not a counterattack; this was the thrust that had seized the Institute for the Alliance. With the high ground in their rear lost, the Falltroop demibattalion in the tenements below would be outflanked and forced to pull back.

But they had not retreated, Kalm remembered. They would not retreat. And less than a thousand man-heights from the battle, Chieftain Second Kalm ha'Nyjuc, limping slightly from a sore heel incurred during the parachute assault, dropped combat gear in the office of the director of the Institute and ordered guardsmen of ChelmForceOccupation to bring in a work table . . .

*This same moment.*

*Time. The Algheran secret is control of time.*

Kalm's mind shield rose into place. The secret was dangerous. He dared not let it escape before he thought of possible consequences. He could not permit others to know. Not even Teeps.

"Carry on, Trooper," he made himself say, and this time he knew that the harshness in his voice was fear. Then he was rushing back through the building toward the basement ramp, not waiting to see if the soldier obeyed his order. He fumbled with the key, then staggered into the laboratory.

He was suddenly weak. Feeling as if he had been beaten,

Kalm collapsed across a desk in one of the office cubicles, gasping like a sobbing child.

Finally his fear began to ebb.

Whatever the Algherans could do, they had already done, he told himself, staring into the gloom. The present remained. The Alliance remained. He remained. His memories remained.

*The world is safe.*

No.

*A place*, he thought suddenly. *Think of time as a place. The Algherans are out there hiding. Waiting to come out of their hole . . .*

With assassins. Hidden armies. To start another war when the Alliance was unprepared . . . a war that even the telepaths could not predict.

"No!" he groaned. "No!"

They must be stopped. Wherever—whenever—they might be, they had to be sought out, and their power taken from them. They could not be left to control the one world.

*Ultimate power.* Could the Alliance be trusted, either?

*A government can keep a secret.* Kalm trembled.

*A government will use a secret. Even the Alliance— If I gave them control over time, they would use it.*

Thunder sounds rang above, then shouts, muffled by the bulk of the building. Cannon fire. An artillery team.

Soldiers. Government. And if they entered the building now? Woodenly, he rose and crossed the floor to the sled.

The Alliance could not be allowed time travel. The Algherans must be stopped without its knowledge.

By Kalm ha'Nyjuc.

*Rispar Kallimur ha'Nyjuc-once-ha'Ruijac*, he thought derisively. *World saver. Traitor.*

*No. A dead man.*

Accept this charge? There was no refusing it.

He touched controls. The sled began to ascend.

There was much to do. The Kalm ha'Nyjuc who was acting director of the Institute would soon be told of these metal-lined rooms and send investigators. There was a fire to arrange yet, there were weapons and tools to locate, before Kalm ha'Nyjuc and all evidence of the Algheran project vanished forever from the one Earth.

# CHAPTER FOUR

"*Two beers, twelve mina.*" There was no "*please*" in the aging barmaid's words, none in her tones.

Dice rattled over a nearby tabletop. Half-heard voices laughed and grumbled; wood scraped against wood as men shifted their stools and leaned against the plank walls. Evening grayness was already masking the colors of the tavern; darkness waited behind a door opening at the back.

Brine should have ridden the night breeze through the low basketweave wall at his side, but Kalm was chiefly conscious of ancient liquor spills and unwashed bodies. The air was warmer than he had expected, his leather jacket uncomfortably heavy. Frowning as the barmaid waited, he reached into his pants pocket, stopped when he touched only small coins, and let the man he had met push paper toward the woman. "Sorry, Farrb."

Outside a carriage clattered slowly through the darkness, the hollow clip-clop of horses' hooves on pavement preceded by a linkman's wheezing yell: "Make way! Huh! Make way, cit-huh-zens! Make way! Huh!" Voices stopped and restarted as people moved to the side of the street, shunning the glow from the lantern on the linkman's pole as if it would contaminate them. As the carriage rumbled past the tavern, the coachman gestured with a raised whip, shaking it in a meaningless threat. Behind the closed parchment of the carriage's side window, an interior lamp silhouetted a woman's head. Horsemen followed.

The men had been without livery and the coach without pennons, which suggested a hired vehicle. From one of the minor Septs, Kalm estimated, watching through diamond slits in the lattice. I'subnoc, Kubal, Crovsol . . . The exotic names had vanished in his time, but they still existed in Fohima Alghera in this Year of the City 315. Or from one of the illegal Associations. A woman in modest but uncommon circumstances, then, perhaps even a criminal. Or a woman leaving a lover, not eager to be recognized. Could that be?

Yes. But despite reason and experience, it was still surprising to find that people long raised to Cimon's realm harbored emotions, desires, petty secrets—the innocent belief that in this momentary return to existence they had significance.

Fascinated but reluctant to probe for information before the other man, he stared after the carriage, letting scraps of memory and imagination tell him what lives people had led half a millennium before his birth.

Hemmendur would be three years old now—if the Algherans had not harmed him. "Sorry," he repeated.

"Sure you are, lad, and shouldn't it be on me?" *A captain's wife, she is, coming from the docks. Foreigner and a halfmind.* Mogglhen Farribiir leaned forward on his stool, gesturing with a narrow chin. The older man wore gray pants. An elbow did not quite go through a hole in his brown shirt. A crease ran along one side of his throat as if it had been cut open and closed much later. A shapeless big-brimmed hat concealed an old scar on his forehead. Three centuries of life had placed crinkles alongside his dark eyes and roughened his skin, but his hair was mostly brown-black and his body was still wiry. Kalm, at forty-five, wondered if he would shed the weight the years had left on him and grow old so gracefully.

"Lad, it's only polite when you be so eager to pay much for a little service." Farrb's voice was soft and amused, untroubled by the images he had seen within Kalm's mind.

A shadow lifted as the barmaid turned from the lantern embedded on the wall by the entrance gate, then came back to the table. Kalm moved his gaze from the back of the departing carriage to Farrb's lined, sparely fleshed face, then past to sailors drinking from steaming tankards in the far corner. An onlooker at the dicing table moved through the door in the back wall. One of the winners carried a pitcher away from the bar and poured from it into empty tankards.

Kalm's attention warily moved from mind to mind. A neuroshock pistol was strapped inside his jacket, but in this age the weapon had not been invented. Half-superstitiously, Kalm wondered if it would work here.

"Yes, my darling?" The older man's words were flat, touched by a concealed thought as he turned.

"Still due five," the barmaid said.

Farrb pretended surprise but handed over the bill he had palmed. The woman took it in one hand without comment, lowered tankards with the other, then retreated to the bar, her steps loud on the plank floor. She stood with her back against the protruding lip, her elbows resting on its top.

Farrb twisted sideways so that the light did not fall across his face. *They don't like our kind here, and be you remembering that.* "Your part." Deadpan, he held out a tankard.

Kalm smiled narrowly until the rank smell hit his nostrils.

"Your part." Farrb's hand still waited in air.

Kalm handed over his pocket change as Farrb apparently wished, then watched the man grin with wolfish satisfaction. Had it been a mistake to look for assistance here? Could he rely on this man? He patted his jacket uneasily, worrying despite the comforting bulge.

"Thought you were letting me off," he forced himself to say. "For my future good deeds." He glanced back toward the carriage, which was still partially visible as it plowed through bystanders, contrasting wealth and the glamour of a sailor's life with the squalid tavern.

"Well, and there's that." Farrb settled back on his stool, displaying a bland patience that matched the surface of the thoughts he exposed. Thin, dark, homespun-clad—that was true to his self-image, but inspection showed Kalm that the dark hair was graying above the man's ears and that there were gaps in the chipped teeth. "Thought maybe I'd be seeing some of the other money you were bragging of, lad."

"The metal is here," Kalm replied. "But you earn it first. That was the deal."

"But surely it is small cost for the pleasure of my company?" The dark man smiled, but his mind continued to circle subjects hidden from Kalm, and the thoughts that came through his screen were harsher than his words, less patient. *They don't like our kind here,* he repeated. *They have laws against us. This was an evil spot you chose to meet, regardless of your money. My side of the bay is clean enough.*

A shantytown, Kalm thought, knowing the image could not be kept to himself but not apologizing. *Teeps and other riffraff not allowed in the city mixed—dangerous.* "I guess I prefer it here." *The work is here.*

"Oh, and it's fine there for me." Pride radiated from the man's mind. "You're just too lazy to walk there, lad." *Like family there. What would you be worrying about among your own kind?*

Kalm smiled without humor. *More of my own kind.* He slapped softly at the concealed neuroshocker. It was sufficient answer.

The older man pursed his lips. *And where's our honor, if we were treating ourselves that way? That's foolishness, lad.*

"Sure. I'm lazy."

Farrb did not smile. *A killer, a traitor, a man from the future—so your thoughts say.* "Or were you making it up?"

Kalm gestured uselessly. *I'd hide it if I could.*

*Oh, and you could have. You had no cause to come meddle in our time. You can see into minds, I grant you, but it's still a high-Sept bastard mucking about in our "shantytowns" that you are. You're our future, lad? That's no cause for anyone's pride, now, is it?*

"Do you want my money or not?" Kalm controlled his face. "I can go elsewhere."

"Lady." Farrb put a finger into his tankard and flicked drops of beer onto the tavern floor. "Don't you be minding all my words, lad. Foolish I am, at times." He sighed, then swallowed deeply.

"Sure." Kalm matched Farrb's gesture, then tasted his beer. It was thinner than he had expected, musty-smelling, rawer, almost nauseating. It had been laced with grain alcohol, he found, probing the bartender's mind. In City Year 315, two years after the death of Mlart the Unifier, as would-be successors fought for control of the defeated Algheran Realm, few drank for the taste. His schoolbooks had not mentioned that.

He sipped cautiously, waiting.

"An evil time, it's being," Farrb agreed softly. "Ever since the young Warder was killed by the Lopritians."

"Sure." It was ancient history to Kalm, unimportant. *You were in the tra'Nornst's army?*

*The Swordtroop of the Realm. Indeed, I was.* Farrb raised his head imperiously, ignoring Kalm's disinterested gaze. *Well, and weren't the most of us?* Skin crinkled at the corners of his eyes; his mouth lifted at the corners. But the smile curdled. *And we won! We had the winning of that war, lad!*

"Sure."

"We did," Farrb whispered softly, sadly. *We should have won. Had the Lopritians running themselves to pieces, as long as we left them somewhere to run. Then with them all being pinned into F'a Loprit and making themselves brave together . . . And one dark night . . . Sallied out and . . . And it cost us our Warder. And then . . . We—*

*You're a Teep!* Kalm cut off the reminiscence curtly. *Why should you care?*

Farrb stared at him.

*That was two years ago,* Kalm pointed out grimly.

*Lad! A thing that mattered so—*

Kalm choked back a curse. *Do you think I've come back to save your precious Mlart? I'd kill him myself if I thought they were trying to save him. Do you understand that, Farrb?* "Do you understand?"

"Lad, he was a good man."

*I don't care.* Kalm swept his fingers across the table, casting aside nonexistent crumbs. *He doesn't matter now. You and I don't matter. Nothing is real, Farrb. The one world, we say—it isn't. It's chaos, and you just don't see.*

*You know, I don't even remember if Mlart was dead by now in my world, and I can't even find out. The Algherans are changing everything, Farrb, and you can't see it. People, their names, the lives they've led . . . Nothing lasts, nothing is real. It all changes constantly every time I go back to look at my world. Everything recorded in history could have been twisted and we would never know.*

*Maybe there wasn't a Mlart once, Farrb. Maybe the Algherans invented him—and threw him away like a broken tool. Maybe all the life you remember is wrong and should have gone some other way. How would you like that, Farrb?*

Kalm scowled. *The Algherans are real and I'm real, and whatever they do I have to oppose, and that's all I can ever know or ever do.*

"He was a good man," Farrb repeated weakly. *For the Normals and for the Teeps. Is it so bad to be regretting him?*

"No one is worth regret," Kalm said scornfully. "And nothing you do, if it's justified."

No more was said until Farrb's tankard was empty; then he pushed it back and forth on the tabletop, staring at it. "So you've no religious sense." The older man put the words forth tentatively, as if expecting a rejection.

*I outgrew it.* "Most people do."

"Most people don't." Farrb mixed amusement and bitter wisdom on his face as he gestured with the tankard. "But you . . . When will you be dying, lad?"

*When Lady Nicole removes her cloak.* Kalm grimaced. When luck ran out.

*And I'll be long gone by then,* Farrb thought. *It's not a notion for a man to be comfortable with, all alone, is it?*

"No."

But it was only a word. Kalm could not truly imagine a world in which he no longer existed, and Farrb's face showed his knowledge of that. He changed his tack.

*You'll be seeing the world changing, lad. When you're reaching my age, or traveling with your little toys. Always changing and always not changing. Weak men rising and strong ones falling . . . dark chaos always waiting under our expectations of order . . . But we go on, and the world goes on. You have to be asking why it goes on this way, don't you?*

*A test,* Kalm suggested, not in agreement but gently confident that he saw the direction of Farrb's thoughts. *At the end of life, you've learned what sort of person you are.*

"Every instant, lad." Farrb's voice was flat. "Every instant."

"Go on." Kalm grimaced, finding the idea unbearably bleak.

*And if there's a testing, aren't there also the testers?*

*Gods, you mean.*

"Gods." Farrb left the word in the air for a long moment. *And then you're wondering who they may be, and what it is they're wanting.*

*To please them and buy a reward.*

*Just to be knowing them, lad.* The reproof was gentle. *And now we're finding and reading these Plate things . . .*

Kalm smiled. *Men left those records.*

For a moment Kalm saw before him a village on a hillside where men tended fields with methods unchanged for millennia and the cycles of life repeated endlessly, peacefully, without alteration.

*My father's world*, Farrb's thoughts told him. *My father's life. His father's, and his. Gone now.* Regret should have touched the words; Kalm found only acceptance. *We've more than them. And if we're taking so much from the ancient world, haven't we to take their faith as well?*

Kalm hesitated, embarrassed. *In my age, Teeps don't devote much attention to religion,* he thought finally. *We have to learn it, because it's on the Plates and— I used to believe, when I was a child, but it's just history for most of us. We don't—*

"It's afraid you are." Farrb would admit no argument.

"It's Cimon-taken afraid we are." The younger man smiled without humor. *We have enough problems without reminding the Normals we killed their God and Goddess.*

"Ah, and so we did."

*It's a story, that's all. What the priests talk about— Cimon's scales of judgment, Nicole's mercy, the miracles of the tiMantha lu Duois—that's myth. Oh, it's in the Plates— I've read those passages—but that stuff isn't in the Chronicles.* Kalm stared glumly at his nearly empty tankard. What a nonsensical argument to have gotten into. His eyes came up slowly and met the other man's without blinking. *Do you want to argue about this, or are you happy believing?*

Farrb smiled briefly. *Maybe it's a test, lad.* He raised his tankard and jiggled it to catch the barmaid's eye.

Kalm only sighed as she approached.

"Twelve mina. First." She remembered them.

"I'm not done," Kalm said.

He was not noticed.

"Why, sure, my darling, and aren't we your best customers? And me a man with unarguable experience, too, according to the lad." Farrb tugged paper from a hip pocket. "Here, with a touch more for your smile." He grinned at the embarrassed Kalm, then at the barmaid as the paid-for smile became genuine. "And aren't you prettier to be looking at than this mewing babe?"

She checked the notes at the light again. "Only because it's bringing you something wet I am. Experience! You old rogue."

A man in expensive clothing entered the tavern behind Kalm's back, staggered, but kept his balance by clutching the doorpost. Thoughtless, Kalm found, checking automatically and recognizing the mental blank left by a Teepblind. *Here's our man, Farrb*.

The older man grimaced, his eyes moving. *Him, eh? There's an ill feel to all this, lad*.

Farrb hadn't truly believed his story, Kalm noted. *Just the 'blind. You're not used to them*.

"Eh? Thank you, my darling." The older man half turned to accept new tankards, then sat back after handing one to Kalm. *There's not a need for haste, is there, now?*

*Probably not*. Kalm sipped at his drink, determinedly ignoring the barmaid as she dodged a pat on the backside from the man who had entered. "'S all right," he heard. Then a hiccough.

The stranger was young, he thought. Young and careless. The clothes suggested that he had money. What had brought him there, if not a mission? Leave? Curiosity? But it was pointless to ask such questions now. Kalm had seen the man entering the tavern earlier. He had not seen him leaving.

Farrb turned and watched openly as the man groped his way toward the rest room, table by table. *A fine-looking sort, isn't he, now? From one of the better Septs, I'd imagine*. Then he hid his inspection behind his tankard. *Too drunk to recognize his own mother—there's a fair match for you, fat Kalm ha'Nyjuc-wishing-ha'Ruijac*.

Kalm swallowed. *If you're afraid, you can leave*.

"Eh?" Farrb stared at him bleakly as Kalm listened to retching sounds from the rest room. "Who spoke of leaving? Calm yourself, lad."

"All right." Kalm slipped a hand into a jacket pocket, pulling forth a paper-wrapped parcel the size of his palm. "Here's your money." In the background, the retching continued. He lifted his tankard deliberately, sipped, then put it down to show his resolve. "If it's not enough, give it back. I can handle this alone."

"Oh, and for sure that's a pity." Farrb unsealed the package, then smiled and put the metal into a pants pocket without the revealing gleam showing to anyone. *You can be relying on me, lad. Any time*. Behind him, a dice player rose and entered the back room, one hand unlacing his pants.

Kalm overheard a curse, a slap, then the sound of a man stumbling into a wall. The drunk thudded upon the floor, one arm reaching through the doorway into the tavern.

"Not rushing off, is he?" Farrb said coolly. *Almost as if he were knowing he was waiting for you.*

Kalm sighed, his mouth sour even without beer. Snoring came from the direction of the rest room, laughter from the dice players. Meanwhile the tone of Farrb's thoughts showed his satisfaction. *A loyalty to foreign lands, but you're needing to come to Alghera for your assistance. Why is that, now, lad?*

*I'm looking for Algherans.* Kalm was intentionally short.

*Aye, there might be that. Or isn't it the knowing there's that which bonds us more than blood ties, and isn't that the taking in of you by the telepaths after your own kin were throwing you away? Isn't it that Nyjuc was wanting of you, not yet knowing you were to be a true mindseer, but willing still to take you in, so as to be giving you a place? Was it not the simple goodness the "Teeps" gave you that you are so afraid to admit?*

Kalm let his breath out slowly. *Nyjuc was well paid by Ruijac.*

"Eh, lad."

"Eh, lad," Kalm echoed sourly.

But after a long silence he gave part of the answer that Farrb wanted. *No, I do not hate them. I appreciate what Nyjuc did for me. But I never felt at home there.* He did not say, "We can work together."

*No one beat you.*

"No one in Nyjuc beat me," Kalm agreed. *Do you call that enough for a bond between Teeps? I escaped as soon as I could, and I'll never regret it.* He looked past Farrb deliberately and watched a man leave the rest room, stepping over the drunken aristocrat.

*Joined the half minded in an army, you mean. A cruel escape, that.*

"Not that bad," Kalm said, dispassionately reviewing memories. *I learned a lot in the Falltroop. And in Chelm-Force.*

*That's your thought, but you've been cruelly treated, lad. Give it up.* The older telepath glanced toward the rest room. *Give him up.*

*What?*

*Give it up, I'm saying. You've no obligation here to either side of your strange war. You've done duty to both your countries, and it's retiring from it you're entitled to.*

*Let the Algheran time travelers go free, to ruin everything?*

*No, I can't do that. It'd be treason all over, and you know it.*

*So, be telling your authorities. Make it their problem.*

*I can't do that, either.* Kalm discovered that he had straightened up stiffly; he forced himself to sip beer and relax. "Don't need them."

*Oh. You must be doing it all yourself. It's not an Algheran you'll be, and not Chelmmysian. You'll be Kalm ha'Nyjuc, whom no one loves and no one trusts, and you'll be running about revenging yourself forever, saying you're obeying a duty to everyone which no one but you is knowing of.*

Kalm's nostrils flared. *If you see it that way—yes.*

*It's foolishness, lad.*

*It has to be done.*

*Oh, and maybe. And what have you been doing at it?* Farrb pointed with a thumb. *Scurrying after the likes of that child, and needing help from me even then? Give it up, lad. Ask the Lord for his mercy and the Lady for peace, and save what's left of you before you're destroying yourself.*

*It wouldn't work.* Kalm swallowed air, half-unhappily. *I'm not like that. I have to be doing things. I can't live, just having things happen to me.*

*If you must be doing things, lad, throw in with your own kind. Maybe, with the aiding of your machines, we'd—*

"No!"

Heads turned around the bar, noticing them. It eased the effect of surprise; Kalm forced himself to cough, slapped at his chest to suggest that beer had gone done his windpipe, and finally let his face redden as if from embarrassment. The unwanted attention went away.

*Don't start thinking that way, Farrb. It's been tried twice, and your religion tells you how it came out.*

*It's only wondering, I was, lad. And it's natural—*

*Don't think about it anyhow. It'll get you killed.*

*Lad, it's your own desires you're fearing.*

*So be it. It's a flaw in me.* Kalm inhaled deeply, unable to flee Farrb's accusation but forced to fight against it. *In all of us. But if you try to tempt me again, I'll kill you.*

"Lad!" But Farrb obeyed.

Eventually the dice players were gone, leaving the drunk in the rest room where he lay, so Kalm and Farrb were the only conscious customers. The number of people outside the tavern had not diminished, but in their voices and their movements he detected the same weariness that had begun to affect himself and his companion.

The beer left in his tankard was flat, warm, and sour-smelling, tasting as weak as the tavern lights. Kalm swallowed, finishing it only because it was there. "About time."

"Certainly." Farrb rose awkwardly, then pushed a table and some chairs aside as he went to the doorway. Kalm moved toward the rest room, stepping over the drunk.

The room was dingy, and the sanitation primitive. It stank of feces and old vomit, of alcohol and poverty. When his eyes adjusted to the semidarkness, he saw that the toilet was simply a wooden box with a hole in the top, mounted over a hole in the floor. A waist-high barrel stood nearby, filled with scum-topped water.

Kalm took off his jacket and emptied its inside pockets, laying the contents in order on the floor.

"Nh-yyeh?" The drunk was light, blond-haired, and regular-featured. And he was young, as Kalm had noted earlier. Very young—little more than a boy. He seemed to show a well-bred surprise as Kalm pushed him onto his back. But it was too dark to see his face clearly, and the sound was only an interrupted snore. Farrb stood in the front door of the tavern, an indecisive look on his face that was not pure playacting. His thoughts showed that the bartender and barmaid were in conversation and unattentive.

Kalm grabbed a shoulder and an arm to pull the drunk entirely into the rest room, then slapped around the body until he discovered a lump on the front right hip. Unsealing the man's trousers, he yanked them down to reveal a money sack. He found no weapon.

The flesh was soft and greasy, overfed and underexercised. Kalm pulled the arms backward, then slipped loops over the wrists and ankles and tugged them tight, working without emotion.

An injection in the throat to deaden the vocal cords.

An injection in the carotid to sedate sections of the brain.

An injection in an armpit's vein to strengthen the heart.

There was nothing that would instantly dispel the effects of alcohol. Kalm settled for dipping water from the barrel with his hands and splashing it on the man's face. When it produced a response, he slipped his fingers under the band that went around the man's hairline and pulled outward to disengage the Teepblind.

The 'blind itself was inside the band, silver-tinted mesh resting on the scalp. Kalm pulled it through the blond hair, then ran the band through his fingers, squeezing out blood through the vampire valves into the barrel. Another drop of blood oozed from a puncture on the man's left temple; Kalm remembered absently that during ChelmForce interrogations it would have been dabbed clean with a sterile cloth.

Still half-asleep, huddled against the side of the toilet box, the man shivered. His mouth made gasping motions.

Kalm threw more water, then slapped him. The mouth opened wide.

Vertigo tugged at him for an instant. The room spun suddenly. Then Kalm was in two minds, seeing through two sets of eyes, listening through two sets of ears.

"You'll tell me the truth," the man standing before him said, and Kalm had time to reflect on the slowness of that voice, of any voice. Simultaneously he felt a blurry surprise at the question and its implication.

Illumination came quickly as sensation told the man of the bonds and the missing 'blind. *CAPTURED!* the mind shouted. *I can't—*

First there was fear, then a sudden sense of pain, of pressure through the man's body. The heart swelled instantly, seeming to explode. In one of his bodies he gasped, loudly enough that Kalm knew Farrb had heard it.

Then there were pictures: a cavernous hangar with scattered levcraft on the floor; men in an open vehicle under the night sky; a girl's head, the forehead inlaid by a green square; men fighting hand to hand; the grounds of the Institute; other scenes from a city five centuries removed.

There were thoughts of memories that must be kept secret by any means. Kalm caught only glimpses; the pictures flashed by his consciousness more quickly than he could understand them.

Fighting. There were many memories of fighting.

The pictures stopped. All sensation but pain stopped.

Then Kalm was entirely in his own body, standing, sweat-drenched. He listened.

The man's heart continued to beat, weakly and irregularly; his breath was faint and rapid, sour-smelling. His skin was clammy. Sweat beaded his forehead.

There was a trickling sound and the smell of urine. Pain.

The mind knew agony. Its understanding was gone.

Kalm had learned nothing useful. He cursed silently.

Then, regretfully but without alternatives, he grabbed his captive in a bear hug and brought him to the barrel.


"Hey! What is this!"

Off balance, Kalm turned as claws struck at him. Then he fell on the floor into a puddle of water.

It was the barmaid, summoned by the sounds of the splashing.

"Oh, Cimon!" But she was half-blind in the darkness and too stunned to be loud or to attack him again. Kalm got back to his feet without interruption.

"Sorry." Farrb was there by then, pulling the woman back. "I was watching the front. In case—"

"Yeah," Kalm said sickly. "Just keep her away."

"You were—" Farrb swallowed. "She heard you, and—"

Kalm remembered a sound: *die die die die die*. It was his own voice, tense and impatient. *Die die die die die*.

Kalm understood now the strain he felt in his throat and the look on Farrb's face.

"I'll be all right," he mumbled. "Just stay out."

"Is he—" Farrb's face was shiny.

"Close." Like Farrb, Kalm used his voice, unwilling to use telepathy. "Get her out."

His eyes closed as he sank against the wall, but the physical damage was minor: a scratch from the woman, mashed fingers and a sore shoulder from struggling with the man. And a sore throat. It was not real pain; it would all go away.

But even with closed eyes, the image before him remained real: a pair of feet protruding from the barrel, pants pulled to the ankles, feet quivering as water slopped onto the floor.

"—like being an accident." That was Farrb's voice in the front, unpersuasive, preoccupied. "And they won't be missing this one, ever, so you've no cause for being worried." A knife was in Farrb's hand, Kalm knew. He wondered if the man could use it if necessary, and if the bartender would—

He could not bear to check the thoughts. Even with a damaged mind, the drowning man had recognized death so *deeply* before panic had erased his sanity. It had seemed an eternity before the young time traveler lost all consciousness.

Then Farrb's voice halted. Water continued to lap in the barrel, but Kalm knew that he was alone in the room.

He barely noticed. He wanted a woman desperately.

A *special* woman.

His throat moved as he swallowed. Mechanically he put his hands in the barrel and reached down the thigh to release the money bag. He put his equipment back in the jacket. He put the jacket on, careless of his water-soaked shirt. He left the room.

Farrb was gulping liquor from a bottle, uncaring as fluid splashed his face and chest. Kalm swallowed again, the taste in his mouth vile, passing the other Teep without words, and threw the bag to the bartender. It hit the bar and slid off; loose coins rattled along the floor.

As he left the tavern, the bartender and the woman were both scrambling for the money.

Many deaths and years later, he realized that details were unimportant.

Kalm, 47,349 L.C.

# CHAPTER FIVE

*M*idpassage. *The Kingdom of Loprit. Summer. Year 312 of* the Algheran calendar, though here, dating from the Establishment of the Kingdom, it was called 207 F.E.

When Kalm left his tent, dew beaded the overhanging tree branches and a morning fog still covered the town on the opposite bank of the Bloodrill River, but he already knew that there would be little to see even after the sun had cleared the view. With barely a thousand residents, Midpassage was a city only by dictionary definition.

It would grow in future years, he knew. Six hundred years hence it would hold a population of two thousand civilians and a small garrison of ChelmForce convalescents. At this moment, however, in the age of Mlart tra'Nornst, even that military distinction was alien to it—Loprit's squabbles with the Necklace Lake states had been fought far to the west, and the southern part of the country had not featured in the more recent wars with Alghera.

Until now. Kalm finished lacing his shirtfront, then swallowed the last trace of sleep with a yawn and went looking for breakfast. Around him, four thousand soldiers of the Strength-through-Loyalty Brigade were rising with the same concern.

* * *

"Officer," Kalm muttered, cutting into the lead of a cook tent line. The word was adequate if not accurate; he barely noticed as blue-uniformed men grumbled but gave way.

Past the rows of serving tables, with white mist about him again, he listened for the gurgle of the river and the jangle of harnesses, then wandered the other way, through the trees, then up an exposed slope. Long blades of grass streaked his boot tops with dew, then waved unwatched in his wake. The mist was cool; for a moment his thoughts turned to the warm jacket he had left inside his tent, but he continued without it.

He stopped by a split-beam fence. A dirt lane lay on the opposite side, then another fence. Dimly, he could see a pair of trees. A brown and white cow was on her knees beside a mud-rimmed pond.

Kalm put his wooden bowls on the ground, then threw a pebble to catch the heifer's attention. She turned to look at him, her large eyes contemplative, then rose gracefully. Her tail lifted as she turned away, then manure *plop-plupped* onto the ground. Liquid splatters followed. The ammonia odor of urine wafted toward him.

*Welcome to Midpassage*, Kalm reflected with amusement. He collected his bowls and retreated, feeling strangely at home. Smiling, he pushed aside the dew-beaded grass with his feet, removed his knife from its sheath, and sat down to breakfast.

Hot broth, soft-crust bread, boiled wheat grain—the meal was ample if simple, and the food was without taint. It was a farmer's breakfast, too, he remembered comfortably. Fresh food. Barracks provisions in Northfaring, during his short exposure to the Lopritian army, had run to hard crackers and lukewarm broth well laced with grease.

Finished, he wiped the knife blade on his pants leg and returned it to its sheath, then stretched out and rested on his elbows. Trees and the brigade campsite still kept the town in concealment, but below the rising sun a horizon formed by rolling hills had emerged from the thinning mists. Other hills lay behind them, he knew, then still others, rising together to form the Near Rim of the Shield. Parallel to them, behind his back, similar hills and small mountains formed the Far Rim. Just off his left shoulder was Shieldboss Mountain.

The Valley of the Shield—a little nation, for all that it was a small portion of Loprit. Idly he wondered how many of the inhabitants had ever left it. *More than I'd suspect* he admitted after a moment. *They're sophisticated, by their own standards. People here won't see themselves as peasants.*

It was always a new realization.

Glitter caught his eye. At the foot of the clearing a man walked past briskly, dressed in the plastic-surfaced breeches and surcoat that indicated wealth in this culture. Spare and middle-aged, Kalm deduced from a glimpse; head movements showed that he sought something or someone. Reflexively, Kalm probed thoughts.

Gertynne ris Vandeign, he discovered. A low-ranking member of the nobility, but important in Midpassage, and the father of a low-ranking officer in the brigade. The Vandeigns had made errors in Lopritian politics, Kalm was aware; they had backed the wrong faction in the civil war that had brought Queen Molminda to the throne twenty years before. That was only locally important; neither Vandeign met the description he had been given of the red-haired man.

"Looking for Team Leader Wolf-Twin." Kalm stood at a narrow counter in a wagon the size of a small house, trying to make sense of the clutter he saw before him. Tiny tables, stools clamped to the floor, boxes overflowing with papers and map rolls ... The center of the brigade was here, in the staff rooms. "Just got here last night. I'll need a billet."

"Wouldn't know about it, Lieutenant. He's across the river." The blue-clad soldier at the nearest desk returned Kalm's forged orders without inspection. "You want to see the Ironwearer, go over to the inn. In the town—you can't miss it. Or come back after evening."

Kalm was surprised by the ease with which the word "Ironwearer" was spoken. In the modern world it was a courtesy title applied to most military officers. Here, closer to the barbarism from which the Fifth Era had emerged, though wealthy men no longer donned metal armor for battle or led their personal retinues in combat, it carried much of the original meaning and legend-given connotations.

*Blankshields. Only Blankshields.* Even in legends, Ironwearers were no more than high-priced mercenaries, their imaginary qualities only magnifications of traits found in many soldiers. The Ironwearers he would find in this age would be ordinary men.

For confirmation, he sent his mind forth. For an instant he

saw through two sets of eyes and inspected memories within another's head.

*An Ironwearer.* Rahmmend Wolf-Twin, quartermaster of the brigade, was such a mercenary, respected by this soldier as a good officer but not feared. He was not a native, for his skin was dark and his height below average. He had been in Lopritian service for five years.

He was not the man Kalm was seeking.

"How will I know him?" Kalm asked, feigning ignorance again.

"Looks like a frog." The soldier laughed. "You meet him, Lieutenant, you'll remember him."

"Sure." Kalm turned away, then back, as if under impulse. "Oh, another thing. If I couldn't find Wolf-Twin, I was told to look for another officer who works with him, a big man with red hair. Very big, I was told. But I forgot his name."

"No idea." The soldier nodded sincerely. "None of ours are like that. Maybe someone with the Southern Corps?"

Kalm snapped his fingers. "It isn't important."

But it *was* important, he knew as he drew away from the wagon. A big, red-haired man had served prominently with the Strength-through-Loyalty Brigade in the forthcoming campaign. At the end of the war, the man had vanished from history, and no further mention of him was to be found in the files of any army at any date.

Yet the man had existed, demonstrating abilities and prescience far in excess of his nominal station. References to him had been made in reports that were in Kalm's possession. A time traveler, then, magically appearing and disappearing in invisible machinery after performing unguessed deeds of wizardry.

Kalm kicked at ruts in the dirt path. Time traveler, he thought again. Another one to get rid of. What was this one doing there?

Or was this fantasy? A mistake? Perhaps this was someone harmless, and Kalm could ignore him.

No. He stepped more firmly. He could take no chances.

It was not a bridge that spanned the river. It was simply part of the road that had remained in place when earth fell beneath it—or so Kalm imagined as he stared across the river, for the road endured without change. Coal-dark without gleam, it ran north to south without turning. Hard-surfaced, smooth and even from edge to edge, the road had been fitted on the earth without dips or rises for as far as his eyes could reach.

Stepping up the concrete ramp that brought travelers from the dirt pathway up to the surface of the road, Kalm noticed instead a pyramidal boulder at the edge of the bank. A green-streaked plate had been fitted to one face; its lettering could barely be read. On the opposite bank, stakes held brown tarpaulins in place. Water lapped at them, almost the same color, flowing westward, just before the bend that redirected it to the north. Absently, he guessed that the river would be just deep enough and strong enough to drown a kitten.

A barrier waited at the end of the bridge, a pole resting on trestles inside a shabby stockade fence that ran at right angles to the river. Ropes fastened to the ends of the pole led to a small overhanging crane. Standing before this was a silver-haired man struggling with knots.

Before the pole could be raised, the three officers ahead of him had already slipped beneath it.

Kalm probed lightly, recognizing minds that had accompanied him from Northfaring in the previous days. "Here, here," he heard the oldster say. "I need to see your passes."

"Passes?" a voice asked.

"Here, Pops—" A coin flew through the air. "If anyone asks, you didn't see us."

Laughter followed, but the old man scurried about regardless. "No, I have to record your names. And you have to check your weapons."

Annoyance filled Kalm's mind, turning to anger as the old man loomed larger and larger in his eyes. Then he felt a shock in his right arm, a comforting impact that expanded pleasurably throughout his chest and face as the old man fell. His knuckles stung.

*Not my knuckles*, he realized, returning to his own mind at the edge of the bridge. *A shove. I—he—hit the old man.*

It was too late to interfere. Delaying, he examined the plaque on the stone. When he reached the gate seconds later, the guard had gotten back to his feet.

"Who was the kid?" Kalm asked.

"What?"

"The kid," Kalm repeated, pointing over his shoulder toward the plaque. "The one who drowned that that plate mentions?"

"Lord Vandeign's brother." The guard blinked, pulling a name forth from distant memory. "Merryn. Merryn ris Vandeign. The older one. A flood. Back in—"

"Sure. I saw the date." Kalm stepped past, then was stopped by the guard's hand. "What is it?"

"If you go into town, I need your name," the old man said sullenly. "Show me your pass."

"I don't have a pass. I just got here."

"You're part of those soldiers. I have to see your pass."

"I just got here," Kalm repeated. "I'm supposed to report to my superior."

"You're part of those soldiers," the old man said once more. "So you have to show me a pass and leave all your weapons. Or go back where you came from."

*Five hundred and eighty years? Not for you, old man.* "I don't have a pass yet. Maybe I'll get one later. Now, are you going to let me through? Or—" He held up a fist.

The guard suddenly capitulated. "You have to leave your weapon."

"What weapon?" He had come bare-handed.

"On your belt. That knife."

"I eat with that!"

"You have to leave it." The guard was adamant. "It's the rule. Lord Vandeign doesn't allow weapons in town."

Kalm stared, but the man's expression did not change. Reluctantly, he removed the sheath from his waist. "Satisfied?"

"It's just the rule. You can have it back when you leave." The old man nodded abruptly, then tucked the knife under his armpit. "Now, I have to record your name."

"Lieutenant Kalm Rispar." He used a Lopritian shaping of his name and a Lopritian rank—the equivalent of chieftain fourth or fifth in ChelmForce, he had gathered. *A demotion of sorts. And no promotion for centuries.* There would not even be a ChelmForce for several centuries.

"Wait. I have to get the book," the old man said, waving a finger admonishingly as he stepped backward.

Kalm sighed, then watched silently as the other man walked stiffly into an earthen hut. The coach that had brought him to Midpassage on the previous night had halted briefly before turning into the rough lane that led to the camp. It had been dark, and he had been too sleepy to pay attention, but had this been the cause of the delay? Had the same doddery oldster guarded the gate?

"Sign here." The guard man had returned with a pen and an open book. "Mr. Lieutenant." Kalm saw contempt in his eyes.

"R. Wolf-Twin," the last signature read. The script was small and meticulous, without personality or distinction. Under it in the same writing were the words "Hand sticks, two knives, iron mittens, strangling cord." Other names had "musket" or "sword" appended.

Kalm, feeling slightly nude in his ill-weaponed state, signed the book gingerly, adding "Table Knife" on the following line. "You want their names, too?"

"Say?"

*"What's that?" Derrauld ris Fryddich wondered. "A barn?" He pointed to the pastel buildings at the top of the hill, making conversation rather than needing information.*

*"Barn, looks like." Gerint ris Whelmner pulled an apple from a nearby tree and looked at the building appraisingly. "We've got bigger ones on our estate. Surprised this is allowed inside the city, though. I thought the hicks would be made to keep their distance."*

*"No one here but hicks." Krennlen ris Jynnich grinned, pleased to have drawn chuckles but not sure enough of himself yet to join in.*

"Those three." Kalm jabbed the pen toward the soldiers farther down the road. "They brought table knives in also."

*"Some women." Ris Whelmner threw the apple away after a taste. "Always women in a town."*

*Ris Jynnich grinned foolishly.*

*"Get you a woman, boy," ris Whelmner promised. "You aren't like Derry. You'll like it."*

*"Bet he won't." Ris Fryddich laughed easily.*

"It don't matter," the old man said.

Kalm snapped his fingers, then wrote down the three names. The old man took the book and the pen away gracelessly, then stalked back to the hut.

It was not really a farm, Kalm realized, noticing the sheds and neatly painted barns on the hillside beside the clover field as he walked by the apple orchard. It bore that appearance, but this was only a portion of Gertynne ris Vandeign's estate. Gertynne, rather than Merryn, by an accident of fate. It had made little difference to history, he suspected.

Farming was a minor occupation for those who worked

here. Metalworking had always been the core of the Vandeign family's enterprises. Plows and luxuries.

Neither of those involved fighting. Yet above the apple trees, black-surfaced cylinders sloped skyward between over-sized solid wheels. Men in dark blue stood in ranks behind them, awkward in appearance even at this distance, as an instructor moved from cannon to cannon, demonstrating their operation. Behind the farm buildings invisible officers drilled hidden lines of infantrymen, their presence revealed even to a nontelepath by exasperated scraps of shouting.

*Militia*. Kalm found himself wondering how the soldiers raised in Midpassage would fare in war.

As he watched, a woman walked from behind the leftmost barn into the clover. She was a worker's daughter, perhaps; her movements seemed young. White shorts, a sleeveless blue shirt . . . She was barefoot, he guessed, and the dew-soaked clover would be cool under her toes. For a moment she looked in his direction, and he saw that she was blond. So she would be sunburned also, with the untroubled expectations of those who lived outdoors and lacked understanding of the men who became soldiers.

Concealed in the purple clover she would find golden-petaled flowers, anthills, and questing honeybees. A lover would come to join her, or perhaps a husband, and they would link arms and talk without concern for men who dressed in uniforms and died alone.

For an instant he thought of sending his mind forth to share her simple adventures. Then memory of his own purposes, and perhaps a fear of envy, forestalled him.

Another woman was close by, invisible as he approached but near, at the base of the riverbank just south of the inn.

A Teep, Kalm discovered, sensing strength that towered above normal minds. But her thoughts were unintelligible. *Who are you?*

*BUSY!* It seemed a shout. Kalm winced.

But there were no overtones of alarm. It was a single mood she communicated rather than a full thought. He asked again. *Who are you?*

His curiosity was blocked by her thought screen. His consciousness seemed to slide aside, then came to rest upon the surface of her mind. Now only her impressions were visible.

"What she's doing?" ris Jynnich was asking.

*"Payning."* Perhaps that was her word. The woman did not turn to look at the men standing above her. She was thin, with black hair that hung straight above her forehead and curled inward behind her at the level of her shoulders. Her breasts were small and high, hidden under a checkered shirt with rolled-up sleeves. Some sort of framework was before her, like a table resting sideways on two legs. A folding platform near her stool held jars, brushes, and other small implements. She was barefoot, wearing faded blue trousers into which the shirt had been tucked.

A dirt trail filled most of the space between her and the river. A stone's toss away, to her eyes, ramshackle piers waited for spring floodwaters. Ropes dangled from a fragile derrick. Beyond that, unattended, a small flat-bottomed rowboat bobbed on the water by a sloping trail that led up to the bank. Across the river she saw doll-sized soldiers moving through the camp. Outstretched, hollowed at the wrist, her hand seemed to swallow marching men and squeeze them in her fist until they oozed beyond her slim fingers. Kalm turned, viewing the same men with unexpected innocence.

"What's *payning*?" ris Whelmner asked, then scrambled down the bank to stand close to her. The other men followed.

"Making pictures." Her voice was clear and very young. She carved a sliver of yellow paste from a jar with a small spatula, then put it on a glass plate. A glass rod went into a jar of amber liquid.

She enjoyed activity, Kalm guessed from the guarded thoughts. Movement, overcoming weights and resistance . . . each of her actions seemed to spark some internal glow of satisfaction that increased as she pictured faceless, awkward people laggardly performing the same task. Delusion, he judged, but her self-congratulation seemed so cheerful and free of animosity that it was difficult not to share in it.

*Not from Loprit. Not from Alghera, either.* Still curious, his mind turned elsewhere, dancing between the men.

"What's this?" Ris Whelmner stuck a finger into the jar. The tipped-up table shape was cloth-covered, his eyes showed Kalm. Glossy splotches of color were on the cloth, a blue almost the shade of the midmorning sky, browns and greens and yellows. The woman's eyes were green as she turned, seemingly half-closed in an odd fashion over high cheeks. Freckles showed on her tanned face, her arms, and the backs of her hands.

"Turpentine." The answer came only after the man had put the finger in his mouth. "Please go away. Turn around." She pushed on his elbow.

Ris Whelmner sputtered. The other men laughed.

"You aren't very polite, are you?" ris Jynnich said.

"Why should I be?" Impatiently, she shook her head and put her thumb over the end of the rod, then raised it from the jar. Kalm noticed that it had been discolored by the fluid for a finger length.

"We're trying to be polite." Ris Jynnich seemed surprised.

Kalm felt a laugh. "The kid wants to screw you," ris Fryddich said.

"Not a chance." The woman lifted her thumb to release drops of liquid onto the amber paste.

The glass rod was hollow, Kalm decided, despite its thinness. *An expensive tool for her hobby.*

Through ris Fryddich's view, he reexamined the woman's appearance. Her eyes were not closed as he had thought; they were actually narrower at the inside corners, so they appeared to slant upward toward the narrow brows. Far north, on the Mother Continent, people were reported to have that characteristic, but he had never met one. What had brought her to Loprit?

Ris Fryddich snapped his fingers. "He's got some money."

"No." She spoke without listening, concentrating on the liquid soaking into the paste. A blond woman passed through her thoughts after the Lopritian's words made sense. Then the image vanished, and she sliced at the paste with the spatula to speed up the process.

"How about it?" Ris Jynnich rubbed the cloth with a finger, concealing hope and embarrassment behind a frozen expression, while near him ris Whelmner made faces and spit. "Blast!" The boy's fingertip was yellow-colored. He held it out for her to inspect.

"Go away!" The woman had become angry suddenly. She stood holding her spatula as if she thought it a weapon.

"If he doesn't, I will." The man's voice was angry also.

*Ris Whelmner.* Kalm saw rage and lust building in him like rising fires. The Lopritian noble had suffered a hurt; he had been given an excuse for retaliation. He pictured a woman whimpering beneath him, her torn body pressed by his weight onto rock and gravel, the pleasures of clenching soft flesh until screams arose, of striking till the warm blood flowed over his hands and of choking with the sticky crimson fingers even while warm spasms transported him into the long black instant where pain and ecstasy were inseparable . . .

"Go away!" She poked ineffectually at ris Jynnich.

Kalm broke into a run.

He was in time.

"Break it up," Kalm ordered nervously. "Step away from them, miss." The woman was taller than he had expected, almost his own height. The men were larger also—and armed with knives, memory reminded him.

Ris Jynnich, standing on the dirt trail, closed his mouth. The woman twisted out of ris Fryddich's hands, unhurt though her face was flushed. Ignoring everyone, she went back to her table and began picking up fallen jars. The tail of her shirt had been pulled free on one side; Kalm caught distracting glimpses of midriff as she moved.

Disappointment registered in her mind, a trace of nausea somehow linked to being uncovered before a pudgy man in dark clothing. Short, swarthy, heavy-browed, middle-aged, panting from exertion, scowling unhappily—Kalm saw his appearance contrasted with that of a thin elegant man with an easy smile and a Teep's brand on his forehead. He looked away.

Ris Whelmner lowered his hand as Kalm turned to him. There was bright red at the base of his thumb; crimson streamed in tiny trails over his wrist. "Why should we?"

*Are you all right?* "Because I said so." Kalm concentrated on breathing more evenly.

"Why don't you go away?" Krennlen ris Jynnich was excited, his face flushed. Kalm saw anxiety in him, coupled with an almost bladder-spilling eagerness. "We're—we're busy here." Incredibly, the young man glared at Kalm with genuine outrage.

In Kalm's imagination he saw three delinquent children, chastised, retreating before an adult's wrath. The image was repeated once, then again, with a woman smiling triumphantly behind the Kalmlike man. He was seeing the woman's thoughts. *Send them away,* he translated. *Get rid of them.*

*Throw something at them if they fight,* he sent back. *Rocks. Very hard. Then run away and get help.*

*No.*

*They can be stopped. But you'll have to get help.*

*No.* She was concerned for her painted cloth, not for him.

"I think the lady wanted you to go away." Kalm squared his shoulders in a futile attempt to seem more imposing, noticing as he looked down at ris Jynnich that the woman had her hand on a pointed stick. *You are a lady, aren't you?*

"My husband thinks so." Those were spoken words. An undercurrent of emotion carried private amusement. Meanwhile, her conscious thoughts showed that three steps would bring her to the thug with the cut hand, two if he stepped toward her . . . Kalm virtually felt the friction of the stick sliding across his palm as she imagined stabbing it into an eye socket and the impact as it jammed against bone. Drymouthed, he sensed her heart accelerate with anticipation.

"Let it go, Krenn," ris Fryddich said coolly. "We can't have fights in public."

"She hurt Gerint," the boy said.

Kalm waited, knowing that speech would be an error. Ris Fryddich did the same. Ris Whelmner breathed heavily, holding a thumb to his cut hand to stop the blood. The woman shifted toward the Lopritian, her hand swinging with the stick in it, and Kalm, able to view her face again, saw that she was beautiful.

*Don't say anything,* he ordered. *Not for me.*

She looked up at the Algheran, seeing herself defiant and triumphant over both the Lopritians and him. *I'm not afraid.*

*I am.* Kalm tried to communicate common sense to her.

*A man. Lover. Both owner and possession. He is brave.*

*I'm not your husband.* Kalm closed his mind to her, penning up emotions.

"Gerint needs some bandaging, Krenn." Ris Fryddich lied easily.

Ris Whelmner shivered.

"Little bitch," ris Jynnich spit. "Deserves . . ." Fantasy filled his mind, scenes of invented cruelty. But as Kalm waited, the insane thoughts lost strength. Parents, superior officers, past teachers . . . Ris Jynnich saw their images also.

"Come on," ris Fryddich urged. "Buy you both a drink." He nodded coolly at Kalm on the top of the bank. "Risser, wasn't it? Kell Risser?"

The Algheran kept his voice even. "Kalm Rispar."

"Ah, of course. Nice meeting you again."

"Sure." Kalm watched the three men as they left, knowing that he had made an enemy.

*Husband/owner/property.* In Kalm's mind a tall male figure confronted a shrunken ris Fryddich. Cowering behind him, looking around the leg he clung to, was a childlike figure within a too-large adult dress. The swarthy face was his own.

*My husband will protect you,* he translated.

Laughter rose infuriatingly over the bank as he stomped off.

The inn was another ugly Midpassage building, a four-story structure of blue-tinted concrete sitting between a Royal Warehouse and a lumberyard. A graying plank sidewalk ran between the building and the road. Posts stood before the inn's swinging doors; two horses had been hitched to the nearer pole. On the other side of the black pavement, Kalm saw wagons parked under colored awnings, and women gossiping. Everywhere there were barrels, sacks of grain, animal limbs packed in ice, bundled clothing. It was a market, he deduced, watching a man transfer armloads of firewood from his wagon to others in exchange for produce or pieces of paper.

A woman dressed in black loitered near a small conical tent decorated with sun and eye emblems. A nude infant crawled before her on the surface of the road, happily tasting twigs and pebbles. KNOW THE FUTURE, a sign behind the child read. GAIN WEALTH, CHILDREN, CURE SLEEPLESSNESS, HOLD LOVE SECURE. Four of the ideograms had been incorrectly drawn. Kalm grimaced, then skirted the horses cautiously and pushed open the inn's door.

"Not open for food," said a man washing glasses behind a bar off at the right.

Kalm noted the plank floor and the cloth-covered walls with their primitive light fixtures. The ceiling was high, allowing a view of three rows of doors and exposed halls. An open stairway ran along one wall. Kalm sniffed, noticing the cloying smell of spice that rose from the wall covers. *People live here?*

"Not open for food. Come by in a tenth of a day." The bartender lifted a corner of his counter. Kalm saw the men he had followed at a table near an unused fireplace and tried not to watch them.

"Looking for Rahmmend Wolf-Twin."

"Open door up there, second floor." The bartender gestured with a shoulder, holding a tray with three glasses level.

Kalm pretended that ris Fryddich was not watching as he went up the stairs.

"It needs doing," the Ironwearer said comfortably. "I'm here, so I'm doing it." Methodically, he poured water in a glass from a clear pitcher, set it down, then sidestepped to the next glass at the table. If he was impatient at Kalm's presence, it did not show.

Kalm had to tell himself that there was no reason to feel shame for his question. He glanced at an open window, knowing that if he looked through it he would see the dark-haired woman on the riverbank and knowing also that she was watching him through Rahmmend Wolf-Twin's eyes. At intervals, her consciousness pushed at his own, always retreating before he had time to react.

*Stop it*, he ordered.

*Why?*

*Because. Just because.* Privately he wondered if reticence made sense, but the habit was old now. *Some things even Teeps have to treat as secret.*

*A secret? Tell me!*

*No!* Irritated, Kalm raised his mental shield even though it left him unable to probe Wolf-Twin's thoughts. Distractingly, the woman's mind hovered over his regardless, the words no longer penetrating to his consciousness but still there behind other sounds like so many insects chittering. It was a game for her, he sensed; his annoyance left her amused.

"Someone else could do this," he repeated.

"Really?" Wolf-Twin seemed surprised. "Lord Andervyll will drink no water, but he will insist upon a full glass. Ironwearer Clendannan will drink what is before him without concern. Ironwearer Haarper will drink no water that has not been boiled. Gertynne ris Vandeign must have some water to pour out the window, but he will not be thirsty. And I will or will not be thirsty without concern for the gods. Who knows this better than I? Who else would be better at filling these glasses?"

It was not an attitude Kalm would have predicted.

And Rahm Wolf-Twin was not what he had expected of Ironwearers. The man's youth—he was no more than a hundred—was no surprise. Nor was the fact that he was short, dark-complexioned, and squat. But Wolf-Twin was ugly.

He was obese, thick-bellied, with wattles of flesh on his neck; the man's face overflowed with plump cheeks and heavy lips. His uniform was outsized, a nonstandard gold and brown material made to seem yellow by his skin coloring, without decoration except for small crossed swords on the collar. The arms inside the loose sleeves were short, with the thickness of a normal man's thighs. His stumpy legs were bowed, his feet splayed outward. A toad, Kalm remembered hearing. A brown-colored toad who somehow radiated satisfaction.

But he was an Ironwearer, a man enacting a myth. In the real world, he had probably been in a grave for five hundred years.

It was impossible to believe.

"You read and write?" Wolf-Twin asked casually, twisting his head as if seeking a fly.

"Yes. I had to." Kalm paused, then invented an explanation. "My father insisted, so . . . And arithmetic. Do you want an example?"

"No." The lazy eyelids blinked slowly.

*Stupid*, Kalm heard inside his head. *Be honest.*

"I'm well educated," Kalm said, not asking where the prod had come from. "Arithmetic. Geometry. Calculus. I could have been an artillerist." His shield rose again, keeping the distraction at bay.

"Ah." Wolf-Twin blinked again. "Would you have liked that?"

"I'm here to obey your orders."

"So you obey orders, Lieutenant?" Wolf-Twin snorted softly, then put down the empty pitcher. "Have you ever really been on a campaign, young Rispar? Or in a battle?"

"Oh, yes," Kalm said softly.

Wolf-Twin waited a long moment. "You saw men die?"

"Many."

"And were you a good soldier, Lieutenant?" The dark man glanced toward the window, then back to the door, as if expecting it to open.

"Only sometimes." Kalm looked back at his life with unfamiliar acceptance and found no excuses to offer the Ironwearer. "I've done what I thought duty required."

"Ah." Wolf-Twin nodded gravely at the table. "We may fight the Algherans, even the great General Mlart tra'Nornst himself. Would that bother you?" He seemed only mildly curious.

*I've done it before.* "I wouldn't be afraid."

"That was not my question, Alghera-man."

Kalm had time to remember that his birthplace had not been asked.

The Ironwearer suddenly stepped to open the door. "Excuse, please. An argument, I think."

"Not very good wine." Derrauld ris Fryddich snapped his fingers. "It was not worth paying for."

"They ordered it." The bartender stood by stolidly, not looking at the blue-uniformed men. He was not a small man, Kalm noticed, looking at his sleek black hair and thick forearms. A wooden club was in one fist, but he had only wiggled it uselessly.

Wolf-Twin flicked a hand at him, bidding silence. "You drank the wine, yes? Pay for it, soldiers."

"No."

"I will be disappointed in you."

"Drink some wine, then." Ris Fryddich sneered.

Against a man, ris Fryddich was willing to fight, Kalm realized suddenly. With two partners at his side, the tall Lopritian was almost eager for the opportunity. He even felt justified, completely sure in his mind that he need not pay for what he decided to take. He owed no excuses for his actions to anyone in the one world.

The man was dangerous. Kalm hesitated, unafraid for himself but wondering how to warn Wolf-Twin.

"Your names." The dark man spoke before Kalm found words.

"Loorins lan Grannym." Ris Fryddich grinned.

"Treln Vandeign." Gerint ris Whelmner was deadpan until the bartender started. Then he smirked.

"Devint lan Deirne." That was Krennlen ris Jynnich, smiling, seeing only poverty and the ineffective resentment of the poor in Wolf-Twin's homespun uniform. Unlike the others, he did not realize the significance of the crossed sword insignia and copied their attitude without knowing their purpose.

"Your pay books," Wolf-Twin said.

"Forgot it," ris Fryddich said.

"Lost mine," ris Whelmner said.

Ris Jynnich searched himself elaborately. "Oh, it's gone!"

"Pay books." Wolf-Twin's voice was slightly louder.

"Sorry." Ris Jynnich grinned.

Wolf-Twin frowned, the toad features seemingly close to tears, his blubbery lips quivering. His eyelids twitched.

Suddenly Derrauld ris Fryddich was falling backward.

Wolf-Twin pivoted and struck ris Whelmner's jaw with the heel of his outstretched hand.

Kalm stared at ris Fryddich, who was still sliding to the floor with his back against an upended table. What filled his mind was the pain from a bitten tongue.

Gerint ris Whelmner fell as well, catching himself with his palms as he slid into the wall. The wound on his hand re-opened. Kalm saw blood spotting the floor as he rolled to his side. Agony showed on his face; Kalm knew he had broken a thumb.

"Pay book, boy." Wolf-Twin's voice was kind.

"N-no." Krennlen ris Jynnich stared foolishly at ris Whelmner writhing on the floor. He turned suddenly.

*Well, do something*, a mental voice told Kalm. The edge of the riverbank flashed before his eyes, then he saw the side of the inn as the woman glared in his direction. She was running toward the inclined path leading up the bank.

*Go away*, he thought back. He reached out and took the bartender's club. He would do with that what there was a need for—if the Ironwearer really needed him. It seemed unreasonably stupid to enter a fight without thinking of how it might end.

He was certain that Rahmmend Wolf-Twin had not worried about it.

*Useless as Dieytl. Well, Tim's on the way, fat boy.*

The contemptuous practicality angered him, until Kalm saw it for what it was. *Wolf-Twin's just fine. Don't worry.* Then, daring fate, he added, *I like him, too.*

*You might do something, then.* But she was mollified.

As Kalm thought about that, the dark Ironwearer skipped two steps sideways and threw out a foot. Ris Jynnich bent forward toward the door, then, overcorrecting, landed on his backside. *Trying to run away*, hindsight told Kalm. *Wolf-Twin tripped him.*

Derrauld ris Fryddich was fully on the floor now, his back against the fallen table, one foot tangled in the legs of a stool. Misery showed on his thick face as he felt his jaw, and blood was drooling onto his fingers.

"Pay book."

As the Ironwearer loomed over him, Ris Fryddich only

stared in disbelief, barely able to move even when the dark man lifted him by his tunic and belt laces and threw him.

Ris Jynnich had just begun to come to his knees as ris Fryddich fell upon him. The impact knocked him over again. He lay coughing for breath under ris Fryddich as the bigger man flopped about, his hands to his groin. Ris Whelmner remained at the side of the room, rocking back and forth on his side and moaning.

It had taken ten seconds to disable three men, Kalm calculated, and Wolf-Twin had given time to conversation. He could have killed them more quickly. And this was an *ordinary* Ironwearer, not one to be noticed in history books, not one to be remembered a century from now, not an important one.

*Of course not.* The voice in his head was pleased with him.

"Pay book." The Ironwearer smiled as he held a hand out to receive ris Jynnich's pay book.

"Rahm—oh." A very tall man had entered the inn. Like the Ironwearer, he wore a brown uniform, but it fitted better on his broad shoulders than the dark man's did. An old scar was on one temple, crossing from pale skin into short red-brown hair. His lips were thin, his eyes gray. The crossed swords of an Ironwearer gleamed brightly on his shirt collar. His square face showed surprise rather than dismay. When Kalm probed for his thoughts, he met a vacuum.

"Need some help?" The redhead's voice was a guttural baritone of indefinite age; it bore traces of tongues that Kalm could not identify.

A woman stood behind him. She was blond, with short-cut hair; large-breasted and thickset, she wore white shorts and a tight blue pullover. There were symbols on the front of the shirt, meaningless words in thick Algheran ideograms: PEACE THROUGH SUPERIOR FIREPOWER. A round scar was in the middle of her forehead.

Another Teep, Kalm recognized. *Who are you?*

The thought was unanswered. When Kalm touched her mind, the picture of the world he saw was his own, brightly colored with her at the focus. Imperceptibly, she shivered. Other images poured into her eyes, showing Kalm and the redhead as if reflected from a mirror.

"Lan Haarper, lin Zolduhal." The bartender bowed his

head appreciatively, then sidled toward the safety of his counter.

"I manage, my friend," Kalm, in the woman's mind, heard himself saying. "These, they left a bill." Paper slapped against a hand as Kalm recognized Wolf-Twin's voice. He heard movement. The woman's viewpoint shifted, and Kalm was seeing the scene from the safety of the bar.

He probed deeper into her mind, meeting darkness, a silent pain, acceptance, and remembered flashes of sensation. She was young, poor, unsophisticated . . .

She was blind.

The woman he had seen on the hill. Blind, and he had thought— Kalm returned to his own mind with horror.

*Lan Haarper.* Strangeness suddenly gave meaning to the name. *Not from Loprit. A foreigner.*

The commander of the town's forces.

And, Kalm suddenly saw, the Ironwearer's thoughts were concealed not behind a Teep's screens but by a Teepblind. The glint of silver in the big man's hair could be nothing else. The redhead was from another time.

He was an Algheran—and an Ironwearer. The story Kalm had read had been true.

Kalm stared, openmouthed. A pay book skimmed his head, to be caught with one hand by lan Haarper.

"Says his name is lan Deirne. Is it?" That was Wolf-Twin's voice.

An Ironwearer. Kalm swallowed, his mind racing. Someone conspicuous. How was he to kill such a man without risk?

"What's the penalty for theft?" Lan Haarper seemed amused, unaware of an enemy's observation. Knowing now, Kalm heard distorted echoes of Speech in his voice. The Teep woman noticed his surveillance but ignored Kalm, focusing instead on the redhead.

"Pay book, lan Grannym." The dark Ironwearer kicked lightly at the fallen ris Fryddich. "A hand. Maybe a foot. What we want it to be. Why, Timmial?"

"Oh-h-h-h-h . . . it'd be fun to believe him." The redhead smirked briefly. "Pay book's got the name of ris Jynnich."

"Ahh." Wolf-Twin seemed unsurprised. "Pay book, lan Grannym." He knelt and slapped at the blond man's sullen face. The Lopritian snapped his teeth together in response and tried to rise. Wolf-Twin slapped him again, then half raised him by his shirt and shook him. The blue fabric ripped; the dark man reached inside to pull free a pocket and a pay book.

"Theft," the Algheran time traveler said evenly. "Maybe murder. A horrible crime directed at innocent aristocrats by common scum. Notice how ugly they are. Obviously serfs. How could they have hoped to pass themselves off as anything else? I don't think any punishment could be too severe for people like this, Rahm. So let's lock them up and notify the authorities about their heinous—"

"Timmial." The blond woman stepped forward, speaking just the one word, too softly for Kalm to read its timbre.

"Oh, all right, Wandisha." The voice was grumbling, though the man smiled. "You telepaths take all the fun out of life."

"They certainly do," Kalm said quickly. The words would make him noticed; he wondered what response they would draw.

"Maybe, *fellow*." Cold gray eyes focused briefly on him, then drifted back to Wolf-Twin. "Dock 'em for the damages, I guess. Send 'em home."

Ris Whelmner screamed suddenly and sprang forward.

There was a knife in his hand, Kalm noticed in one frozen instant, perversely seeing the man as on hands and knees, even though he realized that the soldier was simply crouching as he ran. A table knife—ris Whelmner had remembered his table knife. Rahmmend Wolf-Twin was two man-heights from ris Whelmner and off balance as he rose.

Before Kalm could cry a warning, the red-haired man acted. A table went sideways, spilling stools before it. Then ris Whelmner was rising, snatched at his collar and the seat of the pants. At the apex of his rise, he seemed to hang in the air above them all.

Wood cracked as the table fell, then rolled sideways. A portion broke from the top as it rolled backward and slapped the floor noisily, pulling Kalm's eyes for an instant.

The young Lopritian twisted in the time traveler's grasp as Ian Haarper lowered him, hate bright upon his face, kicking and half twisting as his arms flailed. A blow struck the man carrying him. Kalm saw skin through a cut in the brown pants. Blood drops darkened the fabric along the Ironwearer's leg.

Then ris Whelmner pitched forward to fall facedown. The plank floor seemed to rattle as he struck. An instant later, Ian Haarper released his legs.

Before the Lopritian could react or even catalog his pains, Ian Haarper jumped on ris Whelmner's back. Kalm half heard, half felt ribs crack even as the big man kicked ris Whelmner behind his ear.

The time traveler was smiling—that was what Kalm always remembered. He was smiling.

The Lopritian lost consciousness instantly. A bloody tooth skittered across the floor. Blood drained from his broken nose.

"Timmial!"

"Tayem!"

The cries came from the doorway. They seemed simultaneous.

The voices belonged to the blind woman and the thin Teep from beside the river.

Kalm, gasping, his eyes fixed on the brutally treated ris Whelmner, nevertheless understood that the women hated one another.

"*Bastard.*" Ian Haarper used the alien word without expression. "It's all right, girls. Just a scratch." He slapped his hands together loudly. "Don't worry about it."

Red drops slipped sluggishly over his boot top, focusing the attention of both women. "Just a scratch," the man repeated sternly. "Run along and let me get to my meeting."

They did not move. The tall Ironwearer sighed, then crossed the floor to stand before them. "Don't worry," he said softly, as if reproving them. "I'm fine."

"Tayem," the dark-haired woman said. "You should—"

"I'll put a bandage on it, Kylene. All right?"

"Tayem." It was a protest against an already recognized defeat, and Kalm was suddenly aware that Wolf-Twin, the bartender, the silent ris Jynnich, and the tall Ironwearer himself shared his perception.

"Go back and paint." The man brushed aside the hair on one side of her forehead and kissed the white skin. "Things are all right, Kylene." The low voice had become a whisper.

*Her husband*, Kalm realized suddenly. The Algheran time traveler was her husband. He held his breath, watching the thin woman, who was close to tears she would not shed for her husband's sake; remembering how bravely she had faced ris Jynnich and ris Whelmner, he understood that he hated Ian Haarper.

"I wasn't worried." The blond woman's voice was throaty and amused, with a poorly concealed tone of triumph.

*Season-taken*, Kalm guessed, but her mind showed no sign that the blind woman was in heat. It was emotion that dominated her reactions, not biology. She took pride from her association with the man. How did a woman stand touches from that monster?

"Good girl," Ian Haarper cooed. "Hmmm . . . pretty Wandisha." He kissed her lips firmly, holding her tight against him, then slapped her on the bottom as he released her. "Have fun. See you tonight."

Half memory, half anticipation, Kalm felt the blond woman's sensations almost as if his own body were responding in unending darkness to Ian Haarper's embraces. Involuntarily he flushed—and knew rage.

Ris Whelmner's broken body gave form to his resolution.

*I'm going to destroy him.* Ignored by the Ironwearers as they bent over ris Jynnich, Kalm stared, hating.

*Not here. Not now. Somehow I'll destroy everything he does.*

He began by saving a boy from drowning.

Kylene, 47,346 L.C.

# CHAPTER SIX

*H*arper was back just as suddenly, invisible in the semi-darkness. She heard his footsteps coming up the exterior ramp before she saw him. They were separate, heavy, as if to shake the levcraft or to wake her. Kylene let her art history book slide from her lap to the floor.

How long had it been? Her eyes moved to the timers, then dropped. Minutes for her had been day tenths for him. She had no way of knowing just when he had stepped through the bubble around the time machine to leave normal time behind.

Getting him back was what mattered.

The interior hatchway rose. He came through complaining.

"Kylene, always button this thing up. Don't leave the ramp down when you're alone. Haven't I told you that before?" The voice was tired. His clothing was rumpled. Looking at him, she could see that this once he would not turn argument aside. Still, he made an effort. "I don't want to worry about you."

"What happened, Tayem?"

"I—" He framed words, rejected them, and began over. "I think I drowned myself in what was supposed to go swimmingly. We're screwed, kid. Screwed right to the wall."

Displeasure was plain even in the unfamiliar idiom. She stared at him, feeling equal dismay. "Tayem!"

"Kylene!" He mimicked her cruelly, then sighed. "Never mind, kid. I'll figure out something. Is there anything to eat, Kylene? It's been a long couple of days."

Days. So one question was answered. She moved to the food processor, dialing for stew and a double portion of bread. Plopping sounds followed, then flowing water. "Tell me what happened, Tayem."

"It's a bit different," he said, bending to open the cooler for a mug of beer. "Remember the stuff I've said about worlds looking almost the same and how they split apart and recombine?"

"Yes." She forestalled a lecture. "Except the arithmetic."

He grinned wryly from the depths of his chair. "That's the fun part. Anyhow, what we have here is a world just a little bit different from most of them. Couple years from now there's supposed to be a local noble named Gertynne ris Vandeign, and I figured with a war with Alghera on the horizon, there'd be a job for an honest and unambitious Ironwearer.

"Didn't work that way." He turned away to toy with the controls, but the behavior of the numbers overhead did not change. "Hate to criticize someone's good luck."

An explanation would come much faster if Tayem would let her see his mind directly, Kylene reflected, but she did not suggest it. Maybe talking was therapeutic for Normals, the slowly paced delivery of information balancing sensible and ordinary needs for communication against their suspicion and lack of trust. She twisted the cup in the food processor to increase the heating rate, then added spices. *Telepaths would run the world much better.*

"Ris Vandeign had an older brother named Merryn," Harper said. "Most everywhere, Merryn drowned in an accident about the time Gertynne was born."

"Not here," Kylene guessed. Bubbles rose at the sides of the cooking cup. She added thickeners to the stew, then reduced the heat and opened a side cabinet to find a serving cup.

"Not here. Merryn survived and inherited, and Gertynne became just an ordinary army officer. He didn't tell me this himself, you understand; I spent some time hanging around to get the background."

She murmured agreement and nudged off the food processor. A Merryn substituted for a Gertynne. Both names were funny-sounding, but she supposed that was insignificant. What had made Tayem unhappy?

"So Merryn had kids. Dandy." Harper stared into the depths of his beer. Kylene waited, pouring stew from the cooking vessel to the purple serving cup as silently as possible.

"One of 'em a boy, and the apple of his eye. So three years ago, against his father's wishes, the kid up and joined the Lopritian army. Merryn's kind of a savant in local terms; he got a set of the Plates copied for him and learned Common, and now he's busy trying to re-create everything the Fourth Era described. Says technology does more for people than war does, and *hell*, I can't argue with him. But the kid just called that blacksmithing and went off to enlist."

Kylene did mental calculations that did not work out, then guessed as she carried the stew across the cabin. "Mlart? Was that during the last war?" Close to Harper again, she stared at his bulky shoulders, realizing once more how much larger than other men he was. Silver glinted on his head, treacherous white and gray strands interspersed among the red-brown hairs, fraudulently advertising great age. Under that was more silver: the mind-concealing mesh of a Teepblind.

He seemed tired, she decided. Exertion had heightened the odor of musk that accompanied him, and there was a raggedness to him, like the unkempt order of his hair, that could be noticed but not defined. Crusted blood showed on his left knuckles. Had he been fighting? She wanted to touch him and to be touched by him, and she lingered, hoping, but he did not notice.

"Thanks, Kylene," he said. "No, it was just after that. The Lopritians thought they'd grab some territory from the Necklace Lake tribes to make up for what they'd lost to Mlart. Progress without all that waiting for technology."

Harper chuckled without humor, then swallowed stew greedily, tipping his head back. Grime showed under his fingernails. "So they did. Some. One of these days, girl, I'm going to throw out the Algheran stuff, put in a decent stove, and teach you to broil some steaks."

She would not mind that, she admitted privately. Whether it was the spices or the way it was prepared, Algheran food simply never tasted right. It was nourishing, but she missed the flavors she had learned to expect as a child. "The boy?"

"Got himself killed. Dumb twit walked into an arrow." Harper shook his head in amazement, scratched at the serving cup with a finger, then pulled off the outer layer of plastic.

"So now his father doesn't like the army, really doesn't like soldiers, particularly doesn't like professional soldiers, absolutely doesn't like the Lopritian court. On top of which—"

He stood to bring his cups back to the cabinets, then dropped purple and white film into the trash bin. "On top of which—I mentioned the Plates—he's a convert to Cimon and Nicole and really doesn't want to fight the Algherans at all."

He snorted cynically. "Of all the Cimon-taken things to find as a roadblock! In other circumstances . . . Kylene, this is not a fair world."

"Could you kill him?" It was only a suggestion she made, not yet a prescription. Kylene reviewed Harper's account dispassionately, unsure of his reaction, balancing names and relationships as if they formed equations in the algebra he had made her study, looking for terms to cancel. Then she repeated herself. "Kill him, Tayem."

The redhead frowned.

She tried once more. "Well, drown him. Again."

"Uh-hhh." Harper shook his head. "Forget it."

"Why?"

"I don't drown kids."

"Yes, Tayem." Kylene patiently held back a sigh, being both familiar and bored with the metaphysical underpinnings of his argument. Things should be simple, she felt rebelliously. Going from one year to another should not be more complex than going from one town to another. It was the Algherans' fault that things were not simple. Telepaths would have run things much better.

In a properly run world, time travel wouldn't be allowed.

"Poor put-upon Kylene." He was reading her expression. "All this time travel, just to make simple things complex."

*Impossible man.* "Well, what do we do, Tayem?"

That cost him his good humor. Harper grimaced. "Nothing yet . . . And . . . well, things are pretty crude here in terms of living conditions. Barracks. No place for an artist. Let me get things ready for you. I'll take you a few years uptime to the capital and put you on a stagecoach. Then I'll come back and take the kind of job Merryn *did* offer me."

# Part 2 Midpassage: A Band of Druthers

Timmial, 47,349 L.C.

# CHAPTER SEVEN

*The* morning sun was an arrow's length above the bow of the horizon when the old prospector crossed the gleaming bridge into Midpassage. On the town side of Bloodrill River, he halted on the crescent of ground that lay between the river-banks and a dilapidated wooden fence, then tugged the halters on his packhorses. The mares closed on either side of his stallion, avoiding the knee-high drop at the sides of the road. The stockade gates were open, and only a pole resting on waist-high trestles blocked his entry, but he dismounted and waited patiently, despite the heat radiating from the black pavement. Dust powdered his boots and leggings, but the var-nished rifle stock protruding from the saddle holster might have been store-bought new. Sage and cinnamon scents escaped from canvas panniers, almost masking the taint of old sweat that also rode upon the horses.

Ropes squeaked in ceramic blocks as the pole swayed up-ward. The prospector cast a skeptical eye on weather-beaten tackle and sagging timbers, then shrugged and turned his look away.

The late summer heat had not been kind to the river that framed the town. The dun sheeting that was to protect the banks from erosion was still in place, but naked clay was visible for a man-height beneath. In spring high waters had half covered the sheets, but now there were only grumbling brown streams threading mud hillocks, and scuds of dust streaked the plastic. On the opposite bank, just beyond the eastward bend, a crumbling curtain of earth overhung the pebbled shelf abandoned by the river. Farther north, downstream, a waterwheel was backdropped by the rolling crest of Shieldboss Mountain. Hidden from view except to the south was the Far Rim of the Shield Mountains.

Scattered clouds loitered in the southern skies, too thin to promise rain or offer shade. The traveler turned east, casting his view along the Shield's Near Rim. Closer at hand, animals grazed on sloping pastures. Foothills pushed toward the river, a giant's head and outstretched arms burrowing under houses. Above them, the mountainsides were darkened by stands of stunted secondary-growth hardwoods and tangled brush reluctantly giving place in the heights to spruce.

Tall grasses drooped listlessly across the river, yellowtopped from lack of moisture. Penetrating them was a gap wide enough for a dozen men to march abreast: the great road he had followed from the south. A summer haze obscured the distance; nearby, mirage puddles shimmered brightly over the black pavement. The road did not rise as it spanned the river, though it narrowed slightly. From the side it could be seen that a shallow arch made the pavement material a handbreadth thinner at midstream. Supporting pillars the width of a man penetrated to bedrock at either end of the bridge. Perhaps erosion had uncovered them.

Beyond the gate the road continued through Midpassage and onward without bend. Three days of marching to the north, near the juncture of the Bloodrill and Ocean Father rivers, it turned west to follow the larger river to its headwaters. Continuing through the moraine-strewn depths of the continent, it veered north again within the Necklace Lakes and finally vanished beneath perpetual snowfalls. Where it ended, no man knew.

"Kantomerge," men had called the Ocean Father during the Fourth Era. No name for the Shield Rims survived from that time, but legends in the Chronicles had placed the Gateway rivers within a valley such as this. The tall man now scratching awkwardly between his shoulder blades could recall older names—Potomac, Blue Ridge, Shenandoah—but he would be careful not to use them.

After the wooden barrier had risen, he led the horses forward and pulled a coin from the tail pocket of his leather shirt. The attendants remembered him from his height and red-brown hair, but they weighed his entry fee regardless and gave him their ledger to sign, then watched while the prospector remounted and continued up the road. He had not been sweating despite the heat, they noted with faint envy.

The town was a short distance north, separated from the fence by rolling pasture and a small orchard. Residences lay on the hillsides to his right as he approached, bright in their summer paint and topped by white canvas sunscreens. First a small lumberyard, then an inn and storehouses and a postal station of Her Majesty's Exploration Guild were on his left, between the road and the silent wharfs. Across the river, tents stretched far along the Bloodrill's banks; groups of men and horses moved in what had been pastures. The prospector nodded, viewing them without surprise.

He turned right onto a dirt road at the town's outskirts and right again at the apiary. At a signpost for the Overcome-with-Gratitude Traveler's Horse Restoratory he turned left, then continued to the top of the hill.

Ignoring heat and smoke, men labored over forges and casting pits in open-fronted smithies on either side of the lane. Apprentices with narrow rakes shoved briquettes of charcoal down black-streaked troughs from the outside bins to tiny furnaces. On his right, a man in a leather apron stuck his head into a large barrel, then pulled it out and splashed his bare chest and arms with water. The clangor died as the workers waved at the rider, then was reborn as he continued up the lane to the golden barns.

A whiff of hydrochloric acid escaped from the epuratory as the redhead passed, causing the horses to whinny in protest, but he had expected the odor and kept them under control. Farther along, clover bordered the lane, a field of purple and white extending along the left side of the nearer barn. He turned right, following the lane, then left to pass through an open gate.

As he entered the courtyard, the mares raised their heads and shook their manes, perhaps smelling better provisions than he had given them recently. The big man smiled briefly, then dismounted and lashed reins to the hitching pole. A stained saddlebag went over his shoulder. A yellow-haired dog approached and nuzzled his knee, and he bent to scratch behind its ears, then patted its side familiarly. Neglected, the horses turned to the water trough before them.

The interior of the barn was kept cool by the skillful arrangement of vents in the earthen walls. The walls had been painted yellow recently, a lighter shade than he remembered. The building was well lit by current standards, with overhead louvers and large incandescent lamps. Stable hands were sweeping out vacant stalls when he entered, pushing straw and manure with wooden rakes across the clay floor toward a grating. Through the back gate, horses could be seen under shade trees at the edge of the paddock.

None of the men visible was the one he sought. The prospector ducked through the side door and entered the office.

A thin man sat on a stool at a wall-mounted desk, annotating documents in a minuscule script while his right hand pushed sweat from his forehead into his graying hair. He wore a fine-woven brown coverall and boots with wide tips. His chin was cleft. "Be with you," he muttered. "Have water."

Then he looked up. "Timmial! Welcome back. You're early." His arms went out to give the taller man an affectionate hug.

Tim Harper reciprocated awkwardly, his eyes roaming over walls and ceiling until self-recognition of his embarrassment forced a smile to his lips. He made a fist and jabbed lightly at the man's shoulder. "Some personal matters to shorten the trip. You're looking good, Merryn. Been too long. Water for you?"

"No need." Merryn ris Vandeign returned to his stool. "Now, what can an old man do for you?"

"Need some horses." A crystal pitcher resting on embroidered cloth sat beside three iron bowls on a small cabinet next to the open window. Harper lifted a bowl with both hands, showing every sign of appreciation as he inspected the minute grooves left by the lathe, then ladled ice water into it with a conical metal dipper. As a gesture to the older man, he cast a spoonful of water outside the window; tradition said such hospitality would ease Nicole's thirst. His eyes moved over the view slowly from left to right, from the rickety town gate to the low warehouses at the north end of the town.

It was not an American town, and more than differences in architecture promoted that feeling, though he could not put his finger on the cause for his unrest. The A.D. 1976 Harper re-

membered was ninety thousand years in the past, lost even to
history for all but him. Nor did this place bear a resemblance
to the Fohima Alghera of 47,930 on the Long Count calendar;
that was another country than this, and City Year 893 was
almost six centuries in the future.

"Good to be back," he said.

When he had drunk his fill, he dried the bowl with a corner
of the cloth and replaced it. "Thanks. The stallion's fresh
enough, so I'll hold on to him, but you can have the mares
back. I need another one, though, for riding. Preferably very
docile."

The older man pursed his lips. "How long? A season. For
you? No. Let's see . . . Yes." He slapped his desk top, then
gave orders to the stable hand who had entered. When the boy
was gone, he rummaged through a drawer, inspecting papers
on both sides. "Thought I had something here endorsed to
you—guess I don't. Well, twelve hundred mina for three
horses, two seasons, and you're back early . . ." He performed
calculations on a nearby pad of paper, compared them with a
dog-eared notebook, then scratched something on a second
sheet. "Three twenty-one—call it another three hundred
mina. Just for you."

"Two-hundred," Harper offered. "I take good care of
them."

"Two-ninety, but it's kindness and an aging man's folly."

"Two-fifteen. Since we're old friends." The redhead allowed uncertainty to flash across his face.

Merryn smiled reassuringly. "Two-eighty, just to welcome
you back."

Harper smiled in return. "Two-thirty, since I'm pleased to
see you again also."

"Two-seventy," Merryn said pensively. "If the gods notice,
they may reward my charity."

"Two-forty." Harper clasped his hands reverently. "And the
surety of Nicole's love."

"Two-sixty-five." Merryn frowned at him.

Harper tried fascinated imbecility. "Two-forty-five. Such a
great number, you know. I've always been very fond of it."

Merryn displayed annoyance, then inspiration, shading into
self-amazed decisiveness. "Two-sixty, and I'll give you the
oldest nag on the lot."

Back to bland. "Two-fifty-five, if you'll toss in a saddle
and harness."

The older man raised his eyes to the ceiling. "What are five mina? Only five mina. When my poor orphaned children are homeless and starving, will they be so concerned about a few mina that rightfully should have been their inheritance? All right, Timmial. But you must promise never to tell them, lest they curse my memory." His pen touched the pad again. "Sign."

The original value of the warrant had been for 240 mina. Now it was for the higher figure. Harper dropped the saddle-bag on the desk and smiled wryly as he took the pen. "Your secret kindness is safe, Merryn."

Ris Vandeign grinned, though emotion that Harper could not read showed in his eyes. "Three-year-old mare. Very sound, trust her with a baby. Want to go and take a look? No? Well, you'll be pleased." With a foot, he pushed a stool at the redhead. "Come across anything?"

Harper simulated uncertainty. "Possibly. Got one of your maps?"

"Here." The older man stood to put one sheaf of papers in a pigeonhole above his desk while he pulled more from an-other.

Harper leaned over the desk, selected a map of the Torn Coast region, then traced declination lines with the pen he was still holding. "Above here—the hilly region north of this river. Ironberries are growing wild, and some of the other trees I planted last year are bearing. Copper and lead, of course, but aluminum also. Maybe some other things. I hope . . . Here!" He reached into the saddlebag for strawberrylike beads and let them slip through his fingers to fall heavily onto the desk top. "What do you think?"

"Excellent form." Ris Vandeign sorted the berries by color, then selected a half dozen of the red ones and scraped at the thin skin to expose the underlying metal. Concentration closed his eyes and placed a scowl on his face while his left hand shook back and forth. "Good weight. Mina . . . and three-eighths, I'd say. Very good, Timmial! Perhaps this is the strike that restores your fortune."

"Thanks. Hope so." Harper pushed maps aside to sit on the desk, ignoring the strain this placed on the supporting chains, then scooped berries back into the bag. "Have to do a decent assay first, though."

"Let me know how it comes out. I'll draw up a standard

contract. In fact, maybe a bonus on top. New metal is going to draw a premium for a while, Timmial."

"Oh?" Harper raised his eyebrows.

"Gun barrels," the older man explained. "Our most sovereign temporal masters speak of reequipping Her Majesty's army." He lapsed into silence, then looked away. "Stammis should have been twenty-six yesterday. Yesterday. Ahhhhhh . . ." He patted the hand Harper had placed on his shoulder. "Thank you, Timmial."

Harper shrugged, leaving the hand in place. "Maybe it's just a safety measure? Or some political arrangement we don't understand?"

"No." A growl sounded in ris Vandeign's voice. "It's war with the Algherans again. Rumors are that their Muster has decided to recall the tra'Nornst as Warder."

"We've heard that before."

"These are . . . believable rumors." Merryn paused after that delicate allusion to the telepaths. "They began to circulate two year tenths ago, while you were outside town."

Harper snapped his fingers. "The tra'Nornst being back doesn't prove there will be a war."

"Sunset doesn't prove sunrise. But you saw the camp across the river?"

"Uh huh. Couple of regiments, I'd say. Couple a thousand men. Which force?"

"Ris Andervyll. The Strength-through-Loyalty Brigade." Distaste was clear on Merryn's thin face. "They've been here twenty days now."

*The Hand of the Queen*, Harper thought, giving ris Andervyll his rank. Good. History was coming back to its proper track.

But something inside him regretted the change.

"We're a central point," he said mildly. Northfaring, where the brigade had been stationed, was west of the border between Loprit and Alghera. Moving the force into the valley allowed it to be used as reinforcement for either the southern or central theaters, but both Coward's Landing, one day's long march to the north, and West Bend, two days south, were too small to provide provisions for several thousand soldiers.

He shrugged off Merryn's look of incomprehension. "Who's on the borders?"

"Other favorites," the older man said petulantly.

The redhead suppressed a sigh. "Who's on the borders?"

"Ris Mockstyn. Ris Cornoval is in the south. If it matters."

"Competent men, I've heard." *And loyal to the Crown, as well*, his thoughts ran. Ris Andervyll was not a hedge baron but the uncle of the queen, equivalent to a duke. In a crisis, either of the Lopritian commanders would take directions from him.

And this was also history as it would be recorded. Imperceptibly, Harper straightened his shoulders. "And where is your brother now?" His voice was only politely curious.

"With Andervyll." Merryn was bitter. "He's an officer on the staff."

*Where he can be watched. Used, but kept subordinate.*

*Well, a man who watched his father be beheaded for treason thirty years ago probably can't be trusted with his own command.* For a usurper, Molminda had been remarkably forgiving, Harper reflected absently.

*So I'll finally meet Gertynne ris Vandeign.* Dusty anticipations stirred in a long dormant corner of Harper's mind, then subsided. When he spoke, the words were only pro forma. "Is he looking for people?"

Merryn ris Vandeign blinked. "You, Timmial?"

"If there is a war . . . I—" *I am not eager to do this.*

"Haven't you outgrown that foolishness?"

"No." Harper knew he must not agree.

"I thought that—"

"No." Harper stared steadily at Merryn till the other man's eyes gave way.

"If I had known," Merryn began, then closed the subject with a gesture. "We can discuss this later."

"Sure." Harper stood, concealing his relief. "I'll go—"

"Not yet." The older man nodded abruptly, then tapped at the map on his desk top. "What did you find? Dantry's Glory? Embarkation? Millennium School? I thought we knew where all those were."

*Richmond*, Harper thought sadly. *Another relic of my world.* But his melancholy had to be masked also. "I didn't find any carvings. Hills, but nothing covering a temple or anything, just dirt. If there is something there, it could be older than the Fourth Era."

"Kh'taal Minzaer, you mean?" The smaller man shook his head decisively. "No. I hate to disappoint you—every prospector I've set up in the last century seems to think he's found Kh'taal Minzaer—but it probably wasn't on this continent.

Fryddich's researches indicate decisively that the topography described in the Chronicles can be found only on the Mother Continent."

*Europe, Asia, and Africa,* Harper reflected. *That really nails it down fine.* But an argument was welcome. "If it ever existed at all."

"Of course it existed. No educated man doubts it, Timmial."

"I suppose," he said carefully.

"Of course," Merryn insisted. "We have the records!"

*We have stories,* Harper corrected him silently. *Legends, at best, or myths. History doesn't last ninety thousand years.*

But what legends! Kh'taal Minzaer, home of the Skyborne, who ruled the world for twenty thousand years . . . Two races of men, two Eternal Wars, five eras . . . Millennia-long conflicts bringing down world-spanning telepath-dominated empires . . . Interregnums of barbarism, broken only at great intervals by the periods in which men built cities and thought themselves masters of destiny . . . Cimon, who had first revolted against the tyranny of the Skyborne; Nicole, his wife, who perished by his side; the tiMantha lu Duois, the "Brothers of Men" who came from the heavens long centuries later to side with the Normals in the climactic battles of the First Eternal War . . .

Legends surely. Merryn's "records" had come from a combination Esperanto Gideon Bible and rubber handbook left in a time capsule. But this was an old argument between them, and he knew that Merryn's Plate-engendered faith would in time replace all other religions. "I suppose," he repeated.

The careful words concealed memories. Seven hundred centuries before this date, with the unconscious Kylene Waterfall captive in his time machine, Harper had hovered above the Rockies watching the town she had sought grow from village to metropolis and vanish in an eye wink.

"The City of Silence," she had named it, a refuge revealed to her in dreams. It was supposedly a community of telepaths, growing in isolation before the birth of the Second Era, which all men knew had been ruled by telepaths. Had that been what men remembered as Kh'taal Minzaer? He had not dared approach it.

*Kylene's city. Kylene's birthright.* He had kept her away from it.

"You suppose," Merryn said, with good humor returned. "You admit the Plates exist, don't you?"

"Yes."

"Have you seen a set?"

"No."

"And yet they exist, you agree. Why not accept that other things exist even though you haven't seen them?"

"Cimon and Nicole, you mean."

"Lord Cimon and the Lady Nicole."

The redhead smiled. "Have you ever seen a *Jesuit*?"

"I beg your pardon?"

"Forget it," Harper responded. "Other things have supporting evidence, let's say. I can believe in the Plates because I've met people who claim to have seen them. I see references to them in books. I see devices, such as your ironberry crushers and epuratory, which you tell me are based on the Plates. So that's evidence. I haven't seen a tiMantha lu Duois. No one I know has ever seen one. I haven't seen anyone getting their soul weighed by Cimon. I haven't had my prayers answered by the Lady. I haven't—"

"But you do pray to Lady Nicole?"

"Of course not."

"Then that's not fair evidence that your prayers are not answered, is it?" Merryn smiled ironically. Then he turned earnest. "I believe in Cimon and Nicole, and so do others. You can believe that belief, can't you? The Plates tell us of our Lord and Lady's actions. I feel their presence about me. Cimon does speak when you ask it of him, Timmial. Nicole will answer your prayers.

"Believe that, Timmial. You can accept that much. And maybe it will succeed in starting you on the path to the truth. You want to believe in something, don't you?"

For a moment Harper remembered kneeling at the communion rail, the wafer on his lips while the tortured Christ upon the Cross looked at him from the wall. *If we could each carry His agony for one second*, he had always thought, sure that that would somehow have taken away His pain but never clear how the miracle could be arranged if the Church itself had not done so.

He remembered also the envy he had felt for the priests, the mixed kindness and hardness he had met in the nuns who had once taught him, the perplexing discovery in high school that his Catholicism branded him socially more than being an orphan did, even though he half knew that Protestants were doomed to hell.

*Father, forgive me for I have sinned . . . Our Father, Who art in heaven . . .* Time and intellect had subverted that faith. For an instant, almost telepathically, he understood the other man's hopes, but reason pulled him back from the brink of acceptance. "I don't want to argue, Merryn."

"Another day, then." The older man pursed his lips, eyeing the redhead pensively. Harper thought again of Jesuits.

He was searching for a response when a clatter arose overhead. "What's that?" he asked. "Birds in your attic, Merryn?"

The graying man looked toward the ceiling. "No. Approaching noon. Time for Wandisha to be getting up."

*Feminine gender.* "Who is 'Wandisha'? Not your wife."

Ris Vandeign smiled. "Hereena is healthy and happy, as ever. She'll be pleased to have you visit again." The smile died. "Wandisha is—uh—someone else. She's—well, she's staying here because she doesn't have anywhere else to stay and not much money and she just wanted a place to sleep and change clothes, so she asked me, and I said it would be all right if—"

Harper lost interest. "Oh, a relative. Merryn, it's time I was going."

"No!" The Lopritian waved him back to the desk. "I don't want you thinking that. Wandisha . . . she's a whore, Timmial."

"I—" The redhead shut his mouth. He did not see. He stepped sideways, aiming for the doorway through the corner of his eye.

"Oh, there's no connection between us. Hereena knows, and she doesn't object. It's no secret, Timmial. She just lives in the room upstairs. Everyone in town knows it." *Don't think wrong of me,* his expression read.

"Well, that clears things up. That's fine. I . . . Merryn, I do have to run. If that horse—"

"Timmial! Don't be so—you'll understand when you meet her. She's quite attractive really, young, a nice person and . . . She needed someone to take her in, so . . . I'd like to introduce you." This last was said very quickly.

"Yeah, I'm sure. Uh . . ." Harper suddenly read purpose into the older man's expression, then let his jaw hang, overcome more by irony now than by prudery. "Any time before this, I'd, uh . . . Merryn, I just bought a wife. She's supposed to arrive this afternoon. That's why I'm back. I'm sorry."

*A baron out to marry me off. Wait till Kylene hears about this!* Then memory brought another name to mind: *Onnul!*

Disappointment showed on ris Vandeign's face. "Oh. Well, I'm pleased for you, Timmial. I have to admit, it hadn't been clear to me you were the kind to wed, although Hereena always said . . . That's why I—what is she like?"

*Blond. Young. Almost a man's height and nearly a man's weight, which made us well matched . . . The first time Onnul and I kissed, we were sitting on my bunk in the Station, and we must have stared at each other for ten minutes beforehand without saying a word . . .*

The present returned. Niculponoc Onnul Nyjuc was four years dead in his memory and six centuries in the future, bleeding and coughing on a battlefield of the Final War, telling a dazed and gravely wounded Harper to desert her because she had never loved him. Other memories followed: learning that Project politics decreed that Onnul could not be rescued, leaving the Project in a stolen time machine, running AWOL back to the First Era and vowing never to return . . .

*So long ago.* Harper leaned with sham nonchalance against the wall by the office door. An old man with a concerned expression was to his left, and stable hands on his right were spreading straw over clay floors in the stalls.

"What is she like?" Merryn repeated. "Your wife? You never spoke of her."

*I'll get her back.* "Her name is Kylene," Harper said slowly. "Kyleena, I guess you'd say. Kylene Waterfall chi' Edgart. I met her in the distant west, some years ago. Didn't think anything would come of it, but no one else had made a bride offer yet, and I had some savings still. So . . ."

*Was that convincing?* he wondered. Probably. It was trite enough. Love should be passion and agony and lust and devotion, with dragons to be slain and raging seas to be confronted. Man and woman standing together on mountain crests, defying the gathered forces of the universe while trumpets sound in the distance. But that could not be said. Instead, he had to playact for Merryn, pretending, as he had pretended being a prospector, that all he knew of romance was the timid water-and-milk sentimentality of store clerks. Despite intellect, bitterness fastened on his soul like a fist.

"What is she like?" ris Vandeign asked once more.

*Just a girl. A telepath. Very young.* But it would be an

error to speak that way. Harper put on a smile, hoping the Lopritian would read a suitor's embarrassment on his face. "Small. Well, medium-sized by most standards. Dark hair. She's young. Very thin, but she promised to fill out properly. Pretty. No, beautiful."

All of which was true, he admitted, as Kylene's face rose in his memory. How strange not to have recognized it before! *My little girl ugly duckling grows up. I'm going to slug any-one who doesn't like her.* "Very determined. I'll be hen-pecked." *God help what innocent soul she does ever marry.* His smile turned to a grin again, this time honestly. "Call me a lucky man."

"Lucky man," ris Vandeign said unsmilingly. "I'm pleased for you, Timmial. If you feel sure you can support—marriage is one of the big decisions a man makes in his lifetime. Her-eena and I have never regretted it, and I'm sure that as the centuries go by, you'll be happier and happier with your Ko-limma."

"Kyleena."

"Oh, Kyleena. Of course. Well, I imagine you're going to be busy. Perhaps Hereena and I will see you again sometime soon? Yes, well, till then." Merryn stood in dismissal.

*A strange encounter,* Tim Harper mused as he rode up the unshaded lane. He recalled Merryn's words: "She needed someone to take her in." So Merryn had done a good deed for the woman, just as he no doubt felt he had done several years ago for a hungry ex-soldier. A good thing Merryn was not a telepath!

It was amusing to have the local baron trying to arrange his life, unaware that the reins of the world lay in Harper's hands. Kylene would enjoy the story.

But that kind of thought showed a lack of perspective. He lost his smile even as he waved his way again past the metal-workers. Serfs, they too ruled the world.

To be alive was to exercise influence. A monarch, a miser, a time traveler: the power each had differed in quantity rather than quality. Technology had not put the universe in his keep-ing, only enlarged his God-given responsibility and increased his obligations. Man alone in Creation had been gifted with free will and the light of morality; to spurn those gifts, to refuse to define good and to act in its defense, was to deny one's humanity, to sin as truly as did any conscious evildoer.

At the signpost Harper turned left, tugging the reins of the mare that followed him, then continued north for a block past the apiary. The houses about him on the hill slopes were spindly creations, pastel-colored concrete buildings narrow and long, three and sometimes four stories high, with gables and peaked roofs, and set back on large lots behind fences. *WPA Queen Anne*, he thought as usual, looking about, but normally he enjoyed the quiet old-fashioned atmosphere. *Tom Sawyer's town.*

He was not content now, he admitted. He did not long to be a soldier again.

*Three years of peace*, he reckoned. It had been too long. *I've lost something.*

It had been a real three years, for the Algheran time travelers had found that history could not be altered by here-and-gone visitors. Only the Agents who submerged themselves for long periods of time made changes that were large enough to be noticed by other time travelers.

Three years alone.

"When do I get to have my own life?" Kylene had asked once, seeing years of semicaptivity ahead. "Sorry. This is life," he had answered, ordering her obedience.

But she had earned her own life.

"What do we do, Tayem?" she had asked, there in the gloom of the time machine's cabin, and he had decided it then. He would accept her company, but he would perform the mission without her. It was *his* duty, not hers. Kylene would not grow old in the service of another's country.

Tree branches overtopped the road, making it necessary to bend in the saddle or dismount. Harper ducked automatically, then patted the neck of the horse.

Time did go quickly, he reflected, looking back not to the period spent with Kylene but to all the years that had passed since coming to the Algherans. From boyhood to middle age, though at twenty-six he would not have tolerated being termed a boy, and ten years hence he probably would not see his present thirty-eight as middle age.

He chuckled half-grimly, then guided his horses to the side of the dirt road to leave space for a buckboard wagon descending the hill. The homespun-clad driver ignored him, only slapping the rumps of his team with the reins to keep them in motion. A small girl, blond and ponytailed, dressed in red coveralls, dangled her feet over the rear of the wagon, inspecting the receding landscape. Noticing the redhead, she waved with an outstretched arm and called out words he failed to hear clearly over the creaking of the wagon.

At thirty-eight she would still be young. She would be middle-aged at two hundred but would not show it. Her old age, if she became senile, would last as long as Harper's, but it would not begin until she was in her fourth century.

Looking at the child's face, Harper saw beyond to the woman she might become, imagining her among her own children and their children. Within a family, the centuries could pass quickly.

Three and a half centuries from now, if Mlart tra'Nornst survived the coming war, a quarter of humanity would die in a bacteriological holocaust. The telepaths would be eradicated. The Final War between Alghera and Chelmmys, at the point of the true Present, would be waged with nuclear weapons.

Harper smiled at the child and waved in the same fashion. In spite of the evil future, yellow flowers had blossomed on either side of him, he noticed, and he had seen a bird much like a robin in one of the elms that shaded the road. The temperature was comfortably warm. A puppy barked happily in a nearby yard. The ground before his eyes had been dressed in yellows and greens, the heavens painted white and blue. The one world was ever new, ever exciting to those who viewed it correctly.

History would be changed, whatever the cost.

In a short while he was home.

When Harper first came to Midpassage, he had been boarded in Merryn's barracks for transient laborers. Verisimilitude had been hard to bear; he had actively sought metals on his third prospecting trip rather than killing time in the hinterlands.

He had found Washington, D.C., within a year tenth.

Or had it been Baltimore? He could not be sure that the swollen Potomac had stayed in its First Era riverbed. Perhaps it had not and he had actually located one of the fabled Fourth Era cities. No matter; the discovery had made him rich for a while, giving him claim to the honorific "lan" in his name and raising him in the esteem of Merryn ris Vandeign.

The wealth was eroding quickly, but his house remained atop the ridge, a monument to his nouveau riche status. Unlike its neighbors, it was built from imported oak and redwood rather than concrete, a single-story dwelling sprawling about an open courtyard. High school Latin had left Harper with an unsatisfied taste for atria, and his self-imposed profligacy had made common cause with his esthetics, however much the local craftsmen had initially disapproved. They had built to his design finally, discovering merit in its costliness.

The memories deepened his smile. As he rode through the gateway, he whistled a tune that somewhat resembled—and that he thought *was*—the "Colonel Bogie March."

After dumping his baggage on the front steps, he took the horses to the back stable. The housekeeper was not around, but the sunscreens had been spread. He nodded approvingly.

To add to his pleasure, a barefoot boy with strawberry-blond hair dashed into the shed while he was removing the saddles and offered to finish the grooming. Young in appearance, he was a teenager from his height and looked vaguely familiar. A neighbor, no doubt. Harper handed over a mina, then another as a tip, cheerfully overpaying a fellow redhead.

Inside the house, he carried saddlebags to his laboratory while bathwater heated, then laid out clumps of berries and uprooted plants by the acid trays, using penciled tags and his memory to order them correctly. A prospector's priority, he noted wryly as he finished. Three years had given authenticity to his habits.

In the bedroom, he removed clothing from cabinets and laid it out on the bed: boots without socks, green shirt, pants with black piping and Velcrolike seals. It was an Algheran uniform, except for twentieth-century underwear, but in this year it would not be recognized. Beneath the clothing were metal insignia that he held but did not place on the shirt collar. There was a crystal knife, never to be drawn in anger, but one that had shed blood.

He bathed in a pewter tub, feeling the pleasure that a genuine prospector returning from the wilderness would find in hot water, no longer objecting to the herb-scented soap. This was authentic, too, as were the room's stucco-daubed walls and the rough gray towels.

As was the tinkling metal bell inside the main entrance.

"Come in." Harper frowned, but that was a reaction to outside sunlight. He thought he recognized the caller.

"If I'm not interrupting . . . Thank you." The man on the doorstep stepped forward quickly. He was past middle age, with graying temples, and burly. A wooden box with hinges and a handle like a miniature attaché case dangled from one hand.

"You aren't now," Harper said dryly, closing the door. The bell had been rung at erratic intervals for five of the long contemporary "minutes." He had had time to towel himself off and don his clothes. "What can I do for you, Nallis?" He remembered that part of the name; the ending had escaped his memory.

"Take some information, you got any to give," the graying man said. He stood at the end of the antechamber, facing the living room, his head turning slowly as if he expected to find secrets painted on the wallboards. "Coach coming through tonight; I thought I'd add something to my dispatch, if I could."

*Still the newsman, or whatever they call it.* "Fishing, are you?" Harper thought for a moment. "I can give you a beer. Would that do?" *Alpbak. Nallis lan Alpbak.*

"Sure." Lan Alpbak followed into the kitchen.

"Just got back," Harper said casually, opening the ice cabinet door. Clear glass crockery, damp with condensation, rested on wooden slats; a cube of ice, milk-white and larger than a man's head, was in a tray beneath; quartz walls, downfilled, provided insulation. "So how'd you find me? Been camping on my doorstep, Nallis?"

That was his thought, but the language lacked the idiom. The actual words suggested seizing property after the owner's death, and the newsman paused to read Harper's expression before answering. Meanwhile, the redhead held a two-gallon glass jar at eye level, looking for sludge and molds in dark brown fluid.

"That." Lan Alpbak pointed with his chin. "Saw your housetender food buying yesterday because she expected you soon, and then lan Callares told me you were back."

"Oh." His curiosity had been answered, and the beer looked clean. Harper used a knife from a wall rack to scrape sealing wax from the top of the container, then pulled the serving cork and poured beer into two mugs. "You came here, you must be desperate for a story."

That was idiom again. The newsman frowned for a moment. "Always looking for information," he said finally. "It's my living."

"Sure. Your health." Harper pushed a mug across the table and raised the other to his lips.

"And yours." Lan Alpbak looked about, then left his writing box on the table and went to the sink with his mug held high. Politely, he dipped a finger into the beer, then flicked drops down the drain. "Lady," he murmured.

*There's your story*, Harper thought, watching. Headlines formed in his mind: *Cimon and Nicole cult still spreading. Converts everywhere, religious leaders report. Missionaries not needed as Fourth Era faith conquers the fifth. "Our work already done," priests say. "Where Plates go, knowledge of the true faith goes." Eventually, nothing else, according to time travelers. Our Agent in Midpassage—*

He swallowed beer, stilling the thoughts. "Information gatherer," that was the word—not newsman and not journalist. Nallis was after commercial data rather than history.

Harper tossed his head, then led the way into the atrium. There were flowers, flagstones, a tree—and quiet. There was something peaceful and comfortable within the garden, a healing ordinariness always welcome despite the fact that he needed no healing.

*Refuge*, he thought. *The walls keep the world away.*

Frowning at himself, he sat at a bench, resting his elbows on a concrete table, and gestured with his mug till the other man sat opposite. He heard a child's distant voice, a barking dog, and faint cymbal-clash rings from the direction of Merryn's foundry. Nallis's breath and the scraping of his clothing as he slid along the bench were louder sounds.

A leaf had fallen from the tree to the tabletop, waxy olive-green on the convex top, duller and silver-toned beneath. Harper pushed at it, then watched with simulated interest as it slipped to the ground.

Meanwhile, Nallis manipulated his wooden box, removing the lid and turning the handle down to form a stand so the bottom rested at a small angle from the tabletop. From a flap on the underside of the lid, he took a sheet of paper. He laid the paper over the gel in the bottom of the writing case and placed bends of wire over the corners to hold the paper in place. When he was through, he sipped from his mug briefly, then put it down. Awkwardly, he used his left hand to extract a stylus from a side pocket, then moved it to his right hand. He waited expectantly.

*Something else stolen from the Plates*, Harper noted with irritation. *They don't have the technology to make real writing blocks, so they make substitutes that look like the pictures.* He realized he wished now that he had not answered the ringing bell.

But he kept that knowledge from his voice. "I really don't have much for you. It was a short trip out, and dull."

"No discoveries this time?" Nallis seemed untroubled. His hand held the stylus steadily against the paper.

Harper smiled briefly. "You should ask my boss about that."

Nallis tossed a gesture at him, an open palm turning to a fist as he brought the hand back. Without words, it said that mere information gatherers did not approach nobles. The expression on his face did not change.

Harper felt irritation again. "Maybe something," he said. "South, below Barlynnt's Tower."

"Ah." Nallis's stylus tip dimpled the paper. "Big?"

Harper swallowed some beer. "Can't say yet. There's enough to justify some analysis, but . . ."

*Richmond, dammit! It's Richmond, Virginia, First Era U.S.A., dead, buried, and forgotten, and he's asking if the grave is worth looting, and I'm pretending I want it to be.*

But he had given them Washington, with nothing to gain but his own comfort. He had fed the ghouls already, calling it practicality.

He sighed theatrically, self-consciously aware that this would be misread as reluctance. "It's still too early to say. You look for area and concentration both. Total yield. If things go well, we'll make a claim soon and continue the analysis. Ask me next year. But right now don't quote me on anything."

"On anything?" Nallis frowned, staring at the marks he had made on the paper.

"Anything. We don't have a claim in yet." Harper smiled ruefully. "Told you I didn't have anything."

"Yes, but—" Nallis touched fingers to his paper, staring down. "Is there anything outside your work?"

"Sorry."

Nallis sighed. "Oh, well. I got a beer out of this."

"You got a beer," Harper agreed. "Another if you want."

The newsman considered, then pushed the mug across the table. "It's been a hot day."

When Harper returned, Nallis had his writing case reassembled. He took the mug with one hand and toyed with the case's handle with the other. "Anything else I can't be told?"

"The secrets of the queen's bedchamber," the redhead said lightly. "The shapes of the things that come."

Nallis stared blankly.

"The future," Harper said, relenting. "I will not predict the future for you."

"War." Nallis busied himself with his beer. "Mlart tra'Nornst is coming back. That means war. I can predict that."

"Likely." Harper returned to his bench and his own beer.

Two decades had passed since the young Algheran general Voridon Mlaratin tra'Nornst had smashed the Lopritian-sponsored bandit groups that dwelt on the uneasy border between the two states. In the aftermath, Alghera and Loprit had signed a treaty of perpetual friendship, to be renewed at three-year intervals; war had quickly followed.

Alghera had been victorious in that war and the one that followed. Its size had doubled.

Half prime minister in First Era terms, half king, as Warder of the Algheran Realm and Battle Master of the Swordtroop, the tra'Nornst had shaped his nation's fate during war and peace as completely as Washington and Lincoln had shaped the America that Harper remembered. The changes had been wrenching and were not all welcome to the aristocratic clans that dominated Alghera and its legislature, the Muster.

Mlart had not accepted criticism of his reforms easily. Eight years before, at the end of his fourth term as Warder, he had voluntarily resigned his offices and settled into seclusion with his wife and infant son. Squabbling among the factions in the Muster redoubled; vying for power, the Septs rebuilt their private armies and employed assassins against rivals. By mutual agreement they neglected the dangerously egalitarian Swordtroop.

Many of Alghera's gains had consisted of lands allied with or claimed by Loprit, and Queen Molminda's attempts to seize compensating territories from the disorganized barbarian tribes westward in the Necklace Lakes region had been only marginally successful. Without Mlart to fear, seeing Alghera slip toward civil war, Molminda's government pressed for concessions and bankrolled competing factions. Privately, her advisers urged preparations for war against the hamstrung Realm.

The Muster had dithered, unwilling to rebuild an army and unwilling to be conciliatory.

Meanwhile, hotheads on both sides fought in tavern brawls, merchant caravans were ambushed in neutral lands, and "bandits" reappeared in Alghera's outlying provinces. Lopritian armies were marching to their assembly points.

Now, at the request of the Muster, Mlart had returned to office. He had been given nearly dictatorial authority to deal with the crisis.

The Warder would try to preserve the peace, Harper knew. He would fail. Books would be written that would describe the negotiations between Mlart's representatives and Molminda's court; other books on his shelves, safely hidden from local eyes, described the war that Mlart would wage after the mutilated corpses of his ambassadors were returned to F'a Alghera.

After a few minutes, Harper spoke. "Nallis?"

"Yes?"

"Why are you wasting time on me?"

"How d'you mean?" The graying man inhaled deeply, nostrils flared.

Harper raised a thumb, pointing. "Army unit across the way. If you see a war coming, there ought to be news there."

Nallis made a spitting sound. "Used to be. Last century, I'd have covered it. I was an all-around man—we all were. But sixty, no it was fifty and, about fifty-five years—the Agency got big. Lots of new money in. Anyway, we have *specialists* now." He made the spitting sound again, but his mouth stayed dry. "Specialists do all that military stuff."

Civilization meant specialization, Harper reflected. "Too bad. So what do you specialize in?"

"Everything the specialists don't," Nallis said wryly. "Special requests for wealthy clients. Crop futures. Ingot prices, in three grades for six metals in four weight classes. Population figures. Family fights. Feuds. The health of our subscribers. The birth of their children."

The redhead grinned. "Any of those connected?"

Nallis snorted. "All of them." When Harper chuckled, he added, "Buy a subscription to the local news and see."

Harper laughed again.

"Maybe read about yourself," the newsman suggested slyly.

Harper stopped laughing. "What?"

"Well, there was that first big strike of yours."

Harper nodded. He remembered that. It had not seemed

important. "I don't want to be 'information,' Nallis." His voice was chilly.

"Oh?" The newsman paused. "People usually like——" He stopped again, mouth open, when he saw Harper's expression.

"Once is enough," Harper told him carefully. "Let the people who want to become famous be famous. I'm not ambitious that way." He stood and gestured, then smiled, trying to ease the sting. "Candidly, it is enough for me to cultivate my garden."

"They were little stories," the newsman said defensively, looking upward. "Like about this garden."

Harper raised an eyebrow. "This *atrium*? I hadn't——"

"The at-three-em," Nallis echoed quickly, shaking his head. "And the——the——" He waved a hand. "The little room."

It took a moment for the euphemism to penetrate.

"My pipes," Harper said disbelievingly, slowly, searching without success for a contemporary word for plumbing. "You wrote up my pipes?"

"Was it wrong?" Lan Alpbak was apologetic. "It made such a good piece, I sent it on to regional. They didn't use it in our regular stuff, but they asked——"

Harper coughed. "It was the housekeeper, wasn't it? She told you, and——" He made a fist, then grimaced. "Not your fault. My Cimon-taken housekeeper. *Da-a-a-amn it!*"

The plumbing in the house was primitive but not authentic and had also met with much objection from the local builders. Harper remembered returning to the house one day and finding seven local women standing agog in the bathroom doorway while his housekeeper triumphantly demonstrated flushing a toilet.

"Did she give you a demonstration?" he asked now. "Did she make the water flow around in the little seat?"

Nallis shook his head timidly.

"Did you use it?" Harper asked evenly. "Did she suggest——"

"Oh, no." Nallis seemed startled by the idea. "I didn't know . . . I thought it might be . . . without experience, I mean."

"Did you see the demon?" Harper's voice turned sour.

"No." But-I-looked-hard, the voice said. "Is there one?"

"Of course there's a demon," Harper growled. "There's a whirlpool, isn't there? And doesn't a demon live in every whirlpool? Even very small whirlpools you turn on and off?"

"She said—"

"She said. My stupid housetender said there was a demon," Harper said, snarling. "An *invisible* demon, wasn't it? Waiting to pull you down, if you sit and—"

"It was safe if you didn't insult it," Nallis admitted.

"Did—you—really—write—that?"

"Yes." Nallis shook his head shyly.

*"Lord, luvaduck!"* Harper prayed with teeth bared.

Of course, he realized, even in the midst of this performance, he had triumphed over the silly old woman in a way. At her insistence he had built an outhouse for her to use, but he had connected it, without her knowledge, to the septic tank.

Germs were authentic also, even if the people of the Fifth Era had greater resistance to disease than he, even if the local people did not understand germs or believe what could not be seen with the unaided eye. He had taken precautions uptime; he did not believe he had been exposed to the Janhular's plagues or carried anything infectious when he returned from the First Era, but he could not be sure.

"And the machinery room," Nallis said. "She said I could write about that also, so . . ." He chewed on his lower lip.

The Nautilus equipment, Harper deduced. That was out of the ordinary also, not because the weights and pulleys were so exotic but because scientific weight training was unknown in this era. *Something else we had that isn't in their damned Plates.* He felt an atavistic satisfaction, thinking that. For a second he even looked forward to another session with the machines.

"And the garden," he said calmly.

"The at-three-em," Nallis admitted. "Yes. I sent that to regional also, and they—they said I should send anything I knew about you, in case . . . Sometimes we get special requests and . . ."

Harper raised his eyes. "Lord, give me strength," he said calmly. Then he glared at Nallis and spread his arms wide. "I weigh one point four man-weights. I am one point fifteen man-heights tall. My shoe size is twelve double E. I am thirty-eight years old. I am single. My love life sucks. My hair color is auburn; my eyes are gray; my teeth are good; my temper is gone. Do you understand? *Do you want my fucking condom size?*"

Windows rattled when he finished. Nallis swallowed, one hand scrabbling at the lid of his writing box till he had it open again. "Yes, Ian Haarper, but—" He swallowed again. "What is a 'fucking condom'?"

And Harper laughed until he choked and Nallis came to pound on his back.

"It's not very exciting work," the information gatherer admitted before he left. "Wheat and ingots and hogs. Which is why I try writing about people now and then, even though the pieces aren't bought. But it's kept me a free man. Leiman and Scee has been good to me."

*A free man.* Harper could forgive much to a man who used those words in that tone of voice.

When he was alone again, he crossed the living room and unlatched the door to his study. This was at the western side of the house, facing the center of town, and it shared a wall with the antechamber. The housekeeper was not allowed to enter the study, but the windows and overhead louvers were kept closed, so only a little dust had settled on the furniture and floor. He would mop that up later.

Harper pushed up the skylight with a pole, then moved shutters and windows sideways to admit any breezes that might visit. Next he stooped to view the outside scene from sill level. Good. The full width of the main road was plainly visible in several spots, barely a hundred man-heights away, and he would not have to cut back the limbs of the elms in his front yard.

"Real good." The tripod was still in place by the big oak desk. He opened drawers, revealing heavy boxes of yellow and red cartridges. Green was beginning to cloud the copper but had not obscured the X's he had carved across the points. Then he went to the fireplace and stretched to pinch a corner post near the ceiling. A muted click sounded, and the hollow beam pivoted at its base, dropping into his left hand.

Cords held secure a long object encased in heavy canvas. Its seals had not been broken. Harper removed it from hiding and pulled the wrapping apart under the skylight. Sunlight glinted on a blue-tinged rifle barrel—steel, not the high-carbon iron of Merryn's foundry, though the design appeared contemporary.

"Authentic as all hell." The Algheran time traveler set the gun to his shoulder and took aim at a window, stroking the front trigger slowly till it clicked on the empty chamber. The rifle's balance was excellent, just as he remembered it.

Time and climate might have combined to ruin the weapon's initial alignment, but it could be resighted within a few days.

Match-rifle accuracy, calibrated loads, half-inch slugs . . . Perfect for punching watermelon-sized holes in anyone's head.

When Mlart tra'Nornst appeared, Harper would be ready.

# CHAPTER EIGHT

"**A**nd one more," the warrant broker said. Thin, gangling, with a receding hairline, he spoke quickly with the lilting accent of the capital. He was dressed expensively in pearl gray, and a fashionable checkerboard pattern had been tattooed on his left cheek. Cosmetics made the scar in the center of his forehead seem perfectly round.

In the middle of the table rested a small pile of coins, a mixture of dark iron and gold. Harper wiped moisture away from them with an elbow, then sipped wheat beer from a tankard while the thin man rummaged in an underarm case, humming softly. Liquid-soaked muslin, mulberry-tinted, hung on the wall beside them. He touched it idly, then rubbed his fingertips on his breeches before turning on his stool to inspect the inn once more.

An empty fireplace of white stone was at his back, and beyond it a stand-up bar and the entrance to the kitchen. The floor was unfinished pine resting on concrete, dampened so that swelling would keep the planks pressed together. Mounted at intervals along the wall were tiny arc lights, painfully bright when stared at and hissing like outraged hornets. At his right, four men divided a deck of sixty-four cards and cast dice before placing bets: farmers, to judge from their drab clothing and heavy boots. Then came a vacant table with three empty short stools. Seated behind the farmers were a trio of soldiers, scarlet-jacketed dragoons escaped from their camp across the river. At the bar a blue-uniformed NCO from a line regiment dickered with the bartender.

A tall woman, obviously pregnant, and her husband ate a silent meal in the far corner. Another woman, emerging from the rest room, detoured to pat her swollen abdomen before returning to her inebriated companion. On the plank sidewalk outside the inn, well-dressed men and women loitered uneasily while nighttime insects made strafing runs on porcelain globe lanterns. A youngster stuck his head through the swinging door, then continued on without entering.

Wood *thukk*ed on wood to his left, but no cause was evident. Harper's eyes moved toward the ceiling, catching an older man on the open staircase in descent from the third floor balcony.

"Here you are."

Harper turned back to the thin man and accepted a small slip of paper. A warrant for wages made out in early spring to his housetender for 200 mina, it had been signed off by a local grocer for 195 mina, traveled downriver to a supplier at 170 mina, returned via a farmer at 155 mina, and ultimately been redeemed by the warrant broker at 110 mina. "Little hope all you folks put in my future," he grumbled.

"Travel less, Ian Haarper." While the redhead ripped the note to pieces, the broker grinned and pulled a last 200-mina coin from the glittering pile. The rest he pushed across the table, the remnants of the quarterly installment of Harper's prospecting quitclaim payments. "Still twelve hundred mina, plus. You want it as cash?"

Harper considered, then nodded. Paper was more convenient for carrying and was easily convertible when signed by a reputable broker. But broker notes would not dip below face value, so he would have to pay a premium. "Your warrants, at one percent."

"Two percent."

Harper touched the coins. "Nice doing business, Dieytl."

"One percent it is," the broker agreed quickly. He pulled a pad from his case and began scrawling his signature. As he pushed each new note to the Agent, he took coins from the pile.

*Score one for the Teepblind*, Harper thought wryly. He drained down beer, then put up a hand to attract a barmaid. "Another, but no cinnamon this time. And one for Ian Callares." Then, as the woman retreated, he asked, "Dieytl, who's the girl?" He pointed toward the upper balcony, where a woman had just emerged from a rented room. As he watched, she closed the door behind her, then pulled her fingers through tangled sandy hair.

"Calls herself lin Zolduhal." The broker did not look up.

"Nice build," Harper commented appreciatively. Barefoot, tall, and stocky, she wore a low-cut blue blouse and red shorts. For an instant her clothing seemed translucent as her body was silhouetted by an arc light. She kept a hand on the railing until she reached the stairs, then descended slowly, awkwardly, as a sleepy child might. The movement of her hips was adult. Hadn't he heard that name before? "Real nice."

"She has no . . ." The broker's final word was unintelligible.

"No what?"

Lan Callares said the word again. "Self-discipline," he repeated in Algheran Speech. "You might call it that. It means something else to Teeps than to Normals."

"Oh?" Harper quirked an eyebrow. "Such as?"

The thin man growled without words, then methodically closed and sealed the top of his case. When the barmaid returned, he tilted his head back to gulp beer. "Ah!" His eyes were closed as he lowered his tankard to the table. "A good beer, for the provinces. What do you plan now, lan Haarper? Will you go elsewhere for safety and back to prospecting shortly?"

"I don't think so." Harper tracked moisture rings with his fingers, then dried the fingers on his pants. "I've been here too long to run away, even if another Algheran war is coming."

"It probably is. There are plans to conscript us, you know." *It's what I'd do.* "Merryn didn't say that."

Lan Callares smiled briefly. "Four hundred men, at least. You. Me. Everyone able to march they can get their hands on."

"Couple of companies," Harper mused. *A lot of men for a town this size, but with a three-century life span, I guess it's possible. Draft board heaven.* "They going to spread us through the brigade? Or can you tell me?"

"You'd have found out shortly, so it doesn't matter. Expect three companies, organized as a battalion."

*Four, maybe five slots.* "They have officers yet? Maybe—"

He broke off suddenly, inspecting the beer in his tankard to hide confusion. *For Chrissake! I'm supposed to think like a prospector. And Kylene is coming in, and I haven't even mentioned her.*

"Maybe what?" the broker asked.

The moment for mentioning Kylene had gone, Harper sensed. "Maybe I ought to turn soldier," he said deliberately, defiantly, knowing that she would object. "Got to be smarter to volunteer than wait for conscription." Then he busied himself with his tankard.

Lan Callares raised his eyebrows. "Do you want to do that?"

"Don't know," Harper said honestly. "One time I came here looking for a drillmaster's job, and I would have been good at it. Now . . . Maybe I'm out of practice." But in his pockets the old insignia were heavy, consciousness-filling, and the hilt of the knife in his boot prodded at his calf.

"Used to be an officer, out toward the Western Coast." That was a combination of truths. He hoped Dieytl would not press for details.

"You saw fighting?"

"My share. More than you saw in those diddly campaigns against the Necklace Lake tribes."

"I saw enough." The thin man pursed his lips distastefully, looking at Harper's hairline rather than at his eyes. "You're a foreigner, with . . . questionable ties."

"Merryn?"

"And no rank."

*Made near to major, didn't I? When I was a soldier.* "I've been prospecting."

And he had died as a major, he remembered Tolp telling him. Died in one of the many battles of the Final War, scant days before the Alliance captured F'a Alghera. "You were screaming," Tolp had said. "No one understood the words, but you smiled when they shoved the knife through your throat."

Another man, another Tim Harper, for all that he remembered some of that life. Another Tolipim ha'Ruijac in another branch of history. And another grace knife than the one so awkwardly uncomfortable in his boot top. *That Harper was trying—*

But he would not analyze motives. He leaned to hear lan Callares's voice.

"That. One step up from serfdom, for most men. You come

from nothing, Timmial." The money broker brushed fingers over the signed script. "You will go to nothing."

Harper was conscious of the insignia in his pockets again. "That happens to soldiers, Dieytl."

Lan Callares blinked slowly. "To Blankshields particularly."

"That's life."

"You're foreign," Dieytl pointed out. "And not a noble. It is not likely that any command would be found for you."

"Staff," Harper suggested. "I can read and write. Or run one of the Midpassage companies."

"Do you want that?" the broker asked again.

The redhead forced a grin, sensing that only words preserved his balance on a precipice of events. "I'm open to suggestions."

Lan Callares nodded curtly. "It is not a matter I care to speculate about, Ian Haarper. We have a quarter watch till that coach shows up. Will you share another beer?"

Harper raised his tankard. "Still on this. You want to kill time, there are those married ladies out front. Why don't you seduce one? I'd love to see the fabled Ian Callares technique at work." A danger had been skirted; he could smile genuinely.

The broker smiled also. "I can't teach a nontelepath."

"Give it a try," Harper teased. He looked around till he spotted the blond woman, talking to a man at a table near the stairs. As he watched, she snapped her fingers and turned to lean over a man at the next table. "How far can you get with her?"

Lan Callares seemed to shrink. "Unthinkable!" he hissed.

Harper chuckled. "Come on, stud. Look at the tits. Give it—"

"Be still!" The broker's face was misshapen by anger, the powder blotch that surrounded his forehead scar ashen on blood-flushed skin.

Harper exhaled softly. "Sorry. Dieytl?"

The broker gestured dismissal with his hand. "Drink. Silently. She will notice neither of us." His eyes narrowed, daring the other to speak, then he turned to the muslin-hung wall so that polite conversation could not be continued.

Harper shoved his hands into his pants pockets, feeling folded paper and metal, then let his eyes move from Ian Callares's tight-lipped profile toward the blond woman as she pressed between tables. Perhaps she reddened, but her face showed no expression when she was slapped loudly on the buttocks, and the men who guffawed when a drunken woman repeated the slap fell into silence as she turned toward them.

A uniformed man stood to block her passage. Harper noticed officer's insignia on the dark blue fabric. She sidestepped, but this brought her close to the cardplayers at the next table. One of them rose to stop her. As she turned again, the officer reappeared behind her, knocking over a stool in his haste. Then another soldier, and a third, all officers.

Each man took a step toward her, grinning. One cupped a hand over a blue-clad breast, then pulled her blouse down to expose it and kneaded the nipple with his thumb. A farm laborer grabbed her arms from behind as she tried to escape. He smiled joyously. Others joined him.

*No cops to call. No proper law at all. Not my world. Let the soldiers stop this—those not part of it.*

Harper did not move, though his jaw tightened. A tic showed once on the woman's cheek. She whimpered brokenly, softly. Somewhere a man laughed briefly, shrilly. He heard lights hissing. The soldiers at the bar turned to watch but did not rise.

Three seconds. Two seconds. One second. The wait had brought the woman no defenders, and the time for irresolution had passed. Harper pulled miniature swords from his pocket and pinned them to his collar without concern for Dieytl's start. He smiled as he rose.

A pair of soldiers rose and moved to block him. One stepped away after seeing his insignia. The other Harper shoved aside with a stiffened arm. Coins and glasses clattered behind him. The cardplayers cursed but stayed in place.

The soldier abusing the woman's breasts was the nearest and biggest, a dark-haired man with alcohol on his breath. Harper wrapped an arm about his neck, grabbing hair with the other hand to pry his head backward. "I think the lady wants through," he said, raising his arms to lift the man. "Why don't you animals apologize and go back to your seats?"

Faces turned to him, men showing dismay as they realized that their heads came to below his chin, then horror as their eyes focused on his collar insignia. The officer he was holding made blubbery sounds, kicking and scratching at Harper's forearm. Harper ignored the minor injuries and tightened his grip, then pulled back sharply on greasy hair. Neck bones

made crunching sounds; the man stopped moving though his breath continued. His eyes were open, pleading.

"Apologize," Harper repeated. "Go back to your seats."

"Only funning, Ironwearer." That low voice might have come from the grave. "Just a joke, miss. No harm meant. I'm sorry."

"Sit down," Harper growled to the crowd. With an elbow, he pointed at the two officers who had accompanied the man in his grip. "You twerps also."

Amnesty did not extend to the man he was holding. Harper's arm tightened further, squeezing the carotid arteries without mercy and ignoring the man's feeble struggles until he sagged unconsciously against the redhead's chest.

People had been crowding into the inn to witness the disturbance. As Harper looked about now, conversations were resuming, boisterously, rapidly. The bartender was approaching, a short club raised in one hand. The dragoons had pushed their way to his support and now were self-consciously standing between the officers Harper had pointed to and the doorway. Other soldiers and an uninvolved staff officer were arrayed behind the seated men, holding back onlookers, seeking excuses for not drawing nearer. Their eyes met his, then turned away.

Harper nodded stonily as the man he had held crumpled to the floor. The younger bluecoat stared with disbelief and attempted to rise. A dragoon shoved him down.

In the hush that followed, the redhead put a hand to the woman's cheek, turning her away from the three seated men. *Five feet eight*, he estimated. *Maybe a hundred and forty pounds, maybe one fifty; smaller than Onnul, bigger than Kylene.* Her looks were not exotic—too big to be cute, too broad-featured for beauty: peasant-pretty, he decided. She smelled of sweat.

*Is this what made me a soldier again?* But the irony was there to be noticed rather than regretted.

Her blouse was thin lace, dyed purple rather than blue, he noticed now, with only bare skin beneath. She had retied the front strings so it again covered her breasts, but the right nipple was protruding from the lace, clearly and distractingly visible. Her feet were bare. The legs of her shorts were unhemmed and uneven in length. Heat rash had roughened the insides of her thighs, and a sprinkling of acne ran along her left jaw. A quarter-sized scab was in the middle of her forehead, half-hidden by vagrant strands of yellow-brown hair.

*Twenty-seven, twenty-six*, Harper guessed. An older woman would surely have avoided this situation. *Also, telepaths here usually get rebranded every ten years after puberty.*

There was no exudate in her eyes, but the corneas were cloudy, obscuring blue irises. The pupils were overlarge, irregular. When he moved a finger across her face, her eyes did not track it.

*Glaucoma.* "What is your name, girl?" he asked softly.

"Wandisha, sir." Her voice was timid.

"Wandisha lin Zolduhal?"

"No, sir. I like to call . . ." Her voice trailed off.

*Peasant*, Harper diagnosed. Her claim to gentle birth was make believe. "A pretty name regardless," he said, filling time while he tucked in his shirttail. "You have family here to act for you?"

"No, sir. My family is—is very far from here."

"Ah. Endowed and permitted."

"Yes, sir. I had a second brother."

She would have been turned out of home the moment it became legal, with a five-mina coin as dowry and half-completed marriage certificates already signed by her parents. Disinheritance without onus, but this was a rough world for those without family. Harper felt no pleasure knowing that he had read that hesitation correctly.

What could be done? "Have you been educated?" he asked. Immediately he damned himself for a fool. "Let it go."

The unseeing eyes gave him forgiveness. "I was taught letters once, sir. I sign my name. I do sums. I know some of my prayers."

"Very good." Harper crossed his arms uncertainly. "What . . . Do you have anyone who claims you as family?"

"No, sir."

"Do you have obligations to fulfill? To Lord Vandeign, perhaps? Or elsewhere?" *Are you indentured?* the words meant. *Are you a runaway serf?* Harper hated the euphemisms even as he recognized that the situation did not allow blunt speech.

"No, sir. He has been kind, but—" The girl's head dropped as if to conceal embarrassment. "I don't earn that much," she whispered. "I came with the army."

"Sure," Harper said flatly. "Do you see anything at all?"

"Not with my eyes, sir. If other people—"

"I understand. How long?"

"Twelve years, sir. I believe." She swallowed.

Harper turned to the bartender. "Is this generally known?"

"Yes, sir." The man held his club in two hands, staring at Harper's insignia. "Most everyone knows about her, lan Haar— Ironwearer."

Harper prodded the man on the floor with a boot. "Him, too?"

The bartender looked at the seated men, then moved his head slowly. "Yes. He's been with her several times. He's talked about her being blind. About how—how funny it was. About, about— He had funny ideas."

"Tell me or I ask a telepath."

The bartender swallowed. "This." His voice shrank. "He thought forcing—having a blind woman captive to—to— It would be fun."

Harper said nothing.

"They know, too." The bartender's voice rose petulantly. "They were with him when he—they heard him too. And there are others here tonight who—"

"What did you do about it?"

"Lan Haarper?"

"Ironwearer. This unwiped asshole making threats. I asked you: What did you do about it? Did you warn her?"

"I—I—he's a noble." The bartender had become pale.

"Ironwearer. Did you tell the camp authorities?"

"Ironwearer. Sir. He's noble." The bartender swallowed again. "You know how they—"

"No, I don't. Did you tell Lord Vandeign?"

"No. No, Ironwearer."

Harper pointed. "They noble, too?"

The thin brunet who had snatched at the woman's back started to say something. Harper slapped him backhandedly and repeated the question for the bartender.

"Yes, sir." The man's shoulders slumped.

"What did you do about this?"

"Nothing." His reply was barely audible. "What are you going to do, Ironwearer?"

"Why should you concern yourself?" Harper took the club from the bartender's clammy hand, then moved his eyes to the thin man standing nearby. "Take lin Zolduhal back to the table, Dieytl. Get her a drink. It'll be on the house."

His overt rage was gone, Harper noticed as the couple

moved away. Good, one should not judge in anger.

But what provokes anger must be judged. He slammed the club on the cardplayers' table, drawing all eyes to him.

"This was an act of evil," he began, using somber tones to substitute for nonexistent legal rituals, speaking slowly so his audience would have time to understand his intent. He pointed to the bartender. "Tell them what you told me. Loudly."

"Who saw anything else?" he asked when the man was through. He turned in a half circle, waiting, but no one approached, no one spoke.

"Who will act to protect this woman?" No one moved.

"Who finds excuse for this man?" No answer came.

"Who will take responsibility for his actions after this?" Again there was silence.

"Then I will judge," Harper said somberly after staring slowly at haunted faces throughout the tavern. "Dieytl!"

He brought the club down once, jarring his arm with the impact.

That was enough. The man who had been unconscious now seemed shrunken. The head was misshapen, asymmetrical, and blood seeped from a mashed ear and along the brown hair. Fluid drained from an open eye socket. Blood that had spurted from one nostril dripped to the floor. A urine stain spread across his clothing. An alcohol-ridden stench rose from suddenly loosened bowels. Harper recognized death without the broker's word.

*Population changes. Family fights. Feuds.* Long-ago words There would be a story here for Nallis tonight, he thought coolly.

He pointed to the frightened men. "Whatever he had after his debts and damages here are paid goes to his kin. You three, carry him across the river. That's your punishment."

Dieytl beat them to the doorway and was loudly, violently, sick on the road outside. Others in the room rushed out also.

Red and gray stained the end of the club. Hairs clung to its tip. Harper held it beneath the face of the smaller officer. "Stand up, mister."

Spit landed on his boot. The man did not rise.

"Do that again and you'll live, but your family line comes to a sudden end," Harper said calmly. "Now stand up."

The man stood slowly, raising his head so Harper could see the madness in his eyes. Tears smeared his immature face.

*Just a boy*, the big man decided. *But that's no excuse.* "What's the name, kid?"

"I'll kill you someday." The words came through clenched teeth.

"The famous nobleman I'll-kill-you-someday." Harper snorted, and the dragoons chuckled. "Feared in all the best taverns. Known throughout the Kingdom, are you?"

"I'll kill you someday."

Harper sighed. "Maybe, kid. But before you earn that name, you're going to spend the rest of the night burying your buddy with your bare hands."

He pointed at the remaining noble. "You're helping him."

"You think so?" the blond man sneered.

"Yes." Harper turned to the soldiers who remained in the room. "I'll call out anyone in your camp, regardless of rank, who assists these men. Is that clear?"

"It is, but it won't be necessary." That was the staff officer. Belatedly, Harper noticed that the man's rank insignia were far more ornate than those of his captives. "Will you release your prisoners to me, Ironwearer? I'll see that the sentence is carried out."

"Yes, sir." Harper shook his head awkwardly, unsure as to how Lopritian senior officers were saluted.

The man gestured. Soldiers moved, surrounding the nobles and leading them through the doorway. "Are you known to me, sir?"

It took a second to realize that the question was for him. "No, sir. My name is Tim Harper."

"Ris Timhaper?" The officer frowned.

"Lan Haarper. Timothy lan Haarper."

"Ah. You've enrolled?"

Harper guessed at his meaning. "Not yet."

"You've time," the officer said casually. "If my brother doesn't use you, we still need men, at all ranks."

"That's good," Harper said woodenly.

"Sergeant!" the officer called without looking around.

"Sir!" The sergeant materialized suddenly before the officer, saluting with his right hand parallel to the ground, thumb on left breast.

"Ironwearer's verdict. From lan Haarper. Derrauld ris Fryddich and Krennlen ris Jynnich to bury—with their bare hands—the body of Gerint ris Whelmner. Restitution of damages to this innkeeper. A penalty payment...One day's wages for each of the three, to the whore known as Wandisha. Charges are—" He turned to Harper. "Your charges, Iron-wearer."

Harper started. "Sir?"

"Your charges. The reason for ordering punishment." The officer was brisk.

The redhead hesitated, conscious of attention. "Assault," he said finally. "For the dead man. Whelmner. For the others, abetting an assault. And juvenile delinquency—no—conduct unbecoming, for both of them. Conduct unbecoming an officer."

"Charges of assault and conduct unbecoming an officer. Juvenile delinquency." The staff officer smiled, then repeated the words carefully until the sergeant parroted them. "Convey the prisoners to Ironwearer Clendannan."

"Not Wolf-Twin, sir?" The sergeant seemed surprised.

"He's tired, so we'll let him sleep," the officer said. "Besides, these were Clendannan's men. He'll want to know."

"Yes, sir."

"Keep them out of ris Andervyll's sight."

"Yes, sir." The sergeant saluted again and vanished. Harper did not even see the door move.

"A small world," Harper said foolishly. *Four-century life spans and a tiny population. They all know each other.*

"So I have heard. Do you wish me longer, sir?" the officer asked. "No? Then I have tasks to attend to. You will excuse me." He raised his arm across his chest in salute and left.

*Clendannan. Wolf-Twin.* Other Ironwearers. Harper stared at the swinging doorway, an unformed wish tight in his breast, then made himself turn to the bartender.

"Good little stick," he said with forced unconcern, pretending that matted hair and blood were not adhering to the wood. "Sometimes they splinter." But the man stepped back with raised hands, refusing to accept the club. Harper shrugged and threw it into the fireplace. Perhaps someone would burn it. More likely, someone would take it as a souvenir.

He looked back at his table. Wandisha lin Zolduhal—"the whore calling herself Wandisha"—had been there, in his seat, staring at him with sightless eyes. Now she was gone, leaving an untasted glass of spirits. Harper shrugged again, remembering the ginger-brown hair and half-parted lips, and went back to the stool, pretending that no one was watching him, pretending fatigue had not mounted him.

His actions had been necessary. He would be—was—a soldier again, and across the river were other men who bore the title of Ironwearer. He leaned to rest his shoulders against the wall and finished the beer without permitting other thoughts.

Dieytl did not return.

The coach arrived at last.

Still sprawling at his table, Harper listened with faint interest to the rattle of settling springs and the snorting of tired horses, waiting for the tavern to empty before he stood. He dropped a two-mina coin beside the untouched glass on the table, watched it clatter until it stopped, then went slowly to the doorway.

It was late in the evening now, and the sky had become purple-black behind scraps of cloud, but lights outside the tavern made it difficult to see stars. A lemon slice of moon, the Milky Way, Vega, the distorted shape that might be the Big Dipper . . . Harper moved his gaze to the no longer important Polaris, then shifted his attention to the street. People made way for him on the sidewalk, leaving a pathway to the nearby coach. The soldiers had gone.

Essentially an enclosed wagon, the coach was a narrow box on wheels. A numbered plate was attached to one of the front planks. The pennant of Her Majesty's Southern Communications League drooped from the back whip. Road dust and other grime were caked on the lower portion of the polished wood. As Harper watched, a driver turned a crank to lower the carriage, then moved a set of steps to the side exit. The door opened.

Kylene was the first to appear at the top of the stairs, her almond eyes squinting at the unaccustomed light. At Harper's suggestion she had worn jeans and sturdy boots during her travel, but the high-necked midriff-baring white blouse was new to him. Her raven hair had been knotted loosely behind her head and thrown forward over her shoulder so that the ends dangled below the bottom of her blouse. Before the darkness of sky and road, the lights made her skin seem milk-white, translucent, and accented her high cheekbones. From this distance, she seemed both older and younger than Harper remembered.

He held back, waiting to be noticed. The people he had seen earlier outside the tavern were not so reticent and surrounded her before she could descend. "Molminda lin Chantiel," a spokesman began. "On behalf of the association of parents of school-age children in Midpassage, I'm pleased to welcome . . ."

Harper began to chortle, causing people to draw farther away, as Kylene murmured a denial and scurried across the pavement to him. Another woman appeared in the coach doorway. She was obese, had short brown hair, and was dressed in yellow coveralls; the carriage bounded up, then down as she minced her way onto the steps. The Agent watched with fascination as pendulous breasts continued to rock even after her mighty hips came to rest. The woman coughed a few times while the greeting speech ran down, then spit expertly on the street.

When it came, her voice carried far. "Parenth of Midpathage, ath a humble reprethenative of the Righteouthly Militant and Unquibblingly Loyal Order of Inthructorth of Youth, I am pleathed to be among you today. While theldom accuthomed to thpeak before audientheth, your heartfelt witheth rethound within my breath, and the dedication of your prothperity to inaugurate—"

"Tayem, aren't you going to notice me?"

Arms were squeezing his chest, Harper noticed. He chuckled for an answer, looking down on raven hair and freckled cheeks under almond-shaped green eyes, and patted a white-covered back, then surrendered to Kylene's wishes and hugged her mechanically in return, rubbing his cheek on the top of her head. "Hasn't been that long, girl. Ummm, you smell nice."

"In the wordth of our gloriouth Thovereign Majethy and my namethake, Queen Molminda the Third, mothe fortunate and honored—" A man appeared behind the woman, first standing on tiptoe to peer over her shoulder, then pushing ineffectually at a hamlike shoulder. A schoolmarmly elbow jerked backward with fatal force, thwacking the side of the carriage.

The man vanished. Without dropping a word, the woman continued. "The largeth of thith kingdom itthelf ith not too much to thpend on the education of our thonth and daughterth. And, I thould add, though thurely you are aware, thith include

the thipend of devoted inthructor and inthructorethe. Her Majethy wath recently overheard thaying . . ."

A man came around the back of the coach. Medium tall
and stocky, visibly paunched, black-haired with an oval face,
he was dressed in brown and gold. A leather jacket bounced
on one shoulder. A valise was in his hand. A bushy eyebrow
rose, then he threaded a path through the small crowd.

Harper grinned, recognizing the man who had been on the
receiving end of the fat woman's elbow. He released himself.
"I was wondering if you had survived."

That provoked a quirky smile. "It was a close thing. Of
course, we've been hearing Molminda practice 'thimple appropriate remarkth' the lath theveral dayth—er, days. So I
was, uh, prepared for reaction. Well, I've been with Kylene
for a while. Unless she or I is sadly mistaken, you must be
Timithallin Harper." Hazel eyes froze on Harper's collar insignia. "Yes." After a brief hesitation, the man's hand rose.

"Timithial lan Haarper," the redhead corrected, trilling the
final name in the local fashion as the two men gripped forearms. "Close enough."

"Rispar Kallimur-once-ha'Ruijac." The voice was soft and
overaspirated, not shrill but on the border that split tenor from
baritone. The man's lined oval face was expressionless, the
grip fleshy but turning firm. Firmer than necessary, Harper
realized, but that was typical of the way smaller men challenged his height, and Rispar Kallimur was a head shorter
than he.

Once-ha'Ruijac. An Algheran.

Kylene turned sideways, keeping herself pressed against
Harper. "Kalm."

"Hi, Kylene. Uh—"

An awkward silence fell, which Harper felt constrained to
break. "Nice to meet you. Apologies for my lack of courtesy
—there's usually a sort of party here every ten days when the
coach comes. Everybody gets their mail then and a chance to
meet new people, but—well, things got a bit disrupted tonight, and I'm not sure what'll happen now. I imagine it's
been a long trip, and I'm getting a strong hint that I should be
taking someone home, as soon as her baggage is off. Why
don't I get the wagon while you two say good-bye, and if
you're still in town in a day or two, I'll buy you a drink,
okay?"

"Sure. Uh . . . can't I help?"

"No problem," Harper assured him.

The driver and his helper were unloading the front of the coach as he approached. Kylene's name was stenciled on one trunk and several smaller boxes, which he threw onto a shoulder and carried around the side of the building.

The trunk was heavier than he had remembered. After placing it in the buckboard, he rubbed his shoulder ruefully, then unhitched the horses and drove them around the back of the inn.

Someone was standing on the nearest wharf, he noticed, out on the end, looking up the shrunken river. Despite the quarter moon in the middle sky, it was too dark to distinguish faces, but he stopped the team to watch, grateful for the opportunity to catch his breath.

In truth, he admitted inwardly, he wanted a last moment of privacy. It had been comfortable being Timithial lan Haarper, only once a soldier, bound willingly to a peaceful existence by Lilliputian strands of habit and acquaintanceship. The readjustment forced on him so quickly was not welcome, however necessary it might be.

*Not her fault. She didn't know—didn't even expect I was there.* He did not blame Wandisha lin Zolduhal for what was done.

He blamed Kylene for nothing, either. But it was cruel to know that with Kylene present, it was necessary to become again Harper Timith ha'Dicovys, who was nothing but soldier and time traveler. The prospector lan Haarper she would regard as no more than pretense, and soon Merryn would share her view, and Dieytl, and others.

Then acceptance came, and a silent internal peace.

*N' ha forentimal Dicova taunn.* "I am an Ironwearer of Dicovys."

*Ironwearer.*

The woman on the pier had not turned. He reached for the reins.


No one contended for the use of the road at this time of night, so Harper gave the horses their head after he left the paved roadway, looping the reins around a hook and letting them set their own pace up the hill while he turned and repositioned Kylene's trunk in the buckboard. "So how was your trip?" he asked finally. "Any trouble?"

Kylene snapped her fingers. "Just a trip, Tayem. I went to

the depot after you left me, bought a seat, met Kalm, and that was it. I didn't say anything to anyone to let them know about us. Very boring." Her voice was distant.

Harper listened carefully, pleased to find her Lopritian only slightly touched by Algheran Speech—knowing, however, that he could detect traces of another language and another world. It was always surprising to remember that this teenage girl was a telepath from the age of the legendary Skyborne.

*A.D. 5000. Practically neighbors.*

*Not the Skyborne, at that date. The Skyborne's mother.*

*The girl next door.* Did she blame him for abducting her?

But that was not his business, and she was three years a stranger now. "It was supposed to be tame," he made himself say. "So how did the time go?"

"No particular way." Kylene waved her drawing pad defensively. "I sketched for a while, but the coach bounced too much, so after the first day I mostly watched scenery and slept."

"Oh." He tugged the reins to turn the horses to the left, then put back a hand to push unnecessarily on a box, delaying further conversation until he could feel the weight of the girl's sideward glances. "Made friends with that Algheran fellow?"

"We talked." Kylene looked away. "He was only on the stage the last few days."

"Ah." Harper pushed on the trunk again, pretending that it required his concentration. "So what did you find to talk about?"

"Oh, this and that." Kylene ignored him still, turning instead to look at the elms that bordered the dirt road. "He's a soldier, too."

"Blankshield?" Harper suggested. "What rank?"

"I guess that's the word. He doesn't say much about himself, and he's always so polite." She stressed the final word, making the remark into a complaint, then fell into anxious tones. "'May I get you something, Kylene? Let me carry that for you, Kylene. Try some of this food, Kylene. It's very tasty. Is the carriage bouncing too much for you, Kylene? I can talk to the driver. If you want?'" She giggled wickedly.

Harper took the reins again and shook them to remind the horses that they had a master. "Well—"

"I think he's sweet on me," Kylene said comfortably.

Harper frowned without reason. "Are you going to encourage him?" It could not be a good idea, but he sensed that she would steer a course in opposition to whatever wishes he expressed.

"I might." Kylene mingled thoughtfulness and glee in the words.

"Ummm." Harper pretended the horses needed his attention.

A moment passed, then hands tugged on his arm. "Silly!" Kylene pulled herself across the bench to his side. Harper smelled violets.

Awkwardly, he wrapped an arm around her. "Cold?"

"No." Kylene rested her head on his shoulder. "Just comfortable. Did you miss me?"

"Some." Harper shook the reins with his free hand and patted Kylene's side as she snuggled against him, feeling himself isolated from all human contact. "Sure."

Time passed. Harper listened to Kylene's breathing, keeping thoughts and memories from his mind. Then the warm weight against his side shifted. Kylene stirred. "Tayem?"

"Hmm?"

"You haven't said much."

"Not much to say, is there?" He pulled his arm back, assuming that she would sit up now. "Been three years, Kylene." *We're strangers.* He had no heart for telling her that, but he knew she would see it.

"I'll fix that." She rubbed her cheek across his shoulder. "Tayem, I never would have let—"

"I know." He thought of consoling lies but stayed them. "I did what I had to."

*Strangers.* A thought came to his mind unbidden: Kylene in the white of a First Era Christian wedding, leaving the door of a church with a faceless tuxedoed man. It would not be that way, he knew, but he had never witnessed an Algheran wedding. Kylene leaning over a crib to caress an infant—her child, he told himself. Kylene with other children. Kylene lying in bed by another man. Kylene, matronly, wearing fashions he had never seen but could imagine appearing in the centuries after the Present . . .

Imagination. He let the images pass through his mind as if they were memory, knowing that while touching him she would see them also.

"Tayem—" Kylene shifted. He felt dampness on his shoulder.

"There, now." It was foolish to continue holding a hand in

the air, so he put his arm around the girl again. "There."

"Tayem," Kylene said again, sounding choked. Then she was silent. Her shoulders heaved, but the dampness did not continue.

"There, there." Harper stroked her back mechanically, miserably. "Everything'll be all right, Kylene."

Experimentally, he ran the images through his mind again, substituting for Kylene analogous pictures of himself, but none of them bore the same conviction of reality or lasted for more than an instant. "A good future, Kylene," he whispered. "You got a lot to look forward to, girl."

After too much time, they neared the house. Kylene sat up, and Harper pulled back his arm, though she continued to lean against it. When she spoke, her voice seemed normal. "Tayem? What you did—tonight. To that man. I saw people thinking about it. Is that going to cause trouble?"

"I don't much care," Harper said flatly. Then he relented. "Nothing to affect you. Don't worry."

"But will it change anything? You said when you left me—"

"Yeah, I know." Harper selected his words carefully, not wishing to reveal that he had worried about Kylene's safety while alone rather than the history she might have changed during the coach ride from Fohima Loprit. "It'll be forgotten soon."

"You surprised people," she pointed out. "They thought—"

"They didn't think," Harper said dourly. "They didn't act; they didn't want responsibility. Anyone in that room could have stopped me by saying one word. None of them did. Cimon take the lot of them!"

Kylene was thoughtful. "She was a telepath."

"And a peasant. That's no excuse, either." *Less than an excuse*, he thought angrily. *Americans should not be treated like that girl was; Americans shouldn't have divided into lords and peasants.*

"Yes, but . . . won't things be harder for her now—and other telepaths?"

Harper exhaled slowly, thinking of practicalities. "Probably some nasty thoughts. For a while. But there's only one other telepath in town, and he can look after himself. Anyone really upset will blame me."

Kylene pondered for a while. "Will you make enemies?"

"Only those worth having. And none local." He lapsed into silence, then spit onto the roadside. "Not expecting any trouble. Nice thing about being an Ironwearer: people aren't real eager to argue with your opinions."

"But if—"

"Oh, I guess I got their fur wet deliberately," he admitted. "I know there's no law around here unless you enforce it yourself, but there's good and bad, and people know the difference. So they don't have the guts to tell some jerks no. They won't have the guts to tell me no, either."

He shrugged in the darkness. "Not very idealistic, is it? But you have to figure that, long run, rewarding the good and punishing bad makes life better for everyone."

Kylene shifted her weight. "But can you know that?"

"No," Harper admitted. He scratched a shoulder blade for Kylene as she moved against his hand. "Even the guy with a time machine can't prove it. Let's drop the topic, huh?" The girl murmured something, then pulled away. All he heard now was the clip-clopping of horse hooves, a creaking board in the wagon bed, and the songs of summer insects. Infrequently, a firefly gleamed. Occasional flames flickered behind curtained windows in the narrow houses.

Finally Kylene again broke the silence. "Tayem, if I were . . . if I 'encouraged' Kalm . . . if we . . . would that make you jealous?"

Harper remembered pink-red nipples and blue-veined breasts straining against purple lace, a thin line of curly hair rising from the front of red shorts that surely could be unbuttoned with one move of a hand—his or someone else's. "I'm not going to run your life, Kylene. Do you want to get involved with him?"

"He's . . . interesting." Kylene said no more.

They had reached the driveway. Harper's shoulders twitched, then he concentrated on steering the horses. He unloaded the wagon in silence, piling the luggage in the living room as Kylene watched.

"Not very fancy," he said when done. "Furniture was made locally, and it ought to be sturdy enough. You want me to close the skylight?"

Kylene shook her head, turning about slowly. A fireplace, a chair, two couches, rugs—she seemed to be counting his possessions. "Your walls are bare."

"Put up a couple of your pictures." He felt embarrassed.

"I see. But the room seems empty." She frowned.

"Yeah. Uhh, I could paint them if you want. You have—"

"What's out there?" She pointed to the green curtain covering the high interior wall.

"Atrium," Harper said defensively. He pulled the curtains open so Kylene could see the transparent wall, then pushed to open a glass door. "Show you."

The garden was dark; he gave Kylene his arm to guide her past the nearer flower beds to the stone path. "Lets you live inside and outside at the same time."

She looked at the sky, then at the tree and grape arbor that were the garden's major features. "What did you call it?"

"Atrium."

"I like this." She chuckled softly as she reached for the band that bound her hair. "See, you didn't have to worry."

Relieved, Harper followed her back to the living room.

"Study, two bedrooms, bathroom, workrooms, kitchen and larder, weight room—for exercise. Another bedroom," he said next, pointing in their general directions. "The spare bedrooms are both made up. Why don't you take a quick tour and figure out which one you want this stuff in?"

Kylene leaned against the kitchen doorway as he closed the curtains, her hands behind her. Loose, her hair swept across her shoulders as she tossed her head. Her shoes were off. Calculation showed in her almond eyes. "Will the bedroom I pick stay mine?"

Harper sensed that he had witnessed the first shot of a never-to-be-admitted domestic war. "Of course," he said blandly.

Kylene smiled. "I'll take the one near you."

"Sure." He reached for her baggage.

Kylene frowned, trying to read his expression. "Tayem?"

Harper straightened up with the chest in his arms. "Asses are made to bear, and so am I. Lay on, MacKylene."

When he was through, he took the horses back to the stables alone. He stayed there some while, ignoring the lights that came on room by room to mark Kylene's occupation of his household. At last he cursed and reached for the saddle that he had three times taken from the wall and three times replaced.

\* \* \*

No one stood waiting on the pier. Of course.

Perhaps he felt relief. Now he could return to his horse and his house and not admit embarrassment to an angry Kylene. Blank-faced, Harper turned away from the docks behind the inn.

"Lan Haarper!" He heard the shout as he unfastened the stallion's reins. Rispar Kallimur stood in the inn's doorway.

Stopping would delay a confrontation or provide an excuse to give Kylene. Harper raised a hand in greeting, then slipped the reins back through hoops on the hitching pole. "Be with you in a moment."

"See this?" The Algheran pointed.

"What? Oh." A Leiman and Scee news sheet had been pasted on the tavern door. It was simply a page of bulletins that referred the curious to other publications for details. A name and address in Northfaring had been printed at the bottom of the form; someone—Nallis lan Alpbak perhaps—had crossed them out and replaced them with Nallis's.

TRA'NORNST ALGHERAN WARDER, 7TH TERM, the headline read. There was just enough light for Harper to see that more information would soon be available in Leiman and Scee's *Algheran Report*, Leiman and Scee's *Younger Continent Report*, Leiman and Scee's *World Military Report*, Leiman and Scee's *Industrial Business Report*, Leiman and Scee's *Fifth Era Perspectives Report*, Leiman and Scee's *Regal Affairs Report*, "and others."

"They left out *TV Guide*," Harper commented.

"Lan Haarper?"

"Never mind." Harper shoved open the door and led the way to the table he had shared with Dieytl lan Callares. The iron piece he had dropped earlier still lay there, though the empty tankards and glass had been removed. In the background a handful of townsfolk spoke of nothing important. Harper spun the coin idly, waiting for the other man to speak.

"How is lin Haarper?" the Algheran asked once beer had been ordered.

"I'm—she's fine, that is. How are you?"

"I'm fine." The man lapsed into silence.

"So we're all fine," Harper said evenly. "That's nice, isn't it?" He turned sideways on his stool, inspecting faces in the barroom but seeing no one he was looking for. It was after midnight, he sensed without troubling to convert the local time. Most people would be home and in bed. "The teacher lady ran down finally?"

"A while back." Then silence was restored. The bartender went about the room, pulling small rods from alternate lights to switch them off. The doorway clattered as several people left.

Harper pulled a hand across his jaw, concealing a yawn. When this social duty was done, he could ride home. Kylene would have given up on his return and gone to bed. He could get some sleep without argument. He would think more of being a soldier.

But first he would be polite. "Glad you kept Kylene company. She seems to have appreciated it."

"Oh, well. I liked her." The Algheran flushed, and Harper recognized a young man's diffidence.

"Uh huh. So do I."

"She's Algheran, isn't she? Sept R'sihuc, she said."

"By adoption," Harper said slowly. "It was a while ago."

"Does that make you . . . Are you ha'R'sihuc?"

"Not here." Harper drummed fingers on the table, looking for an honest half answer. "I come from somewhere else. We have different customs."

"Ah." Kalm pursed his lips gravely.

"Yeah," Harper said. "So what about you? All settled in?"

"For tonight I'm staying in the inn. I'll be billeted somewhere else tomorrow."

"You're enrolling, I take it?"

"Already in. Captain's rank, class C, assignment open." Kalm once-ha'Ruijac sipped his beer. "And yours?"

Harper let his eyes run along doorways far above, seeing no signs of life. "Don't know. I suppose I'll find out. This soldiering stuff—have you been doing it all along? For a living, I mean."

The smaller man chuckled briefly. "The standard experience. I was a regular once; I killed men for a while, then moved up to children. Now I just travel around as whim guides me."

*Mercenary? Bandit?* Harper wondered, listening to the cynicism in Kalm's voice. Was this truly a man whom Kylene would consider as a suitor? *"Once ha'Ruijac,"* he remembered icily. Was Kalm a fortune hunter eager to marry into R'sihuc through Kylene, to regain the affluence and respectability he had once known? Surely she would have seen that, wouldn't she?

"You're out of the way here, aren't you?" he asked. "Not many Algherans in this neck of the woods." Women had no sense about men.

The other grinned. "More than you might expect. Mlart tra'Nornst has been building up a fancy new army, but it doesn't have many slots for officers out of the Septs, no matter how much experience we've had. And his new taxes mean the Septs can't afford Housetroops the way they used to."

Harper grunted. Mlart had built up the central government's power at the expense of the Septs. Keeping the great families from subverting the Swordtroop had been one of his better ideas. Whether he had actually expected the improvement in combat that followed was a question that Algheran historians would argue centuries later. So this was what the process looked like to a participant in that revolution: interesting but not earthshaking.

"There are a lot of out-of-work soldiers with experience," Kalm explained. "You wait and you see Loprit's going to be harder to beat this time."

*I doubt it.* "I'm sure you'll all do well here."

"Well enough." Kalm shook his head briefly, then continued. "Not like being an Ironwearer."

Harper shrugged.

"You are an Ironwearer?" the other man asked.

*You make yourself an Ironwearer,* he thought. *You put the name on and then you work at it, and when someone looks at your motives and says you are not an Ironwearer, you cease to be one. But any thinking man has to look at his motives, so—*

"Becoming one," Harper said curtly. His answer did not seem to please the smaller man, but that was not his problem.

"What is it like?" Kalm asked.

Harper snorted. "Call yourself one. Say the words and find out for yourself."

Kalm coughed. "How do you think it'll go?"

Harper raised an eyebrow. "How what will go?"

Fingers snapped. "The war, of course. Mockstyn's corps will block a direct blow against F'a Loprit, so the tra'Nornst will strike from below or above. The south is more probable: it's richer than the northern provinces, better able to support an army—and more apt to stay in line if Mlart bases another campaign on it."

And so it had happened, or would happen, Harper remembered. But he must pretend ignorance of the future. "Think I'll leave that kind of thinking to you old Algies."

Kalm grinned. "You must have some opinions."

Harper thought about it and produced one safe remark. "Your Warder would have terribly long supply lines if he tried that."

"Not my Warder now." The smaller man showed no concern. "No more than he is yours. But he is a better general."

Harper nodded agreement but was not willing to let his argument go unpunctured. "Loprit is bigger than Alghera. It's got more people and more soldiers. If Mlart tried such a campaign, what makes you think the Swordtroop would get north of the Ocean Father?"

Kalm smiled briefly. "I'm just an uninformed captain, Ironwearer. But Mlart can hire more mercenaries. They'll go with him anyhow, since his record is good. Your queen will try to hold everywhere."

"Not my queen," Harper pointed out. "Kylene and I just live here. We're not involved."

The Algheran ignored the interruption. "Stretch your forces all over the landscape and Mlart will beat them in detail."

All too true, Harper admitted privately. Lopritian commanders had shown little understanding of war in past campaigns. But he was not here to side with their conquerors. "So what's the defense?"

"Concentration." Kalm dipped a finger in beer, then sketched broken lines on the table. "Keep the main force together near F'a Loprit, then hit him when he appears."

"And if he doesn't?" Harper asked. "Suppose he just occupies the Valley of the Shield, puts a garrison in Northfaring, and goes home?"

"Without a battle?" The younger man seemed scandalized.

"With a victory. Who needs a battle if you have that?"

Kalm frowned. "Loprit would have an army left."

"Which it wouldn't be able to afford for long. Remember, the tactical advantage lies with the defense. Alghera can afford to leave a big enough garrison to hold the valley if Loprit gives it up."

"Invade Alghera?"

Harper shrugged. "It hasn't worked before. Alghera can always defend itself against an invasion."

"But not Loprit?"

"Different case. If Mlart takes the initiative, he has a strategic advantage. Loprit has to beat him to win the war; he just has to grab something and not be beaten. That's a much easier job."

Kalm frowned again. "What would you do, Ironwearer?"

"What would by my *objective*?" Harper hesitated, looking for a native word to express his thought. "What is my intent? To keep Loprit from getting beat? To wipe out the Swordtroop? To conquer Alghera?"

"Yes."

"No." Harper shook his head. "Those are different things, and they're political matters. Soldiers don't make policy."

"But if they did?"

"Then they aren't soldiers." Harper sighed softly, staring into a bleak distant past. "When I was younger, I thought that what I wanted as a soldier had to be good for the country. I got upset with civilians and politicians who had different opinions, thinking they were wrong in some obvious way. Now I still think I wanted the right thing, but the country as a whole has to make that kind of policy; politicians are just the mechanism that gets used. And soldiers are just another part of the mechanism. They get orders, they follow orders. Or get out. The big decisions aren't theirs to make."

Kalm blinked. "I don't understand."

"I think that's how soldiers save their souls."

Into the silence that followed, Harper grinned wryly. "Anyhow, if I weren't a soldier and I ran Loprit, what would I do? Sue for peace. Stay out of the Cimon-taken war."

"That probably isn't possible."

"War hasn't come yet."

"It's inevitable, Ironwearer." The last word was dipped in scorn.

The big man considered his response carefully. "Conflict between states in some form is inevitable, but individual wars can be postponed or prevented. Economic growth, or scientific progress—you should realize there are ways to change the balance of power that don't involve fighting. And improve things for most people."

"But they're slower ways to change. And just as chancy as a war." Surprisingly, the Algheran had not taken offense. "If the trends are not in your favor, I mean. And aren't wars ever fought for idealism?"

"On both sides? I never have figured that out."

The smaller man blinked. "What if someone attacks you?"

"Some idealist?" Harper shook his head. "Oh, sure. Pacifists lead short lives. Defending yourself you have to do. But..." He waved a hand to encompass the world. "There have been an awful lot of wars in all the eras. Maybe some of them had idealism on both sides, but I can tell you they were all rough on innocent people and real estate. You ever wonder what life might be like if we fought less?"

"No." That was said without regret. "Do you?"

"Now and then, young man," Harper said finally. "Now and then." He turned so that he need not face the Algheran.

Time had passed, he noticed, looking about. Few slits of light played past open door edges above them; none but he and Kalm remained sitting in the inn's tavern. *Where is she?*

"You certainly have created a stir," he heard at last.

"Oh? How is that?" He kept his back turned.

"Well, you know."

"No, young sir, I don't know."

Fingers snapped. The table creaked as the Algheran rested his elbows. From other sounds, he sipped at his tankard. "Good beer, this. A war is very close. People on both sides are planning for it—just like we've been doing—and building up their forces, and suddenly you're an Ironwearer."

"Um huh." The time traveler half turned in his seat and began drumming his fingers idly on the table. "You doubt it?"

The dark-haired man chuckled once more. "Not really. Those insignia didn't surprise your wife, after all. And I've heard a few words about you since I got here."

"Probably. I have famous pipes and a captive demon."

Kalm smiled. "I always wondered what an Ironwearer was like up close and never thought I'd share a beer with one."

"Satisfied?" Harper bit the word off, controlling an urge to sneer.

The Algheran hesitated. "I don't know what I expected. You're big enough to be dangerous in a fight; that's that side of it. I find people regard you as unpredictable but well intentioned. A bit slow-spoken, perhaps, strong-willed, but that's—"

"Pigheaded," Harper said evenly. "Stubborn and stupid. Mustn't forget the pigheadedness. A certain stolidity, even stodginess. A notorious inability to handle money. And no sense of humor, but I value a quiet garden." *Where is she?*

"Sad but true," ha'Ruijac agreed. "Overemotional, though. Kylene says you're like a big bear—"

"Strong, and grumpy when I'm not fed."

"—needing a cage and a keeper."

"Nice to be loved," Harper said wryly. He turned to face the Algheran now, meeting a look with more intelligence and determination than he had expected. "So I've created a stir?"

Kalm shook his head solemnly. "Bound to. The Hand of the Queen was pulled from his bed a quarter watch past because of you. A couple of staff officers will get no sleep tonight, and tomorrow an aide must ride to Loprit to answer questions for Her Majesty. Only another twenty Ironwearers in Loprit, after all, so you've made a stir indeed."

"An interesting prediction." Harper finished his beer and tapped idly on the table. "Very flattering. But speculation."

For answer the man smiled briefly, then held up fingers and pointed at the table when he caught a barmaid's eyes. Reluctantly, she filled new tankards from the barrel beneath the counter.

"Not speculation," Kalm said, watching her. "Not prediction, just fact. I've been listening to soldiers talking. And thinking about politics, as you call it."

Harper sipped nonexistent beer, collecting his thoughts. "Politics is always guesswork. Another reason for soldiers to ignore it."

"I disagree." The man nodded politely, then turned to the barmaid for the pair of tankards. "To your health, Ironwearer," he said after handing one to Harper. "Politics is the surest of sciences, and the easiest. People are simply afraid to admit it."

"Oh?"

"Oh," Kalm echoed. "Everyone wants to be complex and mysterious. They want to be individuals. They want to be good—or to think they are good. And politics works because people are not basically good, because they're lazy and greedy and simple. Very very simple."

"Very very cynical."

Kalm snapped his fingers. "A simple cynicism. Anyhow, Loprit has had four wars in the last two decades and lost three of them. Queen Molminda's family can't last if this continues. So Loprit needs to find Ironwearers."

"To win the war." Harper shrugged. "We can try."

The ex-Algheran smiled nastily. "Loprit isn't likely to win, as you admitted earlier. No, what do you think the Ironwearers are for?"

"I don't know. You tell me."

"To take the blame," Kalm explained. "Loprit will lose, and the court will charge the Ironwearers with betraying it. A few showy trials, with lots of shouting and testimony and factions fighting."

"But they wouldn't convict—" Harper stopped, then tried again. "I mean, telepaths could testify."

Kalm snapped his fingers again. "Teeps testify in a state matter? You know that can't happen. And do you think everyone would believe them if they were at odds with Molminda? Of course not. Besides, who will care if a few old soldiers are executed? Ironwearers are men, after all; they're replaceable. And it wouldn't be just Ironwearers. The court has its opposition, nobles who can be accused of treason just as easily. And killed just as easily. The whole business would keep Molminda on the throne another half year, and that's long enough to live down the defeat."

Harper thought of Merryn's brother and drummed on the table again. "I don't like that picture."

Kalm twisted his mouth into a one-sided grin. "Well, you must be a simple man, Ironwearer."

"Probably." Harper swallowed beer, stalling to let thoughts form. "I guess I'll find out, if you're right."

"Oh, I'm right." Kalm sighed. Behind the bar, the serving girl yawned and slipped into the kitchen. "Well, Kylene and I will miss you after you're gone."

"So you're going to survive?" Harper asked ironically. "Is that your reward for cynicism?"

"For realism." Kalm paused reflectively. "I'd rather make my destiny than be its victim."

"So I'm a victim."

"You will be," Kalm said softly. "You will be."

A long moment passed.

"If that's the cost." But Harper tasted metal.

"That's the cost." The ex-Algheran smiled with sham humor. "I'll look after Kylene when you're gone."

Harper stared, then ran a finger down the side of his tankard. "I do doubt it. Drink your beer, so they can close up."

Kalm put his tankard down. "Is that all you will say?"

Harper continued to stare. "What else are you looking for?"

"Not much." Kalm snapped his fingers. "Just for the truth."

"Too bad," Harper said softly. "It's getting late, fellow, and I don't like this kind of sparring. Stay out of my business, and I'll stay out of yours."

Up on the third floor, a door was opening. All the interior lights had been dimmed now, so he could not make out features, but one of the emerging figures was a man, one a woman. He saw red shorts and a dark blouse; he heard a laugh.

"And if I don't?" Insolence sounded in the words.

"Don't push your way from under Nicole's cloak."

The woman suddenly was not moving. Was she looking at him, using the eyes of others?

"And Kylene, what about her?"

"What about her?" The woman was walking now, awkwardly, with fingers touching the wall to guide her steps. Harper let his eyes move as she did. The man was leaving the inn. The bartender had gone already, he realized. He was alone with Kalm. "She's with me."

"She's not your hearthmate! Whatever you're pretending here, she never mentioned it on the coach."

*I think he's sweet on me.* Harper heard exasperation now rather than a threat. It mirrored his own emotions as he watched the woman confidently cross the darkened room to the doorway, but for Kylene's sake he waited to give the man an answer.

"All right, Algheran. So she's not my wife. I'm fond of her, I look out for her, but—" He sighed, feeling shamed by the metaphor that had come to him. "It isn't your business." *If there were a button in front of me that I could push and fall in love with Kylene, just like that—I wouldn't do it.*

"No?" That was said very quietly.

"No," Harper echoed bitterly. The woman lingered at the doorway, fingering her neckline, looking toward them. She was watching through Kalm's eyes, he knew, listening through Kalm's ears. The knowledge brought anger into his voice. "But remember this, Algheran: Kylene is here for a reason, and I look after her. You cause either of us any trouble and you'll end up very dead. Do you understand?"

The smaller man snapped his fingers. "I'll remember."

"Do that." The Agent smiled grimly. "Cimon guard, Nicole guide. And have a nice day."

She had left the inn as he approached, and now she stood

waiting just outside. Somehow her eyes were pointed toward him.

The moon had crossed the sky to hide behind clouds, and most of the lights on the hillside opposite had been shuttered, so stars could be seen. A breeze pushed a scrap along the sidewalk. A man-height away, Harper's horse shook its head and pawed at the pavement, recognizing him. They had the street to themselves.

"I didn't expect you," the woman said gravely.

"I didn't know myself."

She moved slightly, and Harper saw that she was trembling.

"Are you cold?"

Her eyes blinked uselessly. "No." She trembled again. "I did not mean to cause you trouble, Ironwearer."

"Don't worry about it," Harper said. And when he saw that she would not speak, he asked, "Are you going home?"

"Yes. Why?"

"I wanted—I thought I should check on you."

"That was nice of you." Wandisha nodded gravely, but the hint of a smile dimpled her cheeks.

"Oh, it's nothing. Just . . . it's late. Maybe I should see you home." There, it was said. The words were out despite the thickness at the back of his throat. He waited, knowing fear.

"Will you protect me from the dark, Ironwearer?" The laughter she had suppressed came out now, full-bodied but mercifully short.

Harper breathed heavily. "I'm sorry. It was a dumb idea. Good night, lin Zolduhal." His boots were loud on the empty sidewalk, and he knew she was listening as he walked the long distance to his horse.

Her voice stopped him before he reached the hitching pole. "Ironwearer. May I call you by another name?"

He gave her an unseen nod and kept disappointment from his voice. "Timmial lan Haarper. Or just Tim. Yeah. Call whenever you need."

"Timmial." Wandisha took a step toward him. "Timmial, I'd like someone to protect me from the dark. Please. For even one night." An emotion he could not decipher showed upon her face. "I know it won't . . . but even one night."

Harper moved without awareness across the sidewalk to her, so that she ended in his arms. Her back was firm, he noticed suddenly, and the legs that pressed against him were sturdy. He kissed her all across her sweat-dampened forehead, not omitting the brand scar, while she made whimpering sounds at his breast, and his hands stroked her arms gently before rising to her shoulders. Daring greatly, he brushed her lips with his; as she turned her head to meet him, he repeated the kiss, marveling at the feel of the body in his arms, humbled by her trust in him yet knowing himself ten feet tall and filled with responsibility for all that might happen to this woman.

"Silly," she murmured when she finally looked up at him.

Harper kissed her lips softly. "Very silly," he agreed with a smile. "Mind readers aren't supposed to be afraid of anyone."

Wandisha smiled back happily. "Like Ironwearers?"

He chuckled. "Just like Ironwearers. Shall we get you home?"

"Yes, please." Then concern darkened her face, and she pulled back slightly as he led her to the horse.

"What's the matter?"

Wandisha seemed to be listening. "I hear someone crying."

Harper cocked an ear. "I don't. So it's not our worry."

**Kalm**

# CHAPTER NINE

*A*fter *Ian Haarper left, Kalm continued to stare into the* distance. At the edge of consciousness, insect voices spoke beneath his thoughts: waspish Kylene, bumblebee Wandisha, self-conscious droning from an unidentified male Teep. Below those notes, the chitterings of Normals could not be distinguished without concentration he would not give.

Things went well, he reflected, knowing this was intuition rather than knowledge. Well, but not exactly as expected. The simple substitution of Merryn ris Vandeign for his brother had changed history but not lives, it seemed. Ris Whelmner, Ian Haarper, Wandisha, Kylene . . . Circumstances had changed, but the same people danced the same reel of behavior.

Without thought, without choice. Kalm sensed that if he smashed the world asunder, the survivors would continue their clockwork lives without concern, arriving at the same destinies. Which was no flattering assessment of his powers, he confessed inwardly, wryly.

*Still* . . . Lan Haarper had been a soldier once. Now the thought of war jumbled his conversation; he babbled petty threats and an old man's aphorisms. Hidden as his thoughts were, the man had nevertheless become reduced. He had become timid, ineffectual—weak.

*I wish I were beating a stronger man.*

Clatter stirred him from reveries. The bartender was

straightening tables and stools. As Kalm watched, the man picked up a final glass, then moved to the Algheran's table, skirting a reddish stain on the floor.

"You're staying in the inn, sir?" His voice was deferential but preoccupied.

"Very likely." Kalm looked away.

"Sir?"

"Yes, I'm staying tonight." Kalm gestured with the glass. "My bags are upstairs. I'm just not eager to rush to bed."

"Nor am I, and that's a truth." The bartender shook his head minutely. "This has been . . . It won't help the business, that's for sure. Would you be wanting?"

"Yes." Effort lay ahead, Kalm decided, but he had no need to rush to it. "Another glass, laced this time." He stared pensively at the stained floor until the bartender came back, then tossed a coin, which missed the man's hand.

"I'll get change, sir." The man was deferential even as he bent over.

"Forget it." Kalm paused, making his voice casual. "You had some sort of problem here within the last season or two?"

"No, sir. I don't remember any."

Kalm gestured. "Nothing involving people. A fire, a flood, something like that, I heard. Maybe just a big storm."

"Oh. There was the slide, sir. The landslide."

"That's probably it," Kalm agreed. "Big one? Which way from here? And do you remember the date?"

"Can't say I do, sir. Three to four years tenths it was, but I don't remember more exactly. No one was hurt, and that's the important thing."

"Sure," Kalm said, extracting details from the man's dormant memories. "Just checking. That's the one I heard about. I suppose there was a storm that night or the day before."

"No . . ." The bartender looked high at the muslin-coated wall. "I think back, the funny thing is, there was a storm the next night."

"Interesting," Kalm said, and sipped at his beer. The liquid was weak on the tongue but strong in the throat—about one-third alcohol, he guessed. By chance, he must have found the bartender's tipple.

He looked. He had.

The bartender still stared somberly at the wall. "Another funny thing, sir. You know, I'd completely forgotten that slide until you mentioned it. The man who owned that land was in here tonight, and neither of us said a word about it. Memory is strange at times."

"Sure is," Kalm said comfortably. "It's a strange world."

Silence followed for several moments, till the bartender turned again to Kalm. "Sir, I don't want you to think I was listening to your conversation earlier tonight, but I had to pay attention now and then. Because you might want service, and I'd have to—"

"Yes." Kalm looked at him over the beer. "So?"

The man swallowed nervously. "Did I hear you say you were from Alghera? I wasn't really listening, but . . ."

"Long ago. Like Ian Haarper's new wife."

"Can you tell me—" The bartender swallowed again. "They say, sir, they say—" Then, with the words rushing, he said, "They say no one can own anyone in Alghera, that they don't have slaves there, or even serfs. That even if someone comes there with slaves, they have to let— Is that all true, sir?"

Kalm stared at the man bleakly.

"I'm sorry, sir. Forgot myself. Didn't mean to intrude." The bartender stepped backward, rebuilding his dignity, and as Kalm remained silent he retreated farther, beyond the bar into obscurity.

At last Kalm stirred, standing mechanically, with nostrils distended. Nearby, Wandisha was being fondled. Responding carelessly, she radiated her sensations so that he felt ghost pats along his sides and thighs. Distastefully, he closed his mind off and went upstairs.

In the darkness, Wandisha drew fingertips along the sleeping man's side, knowing that her life had not been changed.

This was hers: her mattress bed, her walls, her armful of possessions . . . her thoughts. Before her in the darkness, the almost-flames of human minds flickered. A bonfire of dreams.

It was illusion, built from self-imposed distance. The individual embers would swell if she chose, growing to separate forms, each with its own shifting kaleidoscopic pattern of color. Closer, they could be seen through, lenses on a world she could witness only through the eyes of others.

Illusion again. Looking through one mind, she always felt the presence of the others and often grew silent among the mesmerizing indissoluble bonds that linked one person to another. There was only a unity, she sometimes felt, one immortal being that was all of humanity, the separate men and women being no more to it than the windows of a building.

And Wandisha herself, standing apart, watching, staring through those windows at the world that included Wandisha? Which window had she become? What watcher looked through her?

She was alone. Unknown. For her there would be no watcher.

She stroked the man softly. Nothing had changed.

He had treated her delicately, with the careful restraint of himself that men thought was gentleness. When she had turned to him at the top of the steps, laughing softly at his unspoken desire, he had taken her body almost shyly, and he had asked for nothing as he used her. She did not believe he ever would.

*The coal the fires would not light*, she thought, seeking to place his concealed mind among the rest of her world, trying to find for the man a uniqueness that transcended his lovemaking.

"A trick," he had said of that concealment. An artificial thing, disconcerting but not to be feared. Necessary for reasons he could not explain but nothing she should think significant. Touching his hair, feeling the hidden mesh hard against her fingers, she could not believe him.

What thoughts did he hide from her? From his Kylene?

His Kylene. Another telepath, by coincidence, her mental images guttering flames above the banked embers of sleeping minds. She had wept before she slept, empty, yearning, alone, but Wandisha knew that the little girl had wept before without reason.

*His Kylene*. She felt a distant pity for them both, knowing them both as people who took their possessions for granted. They would want love on the same terms: a thing to be held and kept forever, something purchased by their labor. Fearful of loss, seeing love as something consumed by the act of loving, they would mistrust emotion, denying love given to them without cost.

Cast together, they had taken each other into possession without conscious intent. That was his doing primarily, Wandisha judged—his fault, if responsibility was assigned, for the habits of ownership were stronger in him. Kylene had recognized that possessiveness and chosen to play with it for amusement; she had been doomed from that moment, being too young to know that experiments turned to habit and that habit became need.

Those were traits to guard against, Wandisha noted as an aside. He would spend other nights with her; he would wish to claim her. And he would leave her life as suddenly as he had entered it. He would be well intentioned, but he must learn that he did not own her life. She must not forget it.

And when he left her? Without envy, she knew that his Kylene would be with him.

An eyelid fluttered beneath her kiss. His chest swelled with inhaled breath, and she moved closer, touching his side gently, marveling at the warmth he radiated.

In response, he tugged her closer. "Still awake?" he asked with sleep-softened throatiness. "Thought you were supposed to pass out when the Earth moved."

"You did," she whispered, enjoying the moment of nonsense, and her hands moved lower as he reached for her.

It was not necessary that her life be changed.

The torch of consciousness that was Kalm once-ha'Ruijac vanished, and Wandisha did not notice.

*Just checking.* Surely it was not necessary. Nothing important could have changed.

*Just checking. Making sure everything goes right.*

He felt neither breeze nor motion, yet Kalm was conscious as ever in his retreat of a rushing, massive presence flowing past him on all sides. A darkness, invisible behind a twilight-like gloom, a thing with its own intent, unconcerned by the hopes of men, untouched by their actions. A fearful thing.

Time.

At the edge of hearing, the one Earth rumbled softly, inexorably.

He breathed shallowly, listening to the beat of his heart. A narrow box rested on his hands; its lid was raised. A heavy pack rested on his back, making him lean forward for balance.

*I must be careful. I must not run risk.*

*It will be simple. There are no dangers.*

*I'm only checking, only making sure of what happens.*

*I don't have to feel guilt for that.*

About him, the world changed. Patterns writhed on a gleaming display within the box: painted lines, red and blue and green. Numbers.

Years.

Ships and men were ephemeral things, gone too quickly to be noticed. He saw the world instead as the gods did, cleaned of its imperfections, a thing itself alive and moving.

As he blinked, seasons passed.

Forest trees tumbled down hillsides, silently overrunning one by one the tiny fences set to hold them back. Gray-brown lumber on the piers behind him faded in color to yellow-white as the waters of the Bloodrill rose, then were replaced by other ancient structures that in their turn grew young and vanished without trace.

Buildings rose and fell about him, swept from being with the abruptness of a child's ill temper. As he watched, they became fewer. The hulking warehouse to one side, even the tall inn, shrank to sheds; then shallow pits took their place. Earth flowed, filling the pits; white lapped over them for a handful of seconds, then the green of grass.

Only the great road remained constant. Trees pushed houses aside to draw near it as Kalm watched, collecting at the side of the black ribbon as if to marvel. The houses gave way grudgingly but surely till only a few lingered along the roadside, crowded between tall elms and maples like a child lost in an adult's gathering.

Darkness snapped into being. Sound. Wind. Moisture.

It was raining. Men shouted.


Flames sputtered from torches socketed in the earthen walls. Straw rustled underfoot on a plank floor. In a corner a uniformed man with a twisted foot rubbed tallow over a padded jacket, not looking up as Kalm entered.

A second barefoot soldier, entering the room with a covered bucket, stepped in front of Kalm to stop him. "Where do you think you're going, boy?"

"Thought I'd take another look at young Merryn," Kalm said. "See how he's doing." Casually, he slapped his hands on his thighs, shaking off water and traces of mud.

The soldier blenched. "Captain!"

"It's the Algheran priest fellow, Raff," the man in the corner commented, looking up. "I'd thought he'd be gone on by now. Better'n we'd not have him running free in here."

"Let me get the captain." The soldier backed away hurriedly, then bent to leave the bucket on the floor and reentered the interior hallway.

The word was not "captain" in the sense of rank that Kalm would have given it. In the soldier's pronunciation hints of an older phrase could be heard: "decision maker," "thinker." "Headman." Kalm waited, brushing water from his hair to the wooden floor, wondering why the passage of time brought words to degradation rather than elevating them.

The bucket stank.

Kalm thought regretfully of the comfortable inn he had left behind and the time machine he had buried in the woods. "Are you afraid of me, too?"

"Not from you, not anyone." But the clubfooted soldier had scuttled sideways just far enough to bring a sword within reach. "You wait and talk to the captain, Algheran."

"I saved that boy," Kalm pointed out.

*It looked that way*, the soldier's thoughts ran, half-fearful and half-contemptuous. *Maybe . . . Somehow . . . Those Algherans . . .* "Wait for the captain, boy."

"What's wrong with being Algheran?"

"Eh-h! It's—" The soldier struggled with thoughts he was unwilling to express.

Kalm smiled. "We're not magicians, despite the stories."

The soldier glared at him. "Not natural, that many people living together."

"Like an anthill?" Kalm suggested, blank-faced. "Some say that. It's made us rich." The soldier growled again.

*Now at Alghera begins the Fifth Era . . .* Loprit too would have large cities someday, but he could not explain that to the soldier. This was not yet Loprit, not yet anything.

"So how's the boy doing now?"

"Like'n you could expect. Wanted to skylark some." Willing to change subjects, the soldier coughed and spit at the wall. "Captain's got him to bed, though."

*Keeping the boy from causing more trouble*, Kalm estimated. It could not be easy having responsibility for a powerful man's son but no authority. Young Merryn would be days escaping from his swaddling now that he was so bound.

"You're wanting to see me, priest?" An officer had entered the room, a stocky, hard-faced man wearing a long-sleeved robe. The garment was a gesture to indoor civility, Kalm sensed, noticing angular shapes beneath the linen; the man wore armor despite the late hour. One hand hovered near his sword hilt, the other cupped a tiny leather bag. "You left us, I'd bethought. Did you come back hoping on a reward?"

*Where were you when the boy was drowning?* "I'd take one," Kalm said at last, easily. "Rather just stay out of the rain for a while, though. Thought I might come and talk some with Merryn."

"The boy's sleeping."

"Not yet he isn't."

"So?" The officer grimaced but did not repeat the lie. "You know who he is, priest." He stepped sideways, letting two more soldiers enter the room. They were armed. Both wore long jackets disfigured by crisscross rows of stitching; ironberry seeds jangled between layers of leather.

"I heard his name." Kalm hesitated, aware the officer was close to ordering his arrest. "That's all, just his name. After I got him out of the water."

"And that's all, boy?"

*He's the oldest son of Terrault ris Vandeign, the oldest son of Dalsyn ris Vandeign, an illiterate, insignificant, two-bit noble in an insignificant, two-bit wilderness that can't even think of being a country yet, and you're a barbarian pretending to be a soldier. You were supposed to be escorting his family in friendly territory, and you let the boy die. You're lazy and you stink and your men stink and you can't do your job.* Kalm smiled and spoke politely. "That's all, sir."

"He's worth ten of you. You don't have to know more."

Kalm waited.

"You understand your place here, boy?"

Kalm counted to five silently. "Yes, sir."

"And you still want to talk to him? Instead of money?"

"Yes, sir. As a priest, I—"

The officer spit, spattering the lid of the pail and Kalm's boots. Kalm stopped speaking.

Hands slapped at him from behind—one of the soldiers, looking ponderously for concealed weapons. He sensed rather than saw gestures behind him. The search was ineffectual, insultingly so.

"You wouldn't be tiring him?" The officer bounced the bag upon his palm, ignoring Kalm's glare. "His mother would—"

"I don't need the money. I just want to talk to the boy for a while. About his soul."

"Well, now." The officer looked about the room slowly, carefully, not looking at Kalm's face. "His soul, eh, boy?"

"His soul," Kalm said sourly. "Give the money to someone who needs it more, sir. Just so I talk to the boy."

"Surely." The officer smiled wispily, then dropped the bag into a pouch on his belt. "You'll follow, priest."

"Of course." Kalm turned to look at the soldier in the corner and traced an X with a finger above his heart. "May the Lord Cimon guard you, the Lady Nicole guide you."

In the hallway they paused to let two women pass. One was at early middle age, with a baby suckling at her breast; the second was an older woman with streaked hair and scarred facial designs.

*The competition*, Kalm recognized with poor humor, listening to the officer's hurried courtesies and scowling convincingly at the hex wife before nodding at the younger woman.

*And a noble's mistress. Not a great beauty anymore, is she?* It took deliberate effort to realize that this was Merryn ris Vandeign's mother and that the nursing infant was Gertynne.

*I kept her boy alive. It was to ruin Ian Haarper, but I kept her boy alive and I can't even be introduced to her. Because I told them I was an Algheran.*

*Enough.* He forced restraint on his thoughts. The Algherans might remake men's destinies without cause or meddle blindly as Ian Haarper did. Kalm would wield his power more carefully and without resentment. *Better aims, better skill.*

"He's in here." The officer pointed to a curtain dangling from the ceiling, then pulled it open to disclose a dark room that was small and mostly filled with a bed.

Kalm hesitated, letting his eyes adjust to the darkness, and discovered a soldier in the corner by an opening in the wall that must have been a cold hearth. *Kitchen on the other side of the wall, so the same fire heats food and both rooms.* This was the house's only bedroom, he realized suddenly. An entire family would sleep here normally, but it had been taken over for one boy.

The room stank of vomit and cheap wine.

The soldier nodded at the captain but did not speak. A candle sputtered behind his back, adding smoke and spice to the reek—the hex wife's contribution, Kalm knew.

"Mama?" It was a child's voice, thin, querulous, and without character. Kalm realized it was the first time he had heard Merryn ris Vandeign speak. *Asks for his mother. Well, he knows his father isn't here.*

"She's all right, boy," the officer said. "She's gone off to give prayers with the witch woman. Don't you be fretting." His voice was gentle now, a courtier's voice.

"Is she—" Invisibly, but clear to Kalm's senses, the boy swallowed. A hand moved across the covers. "You have—"

"Just to the barn," the officer said. "We wouldn't let her go farther, a night like this." He patted significantly at the sword on his hip, though Kalm could not be sure that the boy noticed the gesture. "She's being guarded. Don't you fret."

The boy squirmed, forcing himself backward, and the bed creaked beneath him. When his motion stopped, he breathed heavily, whether from exertion or from exasperation Kalm could not tell. "If she—" He swallowed, hiccoughed, then swallowed once more. "My father would not forgive if—"

"She'll be all right," the officer said emphatically, and gestured at the soldier in the corner.

The soldier shrugged, disloding a sack from his shoulder, and bent forward with a knee on the bed, holding the boy half-upright with an arm as he brought the sack to the child's face. "Hirr you arr, yoong sirr."

"Don't want." The boy pushed the sack away. "Not more."

"Drink up, boy," the captain ordered. "Do you want me to tell your grand—your father you're being disobedient?"

"No," Merryn said timidly. Sadly, he brought an end of the sack to his mouth while the soldier lifted it above him and took a swallow, then a second swallow, then a third.

He coughed suddenly, spraying liquid drops about the bed. More wine spewed from the sack onto his face and the bedclothes. Irrelevantly, standing stolidly as the soldier and the officer laughed, Kalm found himself wondering what the usual occupants of the bed would think when it was returned to them.

*And where are they? The barn, perhaps? Also under guard by these soldiers? And who—the local headman or mayor of this village? A noble's oldest son, after all . . . They'd take over the best house they could find.*

*And make a boy drunk to put him to sleep.* A boy whose grandfather made kings. Kalm's face twitched while his mind came to terms with that.

For a moment, insanely, he wanted nothing more than to flee and return to his time machine, to get back to the Present, as far away as possible from the abyss of prehistory.

*The start of the Fifth Era.* But it was the Fifth Era in Alghera, and only in Alghera. Here and elsewhere the dark age continued, the world not yet transformed by the bright light of learning that shone from Alghera, not yet civilized.

*Our world. We were the first to enter the Fifth Era. Alghera made the one world.*

*And I'm Chelmmysian now.*

Mechanically, he scowled at the officer. "I said I wanted to talk to the boy. Privately. About his soul."

"It wasn't your fault." Kalm shook his head, then nodded, his eyes closed, forehead resting on his palm. *Such a long day, starting on the road with Kylene and—*

*She hasn't even been born yet.*

"It wasn't your fault, lad. Whatever that hex woman told you, people aren't responsible for everything that happens to them." *Not for me. She isn't for me. Lan Haarper's woman.*

*There'll never be a woman for me.*

*I don't need anyone. It doesn't matter.* "There's a world which exists apart from our knowledge of it and—"

"But we know so much." Merryn interrupted dizzily, his eyes closed, not eager to argue with an adult but unwilling to hear religious orthodoxy disputed. "So we . . . Sir?"

Kalm nodded again. *Can you read my thoughts, boy? Can you foretell what will happen tomorrow, or the day after? Do you know the life of a peasant or a Warder or a time traveler? Will you draw the back face of the moon or count the stars the same on different nights? Can you tell me Hemmendur's message? Have you already seen Ian Haarper's face? Or Kylene's?*

"We don't know everything," he said patiently, stretching himself in the corner where the soldier had stood, pushing the back of his head against the cold wall. "So we can be surprised. Like you were when the riverbank gave way."

"That was—" The boy swallowed.

"Someone planned it?" Kalm pursed his lips scornfully, grateful that he could show contempt without observation in the darkness. "Someone *knew* you would stand on the bank when it was raining and—be serious, boy!"

"But—" The boy swallowed again, noisily. "I knew. I had to know, or else . . ."

"Are you—" Kalm stopped suddenly and stared into the darkness, letting his consciousness divide. "Cimon! Did you want to die, boy? Really? By drowning?"

"No." It was whispered. "But if I—"

"Does your mother want to kill you?"

"N-no."

"Does your bodyguard want to kill you? Couldn't they do it some other way if they wanted to? Aren't they here to protect you and your mother?"

"Yes." The voice was timid, sad.

"Do the peasants around here know who you are? Could they guess you were coming? Could they guess you'd stand on the edge of the bank, just there? Do they have a reason to kill you?"

"No." The boy hesitated. "I don't think so."

"So they're acquitted, yes? And your bodyguard? And your mother. And your father. And your little brother?"

"I guess." The boy tried to chuckle, halfheartedly.

"Well, it wasn't you, either. It wasn't anyone. The riverbank just gave way. That was all." Kalm shook his head wearily, remembering the catechisms of his own childhood. "Lord Cimon has given us a world we can live in without guilt. Lady Nicole has given us the ability to reap the most reward in it. It isn't all fixed, it doesn't all depend on us."

"But," young Merryn protested tearfully. "Mama says—"

"She's wrong." Kalm stopped there, realizing that further argument was useless, trusting the boy's native intelligence to lead him from the path of superstition to reason.

It was what a genuine priest of Cimon would have done, he reflected. Soldier, savant, priest—so many roles played, so many more ahead! Would there ever be an end to lying, ever be a time when he could be himself without disguise?

ChelmForce, Swordtroop, Nyjuc, Tagin... What had they all taken from him? What was left of Kalm ha'Ruijac now?

What was left of Timmial lan Haarper?

A soldier pushed his head through the door curtain, and the boy gestured, sending him away. "It's scary," he whispered.

*Cimon, yes!* Kalm thought. "I know it's frightening. I know. But it's real, son. We're free. Cimon and Nicole have given us freedom."

He paused and swallowed, reaching back for arguments that had swayed him as a child to reinforce this child's new view of reality. "The Plates, the thing we Algherans found. Two plus two is four, three plus three is six, and it doesn't matter who does the sums. It's always that way, for good men or bad men or even someone who wants different answers. It's what happens in the world, and no one takes credit for it, no one takes blame. We are not responsible. We are free. Like animals."

"We . . ." The boy shook from head to toe. "We aren't free. Are we, sir? I mean, my grandfather is Lord Vandeign, and some day, when he . . . I can't become a peasant."

Kalm smiled. "We're animals in different pens, eh?"

"Well . . ." Tentatively, a silhouette in the darkness, the boy smiled back.

"That's all right," Kalm said evenly, using words he had already rehearsed. "We're free, but we have restraints on us. We have responsibilities, and sometimes we do things we'd rather not do, because they're the right thing to do. Like Cimon."

"He killed the Teeps, didn't he?" Clearly, the boy had heard little of the Algheran religion until now.

"Something like that," Kalm said. *You did become a believer, didn't you, in the world I just came from? Is that—was that—my doing? Should I have—?*

*Enough!* "Something harder. It doesn't matter now. Someone will explain it to you, someday. Anyhow, in your—your mother's religion, you feel you cause everything that happens to you, so you aren't responsible, and you do what you want, and that . . ."

*That makes you barbarians.* He inhaled sharply, trusting that the sound would seem a sigh rather than contempt.

It really didn't matter what he told the boy. If anything, he was only replacing a bad superstition with a good superstition. He might even be doing good—in Algheran eyes.

"In *our* religion we have freedom," he explained. "So we *are* responsible for what happens to us. And for what we do to other people." He sniffed again, then continued. "We can't control everything, of course, but we are free to act, and so we have to act responsibly. We do what we decide to do instead of letting things just happen."

"But—"

"If you were an Algheran child, you would be responsible for knowing that riverbanks give way in the rain. You wouldn't be allowed to trust that some stranger would jump into the water and pull you out, just for your convenience. You'd be spanked, no matter who your grandfather or father was."

The boy thought about that. "Would you spank me? If I was your little boy?"

"If you were my son, or if you were an Algheran child, and if you knew about Cimon and Nicole and the Brothers of Men, I would have spanked you then."

"Oh," the boy said, and over his head Kalm grimaced, wondering why children took comfort in such threats. "Could —can I go to Alghera someday?"

"If you want." Kalm smiled ruefully, remembering his own desires when he was this boy's age. "It's an interesting place to visit. Why?"

"Is it big as . . ."

*Ten thousand people? It's small now.* "It's very big," he agreed. "It may even get bigger."

"It is . . . My father says you could meet a stranger every day for a year and you still wouldn't have seen them all."

"That's true. It's a lot of people to be polite to; are you sure you'd like that?"

"I think . . . I could."

"You'd have to learn their language."

The boy frowned. "Is it hard?"

*"Of anteftsoon certainly,"* Kalm said carefully in Speech, *"the contemporaneous vernacular dialect of the multitudinous brawling Algheran denizens would be cognizable to most judicial and indisputatious but inconscipulabolous auditors as being inferentialiably correspondential in all but insignificant orts from the veritable and verisimilitudious Lopritian."* Then he fell back into Lopritian. "Not very."

"Oh," Merryn said. "Someday . . ."

"You could build your own city," the Algheran suggested. "It wasn't hard for us."

"Could . . . My father says we don't . . ."

"Well." Kalm gestured comfortably, dismissing the notion, and leaned back against the wall, waiting for Merryn to continue the conversation.

Silence reigned.

"What are you going to do now?" Kalm asked at last, seeing the child's indecisiveness. "With your life, I mean?"

"I—my father—grandfather is—"

"He's one of the great warlords here, isn't he?" Kalm asked, placing a just noticeable doubt in his voice. "A man who doesn't approve of cities? And wants to build a kingdom?

You'll be his heir, after your father; you're probably going to be just like him someday, won't you?"

"I—"

"You'll be an important man, too busy for talking to old priests like me, and you'll probably have forgotten all about this little chat, won't you?" Kalm chuckled hollowly.

"No!"

Kalm chuckled again. "That's all right." He straightened and slapped his leg. "Rain's died down, it sounds like. Time I was on my way. You get yourself some sleep, young Merryn."

"No!" the boy insisted as the Algheran slipped around the bed. "I won't forget you! I'll remember this. I'll remember what you said!"

*I know you will.* Kalm smiled tolerantly. "It doesn't matter, Merryn. I don't matter. What you should remember—when you were struggling in the water—drowning—I came by and tried to get you out, and we were lucky. We saved you, by the grace of the Lady's cloak. Maybe . . . sometime, when you see someone in trouble, maybe you'll help them."

"Yes, sir."

The Algheran nodded politely. "You help people, instead of hurting them, and you give to them, instead of just taking from them, like you could."

"Yes, sir?"

"Well, you do that, Merryn, and you build instead of tearing things down, and you save life rather than killing, and you'll be a happy man with good friends all your life. You'll make Cimon and Nicole happy. And I'll be happy, too, even if you never meet me again. Understand me?"

"Yes, sir." The boy shook his head seriously.

"Cimon guard, Nicole guide. Get to sleep." Kalm smiled and slipped from the room.

Outside the house, in darkness, away from the curious soldiers, with the last driblets of rain streaking his face, his smile was less certain.

A short while later he stepped into spring. Gold and brown leaves were restored in green; dying flowers were again in bloom.

Two hundred fifty years had passed. He wondered if even a single pebble had moved in the leaf-strewn path under his feet.

He cast his mind about, ensuring that he was unobserved,

then reset the controls on his time machine's console, lowered the protective lid, then replaced the box in his pack.

It was natural to be careful with his only time machine.

*Part of a time machine*, he corrected himself. *The important part.*

It was the part he had removed from the cabin of another time traveler's levcraft, a less cautious time traveler, once engaged in the battles that bordered on the true Present but now risen—reluctantly—to Cimon and Nicole.

The legacy had included a belt buckle that was now in his hands. As he turned it, it hissed softly at intervals. Kalm examined his surroundings.

He was north of the town, little more than a hundred paces from the great road, but it was already invisible. Trees were on all sides of him, thin, white-barked, unevenly angled. The land sloped, rising with distance from the road and again in the direction of the town. Beneath his feet a shoulder-width depression in the fallen leaves led indistinctly toward the heights. Lower, and roughly parallel, was a shallow dip in the ground that the trees seemed to avoid. A runoff for rain, he estimated; in centuries it might become a creek.

At the moment it led toward another time machine.

Patiently he shouldered the pack and moved up the trail.

Midday and much of the afternoon had gone before the hissing of the belt buckle changed to erratic static. The noise was a directional clue, if he had known how to interpret it; Kalm turned the volume down and let himself by guided by eye.

Trees, grass, rocks, dirt . . . His eyes moved over the cramped horizon of the valley.

A hundred man-heights farther the valley forked, a nubbin extending into a bend of the hill. Erosion had been at work here, making one side almost a vertical wall with exposed rocks and colored bands of soil. The ground below the talus was smooth and tree-free, the grass seemingly never touched by man until Kalm reached it.

*A dead end*, he thought at first, staring at the heights, but the hill was only steep, not impossible. Nearer, tracing plausible paths to the top, he saw out-of-true saplings and a tree limb with dead leaves pointing downward. It was easy to imagine a man with more strength than skill climbing the hill, pulling himself upward on trees and shrubs to speed his progress, a tall man who would snap off branches that blocked his way rather than bend beneath them.

Stripping off his pack and sitting on a convenient boulder, he felt a sense of anticipation. What followed took patience rather than skill. An outsider of another era observing his actions might have thought he was tuning a musical instrument. Kalm, familiar only with singing and simple percussion devices, would have been mystified by the comparison. But it was not likely that an outside observer would have seen him, anyhow.

He slid through time, moving back and forth over a half-year interval, varying minutely the rate of his travel on each pass.

For the most part, he was in darkness. Total darkness—neither the extent of the boulder nor the ground underfoot nor the hills before him could be seen while he traveled. Overhead a thin blue band crossed the sky, slowly waving north and south. As he increased the rate, the color deepened and the waving motion became faster, but the band was never bright enough to provide lighting. That was the sun, still visible through techniques Kalm did not understand.

Here and there starlike motes sparkled before him, vanishing even as he noticed them. He could not explain them, either, though in some fashion they marked the location of solid earth. They created no sensible pattern; they were unimportant.

Abruptly, an image appeared. It was a gleam lasting briefly, a ghost of a reflection. Kalm sighed gently, then smiled.

On subsequent passes the gleam grew larger. Insubstantial, moon-bright, a shape took being before him. It was there only for seconds, a mistlike thing, seemingly translucent; then he emerged into normal time, and only the ordinary world was about him. But it was there when he traveled through time again.

A *levcraft*, he decided. But it was like no levcraft he had ever seen: a silvery ax-head shape with rounded poll, the sides straight, floating at waist height. It was easily ten man-heights long.

In normal time, sitting on solid rock, staring at the unsuspecting grasses waving before breezes on the imperturbable hills, he whistled softly.

*Troop carrier.*

No. Kylene's memories had not shown that.

Of course, he had caught only glimpses of her thoughts, for all his efforts on the stage from Northfaring to Midpassage, but he had seen enough to know that she and Ian Haarper were alone.

*If only—*

A senseless wish. He could have no allies. Telepaths were no more to be trusted with time travel than Normals, perhaps even less. It was not the Normals who had twice attempted to rule the one Earth.

*Besides, she's obsessed with the man.*

He grimaced. A neurotic teenage girl, a peripatetic money broker, an uneducated whore... *And an out-of-condition soldier. Midpassage isn't exactly seeing the world's most impressive Teeps.* Despite the clear record of history and the advantages of telepathy, the stuff of leadership was lacking in Teeps today.

Only today? Guiltily, he reflected that Cimon and Nicole had been worshiped for fifty millennia. Hemmendur of Chelmmys might be remembered for as long. Of the telepaths who had built and ruled empires during the Second and Fourth eras, no memory remained; their names and deeds were no subject for curiosity even among Teeps.

*Ah, well.* Duty remained for some Teeps, even for obscure minor functionaries of this era's short-lived states.

He did not have the skill to synchronize his passage through time with Ian Haarper's vehicle, which meant it could not be attacked and destroyed, but that was not necessary. The levcraft could be buried; it could be removed from Ian Haarper's control.

The bartender had told him what tools he needed. Kalm reached into his pack for a pushstick.

He was not attempting elegance, which sped matters. Properly attacked, the rocks in the hill walls were eager to fall.

Kalm used the pushstick recklessly, replacing batteries frequently from the supplies in his pack. An upward slash at the earth beneath a boulder, a downward slash from above—the cuts were narrow ones, aimed at depth. The cavities were entries to deeper cuts, then for fist-wide holes that he filled with white canisters. Electrical cables ran from the canisters; Kalm moved backward cautiously, letting the wire slide through his fingers as he groped his way from handhold to handhold. As rock and dirt tumbled down the slope, dislodged by his steps, finger-length shards glittered, soil melted and condensed to dark ceramics by the glazing action of the push-stick.

The cables were short; he was not able to reach the ground, so he scrambled across the top of the talus to connect them to a small box. He looked about for observers, then slipped another battery into the box and twisted a switch into place.

When he was done, he detonated the canisters.

For long seconds it seemed nothing had happened. There was no sound, not even the rumble of falling debris. Then puffs of white smoke jetted from the cavities he had dug: ice crystals in suddenly supercooled air. He heard whip-cracking sounds.

Smoke continued to billow from the hillside, rolling downward and dissipating as it mixed with the outside air. The cracking sounds repeated, flat, distinct.

The noise was loud enough that someone might come to investigate. Frowning, he waited while the cracks continued, louder and more rapidly. Meanwhile, he watched the hillside carefully, half expecting to see the earth bulge through the clouds of smoke. But however large the canisters became, he knew, they were dwarfed by the bulk of the hill.

The noise was high-pitched now, a racket, staticlike and almost continuous. Beneath him, the earth seemed to come alive, pieces of gravel springing free as his feet touched them. When Kalm touched the hill, it seemed to push back against his palm.

The earth coughed.

*Here!* Slowly, majestically, a portion of the hill heaved itself upward. A grumbling sound pressed at him, an all-pervasive shaking sensation within his body, a complaint from the rock that seemed never to end as the noise mounted. The one Earth shook itself.

There was rain around him suddenly, quietly falling on him—not water but dripping soil. Unheard in the din, cables snapped, lashing back toward him like angry snakes. Imperceptibly, the earth began to descend.

Only seconds had passed. Kalm had time to spare a glance at the still-empty ground below the invisible time machine. The boulders that had fallen beneath it had stopped rolling, anvils for the hammer he had built. Bracing himself as rocks bounded down the slopes and the earth shook about him, he

looked wryly over to the safe path Ian Haarper had taken to
the top.

When the echoes had stopped and the falling dirt had settled, he climbed to the hilltop, coughing as he emerged from
dust that would not be laid until the following day's rain. He
was not surprised to find himself at the back of Ian Haarper's
house.

# CHAPTER TEN

*F*ive days later, measured against autumn, he returned.

"Yes?" The woman who opened Ian Haarper's door was elderly and midway to corpulence. Seeing Kalm's uniform, she frowned. "You'll be looking for him, I suppose. He's busy the while, in the atrium." She sniffed, the foreign word associated in her mind with spilled food and broken crockery.

She was the housetender, Kalm recognized. "Perhaps I can wait."

"Aye. No doubt there's your horse to see to." Her hand slipped to the door handle.

"I walked." Recalling his hike from the brigade's camp to the bridge, from the bridge into the town, from the center of town up the hillside by winding road and on to Ian Haarper's house, Kalm smiled, half-reassuringly, half-ruefully. "Perhaps I could wait in the kitchen. And if I could have a glass of water?"

He collected sweat from his forehead with the back of his hand and shook it off as his consciousness split, keeping her attention with gestures while his mind passed through her thoughts. Who else came to see the Ironwearer?

Lord Merryn ris Vandeign and his wife Hereena, he saw. The housetender did not understand their interest in her employer, but they were people of quality and long resident in Midpassage. They had not visited recently; it was a pity that when they did, they came in the evenings and never saw who kept this uncouth structure in decent order. Dieytl lan Callares on occasion, a proper rogue since his boyhood, always smiling at silly young women and half-friendly and half-intent on business with everyone else. Children, generating disorder and mishap. And now an annoying young man of no account in a uniform.

*Fair summation*, Kalm admitted uneasily. *I should be presenting a better image to the world.*

But the opinion of an elderly Normal was unimportant.

Almost thankfully, he saw Kylene lin Haarper as a similar intruder in the housetender's orderly life, disruptive of routine and a foreigner and thus doubly unwelcome. The wife, a lazy, ill-tempered, and unthankful woman, spoiled shamelessly by the man despite her inattention to household chores. She was not present now; the housetender thought she had gone into the town.

The blind hussy she had heard so much of lately had not been in the house; the housetender had searched attentively for blond hair, rumpled bedding, clothing articles too large for Kylene, and other evidence of depravity; so far, disappointingly, she had found nothing to contribute to local discussions of lan Haarper's tomcatting.

"It's only water you're wanting?"

"Just water."

She was still suspicious, Kalm saw. Fruits imported from far away—oranges, melons, infrequently pineapples—were stored in the kitchen. More of his profligacy, since he had come into his money, like the purchase of this house, and surely it was having the less of luxuries that made sensible folk appreciate them the more. Those hard reddish things, now—Kylene had eaten them without concern for the price expended to provide her with such fripperies, then ruined a clean tablecloth by wiping purplish stains and seeds from her mouth. Barely noticed since, one *pomegranate* remained. The housetender had marked it for proper appreciation; she feared that Kalm would snack on it if accident delayed her lunch.

"Just water, please," Kalm repeated. He had drunk too much too late the previous night with Dighton ris Maanhaldur and the others to feel any but the simplest thirst.

*Still* . . . Satisfactions for the Hand's son were easily created. Ris Fryddich could find his own pleasures. Ris Jynnich, however, stupid, young, arrogant— *There's a loaded gun ca-*

*pable of firing itself. If only that anger stays under control
while I point him at the targets Ian Haarper finds for me.*

"Oh, I don't suppose he'd care minding."

"I've a message for him. Army business." Kalm concealed
amusement as his pompous tone confirmed her view of him.

"You'll wipe your shoes, then." Reluctant even after he
had obeyed, she retreated backward from the doorway and led
him up a small corridor.

An Ironwearer's house. Kalm looked about curiously. Outside, the exterior had been brown-painted wood rather than the
pastel concrete favored locally, and single-storied rather than
three. Inside, the house was shamelessly large despite its low
height. The living area alone was twice the size of the men's
dormitory in Nyjuc House. *And two women instead of one.
Must he do everything in multiples?*

In search of questions that could be answered, he turned
his attention back to Ian Haarper's house. Unexpectedly, the
internal walls were still nude, no more than reddish planks
framed by massive beams of the same wood. The ceiling was
wood also and built in shed style, a plane surface that slanted
down toward the outside of the house. Air moved from floor-
level vents to glass louvers two man-heights overhead; looking up, Kalm saw blue sky through the openings.

The floor planks were unnaturally pale, artificially narrow
white slats under clear varnish. Leather-covered couches and
chairs had been abandoned without order on the bare boards.
Small rugs and some cushions lay before a brick fireplace;
ashes and half-burned logs were in the hearth pit, though recent nights had been warm. A closed door was at one end of
the room; in an Algheran home, that would have led to the
summer living area, but here a solid wall blocked his view.
Flower aromas were noticeable. He saw no shelves for books.

At least the floor was clean.

"When will this be finished?" he asked, seeking to be polite.

"Never." The housetender looked around the big room with
familiarity-confirmed distaste. "Likes it this way, he does."

"Oh." Garish red and blue flowers were in white boxes
beneath the too-wide windows. Outside, he saw oaks and elm
trees that had to be older than the town. The sunscreen poles
had been taken down; unlike other houses in Midpassage,
nothing protected the exterior walls from the late summer
heat. A scythe lay in the side yard; a mulch pile was near a

row of white flowering shrubs. A red-blond boy pulled a rake through fallen leaves and damp grass. Kalm probed speculatively, retreating to his own mind without disappointment after finding that the youngster was no relative of Ian Haarper.

Reflexively, he scanned further, finding above the drab backdrop of Normal thoughts three energetic minds: a man in the shifting near reality of dreams; a woman staring contemplatively at roots protruding from an eroded riverbank; another woman, nude, blond, seeing herself wrapped in the arms of a dark-haired potbellied man whom Kalm recognized as the bartender of the inn. Both women raised their mind screens as he touched their thoughts, but he had not sought communication. He turned without concern.

The long wall to his right was covered by green curtains. Voices did not come through, but he sensed other minds. Unimportant thoughts, unimportant matters. Not time travelers, not soldiers. Lan Haarper was present, Kalm could tell, but the Algheran's mind was as invisible as his body.

"They're out there with him," the housetender said needlessly. "Ought to be leaving soon."

Kalm murmured inattentively. Rectangular objects had been fastened to the opposite wall. Too shallow to be cabinets, too complex to be decorations, they had attracted his attention almost immediately, and he crossed the floor to examine them.

They were stretched cloths of different sizes with color on them. *Paynnings*, he remembered, the picture things that Ian Haarper's make-believe wife created. Unlike the half-begun work he had seen days before, these held complete scenes, much like book holograms but only two-dimensional and with less detail. They had been mounted at a height a woman would find convenient; he stepped backward to view them better.

He saw a house built from logs, glass-fronted with a double sloped roof, sitting on a gentle hillside. A forest lay behind it; several of the trees were distinctly drawn. A dark brown path extended from the porch to the right side of the picture. Yellow and red daubs that might be flowers were sprinkled over long grass. In the foreground was a pond, dammed by a thick pile of twigs. An animal's head rested on the water, broad-faced and black-muzzled, staring at him.

There was a mountainside, snow-covered, against a pink sky. Boulders burned within green flames; yellow-outlined

black branches hovered overhead. Orange and scarlet soil lay
under the boulders and within footmarks in the snow. Snarling
animals were frozen in midleap in twisted unnatural poses.
*Dogs*, he thought. But they looked like no dogs in the one
world. Why were the colors so wrong? *Whim. A primitive's
fancy. And unimportant.* His eyes moved on.

A muscular man in blue clothing, hands down, caught in
the middle of a somersault, on a pure white backing. His hair
was brown and red; he seemed to be laughing. *Lan Haarper.
An imaginary lan Haarper.*

A double row of beds made with hospital precision and
stretching into the distance. Cabinets were set in brown walls.
Across the aisle, two men were talking. One sat with his back
turned and a boot resting on a footlocker; the other was in
profile, but a green square was plain on his forehead. *A dormitory*, Kalm guessed. But not in the current year, and not in
the Nyjuc or R'sihuc lodges of the Present.

*Images.* Why had they been displayed here? And if Kylene
wished to record such sights, why had lan Haarper not ob-
tained a camera uptime for her?

"Her things." The housetender sniffed audibly, and Kalm
saw that the "things" were to be kept dust-free but never
touched by a duster. The housetender remembered scoldings;
she had not discovered how Kylene knew when her instructions had been disobeyed.

Lan Haarper by himself was almost as demanding, it
seemed. Fortunately, he was away frequently, prospecting—
an occupation without importance and social status that had
unreasonably enriched him.

"You must have known the Ironwearer a long while," Kalm
suggested.

"Aye. In a ` manner of speaking." Unconsciously, the
woman preened herself. "Not that he claimed to be that all
along. Even when he took to calling himself—"

She stopped to sniff again. "Used to be just Timmial
Haarper."

Kalm could not resist. "You all must be very proud of
him."

"Kitchen's out here." The housetender had tired of his curiosity.

"Sure." In the doorway, Kalm looked back. It was simply
indecent for an ordinary man to live so spaciously.

The water was flat and unpleasantly warm, and the house-tender had poured it from a stone crock rather than using the pumps along the side wall. It had not had time to cool sufficiently, she had told Kalm. "His orders." *His fault*, her mind said, hinting at future rebellion. She gave no explanation.

Lan Haarper's orders, Kalm discovered, had been recently given. Beer was not to be tampered with, but all the water served in his house was to be boiled before it was drunk. Milk was to be heated almost to boiling. The Ironwearer had been frighteningly insistent; he had advised the housetender to adopt the same eccentric habits; he had even threatened her for the first time, telling her that if she disobeyed, he would remove her from her position immediately.

Kylene had obeyed lan Haarper without question. That ensured the housetender's silence despite her objections; the little chit had uncanny luck at determining what others had done and never viewed their actions through charitable eyes.

*Surprise.* Kalm turned and smiled cynically. Kylene had managed Dietyl lan Callares as well. Fear of lan Haarper's violence had deterred the money broker's less subtle advances; Kylene had laughed openly at the hints she finally understood. But he was another Teep, and she had moved quickly from tolerance to liking.

Kalm had not met lan Callares yet, but he had the measure of the man: a light tongue and an easy air. Clearly, the money broker possessed less sophistication than he affected, or he would have found employment in the larger cities of the north. His womanizing would probably be from boredom and the lack of a suitable partner rather than depravity; much popular belief in Teep hypersexuality rested on such flimsy evidence.

Reflexively, Kalm scanned the environment again, finding that neither Kylene nor Wandisha had lowered her mind screen. *Raised against each other, as well as me*, he realized. *But they notice each other. All the time. All of us.*

Teeps! He could not change their lives, but he was responsible for them regardless. For an instant he envied the Normals, who neither knew nor cared what thoughts occupied other minds and felt only those obligations that they had deliberately chosen. Then the feeling passed.

*I'm a Teep. What has happened, has happened.*

". . . and when your daddy and I are back, we'll be able to take the splint off," lan Haarper was saying, his voice clear through the open kitchen door. "Don't let him scratch at it, but don't keep him penned up, either. He'll give himself as much exercise as he needs."

"Yes, Ian Haarper," a child's voice said. A dog barked, not loudly, making the yap required for squirming in human arms. It was a puppy, long-haired and floppy-eared, ancestry uncertain.

"Okay, then. He'll be good as new."

"Lan Haarper?" another child, younger, spoke up. "Will you and Daddy be all right?"

"Cristilla!" The older child was a girl. The younger was male. The puppy had not discovered its sex. It was hungry. It wanted to investigate corners. It wanted to make puddles.

"I'll send the children out," the housetender said.

"Probably, Cristilla, but no one can promise," Ian Haarper continued. "We'll do our best to look after each other, but some of us will get hurt. And some of us may be killed."

"I can wait." Kalm frowned at the housetender until she withdrew to the interior doorway, then concentrated on Ian Haarper's voice, curious as to what it might reveal.

The voice was a low baritone, impure, contaminated with the slurs and tonal swings that characterized the illiterate. Underlying the discordant tones were pauses and unusual stresses that showed Kalm that the big redhead was translating his thoughts from another language. Speech? No. Kalm heard traces of it in his words, but there was enough overlap between Lopritian and the Algheran language to show that the man spoke neither tongue as a native would. What Kalm heard in Ian Haarper's voice was a guttural, harsh language, voiced from deep in the throat like a growl.

It was the speech of a man who had lost the sound of his native tongue. Lan Haarper had been away from the true Present a long, long time.

"Why?" the little boy asked, and in that moment Kalm looked through his eyes. "Daddy doesn't want—"

Lan Haarper sighed.

What strange sights and lands had he seen? Kalm wondered. Did he chafe at the time he had spent in Midpassage, at the tedium of the life he led now?

*Some day I have to get that Teepblind off him.*

"Well. Adults have quarrels sometimes, don't they? Sometimes—" Heedless of Kalm's mental urging, the big man remained standing with his back turned, his right foot on a bench, an elbow resting on his knee. As he spoke, he gestured negligently. Slouching, his clothing rumpled and his hair uncombed, he might have been a farm laborer recounting a bucolic anecdote. "No, I was going to say some arguments get out of hand, but that's really not it. So I won't say that. But Cristy, have you ever been blamed for something that wasn't your fault? You did what you thought was right and you got in trouble? And because you were little, you weren't listened to?"

Cristy—and Kalm—shook their heads gravely. Kalm, simultaneously sipping warm water under the wary eye of the housetender, listened with amusement and inspected the boy's surroundings.

Lan Haarper's atrium was a sort of internal garden, a large, open space in the center of the house with paved walks, trees, and flowers. The roof overhung the walls slightly. It had been painted white on top, Kalm remembered, though the underside was dark. A glass-walled corridor surrounded the garden on three sides; catty-corner to the kitchen an open door revealed the foot of a bed, and Kalm realized with some embarrassment that it belonged to Kylene.

*Not for me.*

His thoughts turned to her again despite that, with questions he still could not answer. Had she become hearthsharer to lan Haarper or was her belief only a hope? She was foreign, he knew. A time traveler but not an Algheran, so not part of any Sept. Which meant she was poor. Probably uneducated, like most people in this world, and thus gullible, despite her mental gifts. The normal complexities were within her, no doubt, but to define her was to find answers.

*Not for me.* Analysis was wasted effort.

"Adults get trapped in things also," lan Haarper was saying.

Kylene was a telepath. *She should have had more sense.*

And why hadn't Wandisha had more sense?

Or the man himself? Was every Ironwearer compelled to behave unreasonably? Wolf-Twin, lan Haarper . . . And why did they make other people so unreasonable?

". . . ago, there was another war in this area," lan Haarper said, his voice softening. "Bigger than anything you can ever imagine, lasting for years. And the people who lived here— where we stand right now—lost it. It took them a long time to accept it, but eventually most of them agreed that the war had ended the right way."

*An Ironwearer's philosophizing*, Kalm decided. Wars always ended up with happy endings. *They're just merce-naries*, he saw, suddenly grasping the fears and petty resent-ments that the Ironwearers hid behind their bland faces and unostentatious uniforms. Men on the edge of death, they mag-nified their importance, compensating for their fear without self-awareness. It was all a little sad, like Ian Haarper's pa-thetic belief that wearing a Teepblind would keep telepaths from understanding him.

"It was about—" Ian Haarper said. "About kids; you're both too young for me to explain. Your dads, maybe . . ."

*Flustered*, Kalm noticed, watching through borrowed eyes as Ian Haarper stumbled through their questions. He had at-tempted to overawe weaker people, and his tongue had be-trayed him to children. A strange justice, but deserved.

And his relationship with Kylene was now explained. Ian Haarper's own weaknesses had compelled him to dominate the girl. The immature Kylene had seen his fantasies and believed them, finding in him more than actually existed.

*Poor souls. Once they must have believed they had love.*

"A war in this area?" Kalm asked when the children had left and Ian Haarper took notice of him. "I hadn't heard of it."

"A ways back," the Ironwearer said, half turning toward Kalm as he pulled apart the wall covering in the living area, revealing floor-length windows that gave a view of his atrium. A roll of white tape was in his right hand. He used his left to loop cords around the green cloth at both ends of the wall, then pushed the windows so that they opened like doors. "Throw some light on the citizens," he mumbled.

Kalm waited, but Ian Haarper did not close the glass doors. He nodded instead, seemingly satisfied with himself, then moved without sound toward a half sofa. "How's the army treating you?"

The leather-covered chair he pointed Kalm to was softer than it appeared but poorly placed. When Kalm tried to in-spect Ian Haarper's face, sun glare reflected from across the garden obstructed his sight. Nearer, small yellow and purple flowers rimmed the flagstones beyond the glass; Kalm could not remember names for them. "Like an army," he replied. "They've got me but haven't figured out a real use for me. There's a bunch of supernumeraries like that."

Truth was foreshortened in his remarks. He had turned

down employment with Ironwearer Wolf-Twin, gambling on higher placement when ris Andervyll's son received a command. He had not expected that ris Maanhaldur would be so reluctant to ask his father for a sizable unit or that the Hand of the Queen would be so unwilling to indulge his child. Now, like Derrault ris Fryddich and Krennlenn ris Jynnich, he was scrabbling for a commission of any sort.

*What do I do if lan Haarper leaves without me?*

Follow, of course. It would be easy for a time traveler. But it would be a blow to his pride.

*Ris Clendannan? Would he use another aide?*

Lan Haarper grunted. "Happens. You've been a regular."

"A ways back," Kalm said. "I saw fighting before, but—"

"Then you know something. Most of these people don't, so—" Lan Haarper made a sound of disgust, then toyed with his roll of tape. "You'll do well if you're patient and don't get killed."

Seated, the man made the half sofa seem almost an ordinary chair. If he felt shame at the room's incompleteness or a discomfort so near the open glass doors, it did not show in his body. His mind was still inaccessible. Wraithlike for all his bulk, to Kalm he seemed constantly on the verge of dissolving.

*How does Kylene put up with this?*

"Yes." Silence followed, Kalm grimacing while lan Haarper waited impassively. "Uh . . . I'm here on work, anyhow."

Lan Haarper raised an eyebrow. "How is that?"

"The Hand of the Queen wishes to see you. I brought a message from him."

"You've met the Hand?"

"No," Kalm said, reaching into an interior pocket. "I went by headquarters to see if they had an assignment for me just as they were looking for a courier, so I volunteered."

All of which was true. Uncomfortable with the sensation, he hurried into other admissions. "There's scuttlebutt you've hurt the Hand's feelings by not enrolling. He seems to have a lot of questions about you." He smiled awkwardly, not hinting at the effort he had spent to make lan Haarper seem no more than an unimportant soldier to the Hand's son. *And to the Hand also.*

"Gertynne ris Vandeign speaks well of you."

"Oh?" Lan Haarper raised an eyebrow. "Haven't met him."

"Uh, you did. That night in the inn. He says—" Kalm decided to skip over that remembrance. "I think the Hand wants to offer you a commission."

Lan Haarper's jaw moved slightly. It might have been a smile. "Tough."

Lan Haarper had intended to enroll, Kalm remembered, rather than be conscripted into the militia, but it was not a matter of open knowledge. Kylene had opposed it. He was not sure why, but it seemed unconnected with whatever mission lan Haarper had, since he had given in to her. "It seems the local lord—Merrn?"

"Merryn. Ris Vandeign."

"Merryn, then. He's been telling ris Andervyll there weren't any soldiers in the town. And then it came out, you'd asked for a troop-training job several years ago and been turned down."

"The Hand's pissed," lan Haarper suggested, smiling again.

*Suspicious, actually. He wonders why the Vandeigns are secretly keeping an Ironwearer and how good that Ironwearer is.* It was not necessary to say that. It was not necessary to explain how he had steered the facts through channels of gossip to the Hand or guessed beforehand how the queen's uncle would react to the news. Kalm snapped his fingers, then held out the letter. "Here it is."

"Let's see it." Lan Haarper was unenthusiastic but methodical as he stripped wax and cloth from the parcel. When done, he slumped against a corner of the couch and read silently.

The Hand's letter was lengthy, and Kalm quickly tired of watching lan Haarper. He had other reasons for discomfort, he realized. "Uh, do you have a toilet here?"

"Room over there." The redhead waved without attention.

*I listened to your hearthsharer last night,* Kalm thought, staring at the walls of lan Haarper's bathroom, rehearsing a speech he would never deliver. *She was looking for things to occupy her mind so she would not cry, and I listened to her thoughts because she was thinking of you and feeling pain. And I didn't find out a thing, because all she could think about was her twisted heart and her loneliness.*

*But I was sorry for her. And you were with Wandisha again.*

*But I've buried your time machine so you can't get it, and*

*you're helpless. You're weak and helpless and ordinary, even
if you don't know it yet, and someday, when I know all your
secrets, I'll destroy you. For her sake and mine, I'll destroy
you.*

He flushed the toilet and returned to the living area.

Lan Haarper had not noticed his absence. Unobserved,
Kalm smiled tightly and waited, enjoying the man's frowns.

Finally the big man snorted, putting down papers. "War is
drivel." Kalm waited, but he made no other comment. By
accident, his eyes drifted to Kylene's colored panels. His face
became somber. Kalm watched in turn, waiting for actions to
show what lan Haarper thought.

"Kylene's stuff." The man had noticed the observation but
misread it. "A part of it." He waved a hand, still frowning.

"Her *paynning*," Kalm agreed. "She did some on the
coach."

Lan Haarper hesitated. "Not likely. *Sketching*, perhaps."

"Yes, *sketching*. She said she was doing *sketching*." What
was *sketching*? Kalm wondered.

But the redhead changed the topic. "How do the troops
look?"

"Just troops," Kalm said. "Most are regulars, but they've
been in garrisons a long while. Most of them haven't seen
much combat, and they have a lot of new recruits, but they
ought to be all right. The militia is something else."

The local militia would need a lot of officers; it would need
a commander. Ris Maanhaldur had almost reached the nerve
to ask his father for it.

"The Midpassage troops." Lan Haarper spoke matter-of-
factly. "That's what I wondered about."

Kalm felt air move as he waved his hands, and when the big
man rose and crossed the room, he smelled a not-unpleasant
odor that must have come from lan Haarper's body. "Militia.
You know."

Lan Haarper looked away from him, staring out the window at his yard. "I don't know. I've heard the men in town
will be enlisted for the campaign, but that's it. No drills. No
officers. No uniforms."

They'll be butchered, his expression said.

Kalm agreed with that. "They need some work."

"Andervyll wants them dumb, so they'll make shock
troops." The bare name of the Hand spoken as lan Haarper
had said it seemed close to insubordination.

*Ris Maanhaldur's opinion also, but some things the Hand won't tell even his child. A good way to get some glory— we've all told Dighton that.* "I wouldn't know."

Really, it was not an important secret.

"You're a junior officer." Lan Haarper made it seem an excuse for any ignorance.

Kalm remained silent, watching the man scowl. Had he discovered yet he could not escape in his time machine? *Ris Maanhaldur will command me, after I work his nerve up; I'll command you, lan Haarper. If things go as I plan.* Almost, he felt a touch of sympathy.

"*Dammitalltohell*," lan Haarper said softly, hammering gently with a fist at the windowsill as he repeated the alien word. "You going back there now, Algheran?"

Kalm stood. "Yes. Do you have a message?" *What defeat are you going to admit to the Hand, Ironwearer?*

Lan Haarper sighed unhappily. "No, I'll just go along with you. I'd better see some people. That letter—officially I'd be under Merryn, as an adviser, but the Hand wants me to take charge of the militia."

Then he smiled at Kalm's expression. "Cimon only knows what I'll have to do to train them."

Kylene

# CHAPTER ELEVEN

"*You look very nice, dear,*" the woman said insincerely, her fingers under his neck touching the cords that fastened the man's tunic. "*No soldier will look better than you.*" In the background, disbelieving children watched from a doorway.

"You look very nice, dear," Kylene repeated, tugging gently at Tim Harper's neck cords, then straightening his collar to make the tiny crossed swords show to advantage. "No soldier will look better than you."

"*Gawd 'elpussall,*" Tayem said, turning to inspect himself against one of the atrium's glass doors. "What do you really think, kid?"

*Baritone*, she decided. He was a baritone tonight, if just only, and thus in good health and good spirits for his silly exercise. Sickness or depression made his voice huskier, turning him to basso, she had found. Reflexively, she probed at his mind, unsurprised when she failed to find it.

*Teepblind. Someday I'll be able to see his thoughts even through that mesh on his head. Meanwhile . . .* There were several long hairs on Tayem's eyebrows that refused to lie flat and needed to be cut or pulled to improve him, she remembered, but in his present mood he would ignore the suggestion.

Her father had been much more docile. Self-sufficient Tayems were difficult to manage, she admitted wryly, though usually she enjoyed the challenge. Perhaps she should be grateful that he was not a telepath and aware of his supervision.

Baritone voice versus bass—was it through such clues that Normal women managed their men? And lies?

"It's an ugly uniform," she admitted. "Couldn't these people do any better for you?"

"Afraid not." Harper slapped at the baggy brown pants he had received that afternoon and smiled wryly at the gap between their ends and his feet. "Last come, last served. We're lucky Wolf-Twin could get us uniforms in one color. If Merryn had started this thing before he did—"

"Then you wouldn't be commanding it." Curiously, he took pleasure from that fact. She would not have been happy if he were only another soldier in the ranks.

"Well." The man looked around the unfinished living area, an unreadable expression on his face. "If you call getting one order out of two sort of obeyed, commanding."

"It's what you wanted. Isn't it?"

He grimaced. "Ask me after I've done this for another three days. Ask me this time tomorrow." He coughed deliberately. "He that outlives this day and comes safe home will stand tiptoe when this day is named. He that shall live this day and see old age will yearly on the vigil feast his neighbors. Old men forget; yea all shall be forgot, but he'll remember with advantages what feats he did that day. Then shall our names, familiar in his mouth as household words—green-eyed Kylene, mud-streaked Timmial, Dieytl and ris Vandeign, Wolf-Twin, Styllin and ris Clendannan—be in his flowing cups freshly dismembered. We few, we sloppy few, this band of druthers!"

"You don't think so, huh?"

*He's happy here*, she realized. *It's not just Wandisha. This town. This house. The people. He's happy.*

He shrugged. "Well, who can say? How's everyone else doing? They all ready?"

"Their wives are all telling them how good they look in their new uniforms."

"And all thinking . . ."

"Yes." She smiled at him, sharing that piece of humor.

"Probably all of them telling their husbands not to track mud into the house when they come back."

She counted. "Three of them did, two intend to. The rest of them know the effort would be wasted."

Sense intruded into the levity, and she went to sit on an arm of the couch and stared at the man evenly. "Most of them would never notice, actually. This place is squalid, Tayem."

"It's no worse than what people normally have, kid. You've been spoiled the last couple of years, that's all."

"Who spoiled me?"

"Me." He turned a hand in the air, one of his standard guilt-averting gestures. "I like opulence, too."

If it had been true, she would have found a way to use it on him. Kylene sighed and patted the back of the couch. "It's still early. That Ironwearer, that other Ironwearer—"

"Wolf-Twin."

"Wolf-Twin won't be ready to lead your battalion out for another quarter of a watch."

"He's slow," Tayem grumbled, but he took a seat beside her and put a warm arm loosely around her waist.

"No, you're in a hurry."

"To show off my fancy new uniform."

"Hmm huh." She leaned against him, and bit by bit his hold tightened. But that was only reflex, without meaning or promise. Long minutes went by in silence.

"Do you like it here?" Kylene asked eventually. It was a careful question. She had seen memories in him that Tayem did not recall. She did not think she should mention them.

"In some ways." He moved his head until it nudged hers. "It is primitive, squalid if you like. I don't like the lord and peasant stuff. But there's a kind of optimism that hits me here. There are people in this town who remember when the Algherans found the first set of Plates, back when everyone was poor and illiterate. And now they have the Plates, and they're building. Just as fast as they can, as well as they can. It's—" He shook his head. "I like watching it. Onnul would have had a field day, dissecting it."

Kylene froze.

"Sorry," he said, reading her stiffness. "Didn't mean that." His voice was glum.

*How can I criticize him?* Kylene asked herself. But the

world seemed flatter, less colorful. She brought herself upright on the arm of the couch.

"Would you rather be back in your era?"

It was not a serious offer, she knew. It was only an attempt to keep a conversation going, a pretense at curiosity.

"Yes," she said flatly. "I'd be worth something there. I'd have a husband. Maybe several husbands, and men on the side."

"Uh." His arm dropped from her back.

"What do you want me to say, Tayem? It's a stupid question, and you keep asking it. Am I supposed to be happy here? Am I supposed to be happy because I can clean your house and wash your clothes and act like a child playing a grown-up because that's all you want from me? Am I supposed to be happy because you tell people I'm your wife, when everyone knows that Cimon-taken blind bitch is with you every night?"

"I'm sorry." His voice was low.

"You're sorry?" She squirmed away to keep him from patting her back. "Don't you think I'm sorry, Ironwearer?"

"I'm sorry." She heard pain in the words. "Do you want me to quit it?" She heard him swallowing. Did the silly name mean so much to him? Yes, it did.

"No. You're stupid, Tayem, but you mean well."

"Such an endorsement!" He snorted softly.

*"Good-Housekeeping-seal-of-approval,"* she said to please him, and patted at his shoulder. "This has to end someday, Tayem."

"I know." He swallowed again. His head straightened, and watching him, she knew that he was looking at one of her paintings. "That was the whole idea, Kylene. We work together, and when we're done, we get on with our lives. If it got complicated—"

"If we had sex, Tayem?" She rummaged her memories for words he had infrequently used. "If we got *fucked* together and you *laid me*?"

"Kylene."

"Well. That's the complication you're so afraid of, what you and Wandisha do every other night."

"Thought you people weren't interested in sex." Which was half justification, half complaint.

"Isn't Wandisha?"

"Uh-hh." Harper rubbed a finger over his chin. "You know,

I don't know. Maybe she's a special case, or . . . It's been her living, so . . . I don't know."

*Poor blind Tayem.* "She wants to be loved."

"Oh." He sighed. She expected him to say, "Dumb of me, I made a mistake." But he surprised her. "Sometimes, kid, you meet someone and you think you can fall in love. So you try, and it doesn't take. And when two people are trying . . ."

"Why her?" she asked. *Why not me?*

He understood. "I keep hearing love and sex are so special for most of you telepaths. You get married once, and that's it. Even if—well, just once. I know, when I came to Alghera— there was a man I really admired."

It was not an opinion to argue with, Kylene realized, but she wondered if he had ever mentioned it to Dieytl Ian Callares. Or Wandisha. Or even to his cow-faced Onnul.

She temporized. "So?"

"So you are beautiful and nice to talk to and comfortable to be with, and sometimes I think I have to run away to avoid yanking you into the sack. And you're very, very young, and you have centuries to live after I'm gone. I won't spoil your life, kid."

He rose and slipped into a jacket, then picked up a pack. "Time I got going."

She wanted to kick him.

She kicked the door instead, when he was gone, and threw things of his that would break into the fireplace.

**Kalm**

# CHAPTER TWELVE

*K*alm woke in darkness, bound, hearing whispers all about.

Slowly his panic receded. His hands were unfettered. Bedding was jumbled about him on the loft floor of a small barn. The accusing voices in the background were wind and creaking straw under other restless soldiers. The lump beneath his neck was clothing. He was not in danger.

Facing the nighttime black, his heartbeat gradually slowed. His breathing eased. He listened numbly to whispered conversations. Triangles, lines . . . shapes formed in the darkness. Understandings.

Midpassage. Merryn ris Vandeign's barn. Alone, in the midst of the Queen's Own Puissant Guards Regiment of the Strength-through-Loyalty Brigade. In Loprit. He had found Timmial lan Haarper.

Success. Kalm peered wide-eyed at wooden uprights and knew he felt no triumph. *Tagin. That scene in the field. When I was a boy. I was dreaming of that. Of her.*

Why had he dreamed of matters long past?

*I wanted you to.*

It was not his own thought.

Who? he wondered, struggling to sit up. Two Teep women, a man—were there other Teeps in Midpassage?

Something like memory brought an image of a thin, dark-haired woman. *Me.*

Kylene lin Haarper.

With that identification, the image faded. Kalm was left listening to the noises of nighttime and his heart, but he continued to sense her presence. *Where's your fake husband?*

He felt anger. He had made her mad.

*Sorry. Where's your straying husband?*

*He'd like that pun.* The thought seemed to mollify her. But her mind closed before he could extract useful information. Stealing horses, she had implied, but the image was unclear.

*What do you want?*

*You were unguarded. I wondered who you were.* Her thought was diamond-clear now, unemotional, with none of the overtones of meaning and remembrance that the words should have born.

*Kalm ha'Ruijac.* Behind his mind screen, he mastered irritation. *The man you talked to on the coach. You knew that. You didn't have to wake me.*

*You were vulnerable asleep. Where is she now, that woman?*

*I don't know.* It was the truth. *It was a long time ago.*

*Afraid.* Kalm saw an image of himself cowering. *You think of her often.*

She thought Tagin was a contemporary, he noticed. He could speak of her without revealing to Kylene the true circumstances.

*Too much,* he admitted. Candor seemed the best defense, a brittle protection against remembered emotion. *She wasn't for me. Even if—no. She wasn't for me. Teeps and Normals don't fit together romantically.*

*Afraid. You should have—* The image changed to a man and woman standing face to face. They were of equal height; the man was a slimmer, idealized version of Kalm. *That!*

Kalm smiled wryly in the darkness. *What would I say to her?*

*I have no idea. She was your problem.*

*It was years ago; it's not a problem now.*

Seconds passed while Kylene digested that idea. Kalm yawned, then propped himself up on one elbow. *How was her love life?*

*But you could have tried.* Kylene's intruding mind had returned.

*I didn't want to try.* Kalm sighed, sensing from the silence that that explanation would not be enough. *She made her opinion clear. I didn't have any business arguing with her.*

*She was with someone else. You interrupted; she got mad. It wasn't really aimed at you. You're simple.*

Kalm's jaw dropped, but the woman was not really there to be shouted at.

*Now you're funny.* Her cool thought was contemptuous.

*Part of being vulnerable and simple,* Kalm admitted dryly, rancor departing as he realized the unimportance of lin Haarper's good opinion. What time was it, anyhow? He heard wind, or whispers that might be wind, and water trickling outside the barn, but no purposeful human sounds. It was fifth watch perhaps, and dawn was nearly two day tenths away.

Dawn. The day promised interesting events. And paperwork.

One day on active duty and he was already falling behind. Lord Clendannan's requests for supply caches that must be established south of East Bend, routing orders for the battalions of the regiment, invoices and receipts for local supplies, authorizations for seizures of metal, payment to the Midpassage innkeeper for the damages to his dining room, termination papers to be filled out for the dead Gerint ris Whelmner, dismissal orders for his friends and a letter of apology to the man's father for Lord Andervyll to sign, purchase of the additional medical supplies that Gertynne ris Vandeign insisted upon. There seemed not an area in which Cherrid ris Clendannan did not involve himself, and there seemed never to be enough time to accomplish anything. *And I thought he was taking me on because I impressed him somehow, but either of the Ironwearers probably would have put anyone he could get to work.*

"Captain, take a note. Make three copies."

"Captain, lead up the guns and charge that paper!"

"Captain, sit without squirming!"

"Captain, sprinkle that mud!"

But administration was army work as much as fighting. Kalm felt neither surprise nor dismay at the tasks he had been given.

And today would be different. Lan Haarper would make it different.

*You're ignoring me.* Lin Haarper was piqued.

*Sorry. Thinking. What are you doing up so late at night?*

*Things.* Her mind screen dropped into place, but not before he glimpsed confusion and sexually tinged embarrassment. *Nothing. I was just awake.*

Kalm probed, meeting metal-hard resistance beneath small girllike pouting. *Things?*

*I was alone, that's all. I was just thinking. I was waiting for Tayem to come back.* Yet there was more, which could not be withheld from another Teep and which honesty compelled her to admit. Thoughts. Sensations.

*Masturbating. Even though you aren't season-taken.* He was incredulous. *That's no better than what Wandisha does.*

*I was alone.* She could not conceal that, either. She was alone—which meant forgotten-ignored-unwanted. But the reference to Wandisha had annoyed her.

Amid her anger and embarrassment, Kalm suddenly noticed other sensations no longer disguised: darkness, humid heavy air pressing on exposed limbs, the rustle of wind past an ajar skylight—the same wind that fell upon the barn and the sleeping soldiers inside and out—smooth sheets and the tiny complaining noises an empty house made at night, eyes and face heavy with sleeplessness and unwept tears, and the lingering memory of unsatisfying physical pleasures.

The impression was a constructed one, he realized. The woman's thought processes were predatory; what he saw within her mind had been placed there deliberately for his inspection.

She wanted sympathy.

She was manipulating him—as Tagin had. Just like Tagin.

*I don't care,* he transmitted to her, feeling his own temper rise. *Your complaint is with your husband, lin Haarper. Don't bother me with your unimportant personal life.* And he had to add, *Not for me.*

*Never for you. Of course not.* Pride and pleasure in the rejection accompanied the words; Kalm understood that he was supposed to see them.

*Better proud and unhappy with him than happy and comfortable with someone like me, eh?* In the darkness, Kalm snorted, then settled on his elbows.

*He's a man. You're a boy.*

A lie, Kalm noticed without surprise. *So?*

*Better unhappy with anyone other than you. You're unattractive. Ugly and nasty.*

*No one likes me, lady. I'm used to it.* Kalm yawned audibly and shifted his shoulders about, determined to find comfort that he could display to Kylene lin Haarper. *Go away and let me get back to sleep. I've other things to do than listen to old truths.*

*Not yet. I want to learn things about you.*

*I'm ugly, nasty, simple, and sleepy. What else do you want?*

*You sought Tim.* The thought seemed impatient.

*Yes.* Suddenly cautious, Kalm attempted to strengthen his mind screen. Wind blew; the drumbeat of leaves against the wooden roof increased for a moment, and he imagined rain. He pictured water in sheets running down the inclined side. *That's what we need for tomorrow,* he commented. *What do you know about him?*

*Everything.* Images filled Kalm's mind: Timmial lan Haarper sleeping, nude, smiling, snoring softly . . . making love with a violent, frighteningly mindless passion on a narrow bed, careless of the blood flowing from reopened wounds on his body as Kylene gasped and wriggled beneath his weight . . . frowning tensely as he dressed in a green tunic, the faded scar on his temple plain in the early morning light . . . patiently shaping Kylene's hair with scissors as she directed him . . . beside a bed, reading children's stories aloud, deliberately making his voice squeak and rumble to amuse Kylene and displaying an obscure pleasure in the activity that neither telepath could identify . . . sitting at a small desk and staring idly through a small window, disordered papers before him . . . kneeling to push sticks into an outdoor fire . . . falling from a horse, pain and surprise upon his face as an unknown assailant struck at him with a sword . . . *See? I own his life.*

Reality or daydreams? Kalm withdrew from Kylene's mind to contrast the memories with what he had observed.

*He doesn't seem to know it.* The thought was too cruel to transmit; he held it back but displayed enough that Kylene could see its presence.

*That's because—* She tightened her mind screen suddenly, so Kalm perceived only wariness. Then that impression vanished.

*Where's he now?*

Kylene did not answer. Deliberately, Kalm resurrected one of her memories, substituting a smooth-faced and serene Wandisha lin Zolduhal as lan Haarper's partner in lovemaking for a guilt-ridden, suddenly timid child. *Is that where is he now? With a woman instead of a little girl?*

The blast of anger he expected did not come.

Time passed, and still Kylene did not return to invade his mind. Kalm sighed softly and lowered himself back onto his disheveled bedding.

How much reality had Kylene shown him? How much was hope so revisited as to seem reality for her? Did it matter?

No. The woman was unimportant, and her petty secrets were unimportant.

But she had annoyed him. Deliberately. He would find a way to punish that.

Eventually he got back to sleep.

# CHAPTER THIRTEEN

"*Spotted them, sir.*"

It was early morning. Outside the barn, the world had tilted downward into blue and white skies. Inside, lights had been turned on to accommodate the waking men, but the interior was still dim. Kalm suppressed a yawn and strained to make out the features of the sergeant who had reported. "How many?"

"Can't say yet. I thought—" The man stopped, his face impassive. He had obeyed orders, he had no reason to explain himself to civilians, and in his mind recently commissioned aides-de-camp were still civilians.

"You were right," Kalm said hastily. Then he hesitated, unsure whether ris Clendannan should be woken. The Midpassage Battalion had left the town in middle night; Rahmmend Wolf-Twin was to have left lan Haarper and his men at least ten thousand man-heights distant; it was inconceivable that they had already returned. Stragglers, perhaps; men who had turned back; innocent travelers . . . Those possibilities were all more likely than the arrival of lan Haarper and his men.

But the old Ironwearer's orders had been clear. "Go find out," Kalm told the sergeant. "I'll wake the Ironwearer." *Three-tenths of a day gone already. Seven to go.*

"Sir." The sergeant saluted sloppily, then turned away, his

mind showing confidence that the regiment would soon be
properly commanded.

Kalm dressed quickly and went to awaken Cherrid ris
Clendannan.

"Lan Haarper's spotted, sir. Maybe," he said tersely when
Lord Clendannan was sitting upright on his straw. Covertly, he
tried to shake pain from his right hand's fingers. He had
pinched ris Clendannan's foot to wake him; the elderly gentleman had kicked him even before coming to consciousness.
*Next time I have to wake an Ironwearer, I order someone else
to do it.*

"Which way?"

The small cell was windowless and its overhead lamp had
been left off, but a crack in the wall of the barn admitted a
white stripe of light that bisected the outside corridor.

It was a veterinarian's work area. Kalm made out shapes of
gray and black: the loose straw piled on the concrete floor, ris
Clendannan's erect torso, the knee-high feed trough and hand
pump fixed to the far wall. The man's face was still a blur in
the gloom, but he seemed wide-awake. He was a nobleman of
Loprit; Kalm saw no evidence in his mind that he felt any
incongruity in sleeping in his uniform on a stable floor.

"No good report yet, sir. I'm waiting on another signal.
Still on the road, I suspect." Moving over countryside, lan
Haarper and his men would travel more slowly. The battalion's early appearance justified his conclusion, even if Kalm
had not already confirmed it by probing the thoughts of the
inner signalmen.

The men from Midpassage were still five thousand man-
heights south of the town, too far for him to examine their
minds, but spotters placed along the road and hilltops were
using flags to transmit their observations. Relayed this way,
messages could reach ris Clendannan's command post at Merryn ris Vandeign's barn within minutes, long before horsemen
could cover the same distance. The scheme was not as fast as
mind-seeing or as accurate; it would be good enough that he
need not worry about revealing his talents by accident.

"Check on it." Ris Clendannan rose to his feet easily. "No
sense waking the men till we're sure." His stomach growled.

"Yes, sir. Er, the cooks are setting up, sir."

"Are they, now? Well, check on that report, young man.
Then you can eat." Ris Clendannan smiled frostily at Kalm's

frailty as he swung the pump handle. "By the way, is there something wrong with your hand?"

"No, sir," Kalm lied. "Just a gesture."

"Oh." Water began to flow. Ris Clendannan dampened his hands below the spout and slapped his face, concealing an unhappy frown. *Clumsy young pup, by all looks*, his thoughts ran. It was most disappointing to find that one of the brigade's youngsters had woken him with impunity. "Well. To your duty, Captain."

Kalm had a long time to wait.

There were no other telepaths in the Guards Regiment, but none were needed. Once contact with Ian Haarper's force had been made, the action followed with a dreadful inevitability. Signals from the hilltops, cavalry messengers endlessly arriving and departing . . . Kalm began to see ris Clendannan as the spider at the center of an invisible web of information and Timmial Ian Haarper as the innocent invading fly. Telepathy gave no advantage in this phase of warfare. That was a sobering thought.

But it still took time. Midmorning had been reached before the full form of Ian Haarper's attack was clear.

The time traveler's force was in two prongs. One company of the Midpassage Battalion was moving along the great road from the south, seemingly ignorant of the purpose of the cavalrymen who charted their progress. A second company traveled parallel to them, two thousand man-heights to the east; trudging through fields and forest trails, they would arrive at Merryn ris Vandeign's barns long after the first force had reached the bridge over the Bloodrill.

They were companies only by courtesy; the first unit mustered barely fifty men, and perhaps thirty were in the eastern force. Accompanying water carriers from ris Daimgelwn's regiment almost outnumbered them.

More than three hundred of the Midpassage men lingered behind them. In ones and twos, the stragglers limped along the great road. Two thousand man-heights from the bridge, they were stopped by one of Rahmmend Wolf-Twin's referees, then transferred to Ian Haarper's lieutenants and grouped into packets to be sent forward to reinforce the attacking prongs.

The whole thing was hopeless, Kalm realized, analyzing reports from the cavalry videttes as they came in. The Guards

Regiment had nine hundred men available for duty. Even allowing Ian Haarper's men to be hit twice rather than once before they were removed from the contest would not reverse the odds.

Besides, the long hasty march had destroyed the Midpassage Battalion as a cohesive unit. There was no chance now that Ian Haarper would capture the barns from the defenders.

*A debacle.* Remembering Ian Haarper's bold claims two days ago, he almost felt pity. *Save it for the local men. They're the only ones being hurt by his egomania.*

"We'll send 6th Platoon forward now." In the background, Kalm heard ris Clendannan's voice, firm, methodical, experienced. "Establish contact, then hold."

A platoon was to move forward, across the bridge, to engage the leading element of the Midpassage Battalion at a distance. *A sensible decision*, Kalm agreed. *Meet them early and wipe them out as they come. Get the misery over with.*

Replacements would be needed to fill the hole. Anticipating commands from ris Clendannan, Kalm reached for writing paper and began preparing orders.

"No problem." The stern-faced commander of the 7th Platoon seemed surprised that ris Clendannan had thought it worthwhile to send a staff officer to observe his operations. "We've had some losses." A wave of his hand indicated reclining, grinning men waiting under the apple trees. "Mud pies, for the Lord's sake! The men weren't taking it seriously at first, you know."

He chuckled. "Finally, I told them we were going to do a lot better than the 6th, and there'd be extra KP duty for anyone getting hit, and that sobered them up a bit. Joke's on me, now."

Kalm grinned back, pleased to see a fellow professional at work. "Could have happened to anyone. Where are they now?"

"Other side of the river, over there." The lieutenant gestured with unconcern. "That fence is in the way, but you see those beehives by the bridge? They're in that direction."

"By the road?" The man's memories were unclear.

"Near it. Too much grass for you to see anything, but they're there. They were closer for a while, but we borrowed a squad from 8th Platoon and shoved them back. Just mud pies, you know, but it sure got them to run." He laughed again, untroubled by the drying circles of mud that spotted his arm and midriff. "We ran out of ammunition. And that's when I got mine."

He spit. "Cimon-taken rabble. I mean, we're supposed to be on the same side, and those people just run away. Cimon only knows how they'd react when they meet real opposition. It makes me ashamed, you know? Who wants to defend anyone so hopeless?"

"Nobody." Kalm let his eyes move around the orchard, counting men in the distinctive dark blue uniforms of the guards. Almost a hundred. Preoccupied, he missed the next thing the man said. "What?"

"I said, tell Lord Clendannan they have an advantage. You have to hit them twice—try explaining that to the men—and with those uniforms, it's hard to see if you've hit them once."

"Aren't the referees watching for that?"

"Yes, but—" The lieutenant abandoned his alibi. "I guess it wasn't important."

"Sure," Kalm said amiably. His concentration was still fixed on the men wandering through the apple trees. "What about the ones you 'killed' out there? The Midpassagers?"

"The referees said they could go home. They all had sore feet. And they wanted to wash their hands before they pissed."

Kalm shared the chuckle. "You didn't get a count?"

"No. Does it matter?"

"Just being curious. Where's that squad from the 8th?"

"Still out there, I expect. What's left of it." The lieutenant snapped his fingers. "Not my worry now, is it?"

"Still mine, though." *And five-tenths of a day to go.*

"Yeah." The lieutenant spit again. "Don't worry. Plenty of us left."

"Let's move 10th Platoon behind the 7th. Have them take extra mud balls. Put the 12th into the orchard." Midday had arrived, and ris Clendannan's voice was unchanged. Merryn ris Vandeign's office having proved too small, a work area had been laid out for him in a corner of the barn. Quickly drawn maps had been placed on boards lying on trestles. Tables taken from the inn served as writing desks. There were chairs from the same source.

Kalm, left with Merryn's office and Merryn's stool, listened with admiration to the invisible voice, contrasting the real Ironwearer with Ian Haarper's mimicry. But his own work had to be returned to.

"Seemed they were falling back again." The messenger from the 2nd Platoon sounded unconcerned by the presence of officers. Streaks of mud plastered the side of his head. His hands were clean; Kalm had been in his mind as he washed them in a barrel of drinking water.

"What shape were they in?" Kalm asked.

"Hard to tell. Pretty fair, I guess." Unwitting admiration filled the soldier's voice. "We saw just three or four, you see, and there was this man they were carrying, so the lieutenant said just go out and finish them off lightly to make it official and let them through, and so we did and they all started running, so of course we had to follow, and—well, you see."

"I see," Kalm agreed dryly. "Three or four of them." He stepped out of the office and stared skeptically at the group of soldiers by the open barn door. A pair of them had the wit to appear embarrassed. Their sole prisoner, a thin local man named Pitar Styllin, grinned without concern, a chicken leg in his hand.

"I figure it was the ones in the trees. I mean, we hadn't thought of that. If the lieutenant had said we was . . ." The messenger had followed Kalm, but his voice tapered off.

*Six for one.* Six elite soldiers of the Queen's Own Puissant Guards Regiment for one corporal in the Midpassage Battalion. Lan Haarper's useless Midpassage Battalion.

Kalm swallowed. "What is happening now?"

"Well, the lieutenant said he'd like reinforcements. Sir." The final word sounded like a plea.

"What if I can't give you any reinforcements?" Kalm asked wearily.

"Well, the lieutenant thinks he can hold on. He'd—he'd like some orders. Since our captain got it, we've been—"

Kalm ignored his other words. "Your lieutenant thinks he can hold. He's not attacking?"

"No, sir. Not until— He'd like orders."

The soldier before him had left his unit an eighth of a watch before. An equal time would pass before reinforcements or orders could reach the 2nd Platoon. Half a day tenth then, with Ian Haarper's eastern prong free to move wherever it chose.

*Cimon!* Kalm went back into the office, where ris Clendannan would not notice the questioning. "How many men in your platoon are left, soldier?"

"About twenty," the man said. "When we left, it was about twenty. And we had a squad from 4th Platoon; the people left from 4th Platoon, that is."

"Thirty," Kalm suggested, looking out the window. "Thirty of you." From a hundred.

"Maybe a bit less." The soldier seemed worried. "Can we get some reinforcements?"

*Wash your head and go back as your own reinforcement,* Kalm thought wearily.

*Don't say that,* a cold thought answered him. *If you cheat, Andervyll will hear of it.*

*I didn't say it, lin Haarper. I wished I could.*

*Don't wish, either.* Kylene laughed ogreishly.

"Sir?" The soldier frowned. "Another thing. Could we get some food?"

"Food?" Kalm tore his mind away from lan Haarper's maddening wife and returned his attention to Merryn ris Vandeign's cramped office. "Mess is—"

"Yes, sir. But the platoon, I mean. We haven't had anything to eat since morning. Sir."

Kalm lowered his head and sighed. There was no way to transport food to the troops in the field, and if the 2nd Platoon was hungry, all the platoons would be hungry. And the water carriers would be hungry.

How had he forgotten that?

Easily. No one had expected the fight to last this long. No one.

No one? Kalm sighed again. "There are apples on the trees."

"Sir?"

One of Wolf-Twin's roving referees stepped into the office at that point. "You're a casualty, soldier. Go wait in the orchard with the others."

In the early afternoon lan Haarper and ten of his men attempted to cross in small boats from the western side of the Bloodrill to the docks behind the inn, then retreated as the 9th Platoon lined the banks.

While ris Clendannan's men taunted the would-be invaders, blanket-wrapped men stormed the bridge, knocking over the beehives that had been moved there two days before.

Amid the confusion, they roamed happily through the orchard, indiscriminately throwing mud pies at previous casualties and untouched troops. When they were eliminated, most of the 9th and 12th platoons were gone with them.

Ris Clendannan moved the 11th Platoon into the orchard, leaving the clover field unguarded.

What was left of the 2nd and 4th platoons were retreating.

Cursing soldiers of the Defiance-to-Insurrection Regiment, bossed by Wolf-Twin's referees, eventually got the beehives upright again.

Midafternoon. Three-tenths of a day to go.

"Sorry, sir, I didn't count." With two Ironwearers and other officers staring at him, the soldier fidgeted.

*Couldn't count*, Kalm saw. Even in a world where literacy was uncommon, it was an embarrassment to be unschooled.

He turned toward ris Clendannan, watching from his work area with the remnants of his lunch about him. "Maybe ten more, sir. It's a guess, but there are that many of the 7th Platoon still unaccounted for."

*If it's just the 7th. If he's—*

He did not want to complete that thought.

It was bad enough that Ian Haarper had deliberately kept back prisoners before releasing them to the referees. Kalm's tabulations had been incorrect most of the day because of that.

Ris Clendannan's troop movements had been based on bad information—Kalm's bad information.

He swallowed. Lan Haarper had been under Nicole's cloak. By accident, by constant activity, he had kept Kalm from seeing his plans and countering them.

*The Lady's cloak.* Only that. It had not been a failing of telepathy. It was not his fault.

Still, he wished he could hide.

"You've learned what you can from this man," Terrens ris Daimgewln said coolly, raising a wineglass. He was a tall man with thinning hair and a narrow face. Army rumor described him as able but a looter; Kalm's probes could only confirm the latter, but the wine ris Daimgewln had brought to share had come from his own estates. "Dismiss him, Captain. Bring in the next."

"Sir?" Kalm looked at ris Clendannan. "I checked. The other men weren't any better."

*A nice trick*, the elderly Ironwearer was thinking, contemplating his own use of Ian Haarper's stratagem in future campaigns of his own. *If we had done something of the sort in '02, we could have had Vrect ha'Dicovys dancing till—* He waved a hand, seeing Kalm's impatience. "Let him go."

Kalm repeated the gesture. The soldier left.

"I'll call in one of my men," ris Daimgewln said, dabbing his lips with a cloth. "They can get a good count for you."

Ris Clendannan looked at Rahmmend Wolf-Twin.

His eyes closed, the dark Ironwearer waited, thinking, then shook his head. "I'm not going to allow that."

Wolf-Twin had slept for a watch after returning to the camp, and it had taken great effort to awake him. Even now, Kalm found, the squat mercenary was a strange mixture of awareness and lethargy. But he would do his duty—what he felt to be his duty—to ensure the fairness of the contest.

Curiously, Wolf-Twin was hoping that Timmial Ian Haarper would win. Ris Clendannan, in his estimation, would be a better strategist in the coming campaign if such a shock restimulated his ability.

Had that bias affected his decision? Kalm looked but could not find it.

Wolf-Twin was drinking water, not from abstinence but from a refusal to accept a gift from a man with ris Daimgelwn's reputation. Involuntarily, Kalm remembered the first time he had met the man, in another world, pouring glasses of water.

*There's the real Ironwearer. Ris Clendannan, Ian Haarper, others—they're only copies. All the legends, the ideas we have in my time about what Ironwearers were—it's all based on Wolf-Twin. And no one remembers the real man.*

*Lord Cimon, you are not fair.*


"What do you suggest, Captain?" Ris Clendannan's voice was still serene as he joined Kalm at the map table. A napkin was in his hand; he dabbed at his lips gently. Ris Daimgelwn was gone, returning to paperwork in the camp. Rahmmend Wolf-Twin had been roving among his referees but had returned during the last tenth of a watch; now he was snacking on the remains of ris Clendannan's lunch.

"I don't know," Kalm admitted honestly, wondering how much he could explain without revealing himself. "It's too late now, sir, but we shouldn't have let them wear those dark uniforms."

"Why is that, Captain?"

Wasn't it obvious? Kalm wondered. "It's hard to tell if they've been hit, and since they have to be hit twice, it—it gives them an unfair advantage."

"Not one they requested." Wolf-Twin's eyes, looking at him, were peaceful, but the blubbery lips were pursed.

Kalm swallowed, wishing the Ironwearer would look else-where. "Yes, sir. But—and another thing, though, it's hard to see those uniforms in the woods, and when it gets dark—"

"Blue will be hard to see in the dark, also," Ris Clendan-nan commented.

Kalm turned back to the older man with relief. "But you wanted to get all of them, didn't you, sir? Make them all prisoners?"

"I thought I could, Captain." The elderly Ironwearer raised an eyebrow, then nodded slowly. "It's not necessary, though."

"No, sir." Kalm could not conceal his disappointment.

"How does the situation look to you?"

Kalm swallowed, then moved to the map table and began speaking, hoping inspiration would come to him. "We're still holding them. 2nd and 3rd platoons are still at the edge of this forest. 2nd Platoon is actually the 2nd and part of—"

"I know that." Ris Clendannan was suddenly testy.

"Sorry, sir. 5th Platoon was told to fall back on the right, to stay linked to the 6th. I assume they have."

But that was only belief without knowledge, Kalm admit-ted. The map here that had seemed so detailed meant little to the men in the field. For them, the landmarks were tall oak trees and stone gates on roads that did not show on the map. The fields were without direction lines or convenient labels; the distances they marched and countermarched were unmea-sured. It was impossible to find equivalences between the lo-cations on the map and the confused images in the minds of the soldiers.

Once again telepathy had failed him.

"1st Platoon is still beyond the bridge," he continued. "Consolidated 1st Platoon. What's left of the 8th, 10th, and 12th platoons are on the riverbank. And—" Nothing was left. He stared at the map glumly. "I guess we can hold on, sir." *Two day tenths to go.*

"You see no problems?"

Kalm licked his lips. "It's getting dark, sir."

"I see that, Captain." The Ironwearer spoke impatiently.

"Yes, sir. It's just that . . . well, I think it's possible that some of the men—some of the men who aren't out of it yet, I mean—some of them may be thinking about going off and . . . They're hungry, sir. And everybody knows the Midpassage men got fed—the referees let their wives take baskets out to them. So they'll—"

"Desert us, you mean."

"It's—" Kalm shook his head slowly. "It's a mud pie fight, sir. They'll think—"

"They are thinking, you mean." Cherrid ris Clendannan was unsurprised.

"So I'm told, sir."

The Ironwearer chuckled. "We won't notice it, will we?"

"Sir?"

"Eh? They'll be back, Captain. As you said, they're hungry. But they won't want to lose, either. They'll sneak off to mess, but they'll be back; it'd take a miracle to keep them away."

No miracles were involved, the remnants of Kalm's reason told him. The fragmentation of the Midpassage Battalion ensured that lan Haarper had an endless stream of reinforcements to assist him. It was the Guards Regiment that had no reserve.

*It was not fair*, he thought in distress. *They know this territory better than we do. They have better uniforms for this than we do. They have food left, and we don't. The women are helping them and not us. The Midpassagers cheated, and I couldn't stop them.*

Who would have guessed that lan Haarper would instill near-Algheran persistence in his stupid little battalion?

"Anything else?" Ris Clendannan smiled, pleased with himself for creating Kalm's surprise. "What would you do, Captain?"

"Consolidate the 2nd Platoon and the 3rd," Kalm said carefully, pointing at the map. "Pull them back to this field."

"A field? How is that better than grass?"

"Uh." Kalm swallowed, his attention and vision elsewhere. "It's a squash field, sir. The map says—"

The elderly Ironwearer blinked. "Squash?"

"Uh, yes, sir. Squash. A plant. It grows close to the ground, so—"

"So they'll have some visibility. I understand. Thank you, Captain. You may write orders to that effect."

"We—we're short of messengers, sir."

"Then you'll have to go give them yourself, Captain." Ris Clendannan was already turning away.

"Uh-hhh." Kalm swallowed. "Sir, while I'm gone, you won't let any women move around this area, will you? The barn and—"

"Women?" The Ironwearer stared at him.

"Uh-hhh. I think—" Kalm thought furiously. "We have maps lying out. They can hear what we say. They might find information and pass it on to their—"

Ris Clendannan smiled tolerantly. "I think that's pretty far-fetched, Captain."

"It's a possibility that occurred to me, sir.'" Kalm pretended that he was not being looked at like a village idiot.

"Rahm, were you listening to this young man?"

"No, sir." Ironwearer Wolf-Twin turned from his snack. "What was it again? Something for the referees to worry about?" He smiled, bits of rabbit meat showing on his dark lips.

"Warning me about hostile women." Ris Clendannan chuckled. "Thinks they're going to attack at the center of our strength."

"Just an idea," Kalm said.

"Take no prisoners, sir," Wolf-Twin said. He laughed along with ris Clendannan, silently, his body shaking.

"It was just an idea," Kalm said sadly.

*SPR-OOONG!* something said, low-pitched, in the distance.

*Splat!* That sound was nearer. And *splat!* Dust spurted from a dirt lane between two fences.

"Missed me!" A man danced beside the nearer fence, waving his arms loosely at the forest and the opposite end of the field. His features were invisible in the twilight.

*SPR-OONG!*

"Get down, fool!"

Kalm ducked, then slipped to his knees beside the nearest body. Five men . . . Ten . . . Fifteen . . . Sixteen.

Sixteen men. Three platoons at strength should hold a hundred and fifty.

"Who's in charge?" he whispered. "Where'd I find him?"

"No one's in charge." The man beside him did not turn. A pile of mud balls lay before him, fist-sized, drying. Mud had caked on his hands and the sides of his uniform. Watching

him, Kalm thought that he looked like a man in combat rather
than a man playing a game. Staring across the field at invisible attackers, the soldier mechanically pushed a thumb far into
each of the balls and filled the holes with pebbles. "We got no
officers left. Unless—"

"I'm not a replacement." *I'd be useless here*, Kalm admitted. But that did not have to be put into words. He hesitated,
wondering what he should say.

*SPR-OONG!*

"Get away from me." The soldier did not raise his voice. If
he had noticed Kalm's rank, it had not entered his mind.

"How long has this—" Kalm waved a hand. "What is
this?"

"Half a tenth. Catapult. We think they have three of them,"
the soldier said wearily. "Get away from me."

Catapults, throwing multiple mud pies at a distance an ordinary arm would not reach. A child's toy. *No one told Ian
Haarper he couldn't use children's toys.*

Kalm wanted to giggle. Instead, he cursed.

"Yeah." For the first time the soldier looked at him. "We
didn't expect it. Surprised us good. And you get hit, it hurts.
Made our water carriers call it quits."

*So they won't be advancing*, Kalm realized.

It was all right. Ris Clendannan had been correct. If it was
not possible to destroy Ian Haarper, it would be enough to
defeat him. The plans did not call for an advance, just for
holding till midnight. "But you can hold here?" he asked.
"They haven't advanced for a while?"

*SPRR-OONGG!*

"Need the trees," the soldier said. "They do. We should
hold." After a moment, his eyes went wide. "Oh, shit."

At the far end of the field, men were stepping from the
forest. They were in groups. It took two men to carry each of
the great forked stakes.

"Look, can I go back?" Kalm asked. "Lord Clendannan
needs me. I promise not to get in the fight, but—"

"Nope." The Requisitionary Corps private poked Kalm's
chest in the center of the drying mud. "You're dead, man. You
aren't going to do nothing."

"But just for a while, so I can—"

"Team Leader Wolf-Twin said we let anyone get away like
you are trying to do and he finds out, he'd have our balls."

"But I know Team Load—Ironwearer Wolf-Twin and—"

"I know him, too. You just wait, Captain." The private laughed happily. "Only got a day tenth to go."

The end came in the orchard, under a gas lamp hanging from an apple tree.

"No sour feelings, Ironwearers?" Wolf-Twin asked.

"None," lan Haarper said. "It was a dandy fight while it lasted."

Outside the circle of light, Kalm watched and sneered. Lan Haarper had made a farce of the contest. None of his jokes would have worked on a real battlefield, and no one would ever attempt to use them. He had used unfair advantages. He had cheated.

What could have been a valuable training exercise had been wasted to feed the man's idiotic ego. Even now, Teeps throughout Loprit were recounting the silly story to each other, and the local correspondent for Leiman and Scee was prancing about the town bragging about the account *he*, instead of a regularly accredited news agent, would write with lan Haarper's assistance.

The Hand of the Queen himself had requested a tour of the mock battlefield and was chatting with local peasants in the crowd like an ordinary spectator at a sporting event. Kalm knew he had lost a large sum betting with Gertynne ris Vandeign on the outcome, just as he knew that the younger ris Vandeign would not have been able to cover a loss.

It was not the only bet that had been placed. Dieytl lan Callares in particular radiated smugness, and Kalm was glad that neither of the Lopritian Ironwearers had gambled on the contest. They at least would not have to confront the smarmy Teep.

Men in dresses, arm in arm with Wandisha lin Zolduhal, danced suggestively through the crowd, spurning sham advances from soldiers in uniform. Shamefully, some of the latter were from the Guards Regiment.

Elsewhere, brown and blue uniforms mixed with apparent amity. Men were gesturing at each other and jabbering loudly, much like the local women, but there had not been any fights yet. A handful of officers were trying to preserve decorum and keep the soldiers with their own units, but with little success.

Children were stealing apples from Merryn ris Vandeign's

trees even as the man watched tolerantly. Everyone involved was being very noisy.

"I have regrets," ris Clendannan said firmly.

"Sir?" Timmial lan Haarper had the presence of mind to act contritely.

"I was warned." The old Ironwearer sighed and pointed to Kalm. "He worked hard, and he wants a line commission. You should find a spot for that young man in your battalion."

Lan Haarper looked toward Kalm. "I'll consider it."

Kalm held his breath, knowing that in the middle of the crowd, lan Callares and Kylene were both watching him and both waiting to speak themselves. Lan Haarper's expression had not been friendly.

Ris Clendannan *tck*ed. "The young man said we should worry about local women stealing information, and we laughed at him. We didn't expect to have our little fortress stormed by women, let alone by men in women's dress."

Lan Callares relaxed. Kylene relaxed.

Kalm relaxed.

Wandisha, uncaring, kicked her feet higher, satisfied by outdoing the laughing soldiers.

"Sorry about that," lan Haarper said. "It did work, though."

"That isn't what I regret." Ris Clendannan touched the drying mud on his forehead and chest. "Now it's over and you've won, I'm just sorry I was attacked by women I wanted to defend myself from."

Wandisha

# CHAPTER FOURTEEN

$S$*he had worked hard that day, nearly a ten-day period after* Timmial's mud pie fight. She had earned the coins she had made, even, she suspected, justified by her deeds her existence on the one Earth for one more day. She was tired and in need of rest and not pleased when Ian Haarper moved from hugging her to stroking her body.

"Pretty girl," he crooned, rubbing his palm along the outside of her thigh. The other hand was just above the small of her back, holding her tight against the too-warm press of his chest and legs. "My beautiful girl."

Soon he would rub his chin against her shoulder, move his hand from thigh to waist and side, then move so she must rest on her back in the narrow bed. Leaning over her, he would ask what she thought of while his fingers massaged her breasts. He would stare happily through the darkness at her, before his mouth dropped upon hers. Later, wet-tongued, he would lick the oozing moisture from her taut nipples as his hands stroked her stomach, and his knee would push between her thighs, knowing that she would move her legs apart for him. He would do all this desirously, inadvertently, innocently—demandingly.

That was his pattern. Each man had his pattern, which must be accommodated if she was to please him and ensure her livelihood. She had learned Timmial's pattern, which he imagined was pleasing to her. It was kinder than most, easier to endure than most, and easier for her to feign satisfaction with than most.

She had been stroked on the buttocks that day by a man wishing to use his daughter and kissed between her legs by a man yearning to repeat a wasted boyhood experience.

"Daddy, Daddy," she had said to one. "If we have lots of time, can we do the things you and Mommy do? Just for fun?"

"Women don't understand men," she had told the other, speaking gruffly, pulling at him crudely till he was erect. "They're weak, stupid, too direct. I do what I can, but real men need other men for real satisfaction."

They were all valued customers. It was her work. And they would be back, for she was good at her work.

She did not want Timmial to be another customer, did not wish to return to her work when she was with him.

"I'm tired, dear," she said softly, inoffensively.

"Too tired?" He was still stroking her thighs.

"Hold me," she whispered. "I'd be so happy to have someone just hold me."

He shifted so she was above him and hugged her mechanically, his gestures already showing knowledge that this was the deepest contact they would share that night. "Sure," he told her, his voice flat. "It's been a long day, and I'm pooped also."

"I love you, Timmial," she whispered when the silence had lasted too long. *Please, love me.*

He patted her shoulder in response, then pulled the blankets up to her neck with his free hand, half-asleep, thinking she was asleep.

A short time later his hands were motionless, limp upon the surface of the bed. Asleep, he was gentle, vulnerable, his mind wandering in the wilderness of unconsciousness.

Wistfully, Wandisha pulled her blanket to his shoulders, twisting it so that a corner fitted over his outsized feet, then lay on her side, her back against his arm so she could feel his warmth without discomfort. She would never explore Timmial's mind, never view his life except through proxies, never understand the scraps of knowledge she had gained.

*"I need five, need five,"* sounded from a dark box by the ceiling. *"Enemy intrusion near the ceramics factory. I need*

*five." A popping sound followed, then static. Conversations resumed. Men in green and black uniforms moved through the crowded room.*

"Five," *a tall, red-haired man said in a low baritone. He wore mottled black and green; crossed swords glinted on his collar. He was kneeling, rubbing dice between his palms.* "I'll go with five." *He snapped his hands apart, spilling the dice onto the wooden floor.*

*One, two, and eight. Eleven.*

"Damn." *He did not translate. Currency was in a pocket on his left side. He opened the flap and drew varicolored notes out, scattered them on the floor, then stood, the leather creaking in his high boots.* "Dammitalltohell," *he added reflectively.*

"Eleven." *A man squatting on his left had taken up the dice and was shaking them now.*

"Ha'Ruppir! You going?" *Fingers pushed at the redhead's right shoulder. He turned slightly to stare at a young black-haired man.*

"Harper." *He shrugged, his shoulders reaching the height of the youngster's ears, then glanced around the mesh-lined room. Two volunteers had already passed through the triangular opening in the back wall. He had no thought of following them.* Pressure seals in place of buttons, carrying straps on the back to tote off the bodies. Different from what we had, but a uniform still looks like a uniform after ninety thousand years.

"Ha'peer," *the shorter man echoed. He shifted his weight nervously.* "I wondered if—I mean, someone said—uh . . ."

"Next call," *he said, watching the dice being scooped up by the next man at the circle.*

"Oh, I thought you had been—"

"Quarter watch to go," *the redhead said, turning his attention back to the tumbling dice. He patted his side pocket impatiently. At the far side of the room, two men in green uniforms went through the triangular doorway. Stale alcohol smells filled his nostrils.*

No smoke, no weed. They don't have those vices. Don't even chase women much. They still fight wars. That's human enough.

*Four, two, four. The man across from him slumped.*

"Uh . . . I was thinking," *the youngster said.* "Maybe if you, I mean if you didn't mind, and if it's only a quarter *watch, so maybe—someday I could do you a favor if . . ."*

*Dice rolled. Seven, two, five. A man exhaled loudly.*

*"I mean, just this once," the brunet said.*

*The redhead knelt again. "You from Dicovys?" he grunted, not looking back. One roll and the dice would be his again.*

*"Minursil, but my Sept—"*

*"I don't owe any favors."*

*"Just this one time," the young man promised. "That's all. I mean, when your Sept was—"*

*"Nicole, cover me. Fifteen. Fifteen. Uh, look after these other guys too, Lady. Thank you. Fifteen."* Complain to Borct, kid. He's running the show. Turn left at the freeway, go back sixty miles and three thousand years.

Make him give me back Onnul Nyjuc while you're at it.

*Five, five . . . The last die tinkled to a stop. A six was on top. He smiled mechanically as his hand went out. "Tough shit."*

*"Ironwearer?" the boy said plaintively.*

*"Six. Come on, baby, six." He shook the dice mechanically, then watched silently, his hand still outstretched, as they clattered over the floor.*

*At last someone nudged him. He shook his head, noticing what he had rolled, and paid in his stake. He remained there, on his knees, pretending interest until the dice came around to him once more, then left the circle. The boy from Sept Minursil had gone away by then.*

*Outside the building, the sky was black. No moon was present, and haze hid the stars from him. Shutters covered the windows of the Settlement buildings to make them seem deserted, and none of the other Algheran Agents was visible. He had the nighttime to himself. From habit rather than need, the redhead touched his scalp for reassurance that his Teepblind was securely anchored, then closed his eyes to acclimate them as he walked, opening them only when he thought himself near the wall that ended the courtyard.*

*Less than a quarter watch to go, he reminded himself, leaning awkwardly with his elbows together on the too-low wall. In minutes, his brief liberty would be up and it would be time to go back to the war.*

*Back at the Station, it was possible to joke about duty tours.* Everyone who went to the Present returned, it seemed. Almost everyone. A war without risk, created by the savants of the Institute for the students of the Institute. Algheran technology and time travel were making war boring.

Here, at the Present, men died. Many men.

The night was warm. He had not needed the short cloak he customarily wore, and it hung limply across his back, no heavier than a woman's arm. He sighed, looking past the wall toward small bushes with roselike flowers. *Someone's garden, he thought, viewing in his imagination a woman tending to the blooms with shears and watering can as a child tugged at her skirt. We took it away from them.*

*We still find children's toys here and there.*

*There would have been explanations for the former residents, he was sure. False ones, with no mention of time travel, but convincing enough for the unwary Algherans. Perhaps the men who explained to the tiny farm community the necessity for abandoning their home had even believed the stories they had repeated.*

*Cover stories. Lies.*

Progress. *Surrounded by mind readers, the Algherans had managed to reinvent duplicity.*

All the comforts of home. *He smiled helplessly.*

*It could not be helped. The Settlement was too near the battlefront of this moment, and for six of the seven years of the war it had been in Alliance-controlled territory. The Algherans who had once lived here would never return unless the Agents who occupied it now were successful.*

*But the flowers remained. That was part of life also. He squinted, trying to remember the names Onnul had once told him. Lilacs, lilies, asters . . . No, none of those.* Onnul. My beautiful, blond chorus girl. If we had wandered on the Esplanade and she had pointed them out to me . . .

*It had never happened. He had never shared a summer with Onnul. She had named some flowers as part of his education, that was all. Had she cared for such things herself? He could not remember, and if he had ever noticed, the memory was gone now.*

*As Onnul was gone.*

I'll get her back, *he vowed.* No matter how often they tell me she never existed, I'll get her back.

They were Ian Haarper's images but not his dreams, not his memories. They were thoughts within him, forgotten, hidden, which Kylene had found but not brought to his awareness.

Meaningless scenes. But what Kylene beheld secretly was exposed to other telepaths. Wandisha had seized this scrap and come no closer to Timmial.

*I could be gaining wealth now*, she thought wryly, conscious of all the exhausted men seeking solace from uncomprehending wives after their daily travails with Timmial. *If he wasn't leaving them too tired for anything which would justify payment. If he weren't exhausting himself also.*

Kylene had watched the man exercising that afternoon, hesitant, waiting to be noticed. She was ignored at first, then dismissed while lan Haarper concentrated on his machinery. The dismissal had been without harsh intent, Wandisha knew, though Kylene had not seen it that way. *So young, so easily injured.*

*So frustrated and lonely.*

*Also, so afraid and stupid.* Kylene's memories showed a time when lan Haarper had been helpless and dependent on her. She had been unwilling to use her advantage, fleeing instead to an older man uninterested in sex after she became season-taken.

*If she had remained and acted sensibly . . . if she had done many times what memory shows she tried once . . . She would have owned him; they would have been happy.* Kylene had understood all that, and yet lan Haarper had been alone for years. Wandisha wondered when the girl would realize her cruelty.

*Normals treat each other that way.*

Lan Haarper's arm moved, and she reached to pat it softly, confident that he would feel her touch without waking. Despite his desires, he had been too tired for anything but hugs and silent companionship recently, and she had given him that, she knew comfortably. *Mine.* She had filled part of his need—and hers.

No one had needed her before. It was a pleasant feeling, a sort of warm internal swelling, though she expected it could grow tiresome eventually. She wondered how long it would be before Kylene recognized that also.

*Never, perhaps.* Sometimes she felt a bit sorry for the funny little girl.

Content with being Wandisha, she turned her head to face the town, though it was not necessary. With a part of her consciousness she could never explain, she looked again into the lights of other minds.

Kylene was out there. And Dieytl. And Kalm.

He did not want to be here. Sleep before another wearying day of Ian Haarper's drill, thought about which man in each of his squads could be trusted with one of the precious rifles, even more foredoomed speculation about Ian Haarper's intentions—they would all be preferable to the girl's sullen temper.

*If she cared, or had any liking . . .*

A pointless wish. Kalm saw in her mind he would never be more than a backdrop for her self-absorbed obsessions. He could be her audience but no more. The knowledge was implicit; she had spent no time thinking of him.

He sighed, looking about Ian Haarper's desolate unfinished living area, beyond the bare wooden floor and walls at Ian Haarper's shabby little town. Then his mind shield rose as he noticed Wandisha's attention.

*I'm his problem.*

It might have been thought. It might have been dream.

Wandisha slid into sleep by Ian Haarper.

Another dream . . . She stood ignored on a wooden floor, watching the men talk, uncaring as the lonely words floated past her. It was only a make-believe conversation anyhow, no more convincing than her make-believe marriage.

Lantern light made the room visible, throwing brightness here and there, while shadows darkened the corners. The kitchen, Tayem's study, the exercise room, the bedrooms . . . the uncaring world itself—all that was around her was empty and dark.

She was unloved. Undeserving of love. Unwanted.

Her hand kneaded an arm of a couch, feeling once-living skin. It was cold, strangely alien, unused—another of Tayem's purchases.

She stared at the men, then moved around the couch to make them notice her. She was in a dress. They stared back at her legs and calves, then upward. She felt a faint satisfaction. But when she was silent, they turned away, looking at the shadows, and resumed their meaningless speech.

One was Kalm, of course, the chubby, too-familiar Kalm.

Irritated privately as he often was, he was forcing politeness upon himself before a man he disliked. The other—

Knowledge of the other man whirled upward from the center inside the center that was she. Uncertainly, she rubbed her bare foot across the floor, rolling a tiny piece of dust back and forth.

In Lopritian terms, he was a nobleman—rich, proud, self-loving, and conscious of his importance. Yet even to her inexperienced eye, he was not a terribly attractive man. A hand-length taller than she, thin, dark-haired, narrow-faced, and young, he had eyes that held adolescent anger, uncertainty—hunger. In his mind, memories were pain-filled but blurred. As he twisted about, avoiding Kalm's restrained disdain, his eyes glanced over her figure, away, then back. He avoided her face.

*Peasant*, the glance said. *Attractive*.

She was flattered by that assessment, even in her all-filling unhappiness. Abstractly, commenting only to herself, she realized that fear held him from direct attention to her. Like Kalm. But Kalm's attention was nothing she would ever want.

This man—boy— She sensed anger seeking fulfillment, lust seeking satiety. And danger—not just from him—that might be manageable.

No. She inhaled, feeling breath expand her chest, knowing that his eyes focused on her breasts, enjoying his attention, pleased by Kalm's sudden edginess. No?

*You feel* . . . Kalm's thought faltered as he sensed her reactions and exposed them to her. She felt sluggish, her arms heavy and unemployed, her legs weighty and immobile. Her body seemed centered at an apex on which she focused despite embarrassment—her groin, the warm unused depths waiting to become part of Kylene.

*Season-taken*. That was Kalm again, cool, somehow triumphant.

She flushed, embarrassed by the accusation and because the men had noticed her confusion. But only Normals deceived themselves about thoughts. She had no choice but to follow hers through.

*Only thoughts*. They had to be accepted, even if they frightened. Yet it took an act of will.

*He's attractive, Kalm*.

*"Attractive."* Is that all? He projected contempt/wariness/anger.

She was silent, thinking.

Love. Rejection. Recovery. Love. It was the cycle of existence for all, Teep, Normal, and unborn unknowable races of the future. Yet life transcended love.

*I am young,* she told herself. *It would not be fair for my life to end here, with him. If only he had loved me—*

*I am alone. As all of you have been alone. I would be doing nothing that all of you have not done. I am—*

*Kylene Waterfall.*

*I was of the valleys. I was of Clan Otter. I was Edgart's. I was Samtha's. True-born daughter . . .*

Yes. The decision took forever, and no time at all.

Yes. Of course. How could it have been anything but yes?

*I won't even like him if—*

But it would be exciting. Through the numb, neglected loneliness that filled her, the sharp blade of welcome danger approached.

The choice was made. Yet she waited, unmoving, as Kalm sent the man away. She had seen his mind. He would not go far.

By then, Wandisha was again in the darkness between dreams.

She had not moved since the door closed. The door latch wiggled. Up. Down. Up.

It would not be Kalm again. It would not be Tayem.

She stared at the latch, waiting, hoping, fearing.

*It will not be Tayem.*

The latch fell and moved no more. She heard footsteps, moving away from the house.

When she reached the door, the space before it was empty.

*Send him back,* she screamed mentally at the waiting Kalm ha'Nyjuc. *Find him. Tell him there is nothing to fear. Send him back.*

In Wandisha's dream, a Teep wept.

Alone still, wounded and ignored, as Earth slept under the blanket of night, she had retreated to bed. Beneath the covers, she raised her knees and rubbed at herself, trying to revive the pleasure she had felt in the past, but it was not the same. Sex. Sensation. Only sensation—and she knew at last that that was all Tayem had received from the women he had known.

She shared his loneliness.

She had never been closer to him than at that moment, never understood him more, never felt more love for him. Unsatisfied, she was happy.

Far, far away, she heard the door latch jiggle.

"Wandisha?"

The voice brought an end to dreams. It was morning.

"Wandisha?" There was concern in his voice, caring. Almost love.

In memory, she relived a final dream: She was watching herself through another's eyes, feeling herself walking in another's body across a cold floor to a bed in which she lay sleeping. Fearing, anticipating . . .

Walking, her body was familiar and strange at the same time, oddly weighted and balanced. She felt an awkward tension in her arm reaching for unrecognized bed covers, an uncomfortable strain pulling them back with thumb and ring finger. She was in a man's body.

She should be waking. To please him.

*Dream. This must be a dream.* She felt—remembered?—a heart thudding, breath rasping through a dry throat, a hand pushing at flesh. Pushing at her body.

In the dream it was her body he prodded, his thick fingers falling suddenly at her groin, and pushing at her inexpertly as she pretended sleep. She grumbled in her dream, turning sideways, but the fingers followed, hard, insistent, and tangled in hair. The bed creaked as he sat beside her. She felt his hip pressing at her thigh, bare skin rubbing against skin. She sensed his nervousness and his frozen smile.

She was tired by then, nearly asleep, and washed in disappointment that would not be dispelled. "Away," she complained. "No!"

He slapped her, still smiling.

Before she could react, he clamped a hand over her mouth and pulled back on her hair to expose her bowed neck. "Keep your mouth shut!" he hissed. "Or I kill you. Understand? You understand?"

Not till then had she understood his intent. Stunned, she could only stare at his silhouette.

He bared his teeth, breathing hard. "Yeah. You understand. Now put your hands under your butt and don't move 'em. Do what I say. Kalm said you were very, very good."

"Go away." She summoned her dignity. "I don't want you now."

But her voice was a whisper. When she realized that, she tried to move away.

With a fist, he hit her belly, cursing.

She was motionless, ignoring the pain and sensing that he would hit again and again if she argued—and sensing that she wished to be hit.

"You understand. You understand." He repeated it constantly as he rubbed his palms over her, then fitted himself between her legs and pushed at her painfully, unsuccessfully. He was surprisingly heavy. Her nostrils were filled with the metallic, unbathed reek of him.

She squirmed, and he moved his thumbs to the base of her neck, pressing at her throat, choking her. "Stay still."

"Don't," she gasped when he released her. "Hurt."

As a response, his hand moved between them, his fingers poking at the lips of her genitals, stretching. "Come on, bitch. Kalm said you wanted it."

She sensed rage. Contempt. Seeing whom he hated, she panted, her breath rapid. She shifted awkwardly to accommodate him. "Yeah. Let me." Her fingers moved, opening herself for him and stroking him.

*Hurt him. Let me hurt him!*

Unnoticing, he pushed himself into her. There was pain— pain, pressure, then tearing. It eased at last.

His body moved. She felt nothing.

She would be bruised tomorrow. And she would worry about it tomorrow. She was bleeding, she realized when he withdrew, not understanding why till she saw the knowledge in his mind.

Blood—a victim's evidence. Fear, suffering, obedience: he was powerful and pleased with his creation. He stopped, lying on her, and put his hands at her sides.

The position was awkward. Before she could realize his intent, he pinched her with both hands. She gasped. Smiling, he shifted his hands upward and pinched again. And again.

There were images in his mind to show her what he expected, the words of protest she was to say, the motions of resistance she was to make that would restore his erection.

Mechanically, she obeyed. Her heart beat rapidly.

"Yeah, bitch!" he whispered, not understanding. "This is what you wanted!"

It was. She hated herself. It was.

This time she wrapped her legs around him, making it better—for him.

Finally he was done, collapsed, weak, lying on her, warm and clammy skinned. He seemed vulnerable, trusting. Unsatisfied still for some reason, she put a hand to his sweat-streaked face, then hugged him impulsively.

"Shouldn't." He was stiff and awkward, lying beside her with one hand hanging loosely behind her back, one lightly resting on her hip. But she heard other words behind his words, saw other images in his thoughts, and felt in his mind and body the silent demands he would soon turn into orders. Obediently, she tightened her hold on his neck and pressed against him, finding warm, unexpected pleasure in the contact.

He mumbled something and tried to look at her, but his breath was foul. She turned her face downward, rubbing her forehead against his shoulder and stroking his side as she had done in the images she had seen. Obeying impulse, she kissed his neck, feeling contentment and time-defying satisfaction.

His hands tightened on her. She fondled him, feeling him stiffen once more; she felt his heart pounding as his breath grew loud; she felt tension tearing at him.

"He'd kill me if—" He was grinning, his voice a whisper.

*Yes, he will.* She pushed against him again, feeling melded into the man, breath with breath, pulse with pulse, half sharing and half enjoying his fear. "I won't tell anyone," she murmured, panting and swaying against him. "He'll never know what . . . No one will ever know. So good if . . . You and me. No one will know."

For this moment, the man was hers. Her slave. Her captive. If that was different from his own feelings, it was unimportant.


"Wandisha. You okay?"

*A dream.* She hated herself for remembering it, for lying there and reliving its pleasures. Then she shivered, entering wakefulness with a man beside her. *Only a dream.*

"Wandisha? What's the matter?"

She sensed motions, air currents. Outside Wandisha it was

morning, and there would be light. In the darkness that was always about her, he would be leaning over her, looking down.

She heard—felt—his breathing.

"Stay with me," she murmured. "Don't go yet."

"What's the matter?" he asked again, slipping into her arms.

She laughed softly, protectively. "Just dreams, Timmial. Scare away my bad dreams."

Timmial

# CHAPTER FIFTEEN

*At summer's end the sun rises grudgingly.*

Scant light came with the chilly morning air that roused the man on the floor pallet. Still half-asleep, he pushed a hand under a pillow of discarded garments, then pulled it back to the blankets. With his head tipped, he could see the gray square that was an open window. His left hand moved slowly, to touch the fingers of the nude woman sleeping at his side. Cautiously, so she would not be disturbed, he edged closer and rested his head between her shoulder and chin.

Only when ready for the ordeal did he extricate himself from the bedding, and he closed the parchment window while half-dressed, trusting his fingers and habit to align the seams of his clothing in the darkness. When he was done, he knelt to kiss the sleeping woman on her lips and eyelids, then stepped quietly around the upended crates that served her as furniture. He ducked his head deeply as he went through the doorway. Hidden beneath his bulky jacket, the sword insignia on his shirt collar were cold against his neck. A jagged scar was visible on his left temple, just under the thin mesh that rested on his red-brown hair.

At the foot of the outside stairs he turned left, walking stiffly and scuffing his boot soles across hard brown earth in the shadow of the barn. His hands were pushed into his pants pockets, his shoulders hunched up as if to guard uncovered ears.

No lights showed yet from the dark buildings on the hill-sides ahead, though far to his left a thin line of campfires traced ther river's course. Nearer at hand was a low mound to show where a soaking pit had been dug. Tree-trunk shapes waited sullenly for the daylight that would give them a golden glow, but only enough sun had appeared to melt the night stars into invisibility; another watch would pass, perhaps two, before the icy lace that fringed the puddles had melted. He coughed, spit morning phlegm onto the ground, then headed across the fields to home, tracking dark streaks across the dew-silvered clover.

As he walked, he whistled softly. The tune had once been known as the "Colonel Bogie March."

Kylene was asleep also.

She lay on her right side on the low bed, her back to a window, her legs curled. One thin hand held her blanket tight against her shoulder. Black hair made a fan on the white sheets, a single strand running across her freckled cheek. Her breath was even.

There was nothing that needed to be done for her. Harper patted uselessly at a fold below her knees and left the room.

Visible through the open doors that faced the atrium, Kalm once-ha'Ruijac sprawled over a couch in the next room, co-coon-wrapped in a drab blanket, his mouth open. His head had fallen from a bolster onto a brown-uniformed arm, cover-ing the rank patch of a junior officer. Harper grimaced to control his feelings while imagination showed the man rising to enter Kylene's room, Kylene's arms, Kylene's . . .

He made himself continue tight-lipped across the court-yard. Kalm was an unwelcome guest, but if Kylene did not object, he had no reason to complain about the man's too-frequent appearance. It made sense in a way: two young peo-ple, unattached, without local roots, and already familiar with each other from that coach trip. Perhaps he could manufacture some liking for the man someday. But he doubted it.

In the kitchen he stacked kindling mechanically in an al-cove, then opened vents to the outside. Kylene had carelessly let soot build up on the fire enclosures, so he scraped off cake from the quartz covers with a wooden spatula before hanging them in front of and above the stacked coal. A double handful of timber shavings went in next, then one sulfur and phosphorus match, no different from those used in his era, sufficed to start a fire. When he was sure the flames would last without his attention, he left to bathe.

The bath reservoir was at middle height, the water within it tepid. He had hoped to find it hot, but this was not the moment to feed a taste for luxury. Harper filled the tub from the cistern and sprinkled it with a miser's pinch of spice before climbing in. A few days hence this might seem the acme of hedonism, he realized, scrubbing his back with a bar of coarse soap. *Assuming I last till then.*

Pack straps had rubbed skin from his shoulders yesterday despite extra padding. Wincing, he rubbed dabs of cortisone cream over the raw spots. There were still a few tubes left, he noticed, but not enough to be comfortable. His First Era medication was running low. Another tie loosening, he noted uneasily; another step into exile.

He found his bedroom dark and musty. The housetender should have swept and mopped the floor recently, but enough grit was under his feet to irritate them. Harper opened shutters, then wiped his soles on old garments before dropping them and his wet robe onto the bed for Kylene to notice. *Remind her to send the bedding to the laundry woman,* he told himself. *Any time today will do. Or tomorrow.* He would not be spending the coming night at home.

Tacked up by the window was a sheet of heavy paper. It held a charcoal sketch of a man's face, squarish, with thick brows and a vertical scar that crossed the hairline. The head arched backward, chin outthrust, with thin lips made to protrude by passion. A water spot smudged the line of one jaw. The crumbled drawing had been in Kylene's workroom days ago, lying near a corner, evidently discarded. He had unfolded it from curiosity on a morning much like this, then taken it away without comment. If Kylene had missed it since, she had not mentioned it.

He was still damp, so he jogged in place a few minutes before opening his clothes cabinet, then dressed in jeans and a plaid shirt. An exploring hand discovered hair in need of a comb, but he settled for patting it down to cover the silver mesh on his scalp. Moccasins completed his wardrobe. When would he dress so comfortably again?

He permitted himself a detour before returning to the kitchen, to stop in the room that once had held his laboratory.

This was Kylene's territory now. An easel stood by the south window, covered in muslin to protect the canvas beneath from dust and inexpert critics. Brushes and narrow spatulas soaked in his dissolving pans, small phials of paint and unidentified cans usurped his storage shelves, and a hammer and triangular scraps of wood lay at one side of his workbench. His carefully tagged branches and metalliferous blooms she had discarded, not even preserving a few for still lifes. Blank canvases tacked to wood frames leaned against one wall, some faced with an undercoat of white paint. Completed portraits and other works were propped up in a corner to dry after varnishing. Harper moved to the easel and lifted the muslin.

A blond man, lanky and disheveled, was crumpled to his knees by a gravel-strewn creek. Blood rilled down his neck and one arm, a crimson stream dripping from an open palm to spread pinkly in the water. One hand was on his black-vested breast, a knife hilt protruding from between the fingers. Fear and surprise had made his mouth an O and closed his eyes to slits. A sword paralleled the bottom of the frame, far enough from the man that Harper could not judge whether it was part of the scene or some cryptic comment by Kylene.

*Grim*, he thought unhappily, looking at the still incomplete work. Most of Kylene's paintings had been based on real experiences; this one, so obviously imaginary, was troubling. *Reaction to Wandisha? She's been acting erratically most of the last week, almost as if season-taken. I need to talk to her and tone her down, but—*

Kylene wasn't eager to talk to him.

*Kalm, though—maybe she's trusted him, or will someday.*

No. Without reason, he sensed that Kylene and Kalm held secrets from each other. There was an embarrassing comfort in the thought.

Meanwhile, his head shook as he stood before the painting. Some ringing note of familiarity was attached to that scene or that figure, something tantalizing he should recognize and know completely.

But as ever, he failed. Defeated, he lowered the muslin.

He was ladling out batter when Kalm came into the kitchen.

"Have a seat," he said gruffly. "Hungry?"

The ex-Algheran yawned. "Not especially. Maybe a bit."

"Not the right answer." Harper patted pancakes with a ceramic spatula while behind him the smaller man pulled a bench to the serving table. "Now's the time for packing on the fat and starch, so I made extra of these, in case anyone woke up early. Use the tongs to put a couple on an eating plate. Spread butter on top, then pour on syrup—the brown fluid in that wide jar. Cut them up and eat them."

A clatter indicated that the smaller man was following directions. Kalm spoke after swallowing, in tones showing uncertainty. "Very sweet. What are these things?"

"Something I picked up a while back. *Pancakes. Flapjacks.*" Harper flicked his wrist with near expertise, taking pleasure in his skill but making sure that this time batter did not stick to the hot center of his quartz griddle. "Either name will do. An old recipe, except that I'm just using the whites rather than whole eggs. For some reason, Kylene keeps breaking them open and taking the yolks."

Kalm mumbled inconsequentially. Then he spoke more clearly. "Nice morning."

"It's okay." Harper stepped backward to look through the closest window. He saw glistening earth under scant grass, dappled by brown and yellow leaves, and a bare elm tree backed by a hedge. *Octoberlike. Or is it still September? God! Are we really marching tomorrow?* "It's an okay morning. You feeling ready?"

"Oh, sure," Kalm said. "How's Wandisha?"

Harper shrugged. "Fine. How's Kylene?"

The ex-Algheran waved an arm negligently. "Fine also. We spend less time together than you seem to think."

"Pity. She going to bear up being alone, you think? If it's necessary?"

Kalm lowered his spoon to snap his fingers. "Why not."

*Because she's not used to any of this, you idiot.* Harper yanked his spatula across the stove top, freeing pancakes. "Just wondering." For a while he was silent, busily stacking pancakes on a wood platter. "Sometimes I wonder if . . . maybe if Wandisha moved in while—"

"Never suggest it." Kalm was curt.

Harper nudged the salt block, making room for his platter, then sat on the bench. "Afraid of that. But—oh, Cimon!"

"Cimon," Kalm agreed flatly.

"I got myself into this, didn't I?" Harper asked of no one. "And yet, I don't know . . . What do you do? You know?"

"Wandisha will be all right, lan Haarper."

The big redhead sighed. "Are you sure?"

"Yes." The younger man smiled reassuringly. "She got by before she met you. And right now . . ."

Right now, an army was in town and Wandisha was taking coin in through every orifice, Harper thought sourly. *Her and a dozen farm girls who ought to know better.* But he had to give her credit for keeping her independence.

The pancakes had a poor taste, perhaps because he had used turkey eggs of uncertain age rather than any from now-extinct chickens. Or was the fault only in his memory? How long had it been since he had returned from the First Era and real pancakes? Four years? Five?

He forced himself to eat. "I suppose you're right."

But he did not care for Rispar Kalm once-ha'Ruijac's casual solicitude.

His eyes swept to the window, the view of the outside world removing memories of the Project's subterranean Station.

"I think my platoon is shaping up." Kalm's voice prevented silence from intruding. "They won't win prizes for drill, but they can keep in step now. More or less. What do you think, Ironwearer?"

*That men pay a cruel price for distant happiness, even when their dreams are clearly seen as delusion.* But that was not a response to Kalm's question, and Harper turned his mind to easier matters.

Accepting ris Clendannan's advice, he had taken on the ex-Algheran as a platoon leader in the Midpassage Battalion, using the chubby captain as a lieutenant. Almost ten days had passed, and he was regretting the choice for reasons he could not clearly define. Unfortunately, he had found no one so much better qualified that Kalm could be replaced.

Forty of the man's sixty men had made it to the finish line in the allotted time in yesterday's exercises. Two had been among the "survivors" in the mock battle that followed. It was not the worst performance among the Midpassage platoons; it had not been the best. "Styllin's men were better. But they had their full set of NCOs."

"Sorry." Kalm showed no shame. "Krenn wasn't feeling well, and Derry had business in town. I'm not worried about them."

That was one reason for his dislike, Harper realized: the men the ex-Algheran had taken as section leaders. And the way he defended them. "Ris Jynnich was being lazy," he said coldly. "And I think you realize ris Fryddich's 'business' was sex with one of the brigade noncoms."

"Is that what Wandisha told you?" Kalm was only mildly curious.

"It doesn't matter who told me. On the march, I want them both to behave themselves."

The ex-Algheran snapped his fingers. "Anything else you think I should know?"

*Damn near everything.* But it was unreasonable to expect West Point—style competence from soldiers in this year, and his annoyance left him in no mood for lecturing. "Morale counts more than strict discipline," Harper temporized. "And numbers. Get all your men to the battlefield. Prevent straggling. People on this continent have always been lousy marchers."

The smaller man raised a bushy eyebrow. "Will there be a battle?"

"What wars are for, isn't it?" Harper busied himself with pancakes and syrup. "Having battles? Don't let me or Merryn down out there."

Kalm dropped his grin. "Don't ask for more than the men can give, Ironwearer."

"War is not filled with voluntary choices, Algheran. If I don't get obedience, I'll get a new platoon leader. Do you understand me?"

"Yes." Kalm's face showed emerging grumbles.

"Don't get angry at me. Save it for your former countrymen."

Kalm tilted his head back for a moment. "Blankshields and Nornst. Those aren't my countrymen."

Harper slammed a fist onto the table. "Cut the crap, fellow. Ruijac's part of that country, too. You left it; you can't criticize it anymore."

Kalm pulled back. "Sorry," he said sulkily.

"Kalm." At the sound of the new voice, both men turned to the doorway.

"Good morning, Kylene." Harper forced warmth into his voice.

"Kylene." Aggravation still showed in Kalm's face.

"Admit he's right, Kalm. You don't care much about that Sept of yours, regardless of what you say." Kylene showed no concern as she moved through the kitchen. Barefoot, she seemed unaffected by the cold floor. She wore gray and blue, a dressing gown that represented high style in the capital floating loosely over faded jeans. Bright against the black, a gold band bound her long hair. Her hips were slim, cleanly outlined as she stretched to reach pantry cabinets. A bruise from some mishap, fading now, was high on one arm.

*Seventeen now, or is it eighteen?* Harper wondered. *No matter.* What was significant was that time passed for her as well as for him. She was not a child anymore.

*Yeah. She throws* adult *tantrums.*

What was he to do with her? This was not a world he would like to be pent up in, but it might be less cruel for her than returning to the Project. Kylene owed the Algherans nothing, after all. And what were her goals? Her art, a husband, children, a life at peace ... If she could find those things here, what right had he to object?

His eyes turned to Kalm, and he watched the man silently watching Kylene as she cored and pared an apple. *A predator's look*, he thought, classifying what he saw. But if Kylene could not see it with her powers, he would not be able to explain it to her.

"You should eat more." Kalm's voice, at least, was gentle. And when Kylene responded that she was not hungry, he moved his hands uselessly, then rose to carry her small plate to the table. His manner was subdued.

*Can I trust you to protect my little girl?* Harper wondered. *You've got flaws, God knows, but she's had a rough life, and it's very important that she'll be loved and live happily ever after.*

But even if he were able to express his thoughts, they would probably be wasted. He pushed the table away with both hands and got to his feet. "I have errands," he said heavily. "I'll see you both this evening."

Merryn ris Vandeign was not in his barn that morning, so Harper chased him first to the rooms of the Queen's Hand in the inn, then to the camp across the Bloodrill.

No one challenged him at the outer line of domed tents. Harper hesitated, waiting for a sentry, but none came forth. Frowning, he moved on. The scene of soldiers gambling or goldbricking in their shelters, laughter from unseen women, burnt-out fires and unpoliced litter, and storage parks without guards brought out the sergeant in him, Harper acknowledged.

But he was not in the chain of command here, and growling at the troops was a privilege best left to their officers. Now and then he saluted a soldier who recognized his insignia. Except for men of the Guards Regiment, few were in proper uniforms.

The camp was pierced by a dirt road, adequate for the farmers on this side of the river but now churned by hoof and boot and rutted by military vehicles. Bullocks jostled complacently at feeding troughs in a small pen, close to pits heaped high with maggot-infested offal. Narrow trenches at irregular intervals held kitchen slops or were uncovered latrines from which wafted upward a fetid odor that rain had only slightly reduced. When he stopped to urinate, the spray fell on bloody feces and pus-flecked diarrhea. Harper scowled, looking at the nearby river.

As a counterpoint to these notes of squalor, he glimpsed farmhouses on the hillsides, neatly trimmed hedges bordering black-furrowed fields, and fruit-bedecked apple trees, the evidence of prosperity—and all fraudulent. This had been cropland a year tenth before, but the army had occupied it, so there would be no second harvest of wheat and potatoes this year, and no farmers left to do the harvesting. *Strip their fields without payment, steal their livestock and forage, then draft them because they lack a livelihood . . .*

It was small consolation that previous wars had not touched this area. Yes, war was hell, but with proper policies the misery could be spread more evenly. Was that Alghera's secret weapon: a centralized government that fostered national unity?

Disputed borders, unequal access to markets, conflicting ambitions—perhaps these were only the symptoms of strife, and the true achievement of victory would be a modern state.

*Wish fulfillment, chum. This war does nothing for anyone.*

He had reached the center of the brigade by now. Larger tents had been pitched around a pair of enclosed wagons. Conestoga-sized, the wagons rested askew on iron-rimmed wheels stuck fast in ruts. A woman, young, brunet, and puffy-eyed, appeared in one wagon's doorway, then vanished as she moved aside. *Sleeping quarters for the noble general,* Harper recognized. *Complete with the whores of war. One of them, anyhow. Is she going to stay parked here until the campaign is over or go back to Northfaring?*

Four men in red livery stood patiently nearby, listening to an NCO who wore priest's insignia. As Harper approached, he

heard the lilting tones of the Necklace Lakes region. Designs
had been tattooed onto their cheeks. Harper passed by wordlessly and mounted the wagon steps, his silence enforced by
the feeling of cold lead in his gullet.

*What better proof of wealth in an underpopulated world
than slaves?* he asked bitterly. But understanding did not remove the knowledge that the ancestors of these men had been
Americans.

Harper removed all expression from his face as he knocked
on the wooden door.

The muted conversation within the van stopped.

"Ah, ris Haarper! Welcome, Ironwearer." A hand came
with the gravel-laden voice, and a burly body was just behind.
The grip on his forearm was hard, an attempt at domination
that Harper met with similar force.

"Lan Haarper," he corrected, not for the first time. The
trailer was small, a single room well illuminated by glass windows but filled with the muggy atmosphere created by men
pent up too long. He sniffed to accustom himself to the smell,
then smiled narrowly at the Queen's Hand.

Her Majesty's uncle was a stout blond man near the three-
century mark. By general repute, he was industrious and intelligent; as a soldier, however, he had had little experience,
though determination to equal his grip showed on his face.
Scars from a youthful duel disfigured the knuckles on his
broad hands. *Well, no one ever claimed the ruling dynasty was
effete.* "Good morning to you, Lord Andervyll."

"Of course, of course. You'll take refreshment, Ironwearer? Yes." The Hand opened the door and shouted without
waiting for an answer. "Servant! A glass for the force leader."

Etiquette overrode his lack of thirst, Harper realized.
"Wine," he called out. *Something bottled far away.* "Thank
you, my lord."

*Wine from the table of the queen's uncle. High company
for a simple prospector, chum. But wasn't life easier a couple
weeks back when I wasn't getting no respect?* For an instant
melancholy touched him, twisting his smile even as he turned
his eyes to the other men.

Merryn, seemingly uncomfortable in civilian attire, his expression cold, nodded negatively when Harper greeted him, so
the redhead decided to wait with his request. Regular officers
in bright uniforms stood by the side windows. And the gen-
erals were there: Ironwearer Cherrid ris Clendannan, Master

of Arms Gertynne ris Vandeign, executive officer of the Strength-through-Loyalty Brigade, Terrens ris Daimgewln and others. Harper shook a head to those he recognized and stepped to the long table at the back of the cabin. The conversation he had interrupted was resumed.

The image on the table showed green mountains, blue seas, and the gray lines of ancient highways. Impressive work, Harper thought. Reasonably accurate, too. The Lopritians were famous for their cartographers. This clay map would have been derived from the relief models of the Earth kept in the Royal Library.

*North America.* But Alaska and central Canada were not shown here. Even this early in the Fifth Era, glaciers covered them.

He made out Quebec, Maine, Vermont, and New Hampshire. Cape Cod was gone from the map and from the continent, swept into the ocean during one of the past ice ages. A thin bay marked the location that had been Boston and was now Fohima Alghera. The river that men now called the Ice Daughter entered the bay from the north, after skirting the Berkshires and the gold splotch that represented the city. A forearm's length west another city was marked out in upstate New York—Fohima Loprit. A black line had been painted across the map from north to southeast—the old border between the rival states, as described by Loprit rather than as surveyed.

"Don't like it one bit," he overheard. "Mockstyn is not moving. Cornoval is not in contact with the enemy."

"He's falling back, Lord Ironwearer. Naturally—"

"Naturally nothing, young sir! Cornoval has no idea about what's in front of him."

"There's enough to make him fall back, we know that."

"Lost the entire Torn Coast region, and no intelligence—"

"Took a beating at White Banner Run—"

"No pressure on the Algherans, and I don't like it one bit."

"Overextended. He'll find our people won't cooperate with him. He'll need garrisons, and that will bleed—"

"Not one bit."

Harper frowned. He knew the major commanders—the Hand, ris Clendannan, Gertynne ris Vandeign—but he could not recognize all the speakers. Ris Andervyll's entourage of young officers had increased in the last few days, most of them inexperienced minor nobles eager for commands as preparation for political careers. The Hand had attempted to place some of them in the Midpassage Battalion; he hoped there would not be more.

At least Merryn was keeping silent behind his experienced younger brother and not parading his ignorance. Not that it mattered; this conference did not seem likely to produce decisions that would need his attention. Harper looked to the map again.

Moving south, Long Island was joined to the mainland, and a river ran past only the western side of Manhattan. Other distortions appeared. Florida had swollen to twice the width he remembered and looked within swimming distance of a bloated Cuba. Rivers were more common in this world, and wider and deeper, though that did not show on a map. The Potomac River had merged with Chesapeake Bay to form a great estuary.

And one tributary of the Ocean Father was the Bloodrill River. Harper moved nearer, looking for landmarks. There was Northfaring, at what had been called the Cumberland Gap, the second city in Loprit after the capital, with twelve thousand residents, half of them soldiers. Coward's Landing, with six hundred people, showed just west of Blue Vista Gap at the top of the Shield Valley. There was Shieldboss Mountain. And Midpassage, with a thousand people, twelve hundred on market days.

Two days' march below Midpassage, at a hamlet named West Bend, the great road turned south, separating from the river. Much farther south was Port Junction, a metropolis of ten thousand residents at the intersection of the road and Six Rafts River. Harper let his eyes glide past, deliberately not focusing on nearby Killguide Pass, looking instead for Barlynnt's Tower, at the very bottom of the Shield Valley. Nearly three thousand people could be found there, but no tower.

No one remembered who Barlynnt had been, either.

Farther to the south, where Georgia and Alabama had been, was the Kingdom of Innings. It had given birth to Loprit, but it would be neutral in the coming war. Eastward, north of the Ocean Father, lay Alghera.

Two hundred thousand soldiers could not be seen on the map.

"Find everything you're looking for, Force Leader?" a singsong bass voice asked. "We've slipped in some more supply caches here, and here along the road." Brown fingers reached past his shoulder to tap at the map. "But to do that, we're depending on boats while possible on the march. I think the good docking points have been found."

Harper looked down with a smile. Team Leader Rahmmend Wolf-Twin of Her Majesty's Artful-or-Industrious Requisitionary Corps was a short man, ugly and stocky, with grizzled dark hair and a fleshy, swarthy face. Scented oil had been massaged into his skin, and the odor of cinnamon radiated from him. When he first met the man the time traveler had thought him half-Hindu, half-black, but the brigade's quartermaster came from the interior of what had been Brazil. Another Ironwearer, this was his third campaign with the Lopritians.

A team leader in the Lopritian army commanded ad hoc units of between company and battalion size, making Rahm roughly a major in familiar terms. Harper's own rank, though equally irregular, as aide to Merryn and de facto commander of the Midpassage Battalion, was one step higher.

"I'll want a list of locations, if it's possible," Harper said. "And I came over to see about more medical supplies."

"We'll have to requisition on the march," Rahm said. "The locals are wiped out. Can you give me a list of what you want?"

*Pencillin, tetracycline, ether, iodine, Thorazine* . . . "Blankets, bandages, and herbs. Still needs Merryn's chop," Harper explained, handing over a short list, not adding that confirmation would not be automatic.

"Axes?" Wolf-Twin pursed his lips as he read.

"Say again?"

"Take some extra axes, just in case."

"Uh, you have some medical stuff in the dumps?"

"The last one." Rahm pointed at the table, lips jutting as he set his jaw. Both he and Harper recognized that the area he had indicated was on the verge of being overrun by the advancing Algherans. "Bandages mostly."

*Probably unsterile*, Harper recognized. Contemporary medicine had not reached the germ theory of disease yet. "Surgeons?"

"The Hand's physician is here. A couple of veterinarians." Rahm seemed satisfied.

"Treating men isn't like treating horses."

Rahm's hand moved in an incomplete finger-snapping motion. "We'll need horses more than men."

*War on a shoestring*, Harper thought grimly. *We're starting late.* Part of that was his fault for insisting upon extra days of training for his militia. He was not sure yet if that had made the men more than a rabble or if history would notice. *My own damned pride?*

*Well, Clendannan did back me up. And Gertynne ris Vandeign.*

"Those caches," he said then. "What sort of allowance are you making in them for contingencies?"

"Twenty percent in excess of requirements for our manpower while along the road here. If we hold to a normal pace, but we may take another day. The difficult stretch for my people will be earlier, as we ascend the river, since the boats may have to be poled against the wind. We're having grain sent from Barlynnt's Tower, but Lord Cornoval's force is also pulling stocks from that area. So." The team leader pursed his lips as if pouting, then nodded. "After West Bend, we must have some quick marching, Timmial."

"That's not a problem." Harper frowned. "I'm worried about illness more than injuries."

"We have some," Rahm admitted. "It's part of war."

"You'll have more. So will we, I expect." Harper looked back at the map, tracing the line of the road with a finger. "Green troops, and they'll probably dump a lot of their kit in the first two days. Scare me up a couple of empty wagons, will you, and that'll cut down on my wastage."

Footsteps whispered behind him. He turned to accept a cold mug from a red-clad slave, then sipped cautiously. Thickened with sugar, the wine was unpleasantly sweet; the aftertaste suggested something rancid.

The quartermaster had been thinking. "Supply carts? I can give you five." A writing pad was in his hands.

"Three will do. One for each company, and we'll be able to release them to the brigade at Port Junction, unless we've found other use for them."

Rahm nodded. "You've more than three companies. Your Lord Vandeign is to lead a regiment. The Hand decided it last night."

"Oh? Where? Where does that leave me?"

"Here. With him. The Steadfast-to-Victory Regiment is being reconstituted."

That meant nothing to Harper. He stared to convey his question.

"It's intended as an honor. The Steadfast was put down after . . . some previous difficulties." The sarcasm was clear even in Wolf-Twin's rumbling voice.

The Ironwearer was referring to the coup that had brought Molminda to the throne, Harper suspected. Past commanders of the Steadfast-to-Victory Regiment had evidently been reluctant to accept the blessings of Lopritian political evolution. *Like the Vandeign family.* "I see."

"It means that Merryn ris Vandeign is . . ."

It meant that having lost his only son in the stupid raid against the Necklace Lake tribes that the Lopritians called a "war," Merryn was not viewed as a threat to the ruling dynasty and was being rewarded for his military incompetence with an "honor" he would despise. "Sure."

"Of course, the regiment includes the Midpassage Battalion. They'll make up the bulk of it, with slightly fewer men from other towns from the Northern Valley." The dark Ironwearer frowned. "Ris Vandeign has not told you this yet?"

"Uh, no. Lord Vandeign and I . . ." Harper shook his head, pretending surprise rather than the dismay he actually felt. *I took up with a woman he once wanted to marry me to, and he hasn't forgiven me for it.* "He takes his time telling me things, and we've been busy at different tasks lately. Ummm. Who will be his adjutant?"

"You, of course. It's a promotion, by the way, though your title doesn't change. Another grade. More pay." If Rahm was envious, it did not show in his attitude.

"Nice." But Harper was unenthusiastic, reflecting instead that of the men present, only Merryn, Clendannan, and the Hand appeared older than he. Rahm Wolf-Twin was over ninety but saw himself as a junior officer. *They probably all see me as an underachiever multicentenarian.* He grinned wryly. "I'm sure I'll find an insect in the oil."

"Pardon?"

"Just an expression. Uh . . . who takes over the battalion?"

"Dighton ris Maanhaldur." Rahm hesitated. "No command experience, and the family is unknown, but it's said despite that that his connections are excellent." His face seemed strained; Harper noticed suddenly that Wolf-Twin's eyes were pointed at the Hand.

*A royal bastard. Dandy.* "What has he done?"

"Planning staff," Rahm said. "Didn't contribute much, but . . . he seemed content there until a few days ago."

"Oh?"

"Yes." The dark Ironwearer shook his head pensively. "But he's been getting funny lately. Found himself a bad set of acquaintances. Drinking a lot, too, with that Algy of yours. That little captain?"

"Kalm once-ha'Ruijac?" Harper shrugged. "He's harmless."

# CHAPTER SIXTEEN

*S*ir: *Harper wrote carefully, ignoring the clatter coming from the bar as the tavern owner prepared for the evening.*

By order of Our Sovereign Majesty of Loprit, Molminda III, a general mobilization of forces has been declared. The provisional Midpassage Battalion is called to active duty and incorporated in the Steadfast-to-Victory Regiment, Merryn Lord Vandeign commanding. You will command the battalion's Third Company, comprising your former Fifth Platoon and the Sixth Platoon, under Dighton ris Maanhaldur, acting major. Your rank will be that of a captain of grade B, with commensurate pay and privileges.

1. Upon receipt of this order, you shall designate an acting commander, with temporary rank of lieutenant, for the Fifth Platoon and immediately inform Major ris Maanhaldur and the undersigned of your selection. This appointment by you shall require confirmation by Major ris Maanhaldur.

2. By order of Lord Vandeign, the Midpassage Battalion shall assemble at daybreak on day 161 (tomorrow) at the front training ground (Lord Vandeign's orchard). Your troops shall be in marching order, equipped with clothing and weapons for service in the field. No time limit is placed on this service.

3. Responsibility for supply shall lie with Her Majesty's Req-

uisitionary Corps and officers of the Strength-through-Loyalty Brigade, but deficiencies may be made up if necessary through purchase at civilian facilities. Purchase vouchers shall be indented to Team Leader Rahmmend Wolf-Twin, Ironwearer, STL Brigade Staff (Requisitionary Corps).

Detailed orders will be provided by Major ris Maanhaldur, but for your information, the brigade is to reinforce Haylon Lord Cornoval's Southern Corps near the town of Port Junction. It is anticipated that, barring a cessation of hostilities, the campaign will be concluded within a tenth year.

> Timithial lan Haarper, Ironwearer
> Force Leader, Adjutant for Lord Vandeign

*So this one is done*, Harper reflected. It was sloppily written, perhaps, with the afternoon light fading and the inn's lamps not yet switched on, but study would make it legible.

Good, for if it was true that armies march on their stomachs, it was also true that they followed paperwork trails. Seven letters to company commanders, three to new platoon leaders, one to ris Maanhaldur at the battalion, one each to the Lord Andervyll and Rahm Wolf-Twin at the brigade, one to Lord Cornoval, and copies to pass on to Merryn. The battalion's road to war was clearly blazed now, and thank Cimon for carbon paper. He signed with a flourish.

He shook his hand, wondering if bruised fingers would count as a war wound, then pulled the cover sheet from his writing pad and stuffed it in an oversized envelope. He sealed it with white tape and addressed it after some hesitation, then whistled for a boy playing outside the inn. "Take this message next. Here's another mina for you. Now run, lad."

His smile fell away when the child's back was to him. Palms on the table, he watched without moving as the boy galloped through the tavern door. *Run, lad, indeed.* A hundred men of Midpassage and more could die following the orders he had just written, but it could not be said their de facto commander had acted unprofessionally, without all dispatch.

Even with a down-filled jacket on, he felt chilly in the tavern, and the coming night would be colder still. It would have been unspeakably pleasant to have a huge blazing fire in that big unused fireplace, with flames dancing as high as his face as he rotated slowly, while searing heat broiled his flesh and penetrated to his frozen bones. But the local people did not recognize cold as he did. A fire would not be kindled until the crisp clear days just before the first snows. Horse teams would compete then to draw in great logs that would be upended in the fireplace and sprinkled with spices. The townsfolk would crowd close to the flames, jostling one another to reach the landlord's gifts of beer and mulled cider. Children would cry, ignored by gossiping mothers, and heavily clad farmers would talk gravely about next year's planting. Young men would race eager horses down the long back alleys, pretending ignorance of the watching red-cheeked girls, while their grandsires munched on sweet wrinkle-skinned apples, affirming old solutions for the one world's ills.

Harper would not be there.

He snorted. *Getting maudlin, old chum.* With a campaign about to start, sentiment was a trap to be feared and fought with activity. He would have a drink, he decided, then look up Wandisha. He could really go for a bottle of wine, a good meal, a soft warm bed, and lazy lovemaking all through the long night, interspersed with eager accounts of growing up in Loprit and the distant land that was really First Era America. *Oh, Midpassage is paradise enow!*

Then he remembered that Wandisha was going to her church tonight, along with those who still took the old faith seriously, while others listened to another of Merryn's public readings from the Chronicles.

"Barkeep! Send over a bottle of whiskey!"

A half watch later a drably clad man pushed through the tavern doors, then threaded his way hesitantly between the mostly empty tables. Paper was in his hand.

"Pitar." Harper waved him to a stool, noticing the rumpled uniform damp with sweat under the arms and the disorderly dark hair. "What can I do for you?"

The man swallowed. "I wanted to thank you." Across his cheek was a wide smudge line that washing would not eradicate. His clothing reeked of gunsmoke.

"You earned it, didn't you?" Once a foreman in Merryn's foundry, the man had been one of the better squad leaders to emerge in the militia. Harper suspected he had been directing firing practice when the boy reached him. The man had a wife, one infant daughter, and a still-living grandfather who

had been a serf. Privately Harper hoped very much that Pitar
Styllin returned safely to his family.

"I hadn't hoped—I mean, there were nobles being squad
leaders in the 5th Platoon."

"Still are." Harper was short. He did not explain that he
had given Pitar the 6th Platoon to separate him from a possibly resentful ris Jynnich and ris Fryddich.

"But—"

"Forget it. Go home to your wife, Ian Styllin."

"Sir? It's just—"

"Officer *and* gentleman, Ian Styllin. You aren't turning
down your commission, are you? I don't think I'd let you. So
go home and tell your wife her name's been stretched. Get
some sleep, and I'll see you tomorrow." He smiled at the
man's look. "Tell your gran'ther, too."

Alone again, he continued to smile. It probably made no
difference to history that an unknown workingman had risen
to upper-class status with several strokes of Harper's pen, but
it would change the life of Pitar's family. And the example
might change the lives of others.

He hoped for that also.

The smile died shortly after, as he noticed Kalm entering
the inn in civilian clothes. The chubby Algheran had company: blond Derrauld ris Fryddich, the thin brunet Krennlen
ris Jynnich, and an even thinner, taller, spider-limbed man in
blue with gaunt cheeks and lanky blond hair. He had seen the
man before near the Hand's headquarters but had paid little
attention.

So that was Dighton ris Maanhaldur. He was doing most of
the talking, it appeared. Kalm and the others were attentive,
providing him with agreement. Harper suspected that the man
would not be a willing subordinate.

Inside the inn, the group went to a table. Ris Jynnich,
looking for a waiter, spotted Harper and pointed him out to
the others. There was subdued talk, then Kalm rose.

Harper watched stolidly as he approached, noticing the
satin-smooth clothing that contrasted so strongly with the
homespun he and Ian Styllin wore. He waited deliberately till
the man was standing before his booth to swallow another
drink and wipe the back of his hand across his mouth. "Well?
Where's your uniform?"

"You're drunk," the smaller man said.

*And you're an ass kisser. But do I throw out cheap insults?* Harper thought. "I'm fighting the cold."

"Are you cold?"

"Not yet," Harper mused. "Close contest, though. Always cold around here, long as I can remember. Cold. Bold. Old. Toll'd. Sold. Cold. I grow cold. I grow cold. I shall wear the bottoms of my trousers rolled. Shall I part my hair behind? Do I dare to eat a peach? I shall wear white flannel trousers— that's poetry, y' know? I grow cold. Eliot—you don't have anything like it. Haven't been warm clear through since I left 'Nam. Are you sold?"

"You're drunk," Rispar Kallimur repeated.

Harper pretended to consider the idea carefully while emptying the last of the whiskey bottle into his glass. "Not yet. Just . . . philo . . . sophical. Say, do you want a drink, if your pals can spare you? Stuff tastes like paint thinner, but you get used to it."

"No," Kalm said. "But I've got questions. May I sit?"

"Be my guest." The redhead swallowed. "What d'ya want?"

"Information." Kalm sat, then tapped the table with a corner of folded paper: Harper's order to him. "You're giving me the 5th and 6th platoons?"

"A temporary loan," Harper said, wagging a finger at the ex-Algheran. "You have to give 'em back in good shape."

Kalm frowned. "Who has the 6th?"

"Pitar lan Styllin." The big man leaned backward, yawning widely. Meanwhile he watched the other man through narrowed eyes.

"A commoner? What's the point of that?"

"He's a good man. You know it."

Kalm's face did not show the war between convention and reason that Harper had expected. He simply changed the subject. "What about Derrauld and Krennlen?"

Harper looked away. "What about 'em?"

"Don't they deserve—"

"What they deserve, they aren't gonna get. And I'm *damned* sorry about that, Algheran."

Kalm's nostrils distended as he interpreted that. "Ris Maanhaldur may have other ideas."

"Tough."

"Well . . . I want ris Fryddich at the 5th."

Harper wasn't surprised. He shrugged, not pleased but

aware of how short the battalion was of capable officers. "If
you want."

"And Krenn?"

"Maybe he'll find happiness under ris Fryddich." Harper
chided himself for that, but the crack had been irresistible.

"He should get a promotion also. If Styllin—" Kalm stood
suddenly and went back to the table he had come from.

His back turned to the nobles, Harper scowled at his glass
of whiskey and took another drink.


"Ironwearer?" Ris Maanhaldur's voice was reedy, overfilled with air, though not unsure.

Harper looked up. "Yes."

"There'll be some changes in your plans." The gaunt man
smiled coldly and sat down. Harper, watching across the
table, noticed that his eyes were bloodshot and preoccupied.
Kalm hovered in the background, accompanied by Ris Fryddich and ris Jynnich.

"Oh?"

"I'll need an aide. I believe Krennlen would fit that role."
Ris Maanhaldur sniffed, then lifted his glass for inspection.
His Adam's apple bobbed for a long moment in falling liquor.
"You'll accept that."

"Sure."

"He'll have a major's rank." Ris Maanhaldur took another
swallow.

Harper waited for him to finish. "No. You're a major. You
can't promote to your own level."

Ris Maanhaldur thought about it, staring past Harper's
shoulder at an elderly soldier. The redhead wondered if the
man was actually focusing on what he saw and how much of
this conversation would be remembered in the next day.

"I can make him a captain, though." The reedy voice was
sly.

"Captain, grade A, if you'd like."

The gaunt man shook his head gravely. "I'll do that, then.
So he'll be the same as Derrauld." He lifted his glass again.

Deadpan, Harper looked at ris Fryddich, then at the
younger ris Jynnich. He raised an eyebrow, waiting till ris
Jynnich had seen it, then smirked cruelly. "Derrauld's a grade
C."

"Make him a grade A, too."

Harper smiled cheerfully at ris Fryddich's transparent contempt. "I'm through with paperwork for the day. Have ris Jynnich fill out the forms."

"All right." Ris Maanhaldur looked wistfully into his empty glass. "Krenn, you fill out the forms for both of you."

"Yes, Dighton." The boy was red-faced.

*Embarrassed at something*, Harper diagnosed. That spoke better for the man than any of his actions to date—or his choice in friends. "Do you want to do something for Kalm, too?"

"Oh?" Ris Maanhaldur put down Harper's empty bottle. "The Algy? What's he?"

"I forgot," Harper said carefully.

"Captain B, sir." Kalm said that as one word, quietly.

"That's right!" Harper held up a finger, pointing it at the ex-Algheran. "He was a captain C this morning. Now he's a B."

Ris Maanhaldur snapped his fingers without a sound. "He's taken care of then. Derry?"

"Sir?" The blond noble bent forward.

"You've been promoted! You should buy me a drink."

"Yes, sir. In fact—" Ris Fryddich turned to ris Jynnich, handing over money. "Get a whole bottle, Krenn. We'll do this up right."

Somehow he managed to sound sincere. He was even solic- itous as he turned back to ris Maanhaldur. "Let's take it up- stairs, where we can be comfortable, sir."

"Sure." The gaunt man pushed at the table. Assisted by ris Fryddich, he came to his feet.

"Join us, Kalm?" Ris Fryddich was polite-spoken even as he steadied the taller man.

"Later, perhaps." Kalm was quiet.

"First time I ever felt sorry for the man," Harper com- mented as the three nobles vanished behind an upstairs door.

"He has—" Kalm stopped. "Ris Fryddich?"

"The Hand. So that's his kid, huh? Illegitimate."

"His wife is barren. Or else—he has this one."

"Too bad. They'll get him to bed?"

"And awake in the morning." Kalm looked up at the closed door. "They won't get much sleep themselves, but he'll look fine. It's—Dighton's not a bad man. He wants to go into politics someday."

"Too bad," Harper said again.

"They have a tradition. It's like the Muster."

"Except the voting is rigged."

"They're called Queen's Beloved Counselors, and—"

"Kalm, I live here. I know that crap."

"Well, he's . . . nervous."

"Too Cimon-taken bad."

"After a while—a couple of days—he'll feel better." Kalm exhaled quickly, a pant. "He wants to do well. And it's just the one campaign. He can't do much harm. After this—"

"You think so."

"Yeah, I think so." The ex-Algheran turned to a nearby barmaid, a coin gleaming in his hand. "A small beer, please."

"You're wrong." Harper was scornful. "That's not a man to trust, any of 'em, and you should know it." And when those words had no impact on Kalm, he reached out to grab the woman's skirt. "Forget the beer, miss. Bring more whiskey. And another glass. This soldier just got a promotion, y' know. We should celebrate it properly. Maanhaldur is going to be a disaster, Algheran. A useless politician out to build a reputation without work."

"Lan Haarper!"

"You had your say, this is mine." The Agent shoved the barmaid off. "Bring us some whiskey, woman! Don't be so Cimon-taken virtuous, Algheran. I'm gonna pay for it, you're chasing my wife, you're brown-nosing that shit, you can pretend to be friendly to me. You're gonna be a soldier, you can have a drinking buddy. Right?"

The smaller man breathed heavily. "You don't understand." He paused. "I've got to get washed and dressed. I'm meeting Kylene for dinner before services, and I don't have time. I'm not a soldier till morning, lan Haarper."

Harper swore again. "You wanted to be a soldier here, and it's too late to back out. You knew what you were getting into, Algheran."

"Let me get ready." Kalm tried to stand.

"Not yet!" Harper grabbed his wrist. "You've been a soldier somewhere before this, haven't you? You had experience. Where'd you get it, Algheran?"

Kalm kept his eyes averted. "These times—not hard to get experience."

"Nicole's tits!" The big man slammed his glass down so that drops of whiskey splashed the tabletop. "Half the clowns in the battalion have been in an army, all the old ones have, and there still aren't enough smarts between them to get out of the rain." He kept his voice low to avoid being overheard, but a snarl sounded in it regardless.

"That's pretty harsh, Ian Haarper. After all, you were in charge of training them, and you told them they were good troops yesterday. I heard you." Resentment was clear in Kalm's voice.

"Yeah?" Harper shook his head as if to improve his concentration, then waited for the barmaid to leave a bottle and another glass. "Yeah, yeah. What was I supposed to tell them? The truth? They aren't soldiers, not yet."

"They'll improve."

Harper sighed. "Not enough. They've had ten days of training, and half of them don't understand yet what any of it's about. The ones who know anything at all think this campaign will be a repeat of that Necklace Lake thing. And it makes me sick," he explained softly. "I'm getting ashamed of everything I've done here."

Kalm poured liquor into both glasses and pushed the fuller one toward the Agent. "I think they'll put up a good fight."

"Better hope so, Algheran." Harper knocked his glass against the smaller man's. "If not . . ." He swallowed half his drink, then coughed. "Dandy targets, us officers. Ever think of that? But it doesn't matter, I guess. You're trapped in the situation, too."

Kalm eyed him appraisingly, one brow cocked, his lips twisted into a cynical smile. "Getting nervous?"

Harper snorted. "No, I'm just going to be annoyed if I get killed with nothing to show for it." Then he hiccoughed solemnly.

"Oh, but you'll be resisting the perfidious Algheran foe, defying the cruel invaders of a peaceful kingdom, and showing the despicable lackeys of tyranny how free men, strong in their patriotism and love of monarch, repel unprovoked aggression." Kalm kept a deadpan expression, his voice almost showing sincerity. "What an example you'll be setting for us all. Did you ever do anything like this before, Ian Haarper?"

"Are you quoting ris Maanhaldur's speeches? I think loving monarchy is a social disease. But I've met the perfidious Algheran, all right." The big man snorted again. "We'll probably go down together."

"Perhaps." Kalm shook his glass to make the whiskey slosh. "Are you scared? With all your experience?"

"Hmmm." The Agent delayed his answer, weighing responses. "True confessions time? Mixed feelings, I guess. I've been in battles, but the conditions were different. If we get into a stand-up fight, that will be new to me. So . . ."

"I've never been scratched," Kalm said thoughtfully.

"Way I see it," Harper continued dreamily, "it's a matter of odds. Thousands of identical characters in virtually the same circumstances. Some of them come through, some don't. It's impossible to predict which set you'll be in, and almost a waste of time to try to influence the outcome. Because you can't control everything, you see? Hmmm? You said something?"

"I get impatient." The smaller man was still staring into his glass. "And sometimes, when I think about dying, I'm not so much afraid as curious. I get to wondering: what would it feel like? What happens next? What would I compare it to? I'm not scared—not really, anyhow—but I want to know. You probably think I'm nuts."

Harper tried to snap his fingers but failed. "Nah, it's a way to be, that's all, Algheran. You'll settle down eventually."

Kalm raised an eyebrow. "Go on. But don't call me 'Algheran.'"

"Well, you adapt to things. Getting old, being unloved, dying . . . seeing your girl die. Whatever kind of misery. War's just more of the same, and you come to terms with it. That's a bad part of it, you psych yourself up for it, and then you go up-country and you find the psyching up didn't do the job, but you got to keep going, so you do. And you get back, and you adjust to that too, and you forget what it was really like."

Kalm peered at him over his glass. "Interesting," he said tonelessly, then finished off his drink and poured another while looking toward the doorway.

Harper followed the glance. "So what's your big truth about fighting, Algheran?"

"I don't have one, Ian Haarper. It's madness, and I never remember any of it."

"I'll buy that. You know what I always wondered?"

"I don't know." Kalm smiled quickly. "I'm not a Teep."

"Yeah. But what I wonder is, what is it like for a telepath, reading minds and being in a battle?"

"Just like it is for a Normal." Kalm's voice was flat. "Because they don't read minds then. I talked to one once. He said someone scared can't be understood, so it's painful to try, and even if it's another Teep, it makes no difference. Teeps die alone, Ian Haarper."

"Too bad for Ian Callares."

"What?"

"I've got dancing girls and a small choir scheduled for the rest of us. But if he's not interested . . ."

Kalm chuckled. "I hear from Kylene he can find his own women. I think she told him so."

*Not like you, I bet.* But there was no point in that remark. Harper smiled wanly and traced water rings on the tabletop.

"You could ask *her* what it's like being a Teep," Kalm said.

"I don't think it would be the same."

"Because she hasn't been in a battle?"

"Not quite." Harper shook his head uneasily. "I don't think telepaths like to talk about their experience. The one you met was an exception. But . . ."

"You wonder." Kalm smiled ironically.

"Sometimes. And sometimes I think I know, and I'm not sure if it would be good or bad."

"I've never wasted the effort wondering." Kalm seemed pensive, but his gestures were still purposeful. "Your glass is empty, Ironwearer. Want a refill?"

"I'll take another. Thanks."

When Harper spoke again, his tone implied that the subject had changed. "Sometimes I wonder about Kylene, too. I worry."

"Don't," Kalm advised sourly. "She'll manage."

*She has to. She'll be young centuries after I'm dead.* The Agent drank with his eyes closed, letting the liquor swirl about his mouth before swallowing. "Regardless. Even if nothing happens to me, you've got a clear path with her, if you want it."

"Wasted effort," Kalm said. He poured another round.

" 'Nother bottle coming," Harper said somewhat later.

Annoyance tightened Kalm's facial muscles, but he regained his control. "Do you drink just to get drunk, Ian Haarper?"

"Prissy, prissy, Algheran. I don't get drunk that often, after all." Harper smiled again, then leaned over the table to pat the smaller man on the shoulder. "I'm doing it now just to annoy you."

"I almost believe you." Kalm blinked wearily.

"Oh, you should, Kalm," Harper confided. Then he straightened. "Oh, hell. Algheran?"

Kalm raised his head, his eyes half-closed. "Yes?"

"Wake up, fellow. I see Kylene coming."

"Then it's time I got dressed." The ex-Algheran got to his feet without haste. Except for a sardonic smile, he showed no sign of the whiskey he had presumably consumed. "Tell her I'll be back shortly." He slipped toward the stairs with no sign of unsteadiness.

"I've been snookered," Harper admitted to open air.

He stood to take Kylene's hand. "You're looking very pretty tonight, girl. Shall we go to another table? This one is—"

"This one stinks of liquor," Kylene said flatly. "Yes, another table. Try not to stumble, Tayem."

"I'm not—" But he was talking to a turned back. Harper shrugged, then followed obediently as Kylene crossed the floor to a vacant table. She was indeed very pretty tonight, he decided. Rose-red blouse with puffed sleeves, full black skirt without decoration, high boots—and very determined. With that stiff back and high head, she had the air of a countess about to slash insolent faces with a riding whip. *Watch your step, chum.*

"I think I prefer your hair straight," he said, sitting down. "Piling up braids is for old maids. Uh, Kalm will be here soon."

"Yes, I know." Kylene patted her hair, advertising disinterest, and looked away so all he could see of her face was a freckled profile. Diners nearby turned away hastily as her eyes passed over them.

"Guess I feel a bit silly." Harper smiled ruefully, but Kylene continued to ignore him. He was still holding an empty glass, he realized suddenly, so he set it down noisily on the table. A moment later he moved it again, without looking, to the table behind him.

There was an immediate polite cough. Harper turned, his embarrassment deepening as his glass was returned to his hand.

"Apologies, my lady. My error. Sorry, Sergeant." He sat the glass on the floor by his feet, trusting that Kylene would not comment on what she was not forced to see. "Yeah. Pretty silly." He forced a chuckle.

"Tayem, stop it!" An angry string of alien words followed.

"Kylene?"

"Stop playing the guilty little boy," Kylene said distinctly, and he recognized with shock that she spoke in fiftieth-century English. "I have seen you do it too often to believe your pretending. And stop moving your hand in the air that way. Close your mouth. That is your 'I am being misunderstood but I can explain everything' act, and I have seen it, too."

Harper's fabricated smile evaporated. "What are you objecting to, kid?" he asked quietly in the same language. "My game with Kalm?"

"Your game with Kalm," the woman agreed. "Do you believe he thought you intoxicated? He did not."

Harper shrugged. "Worth a try. I notice he did stick around just in case I had something to spill." ·

Kylene avoided that. "He does not mean you harm."

"And how am I to know that? How do you know that?"

"I do! Do you not trust me?"

Harper took his time answering. "I don't know, kid. Maybe, within limits. What is Kalm up to, Kylene?"

"What is meant— I do not understand you."

"Yeah?" Harper grabbed suddenly, throwing Kylene's hand so it slapped the table and pressing down with his own. "He tells lies about his background, and he's always trying to pump me. He hangs around you. I don't like his friends. I don't like any of it. Now do you understand me, little wife? He's a snoop. Why? What is Kalm up to?"

"He does not oppose you! Tayem! You are hurting—"

"What is he doing, *dammit*! Who does he work for?"

"Let go! Tayem, let go or I'll tell you nothing." Kylene's face was flushed, anger narrowing her eyes.

Harper glared back at her, then raised his hand slowly. "My apologies," he said tonelessly. "I lost my temper. I don't need anything from you, and I'm sorry I asked. Good day, lady."

Perhaps Kylene cried out, but he was alone when he shoved through the door, and the hushed tavern soon returned to bustling normality.

"Timmial!"

Harper leaned against the railing on the long pier, waiting to hear if the cry would be repeated, and only when his name had been called a third time did he turn.

The dock area was dark and equipment-littered, so it took him a while to make out a shape in the alley between the inn and the warehouse. Wandisha was alone, he noticed, and would not find him unless he cooperated.

He sighed, then went to greet her.

"I was watching the river," he explained after a kiss.

"Were you lonely?" Leaving her arms around his neck, Wandisha turned her head so her cheek rested against his chest. "I missed you."

"Missed you, too." Harper rubbed his chin on her sandy hair, smiling at the tickly feeling, and held her tightly, then slid his hands down from her white lace-covered shoulders to her hips, his fingers gently kneading the firm buttocks tightly draped by a dark wool skirt. "Pretty girl." He purred at her. "You smell nice. What's up?"

"I just wanted to be with you tonight," she said softly in a sleepy child's voice. "Will you stay with me?"

He kissed her scarred forehead and her eyelids and rubbed a finger softly along a downy cheek. "Sure. Are you hungry?"

"No. I—someone else gave me a meal."

"Oh." *Live with it, chum.* "Want to go out on the dock a while?"

Wandisha murmured agreement, her head moving against his chest. Harper led her by the hand, steering her around bales of merchandise and under hanging tackle, guiding her along the ramshackle pier. At the end rail, she turned into the evening breeze, then moved her head as if looking at what she faced. But she stood stiffly, and the hands that gripped the wooden railing were like fists. She sniffed once, drawing in the smell of mud and decaying weeds, then was silent, so water could be heard chuckling as it slapped against the posts below.

"Not a great deal to see," Harper said casually. He stood close to her, one hand on the small of her back while the other gently massaged her rocklike knuckles. Behind him was a gap in the railing, closed by a length of rope, which he had not mentioned to the girl.

"You're looking toward the horizon now. Dark over there. Some campfires. Just a scattering of clouds, and a lot of stars overhead. Lower your chin a smidgen. You're facing at a line of six boats now, bobbing just a bit. They're riding at anchor, waiting for the daybreak. No details visible right now, but they are canoe-shaped, about five man-heights long and two wide, about one from keel to gunwale. They have low cabins about half that size seeming to sit on their decks, and little green lamps at stern and bow. Two small masts, for triangular sails which aren't up now. More boats upstream and more downstream, where we can't see them. This side, there's a fire down by the bridge."

"Merryn's services," Wandisha said, half turning in that direction. "It's a bonfire. People are starting to gather."

"Ah. I guess you know what's there better than me." Harper tried to put a smile into his voice. *It's only with me that she's blind.*

Wandisha murmured wordlessly. Then she said, "Kylene is unhappy."

"Kylene is often unhappy." *Why are we talking about her?*

"You decided not to trust her and walked out."

"I didn't say anything like that." Even to himself, Harper's voice was petulant. "All right. I did do that. But I didn't say it."

"It was cruel, Timmial." Wandisha still refused to face him.

"Called for, I think. She wouldn't—"

"Tayem!" the woman cried out. "Don't you understand? Kalm isn't spying on you. He doesn't need to. He isn't trying to. Tayem, we're so vulnerable, here, so exposed! Don't you see, if he didn't mean well, he could have hurt us long ago." That was Kylene, not Wandisha.

"Dandy," Harper growled. "I'll think about it. Now knock this crap off."

Kylene bleated at him once more, but he ignored it. "How much of that can I believe?" he asked after Wandisha had her body to herself.

"Most of it," she said slowly. "But Kalm—don't trust Kalm, Timmial."

"Don't trust Kalm," he repeated. "Is he spying on Merryn?"

She seemed startled. "Is that what you think?"

"Makes sense, and not much else does. Isn't Molminda still worried about how the Vandeigns will jump during the war? What better way to keep an eye on Merryn than to send someone like Kalm to watch him? And Merryn's favorite Ironwearer."

"No, he watches you." Wandisha moved away, bumping against the wood railing. "I think he hates you." It might have been a remark about the weather.

Bravado seemed out of place. Harper settled for, "Oh?"

*You're a big boy, chum. You don't need to ask for help.*

*I can't get Wandisha involved with this.* That was his next thought. *If there's a real problem, Kylene will tell me.*

"Kylene doesn't know anything about it," Wandisha said thickly, as if reading his thoughts. "She hasn't seen... anything. Like I..."

Harper hesitated. "Is his mind like mine? Shielded?"

"No." Wandisha seemed regretful. "It's like—I couldn't explain it to you, Timmial. Being in Kalm's mind is... painful. None of us like to do it."

*Neurotic,* Harper decided. *I can identify with that. Are Kalm and Kylene— No. I don't have to know.*

Wandisha stared at him. Had he said something he should not have? "Never mind," he said grimly, then smiled. "So I've got him watching me. Green-eyed, I suppose? Jealous?"

Wandisha hesitated, unfamiliar with his idioms. "Kalm is not jealous," she said at last. "Timmial, he is not— We should be going." She sounded miserable.

"Really?" He stepped closer to hold her. "It's all right, girl. He can hate me so long as he fights fair. Or doesn't give me trouble."

Wandisha tried to pull away, then relaxed. "No. He won't give you trouble. If he planned to, Kylene and I would know."

"Hmmm. Kylene." He sighed.

"She—you never should have brought her here, Timmial."

"I know," Harper said unhappily. "It's all so screwed up. I don't know what to do now. You women sure turn everything into a big emotional circus, don't you?"

Wandisha pulled away suddenly. "That's a nasty thing to say."

*Oh, hell!* "Sorry, dear. Just thinking out loud." And when that did not calm her down, he said, "Wandisha, please? I didn't mean to get you mad."

"Well, you did. Timmial, how can you expect women to be everything you want them to be when you aren't loyal to them? You're mad at Kylene."

"Not mad. Just fed up with—"

"You were mad! You told her she wasn't to be trusted, but you put her in a situation where she can't be. Why do you expect her to do anything at all to help you?"

Harper forced a laugh. "My wonderful personality?"

"Timmial, be serious! Did you want to be betrayed by her?"

"I—oh, come on! Don't you be mad, Wandisha," Harper pleaded. "But don't give me any more of that psychological crap. I don't need anyone to help me. You know that. That's what got Kylene upset—not that I don't trust her but that she's trapped in a small town with nothing to do. Ah, why do I have to explain everything? Look at me, please?" *Cimon! I'm begging, and I'm not even making sense.* The situation was absurd, almost funny. Why was Wandisha defending Kylene?

To think that was only a step from asking, once he felt he had regained sufficient dignity. "She's said pretty vicious things about you, after all," he pointed out.

"I know." Wandisha laughed shakily. "But—forget it, Timmial."

*Women!* Harper thought angrily. *"A fool there was,"* he quoted loudly and clearly in English. *"And he made his prayer, Even as you and I! To a rag and a bone and a hank of hair . . ."*

Wandisha understood none of that.

He relented. "You forget it," he said gruffly when she asked. "I won't translate that. I was being nasty without reason, just because I felt you women had ganged up on me. Ah, well, maybe you had cause."

It had not been fairness, he saw suddenly, that had provoked Wandisha's outburst. Whether she understood her own motives or not, in pleading Kylene's case with him she was pleading her own, for his refusal to become involved with one woman only mirrored his unwillingness to increase his involvement with the other. *Kylene makes me angry, since Wandisha makes me guilty. Great. Isn't insight just wonderful!*

But how was he supposed to behave, he wondered. Onnul . . . Hadn't he learned a lesson from that business? He had not been tying down anyone, regardless of Wandisha's words. He had not even tried to. *Damned women; why does every acquaintanceship with them turn into entanglement? Is it my fault?*

*Calm down, chum. It's just the way their minds work, is all. Women and men are different species, no matter how much alike they seem. Got to remember that.*

But what was he to do?

*Call it quits and go home to the First Era? It wouldn't be any different there, and I have work here.*

*Be truthful as possible with them. They can deal with facts, after all, even if they don't want to. And that's just what I've done. Dammit! I don't have a reason to feel guilty.*

But he said none of that. Instead, he pressed himself against Wandisha, stroking her methodically, knowing that would force her to respond eventually.

"Lovely Wandisha," he crooned at her. "Pretty Wandisha." As his lips moved along the side of her neck, he damned himself for deliberately manipulative behavior, but he also took cruel pleasure in the knowledge that the woman's mounting arousal was being broadcast to every telepath within the town. "Sugar-sweet lovely Wandisha."

"We should be going soon," Wandisha whispered brokenly. Harper's arms tightened, and the two of them swayed together back and forth at the end of the dark pier.

At last she stiffened. "We should be going," she repeated. "Timmial?"

He leaned forward, enjoying the feel of her body. "I'd hoped—"

"Please, Timmial? Indulge me just this once." Still breathing heavily, she turned and placed her arms around his neck. "We don't have much time left together, do we?"

"No, we don't," the Agent agreed sadly. "All right. But I wish . . . It's a long walk to that chapel of yours."

"I didn't want to go there tonight. I thought . . . Lord Vandeign's service."

"Merryn's?"

"I wanted to hear the story."

*You and Kylene, both.* "Why are you telepaths so eager to hear old stories? If I were you . . ." *Both my women, dammit!*

"But you aren't." Wandisha chuckled throatily and tugged at him. "It fascinates us, Timmial," she said more soberly. "It defines us, in some fashion. It tells us what we were, and what we might be."

That did not satisfy him, but Harper kept his mouth closed while guiding her to the front of the inn. Slowly, he regained control of his temper.

Wandisha and he walked hand in hand to the services.

"So you're out to transcribe my old memories," Merryn ris Vandeign was saying as they approached the worshipers, his finger tracing the text he was reading from. A bonfire was at his back, a pair of thick logs lighting up the pasture, while torches flickered high on either side of him. No podium was before him, and Harper could see brown clothing through the front of Merryn's self-invented vestments.

*Chronicle of Tomas Reintjes*, Harper identified. *Just at the start. Good timing.* Except that he did not want to be there.

He pulled Wandisha forward, stepping past seated people and looking for familiar features on the dim faces around them. He saw Merryn's wife, healthily stout and serene in appearance; the Hand and other officers, giving way uncomfortably to curiosity or political considerations; a red blouse under dark hair on a reclining woman who might be Kylene; a pair of the neighboring children sitting on a small blanket beside a woman he did not recognize; the fat lady schoolteacher, a sandwich at her mouth, turning away to watch only Cimon knew what; and uniformed men from across the river.

"Raw material, eh, for your histories?" Merryn's voice rang clearly over the crowd, a slightly accented baritone that easily overrode other sounds.

Harper kicked leaves aside, then sat with his legs out, half-turned so Wandisha could lean back against his chest.

Kylene was with Kalm. Her head was on his leg. His hand brushed her hair.

Harper's eyes moved from her to Kalm's face, hoping the ex-Algheran would notice him. But when it happened, Kalm only raised bushy eyebrows and flashed a half smile that might have been disdain or recognition. He continued to pat at Kylene without pause.

*Hate, huh? What the hell else is going on in your head?* Harper wondered.

**Kylene**

# CHAPTER SEVENTEEN

"So you're out to transcribe my old memories;
Raw material, eh, for your histories? . . ."

The words Merryn ris Vandeign was reading floated past
her, having meaning only one by one. Kylene, pretending
carelessness she did not feel, remained in her position as
Wandisha and Harper crossed the orchard and took seats
nearby.

Others had noticed the newcomers also. Without examining individual minds, she sensed awareness of Harper's entrance, coupled with amusement not intentionally aimed at
anyone but galling nonetheless. Involuntarily her arm, loosely
draped over Kalm's knee, tightened. She felt the muscles contract, and a dampened annoyance in his mind.

". . . Third year, I think it was, of Ruppelt's reign—
Cimon's father, himself a warrior,
He who established the present border . . ."

That was the name they had come to hear. *Cimon*. She felt
the townsfolk exhaling as they heard the end of that line.
"Legends," Tayem had said once, speculating more for himself than for her. "A lot of legends. Maybe echoes of a real

274

Fourth Era religion. People do remember Cimon and Nicole's names, and when the missionaries come in, they're already disposed to believe. As soon as they know what to believe."

Those were professorial words, dispassionate—uncaring, like he was.

She glanced at him quickly, seeing a face washed of emotion.

Wandisha, leaning against him, conscious of Kylene's reactions, tugged at his arm, diverting his attention.

Irrationally, Kylene regretted that Tayem had not noticed her look.

Kalm put a hand on her ankle and began to stroke it. For an instant she wanted to pull it back, then she saw Harper frowning at her. She enjoyed *that*.

And Kalm's little pleasures meant nothing.

Her own father, some relatives—who had ever cared for her simply from liking rather than through kinship or the shared bonds of telepaths?

*Even Tayem*. He had been using her.

For the telepaths, he had said. But he had meant telepaths in general rather than particular telepaths. Caring of that kind did not count with him.

*So close at moments, but—*

*Normals don't have our understanding, Kylene. They have to rely on trust to build relationships, knowing at some point it will always fail.* That was Dieytl, from across the town, in what the Normal woman beside him would think a moment of deep emotion. *Always . . . it takes a kind of bravery. And hope.* He kissed the forehead of the woman gently, touched by respect and guilt.

*Hope*, Kylene thought sourly. Harper had hoped, thinking of his lost Onnul. The Algherans fought their war, hoping. Long ago, she had left her home, hoping.

Hope was never a reasoning response. And trust, relying on hope, was doomed to disappointments, even deserved it in some sense.

*Tayem!*

Merryn droned on, but she ignored him, turning to stare at Harper.

*He looks tired*, she thought, watching him sitting patiently and pretending interest in Merryn's readings as Wandisha leaned on him. *Never home at night, drill all day. Does she let him get any rest?*

What did Wandisha give to him? Sex, of course.

She remembered the feeling of bodies locked together, minds apart but feeling linked, and the warm, filled, empty-minded, separate contentment.

More realistically, she recalled the effort and the disappointed wish for contentment, but an aftermath still surprisingly satisfactory. Reaction-induced tenderness mimicking genuine affection . . . she understood that.

Wasn't there more? Shouldn't there be more?

*Not your boyfriend's opinion.* Kalm commented, feeling amusement.

Wandisha and Dieytl were still, watching her reactions.

". . . telepath came, once events forced policy.
Treated us gently, as if we were still free,
Asked us if we'd come to a decision,
And listened politely, without derision."

The singsong words took meaning suddenly, and Kylene felt herself watching a reality: a lean, taciturn man, pensively feeling earth in his fingers, nearly as close to the soil as the peasants he counseled, steering their reactions to him with patient skill.

His face was a masculine version of her own.

But that was not reality. None of the Second Era telepaths had been descendants of hers. Tayem had taken her away before she could have descendants.

Kalm stirred, his mind pressing lightly against her shield, but that was only habit. She sensed that his attention was far removed from her or anyone else in Midpassage. Anyhow, her thoughts were in her childhood tongue; he noticed them only as meaningless static.

*Let it be that way*, she thought selfishly. Kalm believed she was native to this era, but she would tell the Algheran telepath nothing he had not already discovered, keeping secrets from him just as he kept his inconsequential secrets from her and the other Teeps.

". . . West I traveled, myself for companions,
Following the telepath's brief directions.
First time in life I knew true loneliness—
It stamped my heart with marks still impressed . . ."

*Solitude, not loneliness,* she thought, correcting the account. Loneliness was something felt with people all around.

Kalm took her hand and rubbed its back. *Not that bad, is it?*

It was only soft pressure, not the reassurance he had intended, but she let him continue, observing how solicitude coexisted with self-admitted lust in his mind.

*One man at a time, fat boy,* she told him, enjoying the contrast between the cold thought and the sensuous pose she had taken. *You wanted the appearance of seduction to annoy him; it's all you get.*

*I know.* But beneath the crust of patience she saw regret.

*You should have tried yourself, Kalm.* She moved intentionally, sliding so her skirt moved up her hip, knowing that the movement would tantalize him and simultaneously finding the gesture pleasurably erotic. *No telling what you might have been admitted to.*

*Stop it, Kylene.*

*But see what I've been learning, Kalm. So nice . . .* To accompany the gibe, she slid her consciousness through new memories, selecting from them to create arousal in herself.

". . . Yes! We were subjects. We knew we were ruled.
Our veiled captivity left us unfooled.
We hopped up and down at Teep dictates
And pretended allegiance to flea-bite states.
And why not? They were keeping us alive.
Tell me it's liberty for which men strive,
And I'll laugh at dolts. Do you understand?
It's poverty that brings men to the brand.
That—and love for those who on us depend.
A child's smile is worth a knee bend . . ."

*Smile, Kalm/child. Women are traps. Think of what you're free from.*

*I don't need you!* The thought was bitter, contemptuous. Kalm's anger seemed directed at all the world.

*Don't you? Why did you spend so much effort, then? You used me, you used my anger, my trust. What are you gaining, Kalm?*

But she already knew the answer.

*I should have told Tayem about him,* she realized. Harper

would have wanted to know that Kalm was a telepath.

"Don't mention it to anyone," Kalm had asked her on the coach. "Don't use my old name."

It had seemed a small thing, a favor for an unimportant Algheran telepath fleeing some minor peccadillo. She had not thought of Tayem then. "Anyone" had been the drivers of the coach and Molminda. She had not expected Kalm to stay in Midpassage.

But was it really her fault that she had kept quiet? It had not seemed important on her first day in the town, and Tayem had not given her an opportunity to tell him. He had been with Wandisha most of the second day. And on the third day she had not felt like speaking to him.

After that, it had not seemed worth stirring up his anger just to tell him about unimportant Kalm. And when she finally understood that Kalm was not the pure friend he pretended . . .

After that, there would have been too much to confess.

*Why?* she asked. But Kalm only smiled, jaws clenched and lips tight.

*Why?* Dieytl, pausing in his lovemaking, had the same question. Wandisha waited as well, wondering but not expectant.

*It's your fault also*, she told them. *You did this with him. Let him do this—it's the same thing.*

Her eyes moved from face to face, seeing the other furtive eyes in the camp light: Kalm, silent, patient, behind a mind shield almost as rigid as Harper's Teepblind; Wandisha, fearing to disrupt any stability that protected her, afraid of Kalm's strangeness; herself, unwillingly an accomplice of Kalm's intent, whatever it might become; Dieytl lan Callares, distantly observing her and the others as he stroked the cooling skin of the woman he had found for the night, enjoying the testimony to his skills rather than sharing the pleasure it brought the woman, watching, knowing himself watched, and finding a strange comfort in that observation.

*It shouldn't be this way*, she sensed, remembering her city in the mountains. *It should have been our world. We should have been its rulers. Things went wrong; it rules us.*

*Don't think that way.* Kalm's thought was hard, even merciless.

*Is it our fault?* Dieytl sucked gently on an erect nipple, taking in the Normal woman's sensation and sending it to Kylene, continuing until her own breath was ragged and her own breasts stiffened. *We watched you, yes, but you did what you already wished for. You shouldn't blame us.*

*I didn't!*

*You did, Kylene.* Wandisha sighed softly, distantly. She had placed Harper's hands on her breasts.

*No! It's not my fault! I wanted Tayem!*

*Hope for him, then.* Dieytl, ironic, slipped his arms under the woman's knees. Kylene tasted hair on her lips and smelled a fishlike scent. *Is this so bad that you must close your mind and live on hope alone?*

His tongue moved. The woman began to writhe.

Kylene writhed.

Wandisha pressed against lan Haarper, keeping his attention focused on her.

Kalm was still, unmoved.

In the background, Merryn's voice droned on.

"Lan Haarper will be with Wandisha tonight." Kalm's voice sounded suddenly near her ear, quiet, intruding on the senseless words that Merryn spoke. Kalm's hand was on her shoulder.

*Yes.* The word was only recognition of the unwelcome interruption.

*Ris Jynnich asked about you when we were standing around chatting after lan Haarper's afternoon drill. Shall I tell Krenn he can see you again tonight?*

She hesitated until Dieytl read that irresolution and forced his woman to react. She trembled then, feeling the woman's sensations, remembering pinches, remembering bruises, feeling her hips about to rock.

"Kylene?" Kalm smiled at her knowingly, contemptuously.

*Please, Tayem. Don't see this. Don't ever find out.*

"Yes," she gasped. "Yes, yes. Tell him yes. Please. Yes!"

# Part 3: Valley of the Shield:
# The Colonel Bogie March
**Kalm**

# CHAPTER EIGHTEEN

*I*t was early morning of a clear crisp fall day, a canvas prepared by the gods for recording scenes of valor and gallantry.

The order to march had not been given.

Kalm scowled, envying the self-centered absorption of the Normals. Life could be so simple for the half minded.

He stood at the edge of Merryn ris Vandeign's orchard, at the front of his men, periodically sweeping his eyes down the ranks. Two platoons of sixty men, two other officers, a signalman, three runners, an orderly—all his property and his responsibility, as if in truth they all rode astride his shoulders.

Uniformed men sat or squatted in a double line along the berm of the great road, each tending his own lump-filled backpack, canteen, and thick-barreled musket. Here and there a vacancy showed: soldiers bidding farewell again to wives at the end of the column, a few chatting with friends in other companies, and men huddled in prayer beneath the trees with a priest of the old religion.

For the fourth time that morning, Pitar Styllin moved down the line of his platoon, checking straps and buckles. Lan Styllin, he was being called now. His men were already treating him with unexpected diffidence and shaking off his attempts to chat. They tolerated platitudes from him and his nervous attentions, however; that was the natural order of things.

Ris Fryddich's 5th Platoon was more relaxed. Less had been expected of them during training; few of the men realized that, and none thought it would make a difference in the days ahead.

The grumbles reaching Kalm's ears were subdued, untouched by hysteria, but he perceived nervousness and impatience hovering over the men like a low rain cloud, punctuated by lightning flashes of ill temper and cold squalls of concealed fear. Even the handful of well-wishers remaining to see the battalion off radiated annoyance.

"This is the army, Algheran," lan Haarper had quipped earlier that day. "Hurry up and wait."

The time traveler had yawned then, holding his stallion's reins with one hand while wiping the other across bloodshot eyes. It had been a private confession of weakness. Farther up the line, he had loudly assured men of the imminent infidelity of their neglected wives, told them that Algheran troops would eat Lopritians for breakfast and pick their teeth with bullets, and said that the best way for the Midpassage Battalion to frighten "real soldiers" would be to enlist en masse as regulars.

Men had guffawed rather than objected to the coarse language, Kalm had noticed. His own jests, at best, had gleaned laggard smiles, so envy touched him lightly till he remembered lan Haarper's words of last night. This was not humor but the grim, cynical manipulation of innocent men. Lan Haarper had little sympathy for those whose lives he disrupted.

*I'll destroy him.* Kalm remembered his promise.

It was done. He had remade lan Haarper's destiny. It was unimportant that the victory was unsatisfying.

What jokes would the big man tell as men of this ragtag battalion who had trusted him died in combat? When he discovered that his time machine was hidden from him forever? When he was again with Kylene and Wandisha, trapped in the sham existence they had built in Midpassage? What cruel memories would the abandoned time traveler take to his grave?

*I can leave now.* Kalm's time machine was safe in his pack, a secret kept even from the other Teeps.

*No. I'll stay to the end. I want to see what he does.*

Lan Haarper was at the front of the column now, a hundred man-heights away among dismounted cavalry men and staff

officers watching their commanders wrangle with one of the
Hand's aides. Two of Dighton ris Maanhaldur's slaves stood
rigidly nearby, their eyes focused on their master without
comprehension. The dilapidated fence by the bridge provided
a pathetic backdrop.

*A pathetic army*, Kalm thought involuntarily, registering
homesickness and other emotions as he contrasted this disorder with the precision of a ChelmForceLand parade. Even
the battered Algheran armies of the Final War had a better
appearance marching into captivity.

And that was part of reality also. He let the memory surface, finding a strange peace in the recollection.

Men arose before him, thousands of them standing on the
terraces before the Ice Daughter, in worn blue and green uniforms: Eagle Slayers, Forest Guard, Land Watch, Sea Hold,
Falltroop . . . Watching Algherans who had worn those uniforms to the end, he had stood at the north end of the River
Park among the scarlet and russet-clad soldiers of Chelm-
Force, pent within his own mind, unwilling to probe the
awarenesses around him, watching in self-imposed isolation
while the capital's garrison paraded.

The Algherans had been arrayed in the formations they had
used at full strength, leaving a gap for each man who had
fallen. Here and there more than company-sized holes showed
the price of defeat, and the soldiers of the Alliance stood mo-
tionlessly in silent ranks as their foes stacked empty arms.

So had the long war ended.

But it continued here. Kalm eyed his new commanders.

Dighton ris Maanhaldur had a stern appearance even at this
distance, unnaturally stiff on his horse and skeleton-thin. He
was sober, Kalm noticed gratefully. Sober but regretful of the
fact—"hung over" in Ian Haarper's phrase, but concealing the
fact well. He was not a man who was comfortable with responsibility, not one willing to delegate it.

Beside him, tired but attentive, Krennlen ris Jynnich
waited. He was thinking only of the campaign ahead when
Kalm touched his mind. A child's thoughts: ris Jynnich expected to be a hero. Kalm quirked a lip, remembering his own
experiences as an aide. *Charge that paperwork, Krenn. Make
three copies*.

The elderly Merryn ris Vandeign, slouching on his mare at
the side of the road, a floppy hat hiding his face from the sun,
was from a different mold, scrawny and birdlike to Kalm's

eyes despite his trim form. He was silent as he faced the officer from the brigade, leaving most of the speaking to ris Maanhaldur. *Unhappy*, Kalm registered, recalling the boy he had dragged from the nearby river centuries ago. The boy had become a man whose activity forced him to manufacture disappointments. Did he remember his near drowning?

He was no soldier; only politics had placed him in command of the Steadfast-to-Victory Regiment. Merryn had responded foolishly, as a recalcitrant conscript would, determinedly avoiding the use of military manners and phrasing his orders in casual language that his aides had to translate into correct form. *"Noblesse oblige,"* Ian Haarper had once said of his former friend, defining the term in phrases that did not admit ris Vandeign's current dislike of him, and Kalm had wondered at the strength and cause of that unearned affection.

The Hand's messenger was younger than Merryn, physically. Reliable, he could be called. Trustworthy. Brave, once. Never ennobled, but a good man to lead a battalion of swordsmen, a soldier who had survived his and other expectations to see muskets and rifles.

Kalm had plumbed their minds twice that morning, finding less knowledge than he possessed himself, and did not try again. He brought his attention to closer range, just behind his company, where a dozen high-sided wagons waited, their drivers as bored as the plow horses hitched to them.

The men were not townsfolk, Kalm knew, but itinerant farm laborers from Innings swept up for the army by the broom of conscription. Good pay during the campaign and few risks were all they expected, their anticipated pleasures scanted to throat-searing whiskey and amorphous images of easily slaked lust. There was something frightening about their lack of imagination.

After them came an artillery battery discarded by the brigade.

Farther back were more soldiers, resting by a dirt road leading to ris Vandeign's foundry. Distance had dwarfed the men, but the three cannons they serviced could be glimpsed behind caissons and horse teams, unmistakable bronze cylinders sloping skyward to twice a man's height. *The real guns*.

*Waiting for the battalion to move*, Kalm remembered. *After we pull out, they join the brigade artillery section*. Incongruously, it felt unfair for the Hand of the Queen to take away from the battalion something that had been made in Midpas-

sage—particularly when lan Haarper had accepted the small-
est and oldest cannons the brigade had in exchange, simply
because he liked the artillery commander.

It was an error to keep any of the guns waiting, he realized.
In friendly territory, artillery should go before infantry, since
horses moved faster than walking men.

The ships had not stayed, after all, but had departed more
than a watch before, pursuing winds not subordinate to army
timetables. Their sails were already beneath the horizon. Distance shrouded the minds of their crewmen, and only memory
showed that they had ever docked at Midpassage.

His mind moved farther...

Kylene sat in the kitchen of her house drinking a steaming
black liquid—a habit she had copied from lan Haarper. A
hand moving without thought patted back a vagrant strand of
black hair. Folded sheets of paper and a spray of yellow and
red wildflowers rested on the table. Beneath her robe, invisible to prying eyes but obvious in her mind, purplish bruises
were on her stomach. The images filling her mind were alien,
undecipherable, and he sensed no desire for conversation.

Dieytl lan Callares was on horseback on the other side of
the river, speaking about shipping schedules to Ironwearer
Rahmmend Wolf-Twin. His thoughts danced between memories of the previous night and discomfort caused by the coarse
weave of his linen tunic.

Wandisha lin Zolduhal was awake now, unaware of her
dreams, half regretting the loss of the familiar warmth at her
side, half-pleased not to be sharing her bed. Images of
the bartender-innkeeper and several elderly farmers passed
through her mind—she was cataloging the Midpassage men
who were not in the battalion, wondering which would provide her with a livelihood in the days ahead.

Only fragments of thoughts, all of them from Normals,
came from beyond the town. Kalm could discover nothing
new about the progress of the three companies due from the
northern portion of the valley.

Suddenly there was a change in the battalion. Shouts had
halted the drone of conversation, and men were looking toward the front of the column. Kalm saw tension and relief
mapped across his men's faces, and he turned, not knowing
that he shared that expression. The Hand's aide was cantering
off, crossing the bridge to rejoin his master. Lan Haarper had
remounted and was riding Kalm's way. He stopped at the sec-

ond company, leaned in his seat to speak to its captain, then returned a salute and came toward Kalm. Roars followed him.

Lan Haarper's tan uniform was already rumpled. A bulky green and brown undergarment covered his chest, peeking through his unlaced collar. Flattened knife hilts protruded from pockets added to his tunic front and sleeves, and a chain around his left shoulder secured a hip-length brown cloak. The small crossed swords on his collar gleamed like mirrors. Thick-soled black boots rested loosely in oversized stirrups at the level of Kalm's midsection. A leather scabbard below his right knee held a rifle of more than regulation length. The saddle was also not military issue, being raised front and back to provide a deeper seat than was customary, and when moving the big man had jostled from side to side in tune with the jingle of the harness.

*Not a horseman*, Kalm noticed, approaching cautiously. *Well, if I had to ride, I'd probably look just as silly. But for the rest—* His face masked his thoughts as he contrasted the snug fit of his own uniform with the other man's appearance.

"The Hand's going to move out without waiting longer for the Northern Valley boys, Algheran," lan Haarper said casually once he had stopped rocking. "They can catch up to us tomorrow. Ris Maanhaldur will give the order shortly, so get your men up and in kit. When he calls out, make us look good, will you?"

He should have expected this, but Kalm was surprised nonetheless. He blurted out a question he was never able to remember, though lan Haarper's answer was clear enough.

"I'm adjunct to both right now, since the rest of the regiment isn't here except for the gun company. Oh, Jynnich could do the job, but Maanhaldur's using him more as an orderly, and I already know the men, so . . ." Lan Haarper bent to stroke knuckles along his stallion's neck, a piece of Lopritian superstition that the beast tolerated, then turned the hand to Kalm. "Nicole's cloak over you, Algheran."

*Not a young man*, Kalm noted mechanically, registering strands of gray hair among the red and the beginning of crows-feet. *His time is running out*.

Simultaneously, his mind turned to his men. Dinalduln was too old and too fat for a long march and would have to be watched lest he strain his heart. Chilluson would stumble along as if on three left feet. Tibbitur would be too excited in combat to reload his weapon, but he was paired with Derrill lan Nhissun, who had a good noncom's steadiness. Lan Nhissun's son, Theryn . . .

Responsibility. Was it an accident that those men were in ris Fryddich's platoon? Surely young lan Styllin had men who required his worry.

Panic pushed at Kalm. He pushed it away, muttering something trite as he gripped lan Haarper's forearm, then saluted to excuse his awkwardness. His wits came back with the acknowledgment. "Lan Haarper! The same to—"

But the big man did not hear him. "Fifth Platoon," he was calling out. "Those clowns up there think they're better soldiers than you! And louder! Tell me, who's best?"

"Us!" the answers came back.

"We are!"

"The 5th!"

Lan Haarper waved a fist as he lurched forward. "Tell me again! Again! Make ris Vandeign hear you!" Then he laughed through the shouting until it died. "Hey! Who said 2nd Platoon? You? You! Grab him, boys! All right, don't grab him—chase him back to the 2nd! You over there! Sixth Platoon! Who's the best?"

*Not a performance I could equal*, Kalm admitted ruefully, nudging ris Fryddich with a foot. *Or ris Maanhaldur, either, from what I'm picking up*. This was a man who had been an unimportant prospector for three years? Speculation filled his mind as the big man rode on, even as he gestured toward his platoon leaders.

The Agent's evident humor vanished as he drew even with the supply wagons. Kalm, leaning sideways to buckle on his pack after sending runners to corral his missing men, caught a fleeting glint of sunlight from above the river and dropped his gaze just in time to see lan Haarper cuff one of the drivers. His eyes moved again as the teamster scooted sideways on his seat, to see ripples spreading on the water. When he looked back to the road, lan Haarper was loping toward the artillery battery. The shaken teamster was holding his reins in unsteady hands, his bleary eyes staring straight forward.

Ris Fryddich, sitting up with the same expression, yawned and came to life again as he looked around. "Starting?"

"About to." Kalm watched lan Haarper bending over to slap the barrel of a useless small-bore cannon. *Old-fashioned, separate powder and shell—the kind of thing you find fifty pages into the Plates. Junk, but he's treating them like pure iron.*

And the artillerymen, liberated from the Hand's batteries to play with their toys, were lapping up Ian Haarper's praise uncritically. *Doesn't Loprit have any real soldiers?*

Ris Fryddich stood and drank from his canteen, content for the moment with water. "How's Dighton? Still alive?"

"Above ground, anyhow." Men at the front of the column were mounted now, Kalm's senses told him, and he turned to watch.

"Always surprises me." Derry walked away.

There was a pause while men rejoined the ranks and helped each other slip on packs and bedrolls. Lan Styllin and ris Fryddich moved down the lines, double-checking buckles and webbed straps for the last time, their voices muted by shuffling boots and the men's curses as they awkwardly shouldered their muskets. As Ian Haarper rode past again, Kalm slapped hands over his own gear, finding just enough time to transmit a parting thought toward Kylene. Only silence came back to him.

Then the cry came from ahead. "Regiment up! Forward, march!"

"Battalion up! March!" Ris Maanhaldur's voice carried well but was shrill with tension.

"Company up," Kalm echoed after a two count. "March!"

Whatever pleasure marching held vanished quickly.

By late morning, the town itself could no longer be seen but the hills of Midpassage were still upon the rear horizon. A double line of men reached far behind when Kalm turned to look: near at hand, his own platoons, arrayed at either side of the road, then other units, dwindling in the distance to shimmering caterpillar shapes. Toy wagons and horses moved between them, inchworm slow. In all directions, he saw waist-high grass, browning, limp-stalked, unbroken by buildings or fences.

The artillery battery managed to stay with the battalion. Nothing else about it impressed him.

Other horses and riders were at the front of the column, a half squadron of cavalry detailed to that position by the Hand of the Queen. Kalm did not know what purpose the brightly dressed men served; when he examined their minds, he found they did not know, either. Earlier in the day Ian Haarper had attempted to send them forward as scouts, but they had not moved beyond sight of the battalion. After returning one by one to report on the isolation they had observed from the nearby hilltops, they had joined again in a loose formation several hundred man-heights away. Chatting casually, their horses sidestepping to keep pace with the following soldiers, they drifted before the battalion.

"Take a rest soon, Algheran," lan Haarper said, riding past as he had done several times that day. "That tree up ahead. We'll give the men five minutes. Any problems?"

There had been none yet, but the rest would be welcome. Kalm nodded. Lan Haarper moved ahead, passing the message on to the next company commander, and the next. When Kalm came abreast of him again, he was standing at the side of the road, hands on hips while his horse waited nearby. His eyes were bleak.

On the southern horizon, clouds were forming.

"How's it going, Algheran?"

Lan Haarper was sitting on the wet roadbed at a place where erosion had left enough depth for his legs to dangle. Kalm did not see his horse. If the redhead was uncomfortable in damp clothes, it did not show.

"All right," Kalm stopped beside him, willing to take a brief rest. "Some blisters among the men, I suppose. Sore backs. Sore necks. Bruises from stepping into each other." Tired thighs, aching calves, throats made raw by long breaths, dry rations, too much water—he did not think lan Haarper wanted the catalog. "No one liked the rain, but we'll survive."

"Make sure the men sleep with bare feet tonight. Build fires, have them take their shoes off, put them near enough to dry out but not scorch them."

Kalm inventoried the environment, noting the wet grass, a few wet trees, a wet road—and the wet men. "How do we start a fire? Sir."

"You're a city boy, Algheran. Do what the mèn do."

"All right." Kalm took the advice pragmatically.

"Sun's getting low." Lan Haarper glanced past Kalm toward the following brigade. "We ought to get a stop order soon, and we haven't come to a supply cache yet. Nothing to cook, but you might pick a few men to heat water for those who want it."

"All right." It was not pure suggestion, Kalm suspected.

"And I want to put sentries out tonight. Two men from each platoon should do it. One for each watch."

"All right."

"How's *morale*?" It was a foreign word, defining something Kalm had never heard of before meeting Ian Haarper. But by now he had heard the word often enough to guess its meaning. "Good. Not great."

"How are your lieutenants?"

"All right."

"*Where* are your lieutenants?"

"With the men." Kalm looked away, staring at the tail of Ian Styllin's platoon. Above his head, wagons rolled past, wheels rumbling, tarpaulins covering their contents. Teamsters stared down incuriously.

"Didn't see ris Fryddich." He might have been commenting on the nearing clouds.

*Why are you asking this?* "He's up front, I guess. With Dighton and Krenn." *Didn't seeing him prompt this question?*

"Riding in one of the wagons." It was not a question.

"I guess."

"I guess," Ian Haarper echoed. "That's how you control your men, Algheran?"

*I know where each of them is.* But that was still his secret. "Sorry," Kalm said. "I guess Derry wanted to talk."

"He's sleeping."

"He's tired. Dighton kept him up late last night, remember." *While Krennlen was with Kylene.* Kalm pushed at the side of the road, hoping that Ian Haarper would not read his expression.

"I remember. It's not much excuse." The red-haired man paused, staring down at Kalm. "You tell him, after this he stays with his platoon. Or he loses it."

"Hard to tell Derry what to do."

"Tough. You can say it's my order, if you need to."

Kalm considered that. "What if he doesn't agree?"

"Good question. Get him to agree." Lan Haarper stood and nodded, then walked away.

"Who do you have pulling duty tonight?"

Inside his small tent, cold in his chilled blankets, Dighton ris Maanhaldur blinked at the interruption. It was very dark outside. The Midpassage Battalion was encamped along the roadside for the night; his slaves had erected the tent for him, laid out the bedding on mashed-down grass, started a fire, and warmed a supper. Krenn ris Jynnich had kept him company and chatted with him about Molminda's court until most of the men had gone to bed.

The rain had not returned. The sleeping men made little noise, and the irregular insect sounds and hisses from the fire were not disturbing. Even this late, a lantern glowed inside a large tent farther up the column; when he had passed it on his way to the latrines, he had seen Ironwearer Ian Haarper inside, sipping a drink from a small mug, a comforting token of civilization in the middle of desolation. But he was not comfortable himself; the ground under him was uneven, hard in places; his body was already sore from riding, and the campaign was only one day old. Dighton wished now that he had not left home; he wished he had been content to stay on the Hand's staff, with its traveling house wagons and cooked food and padded bunks.

Merryn ris Vandeign was not with the battalion, he knew. He had accepted his brother's hospitality for the night and would be warm and snug in the middle of the brigade. Would anyone blame him if—

His father would. Without asking, he knew the Hand would be contemptuous if he asked to sleep in the staff wagons.

He had been weak, Dighton realized now. That ex-Algheran captain had somehow sniffed out his unexpressed ambitions; then he and ris Jynnich and ris Fryddich had badgered him until he was forced to ask his father for this command. Really, he had only wanted to please his friends, and it was already turning out poorly.

For now he would keep his self-knowledge to himself, so no one would notice it, and tomorrow he would act like a good officer and that would be enough. He would act as his father did and like other nobles he had met at the court, and things would go as well for him as they always did for them. Tomorrow— Tonight was miserable, of course, but no one was watching him, no one knew he was unhappy, and they would not find out, so it was not really important.

"Who's the duty officer tonight?"

That voice again. He did not understand what the question was about. The legs before the front of the tent blocked his view of the fire, and he wondered uncertainly if he could preserve his dignity if he told the men outside to step away with their conversation.

"Ris Maanhaldur, are you up?"

It was the Ironwearer's voice, betraying impatience. He thought of not moving, of outwaiting the big man, but he was not sure it would work, and he wanted the man to go away. "Yes," he said at last, pretending sleepiness. "The duty officer? I—can't you ask ris Jynnich?" Even to himself, it sounded like a complaint. "I mean, he handles details like that. He's probably still up."

"Yes, I can ask ris Jynnich." The voice was patient.

Dighton waited to be sure distance had muffled the footsteps, then reached stealthily for the bottle Krennlen had left. It was still almost half-full, he thought. There would be enough whiskey for the coming night if he did not share any.

What was a "duty officer"?

He had the bottle recapped a minute later when Ian Haarper returned, so there was no embarrassing sloshing sound to explain. Yes, he agreed carefully, hoping the man would stay outside his tent and not smell the alcohol fumes, yes, there should be an officer to supervise the sentries. Yes, it should be a rotating job, held by all the platoon commanders. Yes, he would have ris Jynnich set up a schedule for that tomorrow. Yes, since ris Fryddich was still awake and fresh, it made sense for him to have the duty first, and yes, Ian Haarper could give that order for him.

Left alone at last, Dighton swallowed, feeling that he had escaped some undefinable disaster, and reached for the bottle again. Tomorrow he would be in command of things, he vowed. He could have another drink tonight, and it would never matter. What a man did when he was alone was never important.

Kalm, returned to his own mind, smiled ironically at the walls of his small tent and settled himself for sleep.

That was the first day of the campaign.

# CHAPTER NINETEEN

"*R*is Maanhaldur wants a meeting. All the captains.*"

"Sure," Kalm said. "What about?"

"Things." Krennlen ris Jynnich looked distrustfully at the men walking past. "Just some things."

It was a quarter watch into the afternoon. The sky was pale but unclouded. Sun had not yet warmed the air. The second day's march had lasted just long enough to dispel the morning's stiff muscles but not long enough to reawaken the tedious pain of exercise. The men moved awkwardly, hungry and uncomfortable in still-damp clothing. They were on the road itself today rather than the water-soaked ground beside it, so there was only a single line of wagons between the files.

They still had not reached a supply cache.

Several hundred man-heights ahead, Timmial lan Haarper was riding with a cavalry officer beside the great road, gesturing at grassy hills, but the horsemen seemed no more venturesome than before. At the back of the column, only the black pavement showed behind the three tiny guns; the Strength-through-Loyalty Brigade had been late striking camp.

Kalm unhappily eyed the distance to the battalion commander's wagon, not eager to walk at double time and unpleasantly aware of the weight of his pack. *Why couldn't ris Maanhaldur wait until we've stopped before he starts showing us his leadership?* "Sure."

Ris Jynnich did not move. "You hear what he did to Derry?"

*Yes.* It was not a conversation that would reduce the distance. "I imagine I'll hear," Kalm said, pointing with a thumb. "Him, too?"

"Just Dighton's men."

*We aren't Dighton's men, we're just loaned to him.*

"Let's go."

The artillery captain watched incuriously as they turned.

When they drew abreast of Pitar lan Styllin, Kalm put the lieutenant in charge of the company. "I'll be back soon."

"After your breakfast?" one of the men shouted.

Kalm hesitated, detecting both humor and an emotion that was not yet resentment but that would not be easily dispelled. How would lan Haarper handle this?

"Yes," he called back, knowing truth was inadequate. "All the officers are getting six kinds of steaks for breakfast. Big mugs of beer. And five desserts." He licked his fingers theatrically. "I'll think of you."

His words brought a few laughs. And though ris Jynnich frowned at him, Kalm's own mood improved as they joined the other captains.

Dighton ris Maanhaldur had commandeered an ambulance for his belongings. It was a narrow wagon, enclosed at the rear, with a bed close to the ground and enough headroom inside to stand. Black curtains closed the front and rear of the cabin. The driver's seat was high, with space beneath for poles and canvas; a well behind it served as a mounting place and as a front entrance to the cabin. Stepping onto the moving vehicle, Kalm saw that a poorly folded tent and bedding had been dumped in a storage chest at the side of the well.

Inside the cabin, a pair of benches provided enough seats for a dozen men. On the walls, lowered shelves dangled from hinges. Paper boxes of bandages, pointed rods, short saws, and other implements were heaped in a corner. Derrauld ris Fryddich was raising the back curtain, but the interior was still gloomy.

"Major." Kalm braced his feet against the motion of the wagon but saluted as politely as possible in the direction of ris Maanhaldur. The two other captains echoed him awkwardly, then copied him in removing their packs and rifles.

"Uh, take seats." Ris Maanhaldur gestured hesitantly, as if expecting additional men to arrive. "Uh, I've decided . . . I was talking with Ironwearer Ian Haarper last night, and we decided. We should have sentries at night. Uh-hhh, one from each platoon, I guess. You'll have to pick the men."

"Sure," Kalm said quickly. "It won't be a problem."

"No problem," the other captains echoed.

If anything, ris Maanhaldur became more apologetic. "We ought to have an officer awake during the night, too. Just in case. And I think a lieutenant will be enough. I want to be fair, so I want to use a different man each night. It'll have to be all night, by the way. Lan Haarper says he wants an officer awake 'twenty-four hours a day.' "

The exaggeration brought chuckles, but each of the captains agreed.

"Well. The job should be rotated, then. Uh-hhh-umm. Ris Fryddich had it last night, so I thought . . . Lan Rispar, if you could have, uh, your other lieutenant—"

"Lan Styllin."

"Have him take the watch tonight."

"Sure."

"And tomorrow the second company will have the post for two days, and then the first company. Is that agreed?"

It was. Ris Maanhaldur seemed surprised. "That's it, then."

Kalm stood with the other captains, but as he had expected, ris Jynnich grabbed his arm before he could leave. "We have to do something."

"Do what?" Inwardly he lacked the patience he was displaying, but he lowered his pack to the floor again and sat down, pretending interest as ris Fryddich carefully lowered the curtains. It was very dark then inside the cabin, and no one spoke until ris Fryddich was seated with ris Jynnich and ris Maanhaldur. Kalm smelled a faint odor of whiskey and a stronger odor of unwashed bodies. His hand, moving along the bench, encountered nicks and narrow cuts in the wood.

"You heard what happened to—" Ris Jynnich restarted the speech he had practiced in his thoughts all morning.

"We have to do something about Ian Haarper." Ris Fryddich had his own speech.

"What's the matter?" Kalm asked, already knowing what would be said, already regretting his sham of ignorance. He almost envied the Normals at that moment; for all their half-minded weaknesses, they were never forced to listen to the same conversations time after time.

"You heard what happened to—"

"I heard, Krenn. He went to bed in the middle of the night, and Ian Haarper knocked his tent over in the morning and kicked him awake. I heard about it from the men."

Ris Jynnich frowned at him. "What are we going to do?"

"What can we do? Derrauld, you *were* placed in charge of things, weren't you?" The question was rhetorical; though ris Fryddich protested that he had not been told to stay awake after placing the second shift of sentries, Kalm knew he would have done so if his orders had come from any other officer. He had baited Ian Haarper deliberately, and the Ironwearer had punished him for it.

"That's not it. The question is, What *should* we do?" Ris Maanhaldur spoke at last, gesturing pointlessly. "He's . . . he acts like—"

"Like we're regular army instead of militia?" He deliberately chose an untactful suggestion, flattering to none of them.

"We are, though." Ris Maanhaldur frowned. His true comparison of Ironwearer Ian Haarper was with ris Clendannan and Wolf-Twin. "Can't he be reasonable?"

"No." Kalm enjoyed giving that answer.

"Can we go—"

"Complain?" Kalm asked. "To whom? He's an Ironwearer. You aren't going to get him removed."

"But—" Ris Maanhaldur gestured again. "He insulted Derrauld. A noble, in front of everyone."

*Not for the first time.* "I know. But—"

Ris Jynnich was thinking. "*Why* is he an Ironwearer?"

"Because he says he is," Kalm said. "That's all it takes."

"That's all?" Ris Jynnich was outraged. "That peasant can kill people, like Gerint and Derry—and you and me—without being stopped, just because he says he can?"

"Like worms on the floor." That was not fully honest, but Kalm was enjoying ris Jynnich's discomfort. "For anything," he added, watching the man pale as he remembered his treatment of Kylene. "Even without warning."

Ris Fryddich was still thinking. "Is there a way—"

Kalm sighed. "You can accuse him of not being worthy of being an Ironwearer. The Hand will ask any of the Teeps in the brigade to examine your case, and if the Teep agrees, Ian

Haarper will lose his title. Maybe the Hand would take his rank away from him also, but he is a soldier, and he knows more about commanding a battalion—or a regiment—than any of us."

"What would a Teep say?" ris Fryddich wondered. He seemed genuinely curious.

"How would I know?" Kalm shot back. "Do you think I'm one?"

"No, course not, but—" The blond man sighed.

"*Are* there any Teeps with the brigade? Dighton, do you know of any?" Ris Jynnich was still thinking.

"My—the Hand has one on his staff. He already approved of . . ." Ris Maanhaldur was glum. "There might be another."

"There was one from Midpassage," Kalm said. "A money broker, I think. He's with Ironwearer Wolf-Twin."

Even in the darkness, he sensed that that had provoked frowns.

"That first one, then," ris Jynnich said, breaking the silence. "Can we talk to him?"

"About Derrauld? It's too bad it happened, but that won't get Ian Haarper removed. I've had officers who killed men for sleeping on duty." *In real armies.*

There was more silence.

"Is there anything else about him?" ris Maanhaldur asked. "If not this, is there anything we can show, that—no one's perfect, you know."

*It's trying to be perfect that counts.* But explaining Ian Haarper to his enemies was not Kalm's goal. He only grunted.

"If we knew, or could say, there was something . . . Would the Teep say . . . We could . . ." Ris Maanhaldur's mind raced behind the slow words, looking for a plausible discrediting story to use as an example.

"Forget it," Kalm said curtly. "Even if you bribe that Teep, and even if he tells the Hand what you want him to, every other Teep would know about it, and the story would come out. The Teeps are honest about this kind of thing."

Ris Jynnich cursed but did not argue. "What if—we could tell him he just has to say it once. And . . . after that . . ."

"Kill him before the truth gets out?" Kalm asked.

"Well. Would it work?"

"How do you propose to keep that a secret from him?"

Ris Jynnich cursed again. "What do we do?"

It was ris Fryddich's turn to speak. "Kalm, you said, to be an Ironwearer—it was just saying that. Suppose I said I was one. Or Krenn or Dighton here. We all outrank lan Haarper. Do you think . . ."

He was sincere, Kalm realized with amazement. "Derrauld?" "Yes?"

*Mutiny, perjury, bribery, murder . . .* "I think you'd find being an Ironwearer very dull."

"Oh?"

"It eliminates a lot of your freedom."

"Oh." Ris Fryddich went back to his concentration.

Outside, in the light, men were shouting. Forewarned, Kalm stood casually and put a hand on a shelf bracket. "If you'll excuse me, Dighton, I should get back to my men."

"If you—" The wagon lurched as the driver applied brakes. Ris Maanhaldur and the other nobles were tossed sideways.

Kalm released his grip and looked through the forward curtain as the vehicle came to a stop. A wooden platform, house-size, had been built at the edge of the road. It was covered with boxes of different sizes and rows of barrels. The cavalry unit had formed up on three sides of the platform to keep the men at bay; its officer was conferring with lan Haarper. "Time we showed ourselves. We've reached a supply cache."

They marched only a few thousand man-heights after leaving the supply cache, stopping before evening. That delay cost half a day of marching time.

On the fourth day, a man in the third platoon died.

A teamster, driving without sufficient attention, dropped two wheels of his wagon off the side of the road. Boxes of food and ammunition slipped from under the canvas cover and pummeled two men marching beneath.

One man received a broken arm. The other—a squad leader of about 160 years, a stoker at Merryn ris Vandeign's foundry with a wife and one surviving daughter—had a lung punctured by a fractured rib. He was dead, from shock or hemorrhage or suffocation, before his squad finished digging his grave, even before Kalm's men and the artillery battery got the wagon back on the road and reloaded.

There was no doctor with the battalion to treat the first man, but lan Haarper fastened branches around his arm with canvas so it could not be moved and had one of the cavalrymen ride with him back to the brigade. Kalm never learned what happened to him after that.

# CHAPTER TWENTY

*T*wo days later they were still marching.

In the first days of the march the men had chattered as they walked, commenting on the changing shapes of hills and other bits of scenery and exchanging rumors. Now the conversations had ended. They marched in stolid silence, even their thoughts and daydreams strangely muted when Kalm probed.

There were gaps in the long column. The cavalry unit now grouped itself a thousand man-heights in advance of the Midpassage Battalion; the rest of the brigade was almost an hour's march behind. Looking backward from the rear of the battalion beside the three little cannons, Kalm sometimes saw only empty road and long grass nodding as if with bowed head to deny the existence of other men.

His own company was a hundred paces ahead now, millipede-stepping along the road. Wheels squeaked irregularly as supply wagons rolled past, bored teamsters staring at him for a moment's diversion. Midges were flitting before his face, retreating and advancing as his head wavered. Larger insects buzzed patiently above them. Weeds and strawlike grasses were matted down along the roadbed by soldiers who had sought easier marching.

Haggard, Kalm stepped to the side and closed his eyes as Ian Haarper rode by, returning from a trip to brigade headquarters.

"Afternoon, Algheran." The big man stopped between Kalm and the road, then patted his horse comfortably by his knee as if to draw attention to his still-shiny boots. "You look beat."

"Tired," Kalm admitted, raising his head to focus on the man. On the roadbed, the last of the caissons rolled past, then the three short cannons. A vein pulsed on the horse's neck; Kalm envied its slow tempo.

"Let's talk about it," Ian Haarper said, frowning. He stood in the stirrups and shouted at the column. "Battalion, take five! Five minutes rest!"

"Wish I could do that," Kalm muttered, watching the ranks break all along the line even before the order was relayed from officers to men.

"Just takes practice." Lan Haarper swung from his horse, letting the reins droop to the ground. From his pocket, he took a twist of paper holding a white powder that he held before the stallion's muzzle. "Find a big field where no one minds you and keep calling till your voice carries right. When you're doing it even while someone shoots at you, you'll have it perfect."

Kalm grimaced at the misunderstanding but said nothing. Lan Haarper left the horse untended and led the way to a small hill where he could watch the battalion, then gestured Kalm to a seat beside him.

Seated, leaning backward on his pack, Kalm saw that the man's square face was a mask, piebalded by sunburn, without emotion. Sweat had darkened his uniform's armpits, and dust powdered his legs. The march was making him disheveled also, Kalm realized, thinking of the ruin of his own neat appearance. Mounted, the man had not seemed human. The discovery was jarring. Lan Haarper was unpredictable.

Unpredictable and intimidating. Kalm had become accustomed to viewing Ian Haarper as a duped and easily manipulated victim. But this close to the man, it was impossible to ignore his size and strength or his aura of competence.

It was nerve-racking to contemplate what Ian Haarper would do if he realized that Kalm was an enemy.

Lan Haarper's voice admitted no weakness. "You're weaving back and forth while you walk as if you're drunk, Algheran. But I don't smell anything on you. What's the problem?"

"Just tired," Kalm said. He smiled wanly and slapped his stomach. "I don't think I'm built for this."

"You're losing the gut," Ian Haarper said. "That's not it. How are you doing on sleep, fellow?"

"Not well." With difficulty, Kalm fought back a yawn. He wanted to close his eyelids that very instant and fall asleep. Was his need so apparent? "Thought I was—it's hard, this march. We're going so slowly, but it's still exhausting."

"Takes extra energy to go slow," the big man said. "But we don't have much choice, the Hand is dawdling so. Never mind. Now, you've been marching up the length of your company staring at your men and falling back and speeding up again. Don't do it anymore. Makes me tired, just watching."

"Just checking. In case they need—"

"Find a spot alongside them and keep to it. It'll be a lot easier for you, and if there's anything you need to notice, you'll find out about it. They'll tell you."

"All right. Sorry." The words were automatic; Kalm was actually thinking about the yawn he could indulge himself with when he was again unobserved and safe.

The big redhead lifted his shoulders and let them droop. "Nothing to be sorry about. But how much sleep did you have last night? And the night before?"

Kalm closed his eyes, reckoning. "Maybe a half watch last night. None before. I—I'll be all right if there's any action, it's just that . . ." *If I could only count on both my platoon leaders*. Ris Fryddich was lazy and ineffectual, he had found, but he would not tell that to a mutual enemy. "I'm just out of practice."

"I don't care why. I'm not going to have the officers in this regiment straggling. Understand me? Do you understand?"

"I understand," Kalm said bleakly. "Are you going—am I being relieved?" Only fatigue dulled the bitter taste of defeat.

"I'll think about it."

"I understand," Kalm repeated.

"Yeah." Lan Haarper's voice was soft. "Time we were going." He stood, then assisted as Kalm donned his pack and rifle. "You're carrying too much weight, Algheran. You ought to go through your gear and pitch some stuff. You want advice?"

Kalm turned quickly, keeping the pack from the man's touch. "No. No. I'll manage it."

"Your funeral." Lan Haarper moved his shoulders again,

then put his fingers into a small pouch on his belt. "Here, take this pill, *guy*. It won't accomplish miracles, but it'll keep you going another watch. Report to me this evening."

A man ran past in the twilight, shouting gleefully as he jumped over tent guy wires. He was followed by another man, also laughing, whose arm was outstretched as if to tag him. They were Dighton's slaves; neurosurgery had left them happy as well as docile, Kalm noted. Teep-guided, the operation was comparatively safe, so there was no reason for the faint nausea he felt.

But his world had not known slavery for centuries, and that made him squeamish. Kalm shook his head at his foolishness and only then coughed, drawing attention to himself. "You wished me to report. Sir."

"Ah! Come in, Algheran. Water's on the table." Despite the words, the man on the cot seemed preoccupied.

Kalm hesitated. He felt better now, stronger and more awake, but he was still uneasy. Surprisingly, he lacked hunger, even though his company was already preparing the evening meal under the eye of his lieutenants. Uncertain of his position, he had not issued any orders to them but had prepared his own rations, eating a few bites from habit while reviewing his confrontation with lan Haarper. Fortunately, the men who had noticed his behavior had not thought it of importance, and both lan Styllin and ris Fryddich had asked him to approve their selection of nighttime guards.

Lan Haarper had not relieved him yet. Kalm ducked to fit beneath the tent fly.

Inside the tent, a canvas water sack rested on a low-lying folding table. Next to it was a small glass. Ignored by lan Haarper, he poured one glass outside to ease the Lady's thirst, then filled another for himself. When done, he took a seat on a canvas stool before the table. "This is very nice," he said appreciatively.

Simultaneously, his mind probed outward, finding only vacuum where his eyes saw a man. An involuntary smile rose to his face.

"It'll do. Best thing is, no *mosquitoes*. No flying bugs which bite. Never mind." Lan Haarper touched a shining object that dangled from a string fastened to the tent over his head, setting it asway, then wriggled a hand in dismissal. "Let me finish this chapter."

A coal gas lantern fastened to the ridgepole hissed softly. Kalm regained his face, then looked around the tent with curiosity as his eyes adapted to the flickering yellow light. A canvas floor to keep vermin at bay, a washbasin at one end of the table, writing implements, a spare set of boots, saddlebags against the back of the tent, lan Haarper's scabbarded rifle . . . This was luxury, and the telepath contrasted it unhappily with his own grimy blankets and the tarpaulin draped over a rope that served him as a tent. *And he gets a full-time orderly. He gets to ride, so he isn't tired and sore all the time. And he takes all this for granted. Cimon! His rank is no higher than mine in the real world. How does he rate?*

*Clean clothes, too,* he noted with feelings of scandal. *No dust on him now. Lan Callares couldn't be neater.* The uniforms by the basin—was it Kylene or Wandisha who had folded them for lan Haarper? No one had offered to help Kalm pack.

Lan Haarper, lying on his back with a mass of folded papers in his hands, ignored him. The outsized cot had been made up with two blankets; a third was rolled up for a pillow, and one more supported unbooted feet. Reminded of the man's neurotic sensitivity to cold, Kalm felt better.

Outside, men gathered around unnecessary campfires, seeking heat less than surety in a darkened world. A work party lumbered past, foul of hand and tongue after burying kitchen waste. Splashing sounds located a brook where men filled canteens and washed away itch-generating sweat. In the middle distance, horses neighed. Nearby, a man picked at the soles of his feet with a small knife. Improbably, a dog could be heard yapping.

"Just be patient," lan Haarper said soothingly, and tapped the dangling object again. "Rest your feet. Catch your breath. Maybe close the door there and ignore the world. Just pull that cord and we'll have some privacy."

"Sure." But the tone of his voice carried another message.

Meanwhile, as his fingers moved, Kalm's eyes remained on the swinging object, trying to grasp its shape.

"Relax, Algheran."

A ring of some sort? "Yes, sir."

Lan Haarper sat up and eyed him ironically. "You still look worried, Algheran. Got a guilty conscience about something? Or are you just tired?"

"Still tired," Kalm admitted.

"Hmmm." The Ironwearer touched the dangling thing again, keeping it in motion. "You need to learn to relax."

A little disk. Kalm stared at the swinging object, wondering if he had seen a face on its surface.

"You need to learn to relax," Ian Haarper said.

"Yeah." Was it a coin? From where?

"Maybe I should teach you how to relax," Ian Haarper mused. "Algheran, still here?"

"Uh huh." At the ends of its arc, the swinging thing seemed to float in the air. Kalm could think of nothing more fascinating. "Yeah . . . sir."

"You want to relax, don't you?"

"Yeah . . . sir."

"You're going to relax, then. You are relaxed. Relax. Relax. You're comfortable. You're safe. You're at peace. You're relaxed. But you feel all the weight of your body," Ian Haarper said softly. "Your back, your legs, your arms, your shoulders . . . You feel them all, even your fingers and toes. So heavy, all so heavy. And you're sleepy. Sleepy. Relaxed. Safe. Sleepy. Your head is heavy, your eyes are heavy . . . So heavy. So hard to keep your eyes open . . . when you're sleepy . . . so sleepy."

Kalm murmured.

"So hard. Your eyes close. Just for a moment. You know you can open them, but they're so tired, so heavy . . . Just to rest them, you close your eyes. It feels so good to close your eyes, so good to let them rest . . ."

Slack-jawed, his eyes shut, Kalm nodded agreement.

"Now the weight comes out of your left little toe. It seems to float, and you don't feel its weight. Feel the weight flowing out of the toe . . . Your eyes are closed, and you feel the weight flowing out of the toe . . . And now the toe next to it, all the weight is flowing out . . ."


"Elizabeth's turning down the proposal from the priest, Ian Collins," Ian Haarper said, as if making an explanation. He turned a leaf to his left, and another before putting a marker into place, then shifted to his side. Kalm, yawning, noticed squiggled black lines running across the sheets. Horizontal writing, not in ideograms but broken into irregular lengths like the Plates. What would the man be reading now? What was so important as to require study?

The silver hairs on the Agent's head were obvious in the lantern light, far different from the mesh of his Teepblind. Great age was another weakness, and for an instant, despite the stiffness he felt himself, Kalm's mood turned to pity.

Unknowing, lan Haarper looked up. "Sorry to make you wait on pride and prejudice, but I haven't read it for a while."

"It?" Kalm was polite, willing to indulge the old man.

"A novel," the redhead admitted casually. "With a setting we'd both find rather strange. Makes a good change of pace."

"If you say so." But Kalm could not keep a questioning look off his face.

Lan Haarper laughed. "You should see yourself, Algheran. You look like you'd caught me in some obscene perversion."

Kalm shifted uneasily. "If it's your hobby, I'm not criticizing. I just wasn't aware you knew any fiction writers. Kylene hadn't mentioned it, and there aren't any in Midpassage."

"Jane Austen was long before my time," lan Haarper said dryly. "I never met her. I just liked her stuff. And she had millions of other readers. At one time."

"Pleasant to have so many friends, I'm sure," Kalm murmured, treating the exaggeration tactfully.

"Yeah." The big man dismissed the subject as he swung to his feet. "Now, about you. What's your excuse for this afternoon?" Shadow did not conceal his stern expression.

He had almost been relaxed. Now Kalm quailed. "I—I—"

"Don't stutter. Are you too out of shape to do your job?"

"No," Kalm said flatly, but he was not willing to continue until lan Haarper gestured for more words. "It's just that it never ends. The men—their feet need tending. They don't cook their food properly unless someone stands over them, and they get bellyaches. They worry at night. I don't want to complain—"

"Then don't. It doesn't do any good," lan Haarper growled. He pointed a finger to the tip of Kalm's nose, standing hunched over under the low tent ceiling, so close that Kalm could smell the musky odor rising from his skin. "You have lieutenants to do that sort of stuff. When it needs doing."

He had one lieutenant. It was pointless to admit that he filled the vacancy left by ris Fryddich. "Yes, but—"

"Don't yes but me, man! Soldiers always grumble, and they always have cause to grumble. Haven't you learned that yet?"

"That's a bit callous. If I can—"

"Callous? Can you march for them? Can you shoot for them? Can you fight for them, die for them, wipe shit off their butts for them?"

"No." Kalm clipped the word off, putting a cap on his own rising anger. *I can preserve my dignity.*

It might have been Ian Haarper who was the mind reader. "Give your men their dignity," he said more gently. "Trust them. They aren't children who need potty training. Let them think of themselves as hard-bitten soldiers who fend for themselves. They'll be better soldiers—and better men."

"But—" Kalm stopped, then began anew. "They aren't."

Lan Haarper made his shoulder motion again. "Sure. They don't know their asses from holes in the ground. It'll get a lot of them killed. But they'll find out the difference on their own, Algheran. Let them learn what they can from their mistakes. That's one reason we're on this march, instead of waiting for Mlart to come to us."

"But—" Kalm turned away. "That's so—"

"Cruel?" Ian Haarper mocked. "Mean? Illiberal? Callous? If you think so, I'll give you an order: Don't play daddy for them. Stick to being an army officer."

"I wasn't 'playing' at anything, Ian Haarper."

"*Goddammitalltohell*, Algheran! I don't give a rat's ass! I want your men to stay in formation. I want them to keep their gear in order. I want them to stay in place on a battlefield. And I want them to fight, and if following their orders is going to get them killed, I want them killed! Is that clear? That's their duty. My duty. Your duty. And if you won't do it, say so now, and I'll replace you with someone who will. Is that clear?"

Kalm exhaled loudly. "Yes, sir. It's clear."

"Good." Lan Haarper stood once more, looming over Kalm. "Not easy going up against your own countrymen, I know. If you wanted to bail out and go back . . ." He kicked idly at the stool leg. "People would understand."

Kalm pretended not to be jarred by the impact. "Back to town, and then off to one of Her Majesty's jails."

"Reformation - through - Diligent - Guidance - of - Character Centers, I think they're called these days. Not interested, eh?"

There was no room for two men to stand, so Kalm remained seated, but he forced a grin to match Ian Haarper's. "Better off here, I suspect. It's too late to turn back. Even if—"

Hadn't there been something hanging from the wall of the tent? He thought he remembered something. But it was gone now. It must not have been important. "How do you feel about opposing Mlart, lan Haarper?"

"It's my job. I always do my job, Algheran." Hesitancy showed on the big man's face for a brief moment, then faded to neutrality. "You can keep your company, Captain."

"So." Kalm's buoyant mood collapsed. "Am I free to go now?"

"Not yet." Lan Haarper knelt to open one of the saddle-bags, pulled a long green and brown mottled vest forth, and threw it to the telepath. "This is a spare."

The vest was bulky and surprisingly heavy. Kalm's arm was slapped downward by the weight. "What?"

"Another order for you: Wear this under your uniform. Keep it on constantly till we get back to town. It's *Kevlar*. Bullets won't go through it. Or bayonets."

"Some sort of Ironwearer miracle?" Kalm asked skeptically.

"A miracle from *DuPont*." The redhead smiled mysteriously. "Better living through chemistry." Then he sobered. "It doesn't protect you from cannon, so be sensible. Your body is going to soak up the energy and momentum of anything that hits you. But bruises are better than bullet holes."

It sounded implausible. Kalm lifted the vest, getting some idea of the heft. "Why me?"

"Well, you're senior captain if anything happens to me, for all of Maanhaldur's instant promotions. You seem to have the most experience next to me. And your men trust you."

"Oh?"

"Yeah. Old Silent Kalm, they call you." Lan Haarper smiled. "But mostly it's for Kylene. I think she'd be upset if her boyfriend came home on a stretcher. Or didn't come back at all."

Kalm swallowed, wishing he could disappear. "I . . . Not . . ." Some things could not be said, no matter how alien the man was, however much an enemy he must be.

"What's the matter, Algheran?" lan Haarper asked. "Cat got your tongue?"

Kalm smiled wanly at the image. "Don't you think she'd feel worse if you didn't return?"

"She'd be relieved, I should think. She'd have her freedom."

"You know that isn't so!"

"Keep your voice down, Algheran. Let's assume it is. Anyhow, I wrote her a letter. Something happens to me, she'd know what to do."

*Take the time machine back to the Project. Forget Ian Haarper ever existed. Never search time for him.* Kalm had glimpsed scraps of that letter in Kylene's mind. "Lan Haarper —Ian Haarper, I don't understand you."

"I'm a simple man." The redhead toyed with the novel. "Just ask Kylene." And when Kalm refused to answer, he added, "Or Wandisha."

"I have."

"So you know everything there is to know." Lan Haarper reopened his book. "Time you got back to your unit, Captain."

*Do you know that Kylene thinks you very fragile, Ironwearer?* Kalm wondered. *She thinks that all your childhood, because of your size, you struggled not to disappoint people who misread your age, and it maimed your personality. She thinks that to hide from that you are obsessed with seeking danger, and that you deliberately chose a life which enmeshed you in horrors you can never escape, never acknowledge.*

"Go to bed, soldier," Ian Haarper ordered. "It's late, and when that pill wears off, you'll fall like a rock."

Kalm halted under the tent flap, letting light spill onto the darkened earth. "Lan Haarper, can we speak tomorrow night?"

"Company's company. Sure."

# CHAPTER TWENTY-ONE

*In fact half of a ten-day period passed before Kalm returned*, days in which the Strength-through-Loyalty Brigade completed the portion of its journey along the river. Driven hard by lan Haarper, the Midpassage Battalion kept the lead. When the rest of the brigade turned eastward, it was a day's march closer to the Near Rim of the Shield Mountains.

The weather had turned as well, bringing the latest of the rainstorms that presaged winter. This had been no brief squall but a cold, dreary cloudbuster beginning before dawn and lasting until late afternoon of the following day. Mud had forced the marchers onto the pavement, but the going was no easier, for in places the road was flooded and few of the troops had shoes that kept their feet dry. Fires were not possible, and rations were short; for all that time the men subsisted on grain soaked in water, tasteless kernels with the consistency of iron-berries.

Fortunately, at ris Maanhaldur's request, Lord Andervyll had ordered a pair of rest days to allow the companies from the northern part of the valley to catch up to the battalion, and lan Haarper had added another. So the men were able to stay under canvas while the brigade closed on them. An unlucky few had drawn guard duty or been required to tend to the animals, but their officers had not been demanding. Kalm had not ventured out from his tent more often than necessary. His

own senses had detected no threats, and when he had faced
chagrined half-drowned men huddling between storage
wagons rather than struggling through the mud from post to
post, harshness had been beyond him.

Lan Haarper had ridden past him through the downpour at
one point, headed for Cimon knew what tasks at brigade
headquarters. Kalm had known him only from his size until
lightning lit up his grim, comfort-scorning face. Enjoying the
responsibilities of his rank, Kalm had thought cynically,
watching the big man's mount splash through the encamp-
ment. After days of lan Haarper's exhortations, his sympathy
had been with the horse.

Also, he thought of the sick men behind in the brigade, too
ill to walk, lying in overfilled ambulances and uncovered supply wagons. There were too many sick men, shaking with
fever despite the cold, too weak to void their watery bowels
over the wagon sides so that they lay gasping in their own
bloody, putrid wastes. Too many sick men, trapped below
clouds of greedy, demanding insects clamoring for their dis-
eased bodies. Sick men, too long untreated, with too few attendants, washed clean only by the killing elements.

Rumor had it that the brigade was moving slowly not because of rain but because ris Andervyll was waiting for the
weakest men to die and free space on the wagons for additional sick men. Camp gossip—it was in his power to find the
truth, but Kalm had been unwilling to probe the Hand's mind.

But Nicole had placed her cloak over the battalion—so far.

The good fortune was unlikely to last, Kalm knew. The
cause of marching sickness was not understood, but fatigue
certainly contributed to it. Even with a rest day, exhaustion
and cold weather were cutting the men's strength. It would
take a stay in barracks, with proper discipline and a better
diet, to rebuild the battalion as a military force.

And the Midpassage Battalion was in better shape for
fighting than was the rest of the brigade. Exchanging conversation with Dieytl lan Callares, he had learned that ris Clendannan's Queen's Own Puissant Guards Regiment had
preserved some sort of order, but the garrison troops of ris
Daimgewln's Defiance-to-Insurrection Regiment, removed
from their soft billets and camp followers in Northfaring, were
turning into an armed rabble.

Worse would come. Rain would come more frequently as
the season ran on, getting colder. Within a year tenth, sleeting

rain would give way to snow, and the campaign would be over.

Or so the Lopritians thought.

Mlart tra'Nornst would reckon otherwise, Kalm remembered. He had seen the hostile elements as only another adversary to be defeated; his final campaign would continue without pause until he had blockaded the Lopritian capital. The Swordtroop and Mlart's mercenaries would fall on all the rest of Loprit then, two hundred thousand men blanketing any resistance as thoroughly as snow covered the ground.

Children would be homeless that winter so that Algheran soldiers might be housed; paupers would starve so that the victors might eat. The misery of the conquered would batter Loprit's besieged rulers behind their walls as convincingly as any cannon.

As a schoolboy he had read capsule descriptions of the Unifier's campaigns and remembered only that they were justified and victorious. The sketchy military training he had received in the Falltroop had taught him little more. Ironically, he had gained a real appreciation of Mlart's generalship only after he had deserted the Algherans, in a ChelmForce staff college.

Now Kalm, marching to battle among the Lopritians, was learning to appreciate Mlart's accomplishments from yet another viewpoint. Defeat would not be easy for the Lopritians to accept, and with his knowledge, these last days of summer had a special poignancy. He read a metaphor into every falling leaf, seeing in each one innocence dropping from the tree of truth, which war must soon leave nude and defenseless.

When Kalm's black humor ended and he sought Ian Haarper out again, the Strength-through-Loyalty Brigade had been reunited. The dark cloak of evening was being pulled over the one Earth, and the big man was in his tent, leafing through documents. He was standing, the stool by the folding table occupied by a travel-disheveled man whom Kalm's probe showed to be a messenger from ris Cornoval's Southern Corps.

Nightfall and damp compressed the odors of camp, intensifying them. The mildew scent of stale sweat and unwashed bodies was everywhere, as was the almost pleasant odor of manure. The sweetish smell of putrefying bodies was faint here, fortunately, overtopped by the smoke from burning moss just as lime and a handbreadth of clay covered the corpses—most of them—buried at the opposite end of the brigade. Other smells permeated the breeze that passed over a nearby latrine: the ammonia scent of fresh urine, the sour stench of feces. Kalm no longer noticed such odors consciously; his face wrinkled without his awareness as he stepped from the scrapestone.

The tent had been smudged after the rains, leaving a vaguely citrus afteraroma that stabbed at Kalm's sinuses. A few flies survived regardless, buzzing at the peak of the tent. A brown leather jacket and other clothing hung from the ridgepole. It seemed a lived-in place, a comfortable place, and a portion of Kalm's evening exhaustion lifted.

A steaming cup of black liquid rested on the table, near a candle stub and a barely touched mess tray. Boiled jerky, biscuit, and dehydrated corn, Kalm noticed with revulsion. Black and green flakes speckled the food. Without the spice, it was virtually tasteless except for the odors it absorbed. *Seven days of jerky and corn. Like boiled sawdust, and by now even the spices are monotonous. And he has to eat more to keep going than the rest of us. He's probably even sicker of it than we are.*

"You wanted to see me? Take a seat on the cot."

Kalm obeyed awkwardly, watching while Ian Haarper skimmed over the papers and then scratched a signature on one sheet and handed them all back to the messenger.

"Decisions, decisions," the redhead mumbled after the man left. "Algheran, we're going to hold the battalion up a bit in the morning. I want to get the Northern Valley companies here with the rest of the regiment. And . . . Pardon me awhile."

He pushed the dirty mess tray to one side, revealing a writing pad, and scribbled rapidly. "Excuse-me-I'll-be-back-don't-run-away," he said then, and was outside the tent before Kalm could rise. Even inside the camp, a brace of knives was fastened to his tunic.

*This is the army*, Kalm thought sardonically. *You hurry up, I wait.* But the cot was soft, and he was willing to be patient. He was even comfortable here, he admitted with faint surprise. Frequent exposure to Ian Haarper was dulling his perceptions of the man's defects.

Certainly the man was in his element in the army. Kalm remembered an incident from the previous afternoon, when Ian Haarper had made one of his impromptu inspections. He had been walking past the men, dust-stained as any of them, though a black horse reined to his waist had trailed behind him.

"How's it going, Algheran?" he had asked. "Troops tired?"

"They are," Kalm had agreed curtly. The march had begun early, as if to atone for the previous days of inactivity. While lan Haarper was at brigade headquarters, Dighton ris Maanhaldur had canceled two of the battalion's rest periods, and most of the men had carried empty canteens and sullen tempers. The countryside was unchanging, endless grassland set against a backdrop of rolling hills, so it was impossible to believe they were making progress. The Ironwearer had seemed obscurely responsible for all these complaints, and Kalm had had a blister on his heel that he wanted to pop.

"They need a marching song."

*They need rest*, Kalm thought, but he had simply glared as lan Haarper mounted casually. The time traveler had stood in the stirrups without holding the reins, showing off before the men. "All right, you people, pay attention, then join in!" He hummed loudly to set the tune in his mind, then launched into:

"Mlart! Has only got one ball.
   All those of Nornst are rather awfully small.
   Tra'Cuhyon is somewhat underhung,
   And tra-Dicovys has no balls at all.
   Dicovys has no balls at all!"

The men had taken up the song, and lan Haarper had beamed with obvious pleasure as it spread to other companies. Soon the entire Steadfast-to-Victory Regiment was bellowing the words, and his smile became a grin when the men changed the final lines. "Our Haarper has no balls at all," they had sung. "Lan Haarper has no balls at all!"

Lan Haarper had laughed. "I don't know if they'll scare Mlart," he said before riding off. "But they terrify me. Good men, Algheran." Despite reason and resentment, Kalm had felt reassured.

Waiting now, he pulled his shirt off, folded it along the seams, scratched his sides contentedly, then pulled the shirt between his teeth, biting down when they encountered a hardness. *Turning into an insectivore*, he reflected wryly. *This is the army, Algheran. Hurry up and chew.*

Probably he was encountering seeds and thistles as often as

nits and egg casings. Probably. But distraction would be preferable to philosophy. He let his gaze roam the tent until his eyes lit on the unusual book Ian Haarper had read from.

An artifact such as this he had never seen before: a slippery-surfaced box shape about the size of a hand, with an orange and white cover. He poked at it tentatively, and it stayed in existence. It did not fall part when he tapped it, did not leave traces on the desk top. Kalm put his shirt back on and bit at his lower lip.

Rising courage let him hold the book in his hands and open it. Standing before the desk so he could replace it quickly, he thumbed through the flexible sheets of white paper avidly. The text was completely alien, he found, though it reminded him of the Plates, with minuscule symbols in irregular groups to mark words rather than ideograms. The rows of characters were evenly spaced, most of them the same length. The characters themselves were finely drawn, without blemishes, though they were elaborately curved.

*A code*, he guessed, recognizing no language. Perhaps these were Ian Haarper's instructions. Useless now, with his time machine buried under a landslide, but evidently the man had not discovered that yet.

*Useless for him.* For Kalm, it might have incalculable value.

If only there was a safe way to steal this. Could Kylene translate it for him? Could he find a way to persuade her to translate it?

*Lan Haarper. I can offer her Ian Haarper, can't I?*

"Ironwearer's not here?" A private soldier with a shrill voice entered the tent and put his hands on the dirty mess kit. "Ironwearer's not here?" he repeated, looking about suspiciously.

It was not a question, Kalm realized. This must be Ian Haarper's orderly. "I'm waiting," he said reassuringly as he put the book down. "He'll be back soon."

"All right, then." The soldier shook his head, then left with the mess kit. A moment later he poked his head through the door with a warning. "But you don't touch none of the Ironwearer's stuff, see?"

Kalm smiled. "I won't hurt a thing."

*Even Ian Haarper, if I can avoid it.*

Could Ian Haarper be captured or, better yet, converted to the Chelmmysian side of the war? Admittedly, he would be out of place in the Alliance, but his knowledge of the Algheran time travelers would be invaluable.

Kalm moved around the tent restlessly, thinking. If lan Haarper could be persuaded to help him . . .

"Ironwearer is coming back?" The shrill orderly had reappeared with a clean mess tray and a steaming ceramic pot. The stale cup of black liquid he emptied outside the entrance to the tent, then refilled from the pot. Kalm had already turned up the lantern, but the orderly inspected it regardless.

The telepath sat down on the stool, pretending innocence he did not feel, while the orderly fiddled meaninglessly with the lantern's fuel lever. It was full evening now, he noticed through the tent flap. If he were outside, he would see stars.

"Evening, sir!" the orderly called. "Adjusting your light?"

Lan Haarper nodded. "Thanks, Quillyn. Water for my guest, please, then get some sleep. See you in the morning."

For a short while the redhead tapped fingertips on the desk top without looking at him, then returned his attentions, peering over his cup of liquid. "So what are you after now, Algheran?"

"We're short some supplies. Shoes. Patches for shoes. Some ammunition for practice—you remember, we were shortchanged at that last cache because of the way it was packed."

"Yeah. Wolf-Twin knows. He's got our stuff set aside; it'll just take some wagons to bring it up."

"Okay." Kalm did not rise.

"Anything else bothering you?"

"I don't really know," Kalm admitted. Irrationally, he felt disappointed that lan Haarper had not used his name. "Just restless, I suppose. I wish I had someone to talk to."

"You've got your men to talk to." That was said quietly.

"Yes. But we have little in common. Army matters, but beyond that—" Kalm waved a hand uselessly. "They blame—"

Lan Haarper sighed. "I think you're exaggerating. They have more sense. You didn't start the war, Algheran."

Kalm considered that. "Perhaps. They don't seek me out."

"Hmmm," lan Haarper mumbled. "Why are you so shy, Algheran?"

"Am I?" Kalm was polite despite his surprise.

Lan Haarper shook his head. "Umm huh. Right now, for

example, you're perched over that stool, ready to fly off like a scared bird. I'd think you disliked me if I hadn't seen you act the same way with others who put up with you. Kylene, for instance. And yet I've been told—by people I trust—that you're a very dangerous man. You have no reason to fear people."

Kalm smiled wanly. "That's very flattering."

Lan Haarper murmured agreement, then paused to light a spill from the lantern. He transferred the flame to the candle stub, anchoring it to the desk with drops of wax. "Oh, I believe it. You wouldn't go up to your company before a battle, would you, and ask nicely if they'd like to fight for a while, and tell them your feelings would be hurt if they said no?" While he waited for an answer, he surveyed his hanging clothes and took down a pair of pants.

"I don't believe so." The smaller man suppressed a chuckle, hoping that would cause his face to show amusement rather than wariness. "Is this another test I have to pass to keep my command? What are you leading me to, lan Haarper?"

"No, you wouldn't. You can see how inappropriate it is. So why react that way off the battlefield? Especially when you're the local *James Bond*."

"A Chaimsbonn," Kalm repeated thoughtfully. "What?"

"Someone working for Her Majesty's secret service," lan Haarper explained. He waved a hand negligently, then went back to turning the pants inside out. "A *spy*. Someone running around, getting mixed up in his country's troubles, doing stuff that can't ever be admitted to. Trailing around Merryn and other persons dangerous to Loprit for our beloved Molminda III the Glorious. That's you, I gather."

"I'm not doing that."

"Well, I wouldn't expect you to admit it." A small knife was in lan Haarper's hand now, the blade tip in the candle flame.

Kalm produced a brittle laugh. "Don't tell on me."

The redhead shrugged. "No problem. I expect you've realized by now Merryn is not a threat."

"Maybe *you* are a threat," Kalm said. "Maybe a Chaimsbonn should be after you."

Lan Haarper chuckled. "If I'm causing trouble, I'm not doing it the right way. Anyhow, I thought people like you were swashbucklers when it came to women. What's your excuse?" He let his voice trail off, seemingly interested only in the pants he was inspecting. The knife blade hissed faintly as he probed the garment's seams.

There is an element of torture in a long silence, and Kalm broke first. "Actually, I get along well with people. I just happen to be terrified of good-looking women." A fatuous smile sat on his face, he sensed, suppressing it but not the underlying embarrassment. "Like Kylene." He smiled falsely.

"I expect that's true," Ian Haarper said carelessly. "You'll outgrow it someday."

*I've too many secrets, Ian Haarper. I'll never be able to trust them with anyone.* "Besides, she's a Teep. She'll talk to me, but she already knows I've a foully stained soul."

"I'd have found out more about it if you were really evil, Kalm." Lan Haarper jabbed at his pants once more, then shook his head absently. "Compared to what you might have been, you're in good shape."

Kalm sighed. "Why do you keep pushing me at her?"

"'Cause you seem to be chasing. And lonely. And I'd like her to have someone to look after her."

"She wants you. She wants to be your wife. Really."

"It can't happen."

"Why? You prefer Wandisha?"

Lan Haarper sighed. "No. I like Wandisha."

Kalm waited.

"I'm too old for long-term things," Ian Haarper said slowly. "I'm fond of Kylene, but she's got centuries ahead of her, and I don't. So . . ."

"Why me?" *Why not one of your Algheran time travelers?* "Why not some other fine soldier you know?"

"Because she talks to you. She doesn't get along well with most of the people I've seen her with, but she does with you. And—" Lan Haarper stared at a white-knuckled fist. "That's important."

Kalm realized suddenly that the big Ironwearer envied him.

"I have to leave," he said quickly, knowing he could not remain. "My company, someone just called for me."

Fortunately, Ian Haarper was too wrapped in his own emotions to notice the lie. In darkness, Kalm was able to find composure.

He thought he understood Kylene Waterfall's love now.

He thought he understood Ian Haarper.

# CHAPTER TWENTY-TWO

"**W**hat's up ahead?" he overheard.

"Don't know. Ask the captain."

So there was to be a question for him. Kalm rubbed sleep grains from his eyes, then choked back a yawn. Soil cascaded over his bare toes as he turned, damp, gritty, and cool as the morning air. Nude, his eyes still half-closed as he sipped his breakfast broth, he slowly resigned himself to wakefulness. Hills. Grass, chest high, brown. A scrap of forest lay ahead on an elevation. Clouds filled the sky; the clearness of the air showed that the sun had risen also.

It was a beautiful morning—appreciated by an improved Kalm, he reflected. He tested himself by bobbing on his toes, enjoying the springiness of his leg muscles and the comfortable tension of his stretched calves, then smiled as he slapped his diminishing belly. Town life had been undermining his fitness; the long march was shoring it up.

*Almost ready for a Falltroop induction physical. I'd pass ChelmForceDrop's again now—standards were lower there.* ChelmForce had won with numbers, not quality, he admitted. It was almost disloyal to think that, but it was true. Algheran troops had always been tougher than their Alliance counterparts, better trained and better officered.

He could imagine Ian Haarper as a Land Watch officer, he decided now. Or a Forest Guard sergeant. Something primitive. But the man was too crude to be a ChelmForce officer, too uneducated to qualify for Alghera's Eagle Force or the Falltroop; there was something satisfying in that realization.

*Twelve thousand man-heights marched yesterday, maybe another twelve thousand for today,* Kalm reckoned, looking about the waking camp. *Five minutes of distance in a levcraft, but he never seems bored of this, never seems impatient. He just puts up with it all, like the rest of his men.*

*Ris Jynnich is right. He really is a peasant.*

*I don't understand why the Algheran time travelers trusted him as one of their Agents. But he certainly is here.*

The camp was larger now that the three companies from the Northern Valley had caught up. Estimating, counting the attached artillery company, Kalm thought there might have been as many as nine hundred soldiers in the Steadfast-to-Victory Regiment. Nine hundred men, fifty cavalrymen, and another two hundred teamsters. Lan Haarper was not commanding a small unit anymore, though both regular regiments in the Strength-through-Loyalty Brigade were still larger.

It took an effort of imagination to remember that more men than this had died in one day when Fohima Alghera was captured. More men than this in ChelmForceDrop alone. How much the world would change in so short a time!

His gaze moved down the slopes and up a neighboring hill at the brigade camp, noting cooking fires, a row of wagons holding close-packed men, and men digging holes in a stubbled hillside. Marching sickness—*dysentery* was lan Haarper's term—was still killing over there.

The ambulances blocked the path of the supply wagons for the Northern Valley troops, which meant that part of the regiment would be on short rations. *No supply cache till tomorrow, and it'll be a good while before the brigade gets the train unsnarled. We may have to share some of our food this evening.*

That was more reason for enjoying this breakfast. Idly, he wondered how his fingernails had become so dirty and chipped. Later that day he had some errand to run. He did not remember what it was, so it would not be important.

"Captain?"

He nodded gravely at the interruption, pretending that it had come unexpectedly, while his eyes continued to rove over the lip of his cup, seeing dead brush brown above long grass on the hillsides; a stand of elderly trees, brown- and gold-leafed; gray-white skies tinged with silver to the east; a small clump of violet blooms that had somehow escaped soldiers' boots; and the black road like a knee-high strap from horizon to horizon holding the camps in place. Two thousand man-heights away a lone horseman emerged from the trees and rode toward him, head down. What lay ahead was another long day.

But someone had slipped into Dighton ris Maanhaldur's tent. Men in the brigade were converging on the great wagon that housed Terrault ris Andervyll and his mistresses. Teamsters were gathering their horses, but none had yet placed harness on their teams. The brigade's troops were clumping unnaturally at their mess tents and making more noise than was normal for morning.

"Yes," Kalm murmured. The horseman was distinctly closer.

He looked past the soldier before him. Then he saw through two sets of eyes and listened through two sets of ears. Vertigo struck at him, fear and a lump of hunger jostling for mastery in a gallop-pitched stomach.

Then he was alone in his own mind, wiping the back of his hand across his forehead, feeling surprise at the absence of dust and crusted blood. "We're in for trouble," he murmured, then paused, trying to anticipate the orders he might receive from Ian Haarper.

"I want you and one other man to report to Captain Ian Callares over in the brigade area—the Teep money broker. He'll probably be back by the supply wagons. Or find his boss, an Ironwearer named Wolf-Twin. They've got some stores for us—shoe patches, ammunition. Get whatever you can, for the whole regiment. If they don't have wagons to move our supplies, come back and get some of ours. Do it right now. Find someone who's finished breakfast. And—" He closed his eyes, trying to remember what else needed doing. That errand, whatever it was.

"Sir?"

Cimon, what was it? "There's a little box on my blanket. I wanted—get that, too, and give it to Ian Callares and ask him to hold it for me or Ian Haarper. Do that first."

"The box and the supplies. Yes, sir."

He opened his eyes. "Hmmm? No. First tell the platoon leaders I want them. Then go. Quietly."

*Quietly. Don't alarm the men.* Kalm finished the broth without noticing its taste, simply because it was first on a mental checklist of fear-dispelling routine actons. In his memory, once more the fire crackle of muskets and sharp barking rifles brought him to wakefulness, while bayonets of flame stabbed into the night amid men's shouts and the screams of dying animals. Once more cannon thunder buffeted him, stoppering blood-dripping ears as with hot pitch. Shock hammered through his arm again as his sword struck unyielding bone and a fear-whitened face gibbered meaningless cries before slumping to the ground and he swung at it, swung, swung, swung . . . Dark fluid geysered again from sudden drill holes on a comrade's back, and his own uncontrolled mount stumbled over limp obstacles in its flight.

Breeches. Calf-high padded stockings. Boots. Lan Haarper's bulky vest. Shirt. He donned his clothes before the dying fire, breathing deeply and deliberately, trying to appear unhurried and unworried before his men and not affected by another man's memories.

Motion caught his eye, bringing suspicions that his mind confirmed. Kalm gestured toward pairs of soldiers. "You two. And you two. Get your muskets and stand by the wagons. If the teamsters try to take the horses away, shoot them."

By midday, neither the brigade nor the regiment had moved.

A scowling lan Haarper, ris Maanhaldur and ris Jynnich in tow, had left for a conference with the Hand in early morning, but they had not yet returned. Meanwhile, the first and second companies of the Midpassage Battalion waited in two lines on either side of the road. The Northern Valley companies were arrayed in a square formation on the right. Men on horseback roamed in all directions, before and among the infantry.

Kalm and his company remained at the campsite. He had placed responsibility for feeding the deployed men on Pitar lan Styllin. Derrauld ris Fryddich, whose instincts for this task were more highly developed, had led his platoon back to the brigade and was engaged in "completing requisitions"—stealing supplies needed by the regiment.

Kalm's own consciousness was divided, most of his attention focused on ris Maanhaldur as the Hand's conference proceeded. Nearly a watch had passed in debate, though the handful of known facts were not disputed.

Uneasily, Dighton ris Maanhaldur lifted his eyes toward the window of the wagon, half-curious as to whether the Midpassage Battalion could be seen, but he was wrongly placed at the conference table. His father, Terrault ris Andervyll, sat at the head of the table, Ironwearer Cherrid ris Clendannan beside him; he could not ask either man to exchange seats with him.

Beside the elderly Ironwearer, Terrens ris Daimgewin frowned morosely, a hand fidgeting with papers. Across the table, on the Hand's left, Rahmmend Wolf-Twin studied lading bills, transparently juggling shipping orders and cargoes in his mind while giving only a fraction of his attention to the meeting. Now and then the squat Ironwearer left the conference; ris Maanhaldur had seen him through the window talking to a Teep.

Timithial lan Haarper had a chair near the doorway. One arm rested on the back of a second chair. A glass of water was in his hand, but he had not touched it. He had put his right ankle on top of his left knee, and ris Maanhaldur noticed that his boot sole was wearing down unevenly. Silver glinted in his red-brown hair; his expression seemed alien and distant as he watched the Vandeign brothers.

Tiredly, Dighton managed to keep his eyes open. He had not had enough sleep last night, he had not had his breakfast, and a preheadache tension touched the back of his head. Politely, however, he tipped his head toward Krenn ris Jynnich, letting the man babble whatever it was he insisted on saying, though Dighton paid no attention.

Mlart tra'Nornst had struck at Haylon ris Cornoval two nights before, overrunning the Southern Corps before it formed for battle. Algheran Swordtroop cavalry had pursued Lopritian forces as far south as Barlynnt's Tower, taking unknown numbers of prisoners. A messenger had reported that ris Cornoval and his staff had escaped. The Lopritian general was attempting to regroup, but he promised no date for an advance. He would defend Barlynnt's Tower and the road to Port Junction against the Algherans. He assured the Hand of his loyalty to Queen Molminda. He sent no orders to the brigade, no suggestions.

Dighton knew that Krenn could do nothing to help Uncle Haylon. Wearily, he wished the young noble would stop whispering at him. He wished he knew what lan Haarper was thinking.

". . . not ready to move the men," Merryn ris Vandeign was saying again, insistent despite the numbers against him. "They are not adequately equipped, and they still need training."

"Some more formations and shooting," ris Clendannan said. "That's all that's needed. We can work that in on the march."

"With what?" Lord Vandeign's voice turned petulant. "Slingshots?"

"I beg your pardon," ris Clendannan said. The gray-haired Ironwearer leaned across the table, his expression suggesting that his understanding of the language was incomplete, though he had served in Loprit's armies for more than two centuries.

"Slingshots," Lord Vandeign repeated, looking toward the Hand. "Ask your son."

Silence met the remark. Dighton let his eyes turn to ris Andervyll. Heavyset, dark-haired, his father sat impassively, rubbing his hand against the grain of the table. He looked confident; his dark brown uniform gave him the guise of a soldier, but the reddened flesh beneath his eyes seemed wrinkled and softened. Unhappily, Dighton was coming to suspect that there was some subtle difference between his father and the professional soldiers of the Strength-through-Loyalty Brigade.

"Dighton?" His father's eyes probed at him, hoping, expecting weakness.

Merryn ris Vandeign's obstinacy annoyed the Hand, Dighton saw. The Vandeigns had had ties to the old royal family; they had been among the dissidents when Molminda was raised to the throne, and the Andervylls still found them a quarrelsome lot.

Unfortunately, they still had influence away from the court; he could understand why his father did not wish to revive a controversy. He sighed slightly; his thoughts touched for a moment on a tall songstress in Molminda's court whom he had wished to impress. "Uh, Ironwearer lan Haarper could give a more detailed answer than I can."

"Ironwearer?" The Hand hid his eyes behind a glass of water.

"We've only three cannons, Lord Andervyll, as you know. A regiment ought to have more, but as long as we're supported by the brigade, it isn't fatal." Lan Haarper had not changed his position. Dighton wondered why he seemed untroubled by attention.

"You disagree with Lord Vandeign?" The Hand leaned forward.

"Yes, sir. The Algherans are dispersed because of Lord Cornoval's withdrawal; they must be disorganized themselves now. We should advance as quickly as possible."

Kalm, watching, saw that that did not receive full agreement.

"What do you see as the problem, Merryn?" Gertynne ris Vandeign asked finally. Sandy-haired, neatly dressed, the brigade's executive officer displayed endless patience. A schemer, Dighton's father had called him. But a professional soldier also, and an able one; ability rather than politics had brought him to his post.

Merryn ris Vandeign stared at his spread fingers as if they contained an answer, then waved minutely at lan Haarper.

"Lord Vandeign has another concern," the Algheran Agent admitted, rising to approach the table. "Most everyone in Midpassage had a gun of some kind, but few of them have the same caliber. Making cartridges calls for some specialized tools, so it seemed sensible to pick a standard size of bullet and make a lot of those rather than a few for each gun. But that meant we should have manufactured a standard gun, and we didn't have time for that." He gestured idly with his glass.

"Why not?" Ris Andervyll permitted himself that question.

"Time. A shortage of metal." Lan Haarper frowned, and Kalm remembered that the redhead had once been a prospector. "Those cannons you had us cast could have made a lot of bullets and muskets."

"Ris Cornoval had requested cannons."

Lan Haarper did not argue. He hunched his shoulders up instead, then let them fall into place quickly.

"We have muskets we can spare," ris Clendannan mused. "If we sent the sick back—"

"They're part of our force," the Hand remarked.

"They're not an asset, Lord Andervyll. Not now."

"We'll speak." The Hand gestured. "Later."

"It wouldn't be enough," Ironwearer Wolf-Twin interjected. "We've been supplying our own men with the discards." He turned to lan Haarper. "We can spare more ammunition and powder."

Lan Haarper nodded. "That's better than nothing."

Ris Andervyll waited for disapproval, then shook his head. "Do it, Rahm."

"Yes, sir." Wolf-Twin did not leave the conference. Dighton realized suddenly that the Ironwearer had already anticipated the order and acted on it. He wondered if his father understood.

"How long can Cornoval hold out?" Lord Daimgewln wondered aloud. "He has, what, fifteen or sixteen thousand men? Before his losses? Neither of those cities can support so many mouths."

"They can, can't they?"

Eyes turned. Dighton swallowed, suddenly aware that he had spoken aloud. "I mean—it's past harvest time. We haven't seen any shipments to the north, so there must be stocks. They can eat—"

The Hand frowned. "Would you starve the capital, son?"

"The boy's made a good point, sir." Ris Clendannan spoke before ris Maanhaldur's flush was plain. "If the Algherans control the river, there aren't going to be any northern shipments. None getting through, anyhow."

Dighton exhaled slowly. It was not necessary now to explain that he was repeating a casual remark made by lan Haarper.

"Sir? Sir!"

Kalm blinked, hearing words not noticed at the Hand's conference. A cooking fire was at his side, he saw. Had he been close to walking into it?

"Sir!" It was one of his men. "A cavalry officer wants you."

Timithial lan Haarper dismounted even before his horse stopped and spun about to face Kalm. "Kill that fire," he said to no one in particular. "Where are your boogeymen, Algheran?"

"Top of the hill." Kalm pointed. "And they're real."

"Figures." Lan Haarper looked southward, examining the innocent-appearing road and brush. "How'd they get this close without us knowing it?"

What did "close" mean in this kind of war? Kalm waited, unable to answer either question.

Lan Haarper cursed mildly. "What have you done, so far?"

"I sent for you."

"Cimon, Kalm! No scouts out, nothing?"

He had made a request of the cavalry leader; it had been

refused. Kalm hesitated again, then simply agreed. Behind Ian Haarper's head, something sparkled. Sunlight reflected from weapons. *They're careless up there.*

"How many are there?" Lan Haarper turned and shouted the names of the other company leaders, then gestured till they ran toward him. Behind him, a soldier was kicking dirt into the fire pit. "How many are out there, Kalm?"

"I don't know. Enough to be seen."

"Stop dicking around, Algheran! How many are there?"

"About a company." The words slipped out when he read Ian Haarper's glare. He swallowed, then covered for himself. "Almost two hundred men. That would be doctrine, anyhow. A company, then the rest of a battalion behind them, then the rest of a regiment."

"Pitar, Lerynne." Lan Haarper nodded at other officers, then shouted once more for the cavalry commander. "Go on, Kalm. How far back is that battalion?"

"Five, six thousand man-heights." He looked toward Ian Haarper, pretending not to notice the stares aimed at him. "Behind that company. In addition to that distance."

"Hmmm." The big man looked at the horizon again. "Couple thousand to the top of that hill, would you say?"

"Eighteen hundred and some." That was a lean dark man from a Northern Valley company. "I'm a surveyor normally, and I took a rough measurement of it last night."

Lan Haarper grinned. "Professional curiosity, eh? I look for ironberry bushes, myself."

"Yes, sir." The surveyor grinned back.

"That five thousand a good estimate, Kalm?"

"Closer to six." He made no mention of Swordtroop doctrine this time. "Sir."

"Artillery? They have any?"

"With the regiment." Kalm swallowed. "About like us, but with more. Farther back yet, but I don't know how far."

"Hmmm." Lan Haarper nodded abruptly. "Just about out of supporting range. And I like the odds. We'll attack. Dalsyn?"

"Sir?" That was the surveyor again.

"Spread your men into two lines. Take the right of the road and move out when I signal. Questions?"

The Northern Valley man spit at the ashes of the dead fire. "No problem. What kind of march pace?"

"I'll leave it to you." Lan Haarper turned. "Lan Halkmayne."

"Yes, sir." The artillery officer stepped forward. He made gestures with a hand at his side, signals to his subordinates.

"Nothing for you today, Captain. We want a few left alive to talk to when we're done."

"Yes, sir."

"Sorry about that."

"Yes, sir." Lan Halkmayne actually did seem disappointed.

Lan Haarper turned again. "Ris Thannun. Need your horses for this."

"Sir?" To Kalm's surprise, the cavalry commander had appeared for lan Haarper. His voice bore unexpected tones of chagrin and obedience, though the telepath saw that he would resist commands that threatened the horses.

"See those trees at the top of the hill?" Lan Haarper pointed to the copse at the left of the road. "Mount up double, all you can from Pitar lan Styllin's platoon, and drop them at the back edge of that grove."

"Uh-hh."

"Swing wide if you want. Drop off lan Styllin's crew, then swing around some more while they go through the woods and hit the road behind those Algies."

"Uh-hh." The man swallowed. "If you want an attack—"

"Just take prisoners, Major. Do what comes naturally and they'll fall into your arms. Pitar!"

"Ironwearer? Sir?" Lan Styllin concealed his nervousness well, but it was plain to Kalm. He looked very, very young at that moment, and he did not seem to notice his captain.

"I'm asking a lot of you," lan Haarper said softly. "We got the odds in our favor now, that's why, and—"

"Why, what?"

It was Krenn ris Jynnich. Kalm turned with surprise, seeing both the angry nobleman and an embarrassed Dighton ris Maanhaldur, still sitting on his mare.

"What are you trying to do, Haarper?" Krenn demanded.

"Fight Algherans," the redhead said. "Keep your lip buttoned."

"I—" Ris Jynnich colored. "Dighton, he's going to get your battalion massacred."

The words were shrill. Kalm suddenly realized that most of the men in the Midpassage Battalion had heard them and were watching. For a second, knowing this was also being watched by the soldiers at the hilltop, he wanted to throw his arms up and confess his own embarrassment.

"I'm giving orders to the regiment." Lan Haarper's voice was cool. "Pitar. Those we take out now, we don't have to face later. Understand? Go pick your best men. We'll move in about five minutes."

"No, you won't." Ris Jynnich's words stopped lan Styllin in his tracks.

Then Pitar turned to lan Haarper and saluted. "Five minutes, sir. We'll be ready."

"Get him back," ris Jynnich barked as lan Styllin turned once more. "Let's end this farce. Rispar, get that fool."

Openmouthed, Kalm could only stare. Behind ris Jynnich, still seated on his horse, ris Maanhaldur did the same. He was praying intently that his father would not hear of this incident.

"Krenn." Derrauld ris Fryddich was at Kalm's shoulder. In the corner of the telepath's eye, he saw the artillery commander, deadpan, stolid.

"Derry, he's going to get us killed. Don't you see that?" ris Jynnich asked. "He's a stupid peasant playing soldier and he's showing off, because I've been screwing that season-taken daughter of his and he wants to feel some power and— Dighton, tell him to obey me."

"Krennlen," ris Maanhaudur said, much too late.

There was a long silence. Kalm wanted to be very far away.

"Maanhaldur," lan Haarper said at last. "Curb your dog."

"Yes." It was almost a whisper. Even ris Maanhaldur's mare was motionless.

"Keep him away from me." The words were distinct.

"I will." The Hand's son swallowed. "Give your orders, Ironwearer."

What was horrible, Kalm had time to think as an abashed ris Jynnich moved behind ris Maanhaldur's horse, was that lan Haarper was acting with uncharacteristic haste and without orders and that sensible men were giving him unusual obedience. Ris Jynnich had spoken his own mad words from unadmitted fear, but the young Lopritian had felt that he was being reasonable in the midst of lunatics, and Kalm was not sure he was wrong.

"The left of the road?" he asked thickly, knowing something must be said to end the silence. "Sir? For the battalion."

"On the left." Lan Haarper grimaced alienly. "Platoons aligned, with squad frontage. Couple of squads, put 'em out to link to lan Styllin's men." He seemed dazed.

It was not completely comprehensible, but Kalm thought he understood. "Second company first, then mine, and a link to Ian Styllin?" He glanced at other Midpassage officers, seeing how they interpreted the order, then flicked a hand to dismiss them.

"We're on the left?" Ris Fryddich seemed surprised.

"Yes, we're—" Kalm blinked, seeing the difficulty. The first and second Midpassage companies were in place already, with the third company astride the road, between them and the Northern Valley men. Ian Styllin's men were trotting behind him to the left of the line and joining up with the cavalry, but to shift ris Fryddich's platoon would take more than Ian Haarper's few minutes. "Nicole's boobs!"

"Go up the center, by the road," Ian Haarper said, suddenly taking an interest in the conversation. "On the right. Leave the other companies as they are. Pitar will have men left over; they can link to the battalion without direction."

That was probably true, Kalm reflected. The Algherans had neglected to station men in the copse, so Ian Styllin's men did not face much danger. Still, he was uneasy.

"Will it be all right?" he asked, then wondered why he had spoken.

"Yeah, everything's fine." Lan Haarper spoke mechanically. "Just get your men up."

Ris Fryddich was already giving the orders for that, placing the squads of his platoon in staggered lines and watching as squad leaders inspected muskets. He had even found his own musket, to Kalm's surprise, and was inserting powder and a cartridge as carefully as any of the ordinary soldiers.

He had been an officer before, Kalm remembered. Whatever his defects as a platoon leader, the man had seen action and knew what he should do. Silently, admitting his own uncertainties, he thanked Nicole for that gift.

"I guess we're ready," he said when ris Fryddich shook his head. "You want to give a signal?" Abstractly, watching himself as a stranger at that moment, he noticed that he had not taken up his own weapon, but it did not seem important.

"Yeah." Lan Haarper looked about, peering at ris Maanhaldur and the now frightened ris Jynnich, then raised and swept forward his left arm.

Slowly, five hundred man-heights away, toy horse shapes moved through the high grass. The dark blobs on them were men.

Lan Haarper hopped onto the road, then walked backward several paces. He made pulling motions with lifted hands as he came abreast of the leading ranks.

For a long moment Kalm stared at him, knowing that everyone present shared his uncertainty. But it was too late to stop the man, too late to repeat ris Jynnich's warning.

"Come on, you dog's sons," a man screamed. Another instant passed before Kalm realized it had been lan Haarper.

And then it was much too late. The men were moving.

War. He had thought the Falltroop and ChelmForceDrop had taught him war, but he had never seen a scene like this. On his right, a double line of men advanced parallel to the road, holding rifles before them like religious icons, leaving furrows in the tall grass. Before him and on his left, the Midpassage men moved in distinct rectangular formations, matting down the grass in broad swathes. Far to one side, the cavalry swept forward, disorganized, at no constant pace, not yet aiming at the copse, not yet ahead of the slower foot soldiers.

He stood frozen, watching. Nine hundred men. He had never seen so many acting together. He had never seen so few.

"Let's go, Rispar." Ris Fryddich tugged at his arm.

He jerked free, looking back toward the serenity of the brigade headquarters. It was very foolish to attack without the rest of the brigade, he had time to think. It was very foolish to stand and watch when the equipment in his tent would move him into the future, safely past this moment of danger. But with someone at his side, that refuge was not available.

He tried to smile. He never knew if he was successful.

"C'mon." Ris Fryddich walked, then trotted toward his marching platoon.

*I'd like to know if this is really necessary.* Kalm followed.

It was a manageable distance. He caught up with lan Haarper on the road. For a while he settled for walking beside the man, slowly getting his breath back. When he looked back at the camp area, he saw that they had come only a few hundred man-heights. It was enough distance to make ris Maanhaldur and ris Jynnich look like children. The pony between them was lan Haarper's horse.

The artillery officer—lan Halkmayne—waved. Kalm did not know at whom.

Lan Haarper was without expression. He had turned again

to face the front and walked steadily, economically, noise-lessly. He did not speak. His arms swung freely. Unlike the men, he was not carrying a pack, and looking at his brown-clad back, Kalm realized that the redhead also had forgotten to carry a weapon.

Eighteen hundred man-heights seemed a great distance suddenly, and Kalm could think of nothing to say. Finally he mumbled that he should be with his men and left the road. Lan Haarper said nothing, did nothing to indicate he had noticed.

"I've been screwing his season-taken daughter," Krenn had said. *The idiot.* Kalm wanted to kill ris Jynnich.

He wanted to cry. He wanted to vomit.

But even that would not wipe the words away—or the facts.

Moving through the grass was like moving through water —very thick water—like swimming, upright, with swishing sounds as grass moved past or folded underfoot. He thought about that for a while.

Otherwise, the advance seemed almost silent, until he forced himself to listen. Then there were voices on all sides. Squad leaders chattered at their men. Officers barked at the squad leaders. Soldiers cursed—monotonously, the same blasphemous words over and over, different for each man.

Lan Haarper's boots slapped on the pavement.

Maybe he heard a horse's whinny.

Sixty-two men were to the left of him in ris Fryddich's platoon. Five squads of ten, one of eleven, one officer. Sixty-two men. So many individuals. Deliberately, he closed his mind to their differences, to see them only as a group, and then as soldiers. Big, small, old, young . . . Soldiers.

Men about to fight. Men he knew.

Krenn bragging about Kylene.

He tried to swallow. This could not be real.

Soldiers around him. Soldiers before him. Fighting. Kill-ing. Wounds. Disfigurement. It could not be real.

*Please, lan Haarper. Can we stop and go back? Please?*

He stepped to one side, seeing a man sink beneath the grass.

"On your feet, soldier."

"It's-s-s my shoe, sir. I—I had a r-rock in my shoe."

That was not true, he sensed, even without examining the frightened man's thoughts. He stared sternly, seeing sweat and shaking hands. Barbed pieces of grass like thin brown arrowheads protruded from the man's uniform and his own. "Fix it and get back in line." He tugged at his clothing, yanking seeds through the cloth.

"Ye-yes-s, s-sir!" The soldier had not seen Kalm's own fear.

Were there others hanging back? Kalm stood on tiptoe to look, his hands still brushing his tunic, wishing for once that he shared lan Haarper's height.

*Green troops. Most of them don't know how to hide. Or feel a need to hide.*

Eighteen hundred man-heights. They had only begun.

*I could die here.* Keeping a uniform clean was wasted effort.

He scurried to catch up.

"...a bend in your line, like this." Lan Haarper gestured for the Northern Valley commander.

Dalsyn, Kalm remembered at the edge of the pavement, listening to the conversation overhead. Dalsyn. A personal name, such as friends would use, rather than his family name, lan Plenytk. *When did they get acquainted? He always calls me "Algheran." Why doesn't he call him "Lopritian"?*

"...at the end," lan Haarper said comfortably, "solid, like a fist on an arm. Hit with the fist, not the whole arm. You'll give me my punch."

Lan Plenytk murmured.

"Old idea. Whole armies have done it this way in the past." Lan Haarper slapped the smaller man on the shoulder. "Trust me."

Lan Plenytk shook his head, then went to obey.

"What is it, Algheran? Want to ask for a rest?"

Kalm had not thought he had been noticed. Did lan Haarper have Teep blood? Of course not. He made himself smile. "No."

"C'mon up." Lan Haarper gestured.

*Is this safe?* Kalm looked about apprehensively. On the right, lan Plenytk was laying hands on his men, pushing them with little explanation into the positions he desired for them. Kalm gave a second to admiring that directness.

On his left, the Midpassage Battalion moved forward in a long checkerboard formation perpendicular to the road. The arrangement was surprisingly regular; he did not understand the good order until he realized that the lead files had aligned themselves on lan Haarper. Beyond the battalion, insect shapes wriggled erratically: the cavalry. Lan Styllin's men. *My men.*

The Algheran force was perhaps a thousand man-heights ahead.

Kalm swallowed. "Don't we have to plug this gap?" He waved a hand, indicating the road and the more than ten man-heights that lay between the portions of lan Haarper's tiny force.

Shouldn't lan Haarper take a less conspicuous position? Was the big man trying to get himself killed? *Because of Kylene?*

"We'll manage, Algheran." Lan Haarper glanced past him into the middle of ris Fryddich's platoon. "Hey! Who's thirsty down there?"

Someone shouted. Lan Haarper held his canteen out, then tossed it into a forest of arms. "Pass it down! You soldiers want more?"

There were more shouts of agreement.

"Ask the people ahead of us! Be polite!"

Laughter came even before he pointed.

"Lan Haarper says we can ask the Algherans for water. But we gotta be polite!" Kalm could already see the remark being passed from platoon to platoon. The men would remember the joke. They would remember that lan Haarper had given up his canteen. They would neither notice nor understand the look of calculation that Kalm had seen in the big man's eyes.

Knees lifted high, head down, arms pumping frantically, lan Haarper mimed running while moving at a snail's pace. The men laughed again but fell back into line and resumed marching. In memory, Kalm stared at a line of his former commanders, wondering how he would explain this performance to them.

*An Ironwearer. Doesn't he care about his dignity?*

Lan Haarper stopped his pantomime, dropped back to stand by Kalm, and waved the lines of men onward. "Don't worry," he said patiently. "The gap will plug itself when we make contact. Go back and keep your men steady."

*I'm a professional soldier*, Kalm thought angrily. *Don't try to soothe me.* But it was pointless to say that; he mumbled agreement bitterly and dropped back by his men.

None of them noticed him, though many stared at lan Haarper as they marched. *Not my men, really. His men.*

Even ris Fryddich was watching the Ironwearer.

He had not really been thinking about the Cimon-taken gap.

Gnats whined suddenly. Grass bobbed.

He felt a breeze.

Kalm stopped his hand's motion toward his ear. Those gnats would not be chased by a waving hand.

Grass stems moved toward him, bowing in narrow lines, drawn directly from the insect-high Algherans ahead toward the Midpassage Battalion. He heard muffled popping sounds, thuds like dropped bags of feed. He always thought afterward that he had been the first to notice, the first to understand. Even before lan Haarper, on his elevated roadbed, noticed.

Would he see what old soldiers had spoken of, the bullet aimed at him, the perfect black ball before him just long enough for him to notice, never long enough to react and avoid?

*Five paces. I can go five more paces. Even afraid, I can go that far.*

He swallowed. His heart resumed beating. His foot hit the ground again. He kept marching, looking straight ahead. Five paces. Five paces. Five paces. Five paces.

A gnat screeched metallically, loudly. Then again, in the distance. Another miss.

He heard a thump on the nearby grounds, and footsteps on his right.

"I think I'll check out your hospitality, Algheran." It was lan Haarper.

"Not theirs?" Kalm gestured. His eyes moved over ris Fryddich's ranks, looking for uncertainty.

"It was warm, but there's such a thing as too much concern for company." Lan Haarper looked ruefully at a torn pant leg, the tan speckled now with red, then bent to slap the fabric. "I forgot about ricochets."

"Everything's fine. Keep on." Kalm flicked his hands at curious men, keeping the lines in motion. "You all right?"

"Just a couple scrapes." Lan Haarper joggled his oversized shoulders. "Not enough damage to get a Purple Heart. I've done worse as a kid riding a—a horse."

"Sure." Kalm stared, understanding little of this. "Maybe you weren't polite enough to our hosts." Amid whines, small metallic plumes rose from the roadbed.

"Don't know." Lan Haarper chuckled. "Didn't think I was close enough to ask for anything." He was silent for a moment. "C'mon, Algheran. Time's wasting."

Lan Haarper was not there to chuckle when the first man fell in Kalm's company. He had dashed across the road to talk to the Northern Valley commander.

Kalm had not paid attention. Kylene and Krennlen and lan Haarper—that was another disaster to be faced. Soon. How? Stupid Kylene, stupid Krennlen. Stupid Kalm.

He concentrated on breathing, on his footsteps, trying to keep them evenly spaced, trying to estimate the number of steps he must take to reach the Algherans.

It was still a very large number. Over a thousand.

Kylene and Krennlen and lan Haarper.

Enviously, he thought, *Kylene and Krennlen*.

Fearfully, he thought, *Kylene and Krennlen and lan Haarper*.

There was a flurry of motion to Kalm's left, then the company stopped moving. Men stepped into each other.

"Keep moving. Keep moving," a couple of squad leaders told their men, but their voices were halfhearted. The men milled about in place, their order dissolving.

Ris Fryddich, at the back of the platoon, gave no orders. He stared at Kalm, then across the road, expressionless.

The next company over was still in motion. A gap was opening between it and the third company.

*A perfect target*. Kalm felt naked as he moved through the men. He seemed to float as he pushed his way through the ranks.

"Prellis, sir."

"It's Prellis."

"Prellis was hit."

"Prellis was hit?" he echoed. Then, remembering himself, he said, "Keep moving, keep moving."

"Prellis was hit," someone with a worried face repeated.

*"Nicole's tits!"* he snarled at them all. "Get your asses into gear and *get moving*!"

Those were lan Haarperish phrases. The men began to obey. Were they still laughing at all of lan Haarper's jokes? "Show me Prellis," he demanded, angry with the men and himself.

"Here, sir." A squad leader led the way.

Prellis was still conscious when Kalm reached him, a middle-aged man with brown hair and no distinction as a soldier. He was lying on the ground, with grass and soldiers swaying above him. Red had streaked the hands that held his thigh so tightly, and his face was pinched.

*An old man's neck*, Kalm decided, looking at walnut-aged folds of skin. Prellis might be two-hundred and fifty, or he might be three-hundred and fifty. He should last for another twenty or thirty years. His eyes turned to the blood that had colored the inside of the man's pants leg red. *Flesh wound*, he gauged, dropping to his knee for a closer look. *No problem*. The press of men peering over him was probably more upsetting to the man than his minor injury. "Keep moving, men. How are you doing, Prellis?"

"I don't know, sir," Prellis said, looking up, his voice reedy. He gasped, less from need in Kalm's estimation than because it was expected of a wounded man. "Is—is this going to kill me, sir?"

Kalm forced a smile, pretending he did not notice grass bending about him, did not hear gnat and bumblebee hums, did not smell bullet-scorched plants and unwashed men. "Cimon isn't ready for you yet, Prellis. You've got plenty of time to do some good in your life."

Prellis smiled weakly. "The bad's more fun, sir."

Kalm's grin died. "So I'm told."

Dust spurted nearby, and part of the brown feather plume landed on his leg. He straightened up and pointed at men. "Get back in line. Squad leaders, get your men moving! If you want to protect Prellis, the place to do it is up there, not here."

*Pull the fire away from here*, he meant. It was not until later that he understood it also meant "beat the Algherans."

But men moved. Ris Fryddich passed by, musket in his hands, his face blank. Then Kalm was alone with the fallen soldier.

He kept the explanation simple. "Prellis, you're going to have to be patient. Don't try walking, just wait. We can't move you now. Understand? We can't leave anyone with you. We'll get back. You stay here and behave yourself, and you'll be fine."

"Yes, ris Parr." Prellis stared dejectedly at his leg and his bloody hands, then closed his eyes. His forehead was sweaty.

*Cimon! I should have done that*, Kalm told himself. *If I'd—I wouldn't have had to bribe Krennlen then*. But it was far too late now. "I'm not a noble, Prellis. Rispar is just a name, that's all." *An Algheran name. We don't have nobles.* It seemed best not to explain any more.

"Oh." The man seemed unconcerned by his faux pas.

Kalm hesitated, hearing nearby shots. Without direction, the men were firing too soon. He should get back to them.

Abruptly, he made a decision. "Prellis, I need your gun and your ammunition."

"If—" Prellis swallowed, his face paling, obviously unwilling to release his wound. "Yes, sir. If—you—can get—them—sir." He hesitated, then turned on his side reluctantly, exposing the cords that fastened his bandolier. "There—sir!"

His breath was weak. Slow. Rank. Kalm had to kneel to hear the last words.

His heart stopped while Kalm's hands were still on him.

As he got nearer to his men, the enemy firing began to seem less important. They were reloading, he guessed. It took a trained man a quarter minute to load a musket, time enough for another man to run almost a hundred man-heights. The Algherans would want to be prepared for a rush by the Lopritians. Or else they were shooting more accurately, wasting less ammunition on grass and dirt.

He could not say. He had told Ian Haarper half the truth in Midpassage: Teeps did not use their powers in combat because they could not. Mind reading stopped functioning, probably because it would interfere with the concentration demanded by other senses.

That fact was not generally known. In ChelmForce, Teep soldiers usually gravitated to noncombat positions where they could continue to use their abilities. Normal superior officers assumed they were the best candidates for such posts; Teep personnel specialists always assured them of that.

The outnumbered Teep soldiers described in the Chronicles would have fought their battles with no advantages over their Normal opponents. And it had still taken twelve thousand years and the tiMantha lu Duois to beat them.

*The Skyborne were better than us.*

*Or they used mercenaries to fight for them, Normals like Ian Haarper against other Normals.* Kalm had time to wonder why he had considered that last possibility.

There were other wounded men lying in the grass, not all of them from ris Fryddich's platoon. Some had kept their weapons and ammunition; some had passed them on to other soldiers. If they were conscious, he told them reassuring things that were sometimes true.

He did not think he had seen them all.

There were more dead men.

There were men not wounded. One was weeping behind a small bush, and Kalm only patted his back as he walked past. Others were shamming injury or illness or simply straggling, letting the line pass on as they stood still. He made sure they noticed him, by shouting if necessary. They were inexperienced soldiers; they expected to be caught out, and most of them got back to their units when they saw him gesturing with the borrowed musket. The remaining few obeyed when he aimed the weapon at them.

He was doing a lieutenant's work, he realized at last. Ris Fryddich was already positioned behind the men and could do this just as well. Hurrying, he caught up to the platoon leader and waved at the stragglers. The man's face showed strain, but he shook his head in silent agreement.

Kalm did not stay for a discussion. The men did not need him; they had Ian Haarper if they needed an officer. But he wanted them to see him beside them; he did not want to share them with the time traveler. As he jogged forward, he waved Prellis's musket above the grass and tried to look confident.

"Waiting on you, Algheran." Lan Haarper grinned.

He nodded curtly, panting as he dropped to a walk.

The Ironwearer waved. "Dalsyn, now!"

They were running.

One of the squad leaders fell beside Kalm, but he had only tripped over an obstacle in the grass. Feet pounded past him, then he was on his feet again, running again, just another soldier chasing the platoon.

Rasping, hoarse, sides aching, ears ringing, Kalm managed to stay in the front ranks. Before him, the hillside flickered.

"Yah-hoooo!" Ian Haarper shouted, running ahead of him, waving his arms as he dashed up the road.

Grass waved before Kalm: Ian Plentyk's sudden fusillade, the scattered firing from the Midpassage platoons.

Men in green uniforms lay fallen in the tall grass now.

The Algherans were running.

Kalm leaped over a body as he came to the hill crest, then

looked about wildly, uncertain as to what he should do next.

The grass had been cleared there, cut down by the Algherans as they waited but left to lie on the ground. There was a fire pit, not yet used, and a tarpaulin lying over supplies. Midpassage men were running through the thin line of defenders, their feet tossing grass aside like water from a brook. Before him, they mixed with panicked Algherans.

A man stood before Kalm, tall, red-haired, silent.

Lan Haarper. He had been among the first over the top.

*Enjoying his victory.* Kalm could not begrudge him that.

On the right, the men from the Northern Valley swept forward, running unopposed down the back of a neighboring hill. Behind them, a man shouted orders.

The packed group of men at the end of the Northern Valley line were sprinting toward men running down the road. As they ran, they screamed a distorted version of lan Haarper's cry.

Before them, just on the left, the cavalry unit moved, swarming onto the road amid the main body of retreating Algherans like hummingbirds into bees. Swords flashed as the horses waded into the small column. Blue and green uniforms moved about in random patterns, then individual cavalry troopers were across the road chasing men through the tall grass. There were shouts of excitement, of horror.

Swords continued to swing even after Algherans raised their arms in surrender.

A wall of brown rose before the trees at the left: lan Styllin's men, moving from the copse. Arm-long flames spurted from their muskets as they advanced.

Musket fire continued to sound about Kalm, not with the stick-on-picket-fence clatter it had had before but in isolated booms that barely escaped the noise and commotion.

Behind him, a Swordtroop private blubbered, tears streaming down his face as he waited on his knees. One of the Midpassage men shot him in the neck as he ran past. Nearby, an Algheran noncom waited inside a ring of brown-uniformed men, his musket held waist high, glaring at them. He spit on the ground finally and dropped the weapon, then lurched drunkenly, hit by four bullets.

A Midpassage man on his back flailed with his musket as the Algheran atop stabbed at him. After the Lopritian was dead, two others grabbed the dazed Algheran, but they did not kill him.

A man leaned over the dead Algheran private, pulling things from his pack.

The passion was dying, Kalm realized, listening to his ragged breath and his pounding heart, seeing a man trying to attract his attention and surrender.

The killing was over. He grabbed the Algheran and pushed him in the direction of the brigade. There were already a half-dozen men in green uniforms walking in that direction, weaponless and dazed. The men in the artillery company, muskets in hand, were moving toward them. Men throughout the brigade were looking at the hill, not yet comprehending what had happened.

*We've won.* He let Dieytl know that, knowing that the money broker would tell Wolf-Twin, and the word would reach ris Andervyll. *We don't need help*.

Ten man-heights away, lan Haarper walked about, wading through the grass, talking, pointing, giving orders. Behind him was a tail of soldiers, Midpassage men and Algherans mixed, waiting for directions or only his attention.

Hemmed in by cavalry, a large body of green-uniformed men was coming back up the hill. Kalm could not count the bodies that lay on the road or beside it.

The fighting was done, he realized, looking practically around the little battlefield. It was time to take prisoners off for questioning and to collect their packs and discarded muskets. Time to hear the groans of wounded men and carry them to the surgeons. Time to bury the dead.

It was time to notice tear-filled eyes—and stinks. A stench pounced on his perception suddenly—blood, earth, vegetation, gunpowder, death, his own sweat, and a metallic reek that was none of those things.

Those were a battle's odors. The hilltop would smell of battle till time's end, he told himself, though that was surely an exaggeration.

A musket went off behind him.

Lan Haarper twisted and fell.

An eon passed before Kalm drew the connection. Then he was aware of Derrauld ris Fryddich beside him and of the sharp odor of gunpowder still leaking from ris Fryddich's musket as the man broke it open and shook out the unburned grains.

"Derry. . ." His ears rang. His unheard voice faltered as he looked into ris Fryddich's eyes. They were wide and blind—not sane. "Derry?"

Mumbling as he slapped at his chest, the blond noble stared past Kalm, ignoring him completely as lan Haarper got up on hands and knees. While the Ironwearer shook himself, ris Fryddich lowered his musket butt to the ground and raised a cartridge over the end of the barrel. His thumb slipped; powder spilled onto the ground. Ris Fryddich cursed and pulled another cartridge from his bandolier. Behind him, not yet noticing, another of the men from Midpassage was rifling the dead private's pack.

Lan Haarper was on his knees, his torso rising.

Ris Fryddich poured powder into his musket and dropped in the wadded paper cartridge. Men were turning toward him, mouths open.

Lan Haarper moved, coughing, one hand on a raised knee. Kalm saw no blood on him and none on the ground.

Ris Fryddich bent to seize a ramrod from the ground, moved to avoid a hand reaching for him, and shoved the rod into the musket, compressing the gunpowder.

Lan Haarper shook his head, waving off assistance. He said something—at least his mouth worked.

Ris Fryddich spat a bullet into the barrel of his musket, pushed it into place with the ramrod, then stepped in front of Kalm, using him to block running men.

Lan Haarper looked about, confusion plain on his face.

Ris Fryddich aimed at the Ironwearer.

His musket clicked twice.

It did not fire.

*He didn't prime it*, Kalm realized, stepping to the side, as openmouthed at ris Fryddich's failure as the man himself. The blond man had forgotten to release the catch by the breech that exposed powder to the firing mechanism. The spark had not reached the gunpowder, and lan Haarper was still alive.

Lan Haarper was bent over again, blurred.

He was running—at ris Fryddich.

Ris Fryddich dropped his useless musket. "Gimme!" his mouth said. His hands snatched at Kalm, at Prellis's musket.

It was reflex, not thought, that made Kalm turn away.

Ris Fryddich froze only an instant, then ran toward the trees. No one tried to stop him.

Blundering, awkward in his haste, lan Haarper collided

with one of the prisoners as he turned. No one watched as he got back on his feet.

Men scattered. Lan Haarper had a knife in his hand.

Ris Fryddich ran through a fire pit, then around men reaching for him. Five man-heights from the trees, he tripped on a pair of discarded muskets. Before lan Haarper could reach him, blood spurted from his side, staining the ground beside him.

He shrieked then, reaching uselessly toward the trees. His back arched. Then his head fell, face downward. His hands slid sideways, burrowing under the grass. His shoulders shook. A boot heel twitched.

Blood trickled through the cut grass.

A cavalry sergeant still astride his horse broke open his musket and tapped the breech mechanically against his saddle.

Lan Haarper stood over ris Fryddich's body, shaking his head slowly, the knife in his hand suddenly seeming puny and useless. Pain and bewilderment filled his face.

# CHAPTER TWENTY-THREE

"*. . . and he killed Derry and—*"

Sitting stiffly cross-legged, a writing box on his knees, Kalm nodded at the crouching man. "No, it was one of the cavalry troopers." *Derrauld killed Derrauld.*

"One of his, though, after he—" Krennlen ris Jynnich virtually bleated with dismay. His expression was frantic. The tent fabric shivered behind his shoulder. Behind him, by the fire pit, a squad leader from the first company waved rank patches on pieces of green cloth at blue-uniformed men.

"Someone will hear you, Krenn," Kalm said callously, enjoying the terror that showed on the young man's face while looking past to see the squad leader receiving money. "Derry tried to kill Ian Haarper yesterday. He waited too long, so everyone saw him try it, and he's dead because of it. Remember that. Besides, it's a crime to kill your commanding officer."

Did the idiot realize that ris Fryddich had attempted to protect him from Ian Haarper's anger? No, ris Jynnich was too self-centered to understand.

Kalm snarled. "And you're asking me to join some kind of plot against him. That's mutiny, Krenn. Another crime. Don't you remember that? Are you trying to get the Ironwearer to kill me and Dighton, too? For you?" His voice could be heard outside his tent. He half hoped it would be understood.

"It's not that. It's—it's—we have to protect ourselves. You and me. And Dighton. Against—"

At least the idiot had lowered his voice. Kalm smiled gently at ris Jynnich, realizing how much he despised him.

"Just you, Krenn," he said.

"What do you mean?"

"Just you, Krenn. Captain First Class ris Jynnich. You're the one who screwed his wife, and the one who bragged about it."

"I thought—" Ris Jynnich was white.

"You thought she was a peasant, trying to better herself with a noble, like some slut in your father's fields. You thought you'd have your fun and get away with it, like you always did before. Because *she* wouldn't tell."

"You said—"

"He could kill you this afternoon, Krenn. No one would stop him. Did you ever see an Ironwearer fight?"

"You said—"

Kalm stared up at him. "I know what I said. I said she was mad at him; I said she was lonely. I said she was jealous. That's all. I left her alone with you, trusting you as a Lopritian noble to be polite to your superior officer's wife. What you did after that—I'm not responsible for you, Krennlen."

"You said—" Ris Jynnich's face pleaded for him.

"I know what I said," Kalm repeated. "I can say it again for any Teep in the one world, and they'll say you're lying if you say anything else."

"You said—" The young nobleman was near to tears.

"I know what I said." Kalm lifted the papers in his hands and shook them before ris Jynnich. "Ironwearer Ian Haarper has given me some work to do this morning, the work you should have done for Dighton and didn't. He's going to ask me why if it's not done when he gets back. I think you should leave."

"What will I do?" Ris Jynnich sniffed.

"Go help ris Maanhaldur bury the bodies. That needs doing. Sort out packs. Or help the men collect bullets. Something. He's got every other officer working this morning, why not you?"

"But the men all look at me!"

"Of course! They're waiting for him to kill you."

"Will he?" Ris Jynnich's voice was tiny.

"Get the fuck out, ris Jynnich."

He hated the man, Kalm realized, listening to Krennlen ris Jynnich stumble away from his tent. Ris Maanhaldur had had nerve enough to face the men of the Midpassage Battalion and take charge of burying the dead this morning, because he sensed that the work needed to be done. Ris Jynnich was a coward.

And ris Jynnich had hurt Kylene, hurt a Teep. He could admit that now. The young nobleman was still only an incipient sadist, but Kalm could see the tastes he had begun to develop. In the end he would feast on cruelty even more voraciously than the dead Gerint ris Whelmner had.

But Krennlen had hated lan Haarper; he had dared—once —to offend him. He had shaped himself into a tool for Kalm to use, and Kalm had used the man, sensing that Kylene's infidelity would cause lan Haarper pain. He had not intended for the man to hit Kylene, had not intended to cause Kylene pain, had not intended Kylene to couple lovemaking with the pain ris Jynnich inflicted.

*I made a mistake.*

*She's not Tagin. She's not one of my egg women.*

*If she's been maimed by this, it's not something I'm not responsible for.*

He swallowed. *I only wanted to hurt lan Haarper.*

The tent wall billowed in a breeze. What had Sandibeck promised him long ago? As a servant of the Alliance, he would be proud, bitter, scornful, dominating, guiltless. *A hero, Kalm! Women, wealth, fame—all you wish from life— all you wish to be—we will make that of you!*

"You were wrong, lady," he whispered.

Ris Maanhaldur returned in late morning, surrendering his weary Algheran grave diggers to officers from the brigade, then hiding from the world in his ambulance. When Kalm knocked for entrance, the sounds inside ceased. Numbly, pretending the wagon was empty, he retreated and signed lan Haarper's orders himself, then passed them to other officers.

The Steadfast-to-Victory Regiment was ready to move by midday, but another half watch passed before lan Haarper returned and placed the unit in motion. The Ironwearer was in a bad temper. Kalm did not attempt to speak to him.

Even then the advance was fitful. It seemed as though habit put men on the road that afternoon, not their indecisive com-

manders, habit and frustration that made marching seem a
lesser ill than continued waiting.

The Northern Valley companies took the lead. They were
followed by the second Midpassage company, then the first,
while a pair of lieutenants checking supplies in the wagons ran
to take their positions in line. One of the lieutenants had commanded Second Company the day before. Neither Kalm nor
the officers who had been shifted knew why lan Haarper had
made the change.

A pair of guns went next, then a small file of cavalry, then
more guns—reinforcements that the artillery company had received that morning. Kalm hesitated, reluctant despite the
orders in his hands, then gave way to the feelings of his men.
He formed Third Company along the roadside, ordering the
men to shoulder weapons already in position, then led at double time until they had joined the column. More cavalrymen
rode by on the raised pavement, looking down incuriously
from their height.

Lan Styllin was at the head of his men. Ris Fryddich's
platoon Kalm led himself, pretending that neither he nor the
men noticed the vacancy at his side.

The supply wagons came next, carrying ammunition and
muskets taken from the captured Algherans. Kalm wondered
if somewhere in their midst was the precious crock of foot
ointment and the sheets of shoe-patching material.

Finally, as if getting permission one by one, lan Haarper,
then Merryn ris Vandeign, still in bright civilian clothing, then
Dighton ris Maanhaldur, his tears on his thin face dried,
mounted up and passed wordlessly to the front of the regiment. Dalsyn lan Plenytk and lan Halkmayne were already
there.

Ris Jynnich rode at the back, among the wagons. Earlier,
he had thought of fleeing to his father's estates, till one of the
artillery sergeants had told him the punishments reserved for
deserters. The sergeant had enjoyed the description; Krennlen,
less pleased, had not penetrated his exaggerations.

At the top of the hill, lan Haarper stopped the column.

Accompanied by ris Maanhaldur, he came to each of the
Midpassage companies and gave the same short talk: he
wanted them to count the graves as they marched by. They
would see twelve in which Lopritians rested, twenty-nine for
Algherans. There were wounded no longer with the regiment
in almost equal numbers. The difference was due to the Mid-

passage men being soldiers as good as the Algherans and the Lopritian regulars and to the way they had attacked the enemy instead of waiting passively. He wanted them to remember that lesson and to trust their officers.

Many of the Algherans had died after they had surrendered, Kalm remembered cynically. He wondered if the men were supposed to absorb that lesson also.

He did not ask that. Lan Haarper's face showed strain even Normals could detect, and his awkward little speech had contained no eloquence. In the moments afterward, as the Ironwearer stood before the company waiting for the men to realize he was through, Kalm caught Ian Styllin's eye focused on him and wondered if his own expression was equally wooden.

Ris Maanhaldur told the men that the Hand had praised them and would make sure Queen Molminda heard of their deeds. He was proud to be with them, and there was marching ahead for all of them. He laughed uncertainly, then released them.

The men took it well. They cheered halfheartedly at the queen's name, stomped some musket butts into the ground when Dighton finished, and shouted Merryn's name when Ian Haarper asked for it. Then they went without straggling into formation again at the sides of the road and got back to marching. Kalm even noticed some of them staring at the graves they passed and moving their lips, as if counting.

Afternoon brought them past trampled grass and a line of fire pits, some with embers still smoldering.

More excited by that than by speeches, the men darted away from the road seeking nonexistent souvenirs and points of interest they had never found in their own campgrounds.

Prosaically, Ian Haarper squatted over an Algheran latrine.

The next day began without Ian Haarper. He had left at dawn, returning to the brigade for conversations with other officers. Dieytl noticed him in one of the headquarters wagons, waving his arms over the big relief map while talking to Ironwearer Wolf-Twin, but the Lopritian Teep did not probe to find what they talked about, so Kalm never learned it either.

It was not important. He knew what the Algheran prisoners

had disclosed. The secrets Ian Haarper held behind his Teep-blind were not apt to be significant now.

The man himself seemed less significant, Kalm realized, examining Ian Haarper's accomplishments in the new day's light. Any officer in the Strength-through-Loyalty Brigade—or even the Steadfast-to-Victory Regiment, for that matter—could have led a regiment, backed by a sizable artillery threat, to victory over a company. If Krennlen had been less hysterical, less conscious of his sins, less eager to create a scene, he would have seen the foolishness of his fears. Ris Fryddich would still be alive then. Ris Maanhaldur would have looked better to the men and earned some of the credit they had bestowed on "their" Ironwearer.

Nicole's cloak had covered Ian Haarper. Against a proper defense, the Lopritians would have suffered heavy casualties. But few of the Algherans had realized how green the Midpassage men were; it was the inexperience of their own officers that had cost the Swordtroop so heavily in that tiny battle.

He had done reasonably well himself, Kalm considered. He had been nervous, but he had surmounted that, as he had in the past. He had been one of the first officers to reach the crest of the hill, not far behind Ian Haarper.

The men had thought well of him.

Lan Haarper had shown that he thought well of Kalm.

Smiling at his nonsensical satisfactions, he waved at ris Jynnich and shared breakfast with him on one of the wagons.

By midday much of the pleasure had gone.

Directed by ris Vandeign and ris Maanhaldur, the men marched under the hot sun in an awkward eight-abreast formation that Merryn had discovered in a book and that cast in the air all the dust that had caked the road. The column's motion was checked in front by three small field guns—Dighton's contribution to safe tactics—and much of the cavalry. Droppings from the latter laid only some of the dust.

The coughing men were forced to bunch up at intervals by supply wagons that butted at the rear of the column. Merryn and Dighton allowed them few rest stops, and Kalm waited to overhear angry mutters about the officers, but fortunately the protests that he noticed were seldom verbalized.

That was due to the peasantry's respect for nobility, he decided, tempered by the realization that the peasants had to continue living under the nobility when the campaign was over. He wondered how the men would feel if they knew that both nobles secretly hoped for praise from a former prospector, a man once no higher in status than they. And he wondered also, with something very much like homesickness, how Merryn and Dighton would have fared as officers among the raucous Falltroop companies Kalm had served in.

At midday ris Maanhaldur called the battalion's officers together during a meal break. When Kalm returned to his men, he talked to them cheerfully but did not repeat the false assurances that the brigade was following closely behind.

In early afternoon officers quarreled at the front of the column. The regiment divided, the Northern Valley companies—a battalion in its own right now, under Dalsyn lan Plenytk at lan Haarper's request, Dieytl told Kalm—continuing south on the road while the Midpassage Battalion, under ris Maanhaldur, marched eastward on a dirt lane. The forests stood waiting on the horizon.

A half watch later, between walls of brown grass and shedding ironberry trees, the battalion was halted. The wagons at the back of the column were laboriously turned around. Then the order was countermanded, and cursing soldiers strained to lift and turn the vehicles once more while disgusted teamsters jockeyed their teams back to their original positions.

More confusion arose in the artillery section, complicated by the collapse of a cannon wheel, and a half platoon of Second Company was delegated to shove the now-useless gun to the side of the road. Sounds of argument, which Kalm did not choose to follow, drifted back from the head of the column. Unordered, his men fell out by the roadside to gobble uncooked rations and throw rust-tarnished berries at a sunbathing lizard.

Lan Haarper rode past, ignoring the Algheran's greeting, the big man radiating anger even through his Teepblind. Returning suddenly, he shouted at one of the ambulance drivers, then trotted back to the front of the column. Soon after, Dighton ris Maanhaldur made the same trip, a dazed expression on his narrow face. Lan Haarper's shrill little orderly rode beside him, using a hand to steady the battalion commander in his saddle. While Kalm watched sadly, they dismounted a short distance away and Quillyn half helped, half shoved the shaking man into the enclosed vehicle.

One raw-knuckled hand groped past the canvas flap to fasten desperately on the wagon frame. Kalm heard sobs then—

felt them—and was not able to keep the knowledge from his face.

Lan Haarper had almost predicted this, he remembered, feeling something akin to hatred as the Algheran time traveler rode past, a bottle of whiskey in his hand that he did not attempt to conceal. Wordlessly, the redhead thrust the liquor inside the ambulance, glaring at the men who watched him.

The emotion Kalm felt did not die when ris Maanhaldur's sobs were suddenly choked off.

Lan Haarper must have guessed his reaction, for he halted as he rode by and reached down to punch his shoulder. "I need you now, Algheran," he said tonelessly. "Don't you fail me."

Kalm growled without words and pulled away. Lan Haarper's lips tightened, then he straightened and rode off silently.

The march resumed after that, south again, but at a slower pace. Far to its rear, Kalm's senses told him, the Strength-through-Loyalty Brigade had finally broken camp, reluctantly moving after the regiment as if ropes were tugging at it. Men were ahead of the regiment as well; how far ahead and in what numbers he could not yet tell.

A pair of bewildered men with tattooed cheeks watched from the edge of the grass as the battalion moved out. Ris Maanhaldur's slaves had been stripped of their scarlet finery, but it had not been possible to eradicate the confusion and fear they felt now. Kalm was not willing to meet their eyes as he drew abreast of them, and he turned away with relief as lan Haarper's orderly galloped by, headed north on the Agent's black stallion. Other men on horseback moved to either side of the column and drifted ahead of it in a fan-shaped formation.

*Feelers*, Kalm thought. *Pickets going out. Lan Haarper's taking control again.*

As if to prove the point, the man was continually visible now, whether riding along the column or sitting patiently on his horse as the men stepped by. "Steady does it," he called out when he chose to speak. "Close up. Keep the pace. Close up."

The men marched in two ranks on either side of the dirt lane with the wagons and guns in the middle. It was lan Haarper's preferred formation, the one he had trained them in, and the men were pleased to return to what they knew. Now and then they called out to him as they passed him, but his thoughts seemed distant even when he smiled at remarks made from the ranks.

Beside him, impatient at the men's interruptions, was one of the men he had brought with him from the brigade—a surgeon.

The men obeyed without argument. They were allowed rests at eighth-watch intervals now, and the officers pretended not to notice those who sidled alongside the supply wagons for covert mugs of beer. It also helped that Ian Haarper had allowed them to leave much of their kit in the supply wagons so that only muskets and ammunition bandoliers hung upon their shoulders.

For the men the march was becoming easier. But watching Ian Haarper wipe sweat from his forehead, Kalm remembered almost with sadness the bawdy man who had begun the campaign. When next his company passed by the Ironwearer, he nodded pleasantly, trying to display a smile to reward the man for his effort and assure him that he felt no continued grudge. "Close up. Keep the pace," was all the response he got, but he felt he had been noticed. Kalm was obscurely satisfied.

The ambulance containing Dighton ris Maanhaldur was gone by then, at whose order Kalm never discovered.

It was late the next morning before the battalion came back onto the great road, and afternoon before they rejoined the waiting Northern Valley companies. Nearby, red fabric billowed wearily above a supply dump. There were no barrels of beer and little food. Splintered wood showed where Algheran looters had opened ration boxes. A pallet to keep supplies from the ground had not been laid, so rain and insects had ruined much of the exposed bread and grain. Worse, the wooden vats nearby had not been filled or caulked by the Lopritian suppliers. Some rain had accumulated in them, then leaked out, so only a handbreadth of brackish, foul-smelling water remained.

Stores of salted meat and ammunition had been thrown about, but their contents seemed unharmed. Lan Haarper had the wagons loaded with as much as they would bear. Pillage was not allowed, but the men were told to eat all they could. After that, the order to encamp that Kalm had expected was not given. Instead, the march continued.

As dusk fell, Ian Haarper rode up to Kalm, his red-brown

horse nudging ris Jynnich ahead like a prisoner. "Found this
fellow with nothing to do," he said tonelessly. "You still need
an officer for that platoon?"

Kalm hesitated, regretting now that he had not made a decision before it was necessary to check the men's reaction. "I
thought . . . lan Nhissun would be my choice. Derrill, not his
son. If that's all right with you."

The big man nodded. "I'd have gone with—never mind,
that's a decent choice. You don't want this fellow, then?"

"I'll take him." Kalm pretended reluctance in front of lan
Haarper, despite the looks ris Jynnich gave him. "Would it be
all right if I gave him lan Nhissun's old squad?"

"Just so he does something." The Ironwearer looked
bleakly at both Kalm and ris Jynnich, then rode away.

Krennlen and Derrill lan Nhissun stared at each other.
Kalm was not surprised when the noble's eyes dropped first.

The terrain they met the next day was rolling, round-
textured, not unlike the hills Kalm had known in his youth but
without Alghera's expanses of bare rock. Nonetheless, these
hills were hard on both men and animals, a succession of
green and dun ridges that the road crossed at right angles. The
road maintained an even slope without regard for the vagaries
of the land, so in places it was raised on ramps six man-
heights or more above the ground. Where dirt had been worn
away, it could be seen that the road material continued down
to bedrock.

Infrequently, the Near Rim of the Shield could be seen
from high clearings, the mountains growing taller whenever
Kalm looked, but no closer. There were no streams to ease the
men's thirst. The occasional trees that interrupted the horizon
were stunted, their branches twisted and gnarled and widely
spaced. Clumps of red-speckled bushes grew wild on the hillsides, and silver-colored leaves littered the grass.

It took conscious effort to breathe during the climbs, to
keep walking. Descending the hills, men could shuffle along
at almost a normal pace. On the rises, however, their bodies
failed them, not through unwillingness but from incapacity, as
if only a child's strength remained to propel a man's bulk.
Even the muskets on the men's backs seemed to weaken, their
once jaunty bobbing motion reduced to exhausted weaving as
the fatigued men trudged on. Mirages were always just ahead,
cruelly illusionary pools overrunning the black pavement.

Double teams had been put on the artillery, the extra horses coming from the supply wagons, so the path of the regiment was marked by abandoned vehicles. Much of the food from the supply dump was left behind this way, as if to lure onward the Strength-through-Loyalty Brigade. The ammunition wagons, however, at Ian Haarper's orders, stayed with the column.

The ancient pavement remained smooth, but as the Earth tilted to conceal the sun, Kalm saw men falling behind, unable to keep up the pace. Some continued to stumble after the column; others slumped dejectedly at the roadside, gasping for breath.

Kalm himself felt club-battered with exhaustion, and his throat had become dry and sore with hard breath, but he was not ready to quit until he knew that Ian Haarper would forgive him. Let some other officer drop out first, he decided. *And, Lady, make that soon.*

Fortunately, a halt was called at last, and the men camped on one of the ridges before darkness became complete. Fires were not permitted that night, and water was scarce, but the air was warm. Enough beer remained for each man to receive one mug.

Krennlen's attempts to speak were easily repulsed.

The tents were left on the wagons. Most men were content to wrap themselves and their weapons in blankets on the bare ground, trading an opportunity for a meal for rest. After posting a guard and conferring with Ian Styllin and Ian Nhissun, Kalm did the same. He fell asleep while debating whether to sweep away the twigs and pebbles that lay under him.

The next day had not begun when the march resumed. Soldiers were being kicked awake even before the full disk of the sun had mounted the horizon. There was grain for those who wished to breakfast, but no water and no beer. Those who were willing to embrace risk or who recognized safe plants licked dew from leaves; more cautious men sucked on carefully chosen pebbles.

Ironically, during the night someone had put the discarded beer barrels back into the supply wagons. No other effort was made to clean up the site; instead, the men tossed their blankets indiscriminately into the vehicles even as the drivers hitched their teams. Kalm saw fewer wagons than he remembered.

Fewer men were in the column as well. Little more than seven hundred men were present for duty now, he estimated. Lump in teamsters, officers, and the handful of cavalry, and still one man in three of the regiment was missing. Adding the stragglers who might rejoin would not make up the difference.

The main body of the brigade was now twenty thousand man-heights behind, nearly beyond the range of his mind. The other men, he sensed, were closer, but he still was not close enough to read individual thoughts or estimate their numbers.

Rain began late in the second watch. For most of the day the sun had been hidden behind thickening clouds. In the early afternoon they overflowed, spilling minas of water as if from an overturned basin. The column halted without orders while thirsty men lifted their faces to the sky.

Kalm was among them, rejoicing also as cool drops splashed on him, matting his tousled hair and washing away his sweat. Dust flushed from his forehead stung his eyes, but he was not aware of the discomfort. He shook his head at last to clear his face of water, then knelt to undo the drawstrings on his sodden pant legs and expose his boot-prisoned feet. He was barely conscious of lan Haarper's shouts or of the mud-streaked teamsters who stripped the canvas tops from the supply wagons and spread them to divert the precious water into the empty barrels.

The rain continued all that afternoon. Before it ended, the march resumed.

"Close up. Move on." Lan Haarper's voice sounded again, the shepherd patiently driving his soldier flock. There were other commands as well, brought to the officers by exhausted cavalrymen endlessly in motion around the column. Following those orders, Kalm had an extra ration of meat distributed to his men, then gave a sham inspection to their muskets before they were led off the road to an improvised firing range.

Lan Haarper was here, seemingly impervious to the rainfall, though his brown cloak was tight about his body. He stood alone, slouching, watching gravely as the men formed a line, one platoon behind the other, each soldier not quite a man-height apart from the others. A stone's toss away, a head-sized piece of red cloth had been draped over an ironberry tree, moving only as rain or wind pressed at the branches below.

Lopritian largess had not extended to uniform coats or rain gear for the militia companies. Watching the wretched men in the ragged garments they had brought from Midpassage, Kalm thought he had never seen prisoners so dispirited.

"There's your target, Algheran." Lan Haarper's baritone carried well through the rain. "One volley as they stand, one on their knees, then each man fires two rounds prone."

"Prone?" Kalm stared, then repeated the word with dismay, while men looked at each other like rabbits awaiting butchers. Firing from the ground had been part of lan Haarper's instruction in Midpassage, before Kalm had joined the battalion, but no one had taken it as more than an Ironwearer's foible.

Injured men, released from the battle, lay on the ground. Soldiers fought to their feet so they could advance.

"Prone—means on their bellies." Lan Haarper took the reins of a black horse from Quillyn, stepped up into the saddle, and reached past the covered rifle hanging there to pat the animal. "Not much cure for buck fever, Algheran, but it's all I can arrange. Have a good day."

Of course it was not a good day. Kalm attempted dutifully to comply with his orders, but neither the weather nor the men were obliging. The troops were willing to fire en masse at the too distant target while standing, and a flicker of the red cloth indicated that someone had hit it, but the rain picked up after that. It was not easy to see the target through blinking eyes, and only a few men could be persuaded to kneel or lie on the wet ground and fire at it. None of them made the shot.

Fortunately, lan Haarper's aide had also gone by then, so no one was present to force embarrassment on him, but Kalm was not pleased. Something close to masochism made him fire. He shot four times before the red cloth jerked. When he stood up, his uniform was muddy and powder blasts had seared his cheek black. The rain made the abraded skin sting. His ears rang.

The men would not look at him. Kalm scowled as he swung the inverted musket over his shoulder and refastened the carrying strap, clenching his teeth to fight the pain. *Lady, you sure aren't being helpful. Can't I get a scrap of cover from that cloak of yours?*

The men had done well, he shouted through the downpour at lan Haarper, irritated by the mud oozing along his elbows and legs, by his sopping uniform, by the inhuman patience lan Haarper's horse displayed. They could be released.

The horse eyed him skeptically.

Lan Haarper's mouth twitched to show that he recognized the lie, even as he agreed, and that was irritating also.

But dishonesty had been forced on them both by the circumstances. Kalm could not be sure all his men had aimed poorly or know whether they had all fired their muskets. Rain dampened the powder in some cartridges, no matter how well waxed, and musket barrels got wet, so misfires were likely. In ChelmForce, experienced squad leaders would have overseen the shooting. Here, in miserable conditions, he had been required to guess.

As a final annoyance, the rain made plans for battle senseless, and the men realized it as well as he did.

*Never ask more of the men than they are prepared to give,* Kalm thought grimly, remembering advice lan Haarper had often ignored. Cimon take the martinet. Cimon take the dumb men who did not recognize their limitations. Thoroughly displeased with each part of the one Earth, he led the men at double time back to their place in the column, pretending not to notice as skylarkers stashed their muskets in passing supply wagons.

Rain-diminished, the crack of gunfire could be heard ahead. Lan Haarper was drilling another company.

# CHAPTER TWENTY-FOUR

*If bad weather made battle impossible, Ironwearer Timithial
lan Haarper would not admit it, Kalm soon found.*

The regiment had entered a forest, and the world was tipping into an unseen evening sky when the big man called a
conference of officers. Lan Haarper, Lord Vandeign, the three
Midpassage captains, Dalsyn lan Plenytk, lan Halkmayne, an
anonymous pair of riders, one of them replacing the marching
sickness-seized Thannun . . . *Not many of us left,* Kalm
thought, seeing the changes time had made. For an instant he
felt trapped in a child's game of make-believe that the weight
of his musket did nothing to dispel. How could any of these
unimpressive men pretend to be soldiers and leaders of soldiers?

The rain had stopped, but water still dripped on him from
the silver-skinned branches above. Along the roadside, water
spilling from the pavement carved tiny channels in the red
soil. In the background, cursing men attempted to keep fires
lit. Sparks and muted popping sounds rose at intervals as pale
flames reached grains of gunpowder strewn on the wet wood.
Behind the restraining stockade of the wagons, horses neighed
disconsolately, nuzzling one another for comfort.

The sky over the trees remained gray, the one Earth filled
with gloom. With evening the air would turn from cool to
cold, Kalm knew. The best the men could hope for would be

keeping the wind at bay during the long night. Huddling together in their damp clothing would not give them warmth.

*Getting time to retrieve my jacket,* he reflected, fondly remembering one he had left in Midpassage. The feel of leather
would be welcome now, its yielding stiffness like soft armor,
the concealed strands of heating circuits a comforting cage
that would surround him as he traveled through time, away
from all peril—soon, very soon.

Would lan Haarper understand when he found Kalm missing?

*While I'm thinking of such things, I should break off a bit
of patching material and thicken my shoe soles. Assuming
someone does get a fire started. A practicality.* He smiled
ironically at the men around him, realizing that he could travel
through time more easily than he could walk back to Midpassage. *I should have stolen lan Haarper's levcraft instead of
burying it.*

A twig snapped under a careless foot, bringing him back to
his surroundings. *What are we waiting for?* the telepath wondered in the uneasy silence that followed. *I should be eating
now, with my men.* Bile surged at the back of his throat, the
salt taste of preserved meat strong in his mouth for one moment as he remembered his last meal.

"Er, Lord Vandeign?" Lan Haarper sounded apologetic; his
face was neutral, his stance that of an uncertain gambler. A
rising fire showed drops of water that fell along his jaw and a
pale scar along his hairline. Knife hilts seemed dark blotches
on his tunic front. "Your meeting, sir."

Merryn only shook his head, his face invisible under a
broad-brimmed hat. Kalm's mind reached forth, finding unruly frustration, a thunderbolt of rage, black-edged self-pity, a
longing for the peace of his hearth and family, and anguish at
the futility that enveloped all his wishes and plans. The gray-
haired man gestured suddenly, snapping his fingers and pointing at lan Haarper. "Do as you will, Ironwearer." His voice
was drenched in contempt, audible to Kalm even without his
special senses. "I've no way to stop you."

"Yes, sir." Lan Haarper stood with downcast eyes, scraping leaves aside with one boot to expose dark soil. Kalm,
watching Merryn withdraw with one of the riders, contrasted
the two of them: lan Haarper, tall, bulky, rumpled, in tan
uniform; ris Vandeign, slim, aging, almost elegant in his red

and gray clothing. What strange common interests had once made them friends?

Lan Haarper sighed to break the hush. Tree limbs wavered, and a gust of wind threw raindrops to patter on the silent men, to bombard the bare earth with water and tiny craters. "Thought Lord Vandeign was going to say something a little different there. Well, gather around, people. Now, one hill ahead . . ."

The Strength-through-Loyalty Brigade was then twenty-five thousand man-heights behind them.

"Ammunition! The Ironwearer says pass out all the ammunition!" The cavalryman who had blurted that had ridden past before Kalm had time to react.

So this rest period had come to an end. Kalm nodded absently, then gestured with a finger to bring two squad leaders to their feet. "Get six boxes of ammunition from the wagons. Full boxes."

His eyes swept past them to the gray silhouettes that were his other soldiers, looking for men without their muskets. If only they could hear his orders without speech.

But that was not so. Wearily, he levered himself to his feet, feeling centuries older than his true years. His shoulders were board-stiff, tension-knotted, and a deep ache filled the bone socket in his left hip. He stood unsteadily, marveling at the small miracle, then turned to eye the camp.

Men were asleep on the hillsides, their uniforms indistinguishable from the mud that lay everywhere. Horses were muzzle-strapped to keep them from neighing. Small boxes sitting on wheels to be pulled after the cannons were seemingly abandoned now by the golden-bronze guns. Supply wagons parked without order obstructed the road. *Looks as if Ian Haarper's lost already.*

He forced a smile in reaction to the thought, then walked along the roadside and up the slope, kicking lightly at men too exhausted to react. "Back to the wagons, soldiers. Get your muskets. Come on, men, move." His shoes squelched.

His men could not see his face, fortunately, or penetrate his shielded mind. Kalm marveled at their stolidity and their easy companionship, knowing himself isolated as he had never felt in ChelmForce.

Beyond the reaches of his eyes, three thousand men waited, innocent of his existence. The familiar textures of

Algheran thoughts tugged at his mind, candle lures for the darting moth of his attention. Friends, brothers, ancestors . . .

And he had friends around him. Kalm fought to still nausea on a darkened hillside in an alien world.

*Lady, Lady.* But there was nothing to ask of Nicole.

*Cimon, Lord, let me bear what must be. Grant that honor is in my deeds regardless of the opinions of men. Grant me the qualities that you esteem. Grant me fair judgment and the courage to face judgment.*

The gods gave no answer to him. They never did.

There was no gap in the dark clouds overhead. Elsewhere in Loprit and the Algheran Realm, men slept beneath the same clouds. Families had eaten evening meals under them, waiting for the rain, perhaps discussing sagely before bedtime whatever news of the day had reached them. They were well fed, warm, snugly housed, untouched by fear, undreaming. On the far side of the world, morning had come during the last watch to press aside night's dark cover and wake the sturdy peasants of Chelmmys, who were yet to dream of world unity.

For an instant, Kalm viewed humanity as the gods might, seeing the two races of mankind unbreakably intertwined in a fraternal embrace that neither had the courage to admit, the millions of individual lives that sprouted in flowerlike diversity, bloomed, blindly cast seed upon the winds of fate, wilted, and fell . . . Cimon-guarded, Nicole-guided, the many were one.

Near and far away from him, in the dark cave of war, seven hundred men rested on a hillside. Some of them watched the rain.

There was still time to act, Kalm decided, but not enough time to think of implications. He nodded abruptly, then descended the slope to the supply wagons, limping slightly to ease his hip.

Rain thickened as he was browsing through tents and baggage. Trying not to show haste, he tugged his pack from the wagon, then leaned against a wheel with it resting on his knee as he plumbed its contents.

An extra bandolier of ammunition; cartridge extractor for handling misfires; clothing, smelling of sweat but dry; mildew-scented foot wrappings; a wooden box; the bullet-repelling garment Ian Haarper had given him . . . Kalm smiled as he changed clothes and slipped into the Kevlar vest. *The men couldn't understand why I didn't take souvenirs.*

Box under his arm, he rejoined his company to watch as men shaken from the hillside tumbled into loose formation and his lieutenants handed out ammunition to their platoons. Soldiers nodded at him respectfully.

He watched guiltily, flinching slightly as cold drops of water struck him, hugging the box against him as if for warmth, then set it down, postponing the anticipated moment. Mechanically, he made himself ready for battle as they did, filling his bandoliers with ammunition, stowing a spare in his pack, and sliding the cartridge extractor into a side pocket.

Numb then, sad, knowing that the excited men would not notice his absence immediately, he carried his box back to the supply wagons. Stealthily, he opened it and set the cold controls. *I wonder if any of them will miss me.*

It did not matter. It could not be allowed to matter. Eyes shut, he turned the power knob.

A raindrop struck his head, rolling down his forehead across an eyelid. Another hit his hand as he raised it.

Nearby, a pair of teamsters exchanged mutters.

Coincidence! The dials were set wrong.

Hunched over, he reset the controls and turned the power up again. Water trickled over his neck and down his back.

"Are you all right, sir?" an artilleryman asked, reading his rank from shoulder patches.

"Looking for something." Kalm stood, gasping, chilled as completely through as a statue of ice. "Didn't find it."

"Want me to look, sir?"

"No," he said sadly. "You won't find it."

"All right, sir. That's a right pretty box, there."

"Yeah." A right pretty box. That was all. "I got it from the Algherans."

"Oh! You want to sell it? I'll give you ten mina."

He swallowed. "No. No. Not today."

"Fifteen, then? My brother'd like—"

"No." He sniffed, trying not to cry.

"Not worth more'n that, sir." The soldier reached out.

"No!" He turned to protect the box. "It's not for sale. It's —it's a personal thing!"

*It's not worth more than that.*

*Go away. Go away. Go away!*

"Well, I can find some things of my own tomorrow; they'll be nicer'n what you got." Mercifully, the soldier left.

Water had swamped a gap between ghost-fluid channels;

that must be it, he told himself. It was all the rain; nothing could have gone wrong with the time machine itself. He could dry it near a fire; it would be good as new.

Lan Haarper had not allowed any fires.

Teamsters were approaching. Men were leading horses forward. Soldiers strained at the guns to position them. His own company was formed up, waiting for him. The man on horseback far ahead might be Timmial lan Haarper.

He did not have time to start a fire.

It was a mechanical thing. Jostling in the wagons had shaken free a connection. It could be set right once he opened it up and looked at it in a good light.

There would not be light until morning.

Panic hovered over Kalm. He held it at bay, trying to freeze himself in one moment, to see and comprehend all about him before he allowed himself a reaction.

The moment extended, a drawn-out pause between exhaling and inhaling. When he willed, it would collapse, crushing his sanity.

Stepping lightly, he walked back to his company, the worthless time machine bouncing against his back. He took his place silently by lan Nhissun and stood like a statue in the rain, not blinking as water drops like tears raced down his face, waiting to repeat the march order. With no emotion.

"Third Company, halt, attention! Ready for duty, sir!"

Pitar lan Styllin's boyish voice incongruously parroted a regular officer's phrases. Men stopped marching, then straightened themselves around him, pretending attentiveness.

It should have been his command, Kalm remembered slowly. He had not thought to give it.

It did not matter. Nothing mattered.

Ris Jynnich stared at him sullenly. Kalm turned away, ignoring lan Nhissun's anxious look.

Lan Haarper approached on foot, walking back from Second Company. The tapping of his boots on the pavement was low-pitched and evenly paced. Wind was blowing sternly, but his cloak was wrapped around his body as if molded in that shape. Periodically he threw it open, but it always swept back into place as if the rain had pushed it shut. Water had darkened his hair, making it almost black even when he was close to Kalm.

At the side of the pavement, a man cursed and shook damaged fingers over a box of gunpowder. It was the soldier who had tried to buy the time machine. Other men, shouted at by sergeants, shoved at cannon mounts, chivvying the guns into position.

Captain Ian Halkmayne watched from between his guns, transparently waiting for the infantry to pass so the training cables could be connected. A Blankshield, Kalm noted absently. Another mercenary, highly paid for his expertise but with little standing in polite society for all his family's service to Loprit. Despite that, the man radiated an untroubled sense of competence as well as the comfortable foreknowledge that flight was always easier for artillerymen.

What did the man think now of his friend, Ian Haarper? Kalm wondered. But the artillery officer's mind was in the present, not his past.

"Break ranks," Ian Haarper ordered loudly. "Gather around. Gentlemen—hey! Quiet, you jokers! Everyone hear me? Okay, it's been a rough couple days. I bet you'd all like me to give you some soft beds out of the rain, a good hot fire, a meal—"

"Beer!" someone shouted. It was repeated. "Beer. Beer."

"Dry clothes."

"Boots!"

"Women! Then beer!"

"Beer," Ian Haarper agreed. "Me, too. Don't know about the women, but all the rest of it's down there. You know how to get it, don't you?"

"Ask politely!"

Ian Haarper laughed as if hearing that for the first time. "That's not going to work this time. The folks down there aren't expecting us yet. They'd like a couple days to get ready.

"We aren't going to give it to them."

"Where's the regulars?" someone called, and Kalm heard raindrops strike the pavement.

"Not here," Ian Haarper said flatly. "They're late, but we can't wait on them. Cornoval's in big trouble. Mlart's going to eat him up. If we're going to save his ass, we do it here and we do it now. Any questions about that?"

There were none.

"It's going to be hard. I want you to know that now. You're not going to just walk over these people, like we did before. You understand that?

"But you're the best men in Loprit for this. I wouldn't ask you to fight if I didn't know you could do the job. And if I had my choice of the whole Cimon-taken army, right now, I'd ask for you people from Midpassage. You understand that!

"All right, then! You get down there, stick close to your buddy; look out for him, make it easy for him to look out for you. Keep close to the ground; let them shoot over your heads while you're getting them in the belly. 'Member, mud's better than dead. You can handle mud, can't you?"

He smiled at the shouts. "Who needs regulars, then? Hit these people hard—they won't be better than the Guards. All right! Follow your officers, keep your heads up and your tails down. Go to it, boys."

When the cheers stopped, he pointed at them paternally. "Back in line. Keep quiet till the time comes. I'll meet you down there." The soldiers obeyed as children might, skipping through falling leaves.

Kalm returned to his position and his thoughts. Wind slapped at his face; the insolent fingers of raindrops traced his body. Behind him men chattered of inconsequential matters, of what lan Haarper had told them.

*Lan Haarper. Lan Haarper. Lan Haarper!*

Kalm ran down the road, barely restraining his screams.

"You sabotaged me!" he screamed, careless of the attention it brought.

Lan Haarper stopped and turned. *"Damfuckingstraight, sonnyboy."* Then he switched to Algheran Speech. "You just tumbled to that, huh? What of it?" He seemed untroubled.

"My time machine!" All caution had fled.

Lan Haarper waited till he was at arm's length and rain no longer overpowered voices. "It doesn't work now. You took the battery out and got rid of it. Tough."

Kalm stared in disbelief. "You've slain me!"

"Not yet. That's still option B."

"Why? Cimon and Nicole!"

"Why?" Now lan Haarper seemed surprised. He reached and poked Kalm in the chest, denting the rain-soaked jacket. "We're enemies, remember, Chieftain Second Kalm ha'Nyjuc of ChelmForceDrop. Remember? Different sides? You would have killed me."

"Oh." Kalm watched sanity prepare to flee. "You found out."

"I found out. How about that? Yes, I found out. Finally.

Without much help. So I know about you, and you know about me." Lan Haarper had not raised his voice. "Get back to your men."

"Oh." Breathing was difficult, Kalm noted absently. The wind was pushing his damp pants legs against his calves, and they were becoming uncomfortably cold. Treetops were swaying. The same distant mental processes told him that lan Haarper was mad at him. He could not defend himself by saying that this situation was not his fault.

And that left him without defense. He would die here.

"Go ahead," he said quietly. Ris Fryddich had shown that it was not possible to run away. "How did you find out?"

Lan Haarper nodded. His eyes squinted against the rain. "You never should have flushed a toilet, ha'Nyjuc. There were other things, but that was the first giveaway. And then—I ought to kill you for what you did to Kylene."

"It wasn't me, it was Krennlen!"

"Shut up, ha'Nyjuc! I don't have time to waste. You're still alive. Think about that." Lan Haarper's words snapped like a whip tipped with scorn. "Now, you get your ass back to your company and you fight!"

# CHAPTER TWENTY-FIVE

*A*pprehension *pressed against his mind. Exhilaration,* scraps of prayer, questions, unrecognized memories—from outside, from the soldiers around him. Kalm closed his mind against the intrusion of others' thoughts and tried to erase his own consciousness.

*Warmth,* he told himself, listening to his breath. *Warmth. I am gigantic, and my warm breath fills caverns. Inhale, exhale. I shrink. Inhale. Floating, floating. Exhale. I float on a warm sea, tiny, insignificant. Floating. Floating, inhale warmth, inhale light. Nothing is expected of me. Exhale. I float. I am at peace. The mother-gentle warm waves raise and lower me. Inhale. The summer-warm light laps at me, permeates my body. Cimon watches. High above, Cimon watches, Nicole standing beside him. His face is before me. Titanic, his face reaches to the clouds above. Inhale. His eyes focus on—*

*No.*

It was not Cimon's face he saw. It was not Nicole's.

He saw Ian Haarper's face. Lan Haarper's wrath. Kylene, hating.

"What'd he say?" Krennlen ris Jynnich asked, pressing against him nervously. "Kalm? Did he mention me?"

"No!" Kalm gasped, opening his eyes to return to the one Earth. Ris Jynnich's face was a gargoyle mask in the darkness. Rain was a damp asphyxiating blanket about him, a rustling curtain drawn over the yielding leaves, splattering drum taps upon his jacket, and he was alone, neglected, forlorn in an uncaring world. He was on his toes, crouched, thighs aching, on the wall of a small gully. Fingertips pressed into cool, slick clay. Men were on either side of him and below. A growing brook made baby gurgling sounds. He was all alone.

"He didn't mention you, Krenn."

*Accept. Accept,* he willed. Slowly the breakers of emotion ebbed, leaving a sheltering wall of bleakness.

"Load up," he murmured, then he repeated himself louder as he reached about to prod the men around him. "Load up. Time to get ready."

Men obeyed without question.

*Lan Haarper's enemy, and they still trust me.*

Limply, he fell back against the bank of the gully, careless of the mud that clung to his jacket, and reached for his musket.

Six hundred man-heights to his rear, their hands gleaming in the light from sealed lanterns, men gathered under a small canopy were forcing metal-bound jars up cannon throats, wadding them tight with plump fist-sized cloth packets. Other men in darkness traced ropes between trunnions and tree trunks with expert fingers, sealing loosened ends of fiber to the hawsers with hot pitch. Yet others dragged caissons forward by hand.

Kalm reached down mechanically, plucked a cartridge from his bandolier, then brought the musket barrel inside his jacket. Tallow protected the cartridge from the rain. He scraped an end clean with his thumbnail and extracted the bullet, then poured the powder into the barrel. The folded paper went in next, then the round bullet. He wiped the ramrod on his knee and tamped the charge down.

The musket was, he realized numbly, a thoroughly modern instrument. Centuries hence other devices would replace projectile-throwing weapons, but that did not make this musket any less functional, less dangerous, or less brutally fascinating.

Ironberry prospectors, coal miners, epuratory refiners and forgers such as Merryn ris Vandeign, lathe operators and leading artificers such as Ian Styllin, industrial chemists, powder grinders, stone shapers, woodworkers—all the Fifth Era world, in all its unappreciated complexity, had cooperated to build the weapon in his hands, to equip him for battles that would in turn shape the world and its short history.

*The one world. My world.* The thought was humbling yet strangely satisfying, an antidote to his bleak melancholy.

Sound reached him.

The explosion had touched the gun crews even before an awareness of it could percolate through slow brain stuff. It was more than noise heard at close range; it was a brick-hard wall of racing air that, near the muzzle of the gun, would throw a man farther away than his height and that squeezed against those who stood in safety. Even muffled by the rain and rubber earplugs, the shock wave from the gun hit eardrums with ice pick blows, leaving men who would be deafened for watches to come.

Recoil threw the cannon backward, only at a walking pace but seemingly beyond restraint. The wheels on their carriages had been remounted to deal with this; axles shifted up and forward from the center of gravity to make the wheels turn against the reaction force. The hawsers mooring the guns stretched but held, their string bass twangs a low-voiced counterpoint to the shattered snare drum crack of cannonry.

Six hundred man-heights away from the rolling guns, men faced a seemingly empty sky but were already hearing the steam calliope roar of incoming shells. Within those shells burning fingers of fuse groped eagerly toward yet untouched handfuls of powder.

Kalm hooked one end of a carrying strap to his belt, another end to the trigger guard on the musket, then slung it over his shoulder, stock up so it could be seized and fired in one movement. A twist of tree root had emerged from the gully wall just overhead, and a brick-sized rock was embedded in the clay to his left—step on the rock, grab the root, dig a foothold . . .

Firefly flames appeared in the air, two, three, then four and five, vanishing almost before afterimages could be formed.

*Ka-blam! Ka-BLAM! Ka-Ka-BLAM-BLAMM!*

The world rocked. Kalm teetered on one foot, off balance. *Gods slamming doors*, he thought insanely. Then his hand fastened on the root, and he was once more secure.

*Gods slamming doors on Algherans.*

Fifty paces apart, thumb weights of glass hailstormed the protesting earth, tearing air aside in their haste to reach firmer flesh. Men died with insufficient time to scream, slain by

objects whose passage they would never hear. Only then came
the tearing sheet-metal scream of shrapnel, joining the mon-
strous splatters of outraged earth, the fountain splashes of falling debris, and the giant's flung pillow of shock. *Ka-BLAM!*

A voice could be heard at last, a pure soprano cry so high
and evenly pitched that it carried no suspicion of agony, no
contamination by merely human tones—an angel's exaltation.

Behind, beyond the lip of the hill, amid still settling
smoke, men readied another blow, spongers feverishly swab-
bing out the cannon barrels while artificers screwed new percussion caps into place and carefully deliberate master
gunners checked firing angles and wheel alignments. Runners
were drawing near, carrying sacks of powder from dispersed
caches and scribbled notes from observers on the front of the
hill. Near the bottom of the hill, forty men crouched on horseback, cantering down the ramp to the bridge that led to the
Algheran camp, too watchful and too fearful to observe the
murderous sky.

"Go!" Kalm screamed. "Let's go!" Unthinkingly, he pulled
on the root and scrambled for footing, seemingly raised skyward by emotions he could not identify. Others matched his
shouts, bumped against him as they swarmed over the lip of
the gully, and ran slipping and stumbling up the slope of the
hill toward the Algherans.

"Go!"

"Go!"

"Loprit!"

His men.

"Loprit! Midpassage!" Kalm ran blindly, his face awash in
rain and tears.

Cold rain continued to fall. The rills that flooded the autumn grass knew nothing of slaughter, the greedily swelling
stream ignored human distractions. Only the passive earth had
been tainted with a bloody pox.

Pustules spurted amid human shrieks—weapon fire.

Above the rain, lightning flashed.

Kalm passed by a clump of weeds, a hollow depression
arched by grass, a jagged tree stump, a dark flower. A waist-
high bush lay ahead, too thinly leafed to conceal danger. He
dodged a fallen tree trunk and skidded around a knee-high
rock. It was not yet time to fear.

When he reached the bush, he promised himself. He could

be afraid when he reached the bush, where it would be safe.

He heard shouts from higher up the slope, and thunder above. Kalm bounced off a tree trunk looking backward, then scrambled to his feet without noticing pain from the impact.

Invisible men stumbled on wet grass and splashed through puddles. Footsteps sounded beside him, then passed by. The gasps of exhaustion he heard came from his own throat. Commands and responses were being shouted in Speech.

"Stick with me!" He yanked ris Jynnich's sleeve, tugging the stunned man forward.

"Loprit!" one of his men cried.

Twice as many men were before him as behind. It meant something, but what?

Feet slapped the ground. Water was thrown up from a puddle.

There were shouts. Constant yelling. Muskets barking. Rain pattering against leaves.

No, musket balls. A severed twig struck at him and fell to the ground. He saw a white face, red-tinged for a moment, immobile despite the rain that fell upon it—a body holding still upon the ground, in a uniform he did not recognize.

Kalm shouted wordlessly and pointed.

No excitement rose to meet his own. The face did not move.

He could feel fear soon. He remembered that.

What was fear? Kalm sank to his knees and aimed his musket. Recoil pressed his shoulder. Powder stung his cheek.

No. Lightning showed a stomach wound. His target had been dead already. There had been no need to shoot; there was no need to feel pride.

He stood slowly, his jaw distorted with embarrassment while thunder shook the skies.

But his actions had not been noticed. There was an instant left to him as he broke his musket open to think, time as he inserted new powder and bullet—carefully, carefully! don't shake loose primer—to plan his next action. Or there was—

Noise. Earth flying at his face. Celestial shrieks.

"Loprit!"

Yes, Loprit! It was easier to shout. Kalm rushed forward. He could fear later. Whatever it was.

* * *

Where was everyone? A couple of men in brown uniforms were ahead, big spaces between them. A screen of green uniforms pulsated toward the few Lopritians, then away.

Where were the other companies? Where in Cimon's name was everyone else?

Kalm somersaulted as fountains of dirt sprang into being before him, unaware that he was running, not hearing his own screams.

A fat man with his hand high looked up at the lightning, his back turned against the rain. Kalm took aim, pulled his trigger, and watched the man topple to his side into a puddle as if puppet strings had been released.

There were screams about him. Cries. A din he could not believe. How had he not noticed the noise until now?

There was an explosion; red mud gleamed on his knees till light faded. A whine filled his ears, and he turned as someone tugged at his leg—no, it was a bullet. His leg was uninjured, but the pants leg was torn, the fabric warm to the touch.

*Nicole's cloak.*

At his feet were flowers. They had looked violet-colored, bowing at him as wind and rain pushed at them, as if the battle were less important than Kalm's presence.

Reloading, he wiped mud from his boots, trampling the flowers without thought as he looked for targets.

Time went away. Fear went away.

Someone kneeling beside him, shouting. Kalm ignored him. A body lay to his left, an empty boot on his right. Grooves had been carved into the ground—bullets had done that.

A hand shook his shoulder, and he turned, raising his weapon.

In the glaring white light, he recognized a Lopritian.

"Could have killed you, boy." He shouted it again after the thunder had passed, then dropped the musket. The stranger was a lieutenant, ridiculously young and formal, as if to deny the layer of mud that covered his uniform. He was not one of Kalm's.

Lightning flashed. Kalm saw red at the lieutenant's cheek.

"Captain Ian Harniman's dead, sir."

He had to reload. Kalm pawed at his chest, finding no bullets, then grasped hungrily at the lieutenant's bandolier to extract ammunition. *Reach. Reload. Reach. Reload.*

Thunder boomed. "The captain's dead, sir! They killed him!"

Blood rilled down the young officer's chin and dropped onto the ground. Didn't he realize how silly that made him seem? Kalm pulled a trigger, not caring what he shot at, then swiped again at the lieutenant's bullets.

"He's dead! He fell on the ground and didn't get up and there's a hole at the side of his head and it's bloody and he won't get up. Sir!"

*Hysteria*, Kalm recognized. *How do I get him to go away?* He stopped firing, giving attention to the problem. "Lan Harniman's dead? Well—" *Tell him to be more careful.*

Shouting made the meaning penetrate. A man was dead— an officer. First Company was leaderless. It was necessary to cope with that. Faces appeared before him, then names.

*I'd give him ris Jynnich, if anyone knew where ris Jynnich was. He always thought he'd be wonderful in such a spot.*

*Doubt if anyone'd like to have ris Jynnich, though.*

*Derrauld. We could have used Derrauld.*

"Souvenklil!" he shouted at last. The man was a jokester, but intelligent. He had been a squad leader till lan Haarper had demoted him for some prank, and he was likely to regain that rank. Men did not dislike him. He would not make foolish errors. "Take the company and tell Souvenklil to take your platoon! And . . . Railstenn! Railstenn, if something happens to Souvenklil!"

"Dead!" The lieutenant was regaining his control. "Railstenn's dead!"

"Lehmell! Lehmell, then!"

"Lehmell!" The lieutenant repeated the name.

"Lehmell!" *When did I take the time to learn who these men were?* Kalm wondered.

But it was not necessary to answer that; it was not necessary to explain himself, he realized slowly. It was just part of the job.

Below the thunder, he looked for another target.

*Out of Midpassage with one hundred twenty men*, Kalm computed dispassionately, lying on his elbows and watching other men fight. *Ninety-nine at daybreak. Stragglers . . . Ninety-one left before we came down the hill . . .*

Five men's fears had left them cripple-cowering alongside the brook. Another five hugged ground not far away. He had seen eight men killed, eight seriously wounded, and six lightly wounded.

He had at most sixty men left to force back five hundred; it was probably more like forty.

Twenty of them might be shooting at the enemy. Ten might be able to advance under fire without being pushed. Two might realize the need.

Lan Haarper had asked too much.

Surrender, run, wait—all those actions had perils attached. He sighed and looked for cover.

The nearest piece of apparent safety was a tree stump, but it was a trap, with nowhere to go next and not enough protection. The man lying belly up with no jaw proved that.

*Th-wanggg!* A rope parted nearby, struck by a bullet. A hole had appeared in the side of the fallen tent. Kalm went to one knee and tried to judge the direction of fire from the tiny spurts of earth before him.

The rain had stopped. The immediate obstacle was the Algheran line to the right of the latrines. *Wait for the muzzle flash. Shoot, you bastards, so I can run. Shoot!*

Kalm ran toward the tree stump, then away to the safety of the edge of the clearing.

The body lying beside the stump jerked behind him, then settled into another position as if asleep. It had been in a dark-colored uniform—green.

He had escaped one danger. Kalm stood close to the tree, hands at his side, breathing heavily. Mud was splashed over all his uniform, he noted absently, and a semicircular groove showed at the very tip of his right boot. He had a stitch in his side.

What was the strange smell? It was sweet, almost familiar.

A whine sounded. A white line appeared at head height on a tree in front of him, like a good ax blaze. Ricochets thudded nearby. He looked about, seeing one man in brown at the edge of the clearing.

Kalm detoured, slapped a back with the butt of his musket, and gestured with it. The man followed.

*Lan Gunnally. The cobbler. 5th Platoon, third squad. Can't these people do anything for themselves?*

He found another recruit.

Then he found two dead men, poised with rifles against each other as if to slay a rival. Both wore brown.

Another recruit. Another.

A screen held up beyond the tree trunks: men, with faces pointed his way. Algherans. He grabbed jacket collars and forced men to lie down. The cobbler was the closest. Kalm crawled on his stomach till their heads almost touched.

"You're in charge," he whispered. "Stay low and keep firing at them. I'll get more. Understand?"

He slapped the man's shoulder before an answer came, then crawled away backward till he could see no Algheran faces.

Eventually one shot was fired. Then another. Kalm dropped to the ground, but the return fire was badly aimed. None of it came near him.

*More men, more men. I can't attack with only five.*

He slipped along the edge of the clearing, patting at men and pushing the ones who responded to the left.

A foot stopped with a jar as he stepped through a puddle. His toes hit an obstruction: a stick with a bent twig lashed at its ends. He spotted a space ahead with no bodies visible—a safe place, or a place where the Algherans had not been attacked. He pointed, then prodded men into moving that way.

*Pick up more men. Gunpowder, sweat, no, not those. Try and push them forward. What is that odor?* Had anyone else noticed it?

Lan Gunnally was still alive. So were three of the others he had left. He pushed men into position: five men in front to fix the Algherans' fire; five behind, staggered. They all carried muskets—maybe some would be able to shoot. If not . . . Fear-crazed, they still showed a puppy's eagerness to please, a puppy's obedience, as he shoved at them. He recognized few of them.

A *crmpff!* sounded ahead, birthing a violet-tinged wall of white. In the red and black afterimages the men beside him bore gray skulls in place of faces. "Go," he screamed, pounding at them with his arm, and they ran despite their blindness. Flames rose from the ground across the center of the camp, the earth itself red and crackling. In the midst of fire, a man turned, back arched, musket held high with one hand, his mouth open.

A tent glowed sullenly, then flashed into flame.

Seven of the Lopritians reached the latrines.

*       *       *

He had reached the corner of the Algheran camp, he understood—the southwest corner, which Second Company was to have hit.

Third Company had hit its target, pushed through, and moved a hundred man-heights across the camp. That meant that the bulk of the surviving Algherans were to the right . . . which meant that Second Company had mixed with his men or failed in their attack.

Then the Midpassage Battalion had not pulled the Algherans to the side as they were supposed to, and the Northern Valley men were facing more than Ian Haarper had anticipated.

Which meant . . .

*Failure.*

The sticky sweet odor behind him was the odor of decaying bodies. He had pushed men to attack from a graveyard.

The man was dead. Shaking did not attract his attention.

He crawled on hands and knees to the next body and slapped a shoulder. A face turned to him—half a face, missing the right jaw and cheek. Tiny chips of white were scattered over the ground. Below the insane eyes, a tongue yammered soundlessly, caked in blood and dirt.

In the background, fed by gunpowder stores, flame roared.

A lieutenant's shoulder patch gave him an identity, one of his. It was the 6th Platoon leader, the one who was not Ian Nhissun.

He slapped the man's back and pointed toward the latrines; then, when the lieutenant did not move, he grabbed his shoulder and hand and pulled to make him move.

Prodded, the lieutenant slithered forward on the wet ground, snakelike.

An Algheran crawled nearby on knees and one hand. The other hand was crimson, pressed against his side. Loops of brown and red material like beads waved from beneath his hand. Blindly, he collided with the lieutenant and collapsed against him. For a long moment they stared at each other, faces almost touching.

The Algheran's hand moved to a knife.

Kalm flopped on his belly behind a dead man and fired. The Algheran fell backward, the knife slicing through his intestines.

Kalm reloaded. The lieutenant looked back at him, eyes wide, pleading.

Kalm crawled away, slapping at other shoulders.

He tripped suddenly on an obstacle he had not seen and was brought down hard on his knees. He rose mechanically, pushing a hand toward the front line of the battle.

One hand only. His left leg could not be raised.

He had damaged it in the fall. He had bruised the knee or numbed his leg on some unseen rock on the ground. There had been pressure rather than pain. It was manageable; it would be manageable. He reached back to push mud aside, to touch the bruise that hampered him.

There was no bruise.

His boot sole was missing, and part of the heel. Liquid was welling up, soaking into his foot cover. When he touched it, the skin beneath his fingers was torn—ripped apart for half the depth of a finger's length.

He could see white under the flesh. Bone.

Blood flowed over his hand.

He had been wounded.

Suddenly the noise about him was twice as loud.

Wounded.

It was cold. No—he was cold. Very cold.

But he could not give in to that. Kalm fell to his knees but held back tears. Weeping men were the first to be ignored by their friends on the battlefield, the first to die. He could not afford to be seen crying.

There were so few Lopritians ahead of him now. So few behind.

Help. A bandage. He could do that.

Find a bandage.

He saw a tent, still standing. There might be cloth there.

Kalm stumbled on hands and feet toward the tent, falling without pain when his injured leg tangled with a length of rope. Somehow he held on to his musket.

He stared at the gun stupidly. It was empty; he had not fired it for a long time. What would he do with it now? Where was everyone?

There was the tent. Gasping, he crawled toward its entrance, dragging the useless musket and the useless leg.

\* \* \*

Movement stopped him. Something had moved inside the tent.

Cautiously, knowing he had to reach the tent, he edged closer, to the side.

A musket pointed at him. Mouth dry, he waited to die.

It did not fire. Slowly, fearfully, he crept sideways.

The musket barrel followed.

He saw a face and additional guns.

It was ris Jynnich—in tears.

*All alone. He hid there.*

Relieved, he crawled forward—and stopped, seeing the gun still pointed at him.

*Insane.* Ris Jynnich looked insane. *He'll kill me if I stay here.*

Blood filled his boot toes. He would die if he did not get inside. Helpless, he stared at the tent, cursing the Lopritian silently till ris Jynnich decided that he was no problem and retreated from the doorway.

He was all alone. Ris Jynnich had left him all alone—with a body before him. The uniform was dirty. It might have been from either side.

He would not die all alone. On his knees, grunting to himself, he pushed the body over, searching it for ammunition.

Nothing. He pointed his gun at a man aiming at him and uselessly pulled the trigger again and again.

All alone. He would die alone. He wept.

Hands pushed him forward. He fell on his face.

Legs were before him, green-clad, muddy. An Algheran. He could see the legs moving as the man reloaded his weapon.

*Please.* He tried to move. He tried to say the word aloud, tried to raise his arms to show he would surrender.

The man was not listening. There was pressure on Kalm's back—a foot.

*Please. No. Please. I've been hurt.*

*Please, Krennlen. Shoot him.*

*Please, soldier. Let me go. I won't hurt you if—*

*Please don't hurt me. Not any more. Please.*

*Please, Krenn. I'll give you Kylene again, I'll give you Sonol and Einulko and—I'll give you Tagin! Please!*

*I've so much to do. I shouldn't be here. Please. Please. Please.*

Kalm turned his face to the ground, sobbing as the Algheran shoved his weapon into the nape of his neck.

He heard noises. Grunts. Shouts. Other sounds.

And did not die.

Slowly he raised his head, wiping his eyes on his arm until he could see beyond the nearby ground.

A man on horseback was before him—a man dressed in brown swinging a rifle with one hand, felling men in green uniforms as though they were so many plants before a scythe.

It must be fantasy. A vision before dying. A symptom of delirium.

But at his side another man was dying, blood spilling from his side onto an Algheran musket—a loaded Algheran musket.

Kalm bit his lip and reached for the musket. The effort lasted for hours.

He held it. He pointed it. He found a target. He pulled the trigger.

A man in a green uniform fell down.

He pulled himself toward the man dying beside him.

*A knife. In his boot.* In his time, Algheran soldiers kept knives in their boots.

There was one there. Frantically, carelessly, he grabbed the knife and jabbed it at the dying man's throat. He did it over and over till contractions pulled the man's head back, making the hole in his throat gape like a second mouth.

His hands were wet with sweat, blood, and the dead man's tears. He breathed deeply, satisfied, enjoying the stink of death. *I'll kill you, ris Jynnich. When I can walk, I'll kill you.*

"Algheran!" His rescuer's shout went unheard, but was clear on his lips. Kalm could not make out other words.

A man with red hair wavered beside him. A big man with a rifle dripping blood like a sword. A hallucination. In the background, men rode by on horseback, arms swinging methodically as they advanced, forcing Algherans back to the flames.

*Surrendering. The Swordtroop was surrendering.*

*Lan Haarper had won. A hallucination.*

No. Lan Haarper had won.

Numbly he reached with a hand to pull his foot up and show his wound. The big man snarled, then knelt over him.

Then his boot was pulled free and the agony was real.

Kalm fell back, groaning as Ian Haarper probed the wound, his head turned to avoid watching.

He saw ris Jynnich instead, leaning from the tent, a musket in his hand, looking toward Kalm wildly, recognizing nothing.

*"Krennlen!"* he screamed. *"Shoot him now!"*

# CHAPTER TWENTY-SIX

*T*he red-haired man had been dangling a quarter of a watch when the officers assembled, and there was little capacity for pain left in him. Only the stubs of his arms remained in his awareness, seemingly fire-seared extensions of bruised shoulders. The hands he no longer felt were high above his head, palm to palm, lashed together as if to parody prayer. Now and then a muscle spasm shook his long body gently, like a stifled hiccough, so his torso swayed back and forth and the rope behind him swept in a lazy taillike arc. Blood dripped from his poorly bandaged leg. More had crusted on his cheek after seeping from puncture marks on his temple. Perhaps the tree limb he was hanging from bobbed.

His toes dangled at too great an angle. During the last part of the night, after they had cut through his Achilles tendons, kept away from the other men, understanding then that he would never walk again, never be allowed to walk again, he had cried, realizing his failure.

In daylight a gag had been forced between his jaws to preserve a soldierly decorum, and his gargoyle face was a frozen depiction of emotion only demons could know. After the gagging, one of the guards had kicked his groin as he knelt to make him tractable. He had thrown up as they refastened his wrists before him, but the gag was not removed and vomit had burned through his sinuses to spurt from his nostrils and streak his cheeks with slime. Disembodied from the thing he had become, he had forced his chokes to subside, then gasped down bit by vile bit some of what he had spewed forth.

Three of them had dragged him across the clearing that had been a battlefield and kicked him unconscious as the other captives watched. It had taken three men. Humiliation had not tamed him. But in the end pain had come to blot out terror and future, to cut shame and past away from him. Identity and time fled together, leaving him as ego without awareness poised above the unending present. He had neither cooperated nor resisted as they pulled him under the trees, fitted a leather band about his wrists, and wrapped that with a hanging loop of rope.

With rude mercy, an officer had slammed a boot into his groin, doubling him over. Unconsciousness had not come, but he had not noticed the moment his feet left the ground, or heard the grunts of the men tugging at the rope, or heeded the dragon jaws that chomped at his arms and torso as they swayed him upward, then snubbed an end of the line about the tree trunk.

A sour sick taste filled his perceptions, wiping away knowledge of the clot-filled mash that caked his distorted tongue and mouth, the metal and beetle tang of sweat, and the gut-wrenching blows at his belly that were attempts at speech. Fecal matter gushed forth at some point, a spout that stained the seat of his pants and a leg with thin, foul-smelling liquid that trickled across his toes and pitter-pattered brown upon the leaves below. The weight brought his loose pants down on one side, half baring his buttocks to cold air and the impersonal erotic caresses of dangling rope. Mucus blocked the vision in one half-opened eye and dimmed it in the other.

His feet drooped limply now, uncontrolled, only his toes rising parallel to the earth, and only then his truncated consciousness made him aware that others were watching. There was a justification for his existence, he felt, which he might communicate to them, but he could no longer remember it, and when he had been able to speak he had kept himself from talking. Sadly, he could not explain that much now, for the necessary words were no longer in his vocabulary and the few moans he created were muffled, unformed sounds.

He had spoken something to his wife, he thought. Had he had a wife? Had she been present? Had he said the final words she wished to hear, whatever they had been, or shared some part of his perceptions with her? He thought he had, after they hurt his head. Was he speaking to her now, or—

Illusion. He could not see a wife. Bubbles of memory, floating up, showed faint glimpses of women, but none were clear to him. Blond? Dark? A freckled face? He could not remember a wife. Had he ever known a woman at all? He could not remember.

Flame filled his mind, red and burning, without meaning, then vanished, and only gray remained. He felt no pain, had never felt pain, and there had never been any existence but this, never any other minds. Only gray.

Sensations he could not identify made his eyes open and twisted his weary head so he could see shapes without meaning. Green-uniformed man-beings had formed a line before him, stiff and erect upon their hind limbs, moving their upper bodies in meaningless unison. Other beings were arrayed behind them, in darker garb, frozen in unnaturally even lines. A great weight was fastened to his ankles, holding him still.

Some sense of recognition tugged at him, a prodding familiarity that could not be put into words.

Reflex brought his head to the side in response to a sudden sound. He did not notice the flickers of red that stabbed at him, the thunderclaps that broke the world asunder, the bludgeons that tore through his flesh, the frenzied spasms that marionette-danced his legs free from grasping hands and yanked his arms from shoulder sockets, the pressure pulse that brought him erect and spurted dampness on his loins.

Ecstasy filled him, too intense for thought or image. It lasted for all of eternity.

**Dieytl**

# CHAPTER TWENTY-SEVEN

"*S*ir," he said nervously when he entered the wagon. "Sir." And though he was not eager to speak, it did not seem important that he had interrupted the Hand of the Queen.

"What is it, Dieytl?" Rahmmend Wolf-Twin asked, looking up from papers. He saw ris Clendannan and Gertynne ris Vandeign staring at him from beside the map table and ris Daimgewln looking at him over the Hand's shoulder.

He swallowed, knowing death was near, knowing that Kylene watched.

"The Midpassage Battalion. Lan Haarper's regiment. I—" He could not explain how he had learned it.

But he was without choice.

"Lan Haarper fought the Algherans. Last night, at Killguide Pass." He swallowed, seeing ris Andervyll turning.

"What happened?" ris Daimgewln asked, and Dieytl felt surprise, expecting ris Vandeign to have spoken first.

"They lost, sir."

"Teep," ris Andervyll snarled, "this is *not* allowed. By the terms of the Second Compact—"

"You'll hear him out," ris Clendannan snapped. "Terrault, if you grab a cheap excuse for an execution to justify another Cimon-taken delay, I'll quit on you and go back to F'a Loprit. The war's as good as lost already, and *by the gods, man!* if I have to I'm going to tell Molly myself who lost it for her."

"If Cornoval had—" The Hand blanched.

Ris Vandeign slapped the table with a pointing stick, making the miniature mountains and lakes shake. It turned attention to him. "Let's hear the Teep. What happened?"

"Lan Haarper attacked—"

"The tra'Dicovys." Ris Clendannan had understood he needed a name. "At Killguide Pass. The Algherans had a division in that area, if Cornoval's reports mean anything."

"Thank you, sir. He beat them."

"You said—"

"I thought—"

Dieytl stared at the nobles till they were silent, till they all had become ordinary men. "He beat them, and one of his men shot him. A—a traitor. The Algherans won after that."

"Cimon!" It might have been ris Daimgewln.

"They're prisoners." It was almost the end of the account. "The Algherans are still holding them. They haven't moved—" He swallowed, stopped by ris Vandeign, and touched the map. "That's where they are, sir. If—"

"You want them rescued?" ris Vandeign asked.

"If it's possible. Sir." It was nearly a whisper.

"Out of the question!" ris Andervyll shouted. "This is absolutely forbidden! This Teep is—"

"Shut—up—ris—Andervyll." Gertynne's voice was bitter. "How is Merryn, Teep?"

"Lord Vandeign." Dieytl swallowed sourness. "The river —he is dead."

"Did he drown?"

*How had he known?* Mutely, Dieytl shook his head in affirmation.

"It was his worst fear." Ris Vandeign turned and stared at the Hand. "It was his worst fear, Terrault. What is yours?"

"I'm sorry." The Hand gestured meaninglessly.

"Your worst fear. I believe that." Ris Vandeign turned away, and without mind-seeing Dieytl understood that he had watched all authority leave the Hand of the Queen. "They captured the Ironwearer?"

Terrified of what he saw in the man's mind suddenly, Dieytl stared at Merryn's brother, understanding that the other men in the room shared his realization.

"A long day's march, except by lan Haarper's standard."

Ris Vandeign traced a finger across the map, musing. "If we sent a regiment, would it be enough? Would it get there in time?"

Dieytl wanted to flee, but Wolf-Twin had moved toward the door. The squat Ironwearer's gaze kept him in place like a fly knowing himself watched by a toad.

"Teep?" ris Vandeign asked.

He stammered.

"Teep." And that was not a question.

"Yes. Yes, sir."

"Yes?" Ris Vandeign crooked an eyebrow. "Yes, what, Teep?"

In his mind, he asked, *Who will support me?*

And now it was the end, now there was no escape by equivocation, now he had violated the Second Compact. Despairing, he stared at Terrault ris Andervyll, watching the man rise from the table and step toward the wagon door.

"Ironwearer ris Clendannan will support you, Lord Vandeign. Ironwearer Wolf-Twin will support you. Lord Daimgewln will support you for a price—not a large one—and he'll switch back if you start to lose."

"Ah." Gertynne spoke softly, glancing at ris Daimgewln. "Ah, yes. And Lord Andervyll?"

Andervyll ran, colliding with Wolf-Twin.

Pain filled ris Clendannan's face and mind.

"Lord Andervyll, Teep?" Gertynne appeared not to notice what had happened in the doorway as the Hand of the Queen fell into unconsciousness with Wolf-Twin's hands upon him.

Evasion was not possible. He wondered briefly if it ever had been. "You're going to kill him, Your Majesty."

"I believe so." Gertynne turned to ris Clendannan. "Take your regiment to Killguide Pass. Get those men free and fall back. It's too late to do anything for Cornoval."

The elderly Ironwearer touched his collar. "You'll accept my allegiance without these?"

"I think you should keep them," Gertynne said calmly.

"No, I don't." Ris Clendannan dropped the insignia on the floor. "My regiment will move in a quarter watch, King Gertynne."

At the door, he stared at Dieytl. The telepath stared back, then looked about the room, facing the men who had just condemned him to die also, knowing that they knew what they had done.

Knowing that, he struck them with his final blow.

"The Algherans killed Ian Haarper."

# Part 4: Midpassage: The Service of Another's Country

Dieytl

# CHAPTER TWENTY-EIGHT

"*H*old it there, Kalm." Unobtrusively, Dieytl brought his musket to bear on the walking man. The action was unfamiliar, just as the darkened inn had become unfamiliar, but it was somehow appropriate, just as the orchard and buildings about him had seemed appropriate when he lived here.

It was all different now.

Midpassage was almost deserted, its residents having fled to the countryside and cities farther north. Not even ghosts seemed left in the darkened, suddenly old buildings.

Overhead, a half moon passed reluctantly through dark purple clouds. Stars glittered. The sky of another world, Dieytl felt, a scene he could see but never grasp—like an ordinary man in a room of nobles.

It felt as if there were watchers up there, judging but unable to change what happened. He knew that sensation also.

In the coach beside him, a man moaned.

Kalm turned awkwardly, the box on his left foot somehow diminishing all other characteristics. His face was bright in the moonlight. "Isn't this just a rest stop, Captain?" the ex-Algheran asked lightly. "Before we convalesce in F'a Loprit? I was just getting exercise." He seemed amused, but his head trembled as he inspected the empty houses on the hillsides.

Spoken words. They meant nothing. Dieytl answered the

question that lay beneath what Normals heard. *Kylene wants you alive, if possible.* "They'll be changing horses."

The words held overtones and asked for inferences. No Teep's thought carried a single message, and he could see that Kalm ha'Nyjuc had understood all of them. With the officer in charge of the ambulances looking away from him, he was free to raise the musket till it pointed at the man's midriff. *Try and create trouble, Kalm. I've never trusted you or liked you, any more than you trusted or liked us. I'd be just as happy if you caused her trouble so I could—*

He had never been able to afford friends, especially among the people who dealt with him. Yet many of the Midpassage men, equating money and trust, had thought he was a friend. They were customers. He had lost only customers. But he had been as used to them as they to him. It would be hard to replace those relationships, hard to forget them. *Try to run from me, Algheran.*

*I'm not an Algheran.* It was a thought that Kalm repeated now every time he was called an Algheran.

South of the town, the sky was pink for a moment. Kalm's eyes flickered, covering calculations that Dieytl no longer troubled with. In the flash, he saw soldiers leading horses down the hills from Merryn ris Vandeign's barns.

*Algheran, Kalm. Lan Haarper called you that.* That was a triumph of the dead over the living, he knew. In lan Haarper's memory, he tormented his tormentor.

He hadn't really trusted the Normal, either, not the way one trusted friends among Teeps, particularly when his secret thoughts had been so shielded, but looking back now, he had liked the man's attitude, and maybe the man himself, more than he did Kalm ha'Nyjuc's.

*Lan Haarper's dead.* That was the Algheran's response to every mention of the man. *Things have changed. Let me go. Cooperate with me. I could make you rich, let you find pleasures* . . . The thought was mechanical. Kalm continued to make the offer long after both of them understood that Dieytl would not accept it.

Grumbles swept over the horizon, like low-pitched thunder, then more sounds of some distant collision. Artillery. The armies were less than a day's march distant.

*You're stalling.* Dieytl wiggled the musket, restoring Kalm's attention to him, and increased the tension on the trigger. He would kill the man, then explain that Kalm had gone berserk hearing the barrage.

*The drivers will stop us. They'll say we're deserting.*

*No one cares now, Kalm. Get your pack; stop telling lies.*

*It's too heavy. I've got a Cimon-taken wound and—*

*He can crawl if he must.* Kylene's thought intruded.

Dieytl repeated it aloud for Kalm. *Don't make her madder, Algheran.*

*I'm not an Algheran.*

*Don't make her mad.*

*She'll let me go. You'll see.* Despite the brave words, Kalm obeyed, then moved slowly toward the road leading up the hill.

Dieytl followed. No one noticed.

In the distance, the Algheran artillery barrage continued. The remnants of what had been the Strength-through-Loyalty Brigade continued their retreat.


"Wandisha's dead," Kylene said. Those were her first words after she had closed the front door and led them into the big living room. She head a weapon in her hands, too small to be a true gun but large enough for Kalm to show intimidation. Feeling relief, Dieytl left his musket in the antechamber.

The living room was dark, the curtains drawn, pairs of candles on the fireplace mantel providing the only light. Foolishly, Dieytl thought of bloodstains on the unfinished walls and of bodies lying in piles in lan Haarper's central garden.

"When?" Like Kylene, Dieytl used words, preferring the unemotional sounds just then to mind-seeing.

"Six days ago. I told her about him. The next morning one of the soldiers found her in the pasture in a watering trough."

Kalm smiled. No, it was a twitch that left his face half-frozen for them to see. He felt— Dieytl did not want to see what Kalm ha'Nyjuc was feeling.

Wandisha was dead.

"Cimon." The walls of lan Haarper's house seemed close to collapsing on them, though he knew that was not true. "Didn't you see it coming? Couldn't you have stopped her?"

"*. . . Any man's death diminishes me . . .*" Lan Haarper had said that once, drinking late at the inn, in his first year as a prospector for Merryn. As they came back to Dieytl's memory, along with lan Haarper's face and voice, for an instant he thought he saw Wandisha as lan Haarper had seen her—which was another view into lan Haarper's hidden soul.

He was sorry then that Wandisha was dead, sorry for the woman herself rather than for the disliked ally in the unspoken war between Teep and Normal.

"I couldn't stand the bitch," Kylene said, cutting through his sentimentality without pity. "Get him in here." With her chin, she indicated the door to the front living room, one that Dieytl had never seen open during any of his visits.

"Kalm?" He reached the man's pack. The ex-Algheran did not meet his eyes.

"Tie him up."

Dieytl saw rope on the desk, a pair of chairs, and shelves. "Is it necessary?"

"I'm not taking chances. Tie him up." Kylene moved to keep the corner of the desk between Kalm and herself. The weapon in her hands never wavered.

Fortunately, Kalm did not create trouble. His mind seemed to be far distant, as if he were an adolescent Teep just learning to use his powers, leaving his body untenanted. For a moment Dieytl was afraid the ex-Algheran had taken just that escape, but he was reassured when he checked.

Kalm stared passively at Ian Haarper's shelves. *Books. So many books.* Dieytl could not understand his interest.

"How bad is that foot?" With Kalm tied, Kylene could gesture with her weapon.

"It's a flesh wound. More than a scratch, but—" Dieytl imitated one of Ian Haarper's shrugs for Kylene. "Not as bad as he convinced the doctors it was. It'll heal; he'll walk without that box in a couple of year tenths. He just wasn't eager to see more combat after—"

*After he did what he came here for,* Kylene said silently.

"Well." Dieytl was still not clear what Kalm had been trying to do—or what Ian Haarper and Kylene had been doing.

"Ian Haarper wanted to defeat Mlart." It was the first thing Kalm had said since entering the house. "I would have let him alone, if . . ." He sighed wearily. "I was afraid he would."

"You were a traitor," Dieytl said slowly as the sense of Kalm's words penetrated. "You were the one who—"

"No! It was Krenn. Ris Jynnich shot Ian Haarper! He was afraid Ian Haarper would kill him, because—" Kalm stopped suddenly, sourly. "It was your fault, too, lin Haarper."

Kylene hit him. Dieytl thought it was a slap till he saw metal gleaming in the hand she had swung. Kalm's head rocked with the blow. Blood dripped from a line on his cheek.

"It's all right, Dieytl," she said, breathing heavily when he got between them. "I won't hit him again. He had that one coming, but I'm not going to mark him any more."

"All right." She meant it. He let her hands down.

"What happened to ris Jynnich?" She had seen something of Dietyl's thoughts before he raised his shield.

"He died." Dieytl sighed. "When ris Clendannan liberated your husband's men from the Algherans, after they cut your husband down, he tried to find out what had happened. Kalm told him how ris Jynnich shot Timmial. And I backed him up." He swallowed. Was it for that reason that Gertynne had sent him along with ris Clendannan? To justify another killing?

."They killed him." Kylene was unconcerned.

*Ris Clendannan got two volunteers to take ris Jynnich back to Gertynne for judgment. Styllin—one of Pitar Styllin's men, and an artillery captain. They tied his hands to their stirrups between their horses and left at a full gallop.*

*Ris Clendannan's idea. Wolf-Twin would have given him a cleaner death. But ris Clendannan was taking advantage of not being an Ironwearer when he did that.*

"Normals. Who cares?"

*His left arm was pulled off before they were out of sight. He screamed, Kylene. He knew he was being killed.*

"So did Tayem."

And that had no answer. Dieytl swallowed, remembering the events he had lived through.

Kylene upended Kalm's pack, spilling clothing and other things on Ian Haarper's desk. "Dieytl, that package you were given, the little black one—yes, that one—you still have it, don't you? Go get it."

The box was in his own pack. He had forgotten it till now, knowing that he was to give it to Ian Haarper. He had not thought to give it to the dead man's wife. Nervously, he obeyed, trying to forget the fears that remained in him.

"You've lost some weight, Kalm. You could almost be handsome." The man flinched as she reached for him, but she did no more than draw a finger across his cheek, brushing flecks of dried blood away. She did not let go of the gun.

At her elbow was a complicated box, open, with knobs and different colored dials protruding. Dieytl thought it had come from Kalm's pack, but there had been a cover on it then.

"Thank you, Kylene. You could almost be kind." The Algheran's voice was half-serious, half-ironic. "Can you untie me?"

They stared at each other, half smiling. Dieytl dropped the little black box by Kylene's hand and retreated.

For a while he remained in the living room, listening to spoken words, his mind shield raised. Lan Haarper, his wife, Kalm ha'Nyjuc, even Wandisha—their lives had had complications his had never felt and had been intertwined as his had never been. Only lin Haarper and the Algheran remained now, and their behavior told him that they were settling the terms of whatever relationship they had had, or could have had.

He did not think he would understand what they had to say to each other anyhow. He could give them some privacy.

A curtain billowed, revealing that one of the glass doors to lan Haarper's strange *atrium* was open. Half smiling himself, he went out to enjoy for the last time the peace of his friend's garden.

"She's gone," he said when Kalm came through the curtains. It was still dark then, but birds could be heard.

The armies were rousing also.

Ris Clendannan would not make a stand in Midpassage, he knew. The Strength-through-Loyalty Brigade—or whatever King Gertynne had renamed it—and the men who had served with lan Haarper would retreat again till the old Ironwearer had reached the safety of Northfaring.

In Merryn ris Vandeign's barns, the men guarding the horses were rising, finishing their own preparations for leaving the town, following not the orders that had never reached them but some strange soldier's instinct that sometimes served Normals as well as their senses did the Teeps.

Mlart would follow, pressing them north. And then—

"Yes. She's gone." Kalm shook his head almost shyly. "You're thinking there will be a civil war."

Dieytl sighed, seeing the other man across the concrete table only as a silhouette. "We'll be torn up by it. Between Gertynne and Molminda and Mlart—I saw what Loprit did in the Necklace Lakes region a few years ago because those little tribes couldn't cooperate against us. Cimon help us when the slavers come."

"That's a made-up problem," Kalm said, and Dieytl heard again, for the last time, an echo of the confidence lan Haarper had often shown. "Either Mlart or Gertynne will be better for you people than Molminda and her relatives. Two chances out of three are not bad. Besides . . . the Algherans will have problems of their own, Dieytl."

There were no thoughts behind the words. Reflexively, Dieytl probed, striking the same vacuum he had always met when looking for lan Haarper's thoughts. As always, it was frightening.

"A Teepblind," Kalm said, guessing correctly why he had gasped. "It was a spare of lan Haarper's. She gave it to me so I could concentrate on—other things."

*What other things?*

"I'm sorry, you'll have to keep using words."

"What other things?"

"Political things." Kalm stared at him, his moonlit face showing more understanding of Dieytl than the Midpassage man had ever anticipated. "They scare you?"

"Yes." Dieytl remembered Gertynne ris Vandeign's face when he heard of his brother's death, the ambitions and intentions that had suddenly gelled and the actions he had taken using the murder-justifying excuse of Merryn's and lan Haarper's killings.

Suddenly the tranquillity of the garden evaporated. "Yes."

"Kylene said so." Kalm put his boxed-up foot on the bench beside him, staring intently.

Dieytl trembled, feeling captive.

"C'mon." Kalm snapped his fingers and led the way back to lan Haarper's private room.

A post in one corner of the room had been opened, showing a hollow. A gun was lying on the desk, not a musket but a rifle, even to Dieytl's inexperienced eye. It looked expensive, and as Kalm raised it, Dieytl knew that it was lan Haarper's property.

But lan Haarper was dead, and Kylene was gone—somewhere. Dieytl stared out the open window as if expecting to see the woman in the yard, but there were only bare-limbed trees and a distant view of the great road at the bottom of the hill. Bewilderment came to accompany his fear.

"Kylene tells me you told Gertynne he could mount his coup. 'You'll have ris Clendannan if you announce and lan Haarper's people, and ris Daimgelwn's if you pay him enough. Wolf-Twin will go with you if ris Clendannan does.'

You told him that." Negligently, Kalm lifted the rifle and broke it open.

Dieytl stared at him. *I shielded that. How did she know?*

*I had to do it, to save the rest of the Midpassage men. Ris Andervyll would have let them all die otherwise. The only person with a reason for saving them was Gertynne.*

But ingrained Teep honesty kept him from denying the truth. He shook his head and waited, hollow-stomached, to be killed.

Kalm chuckled. "No one knows but me and Gertynne, Dieytl. And Kylene, who isn't here and has ... special talents." He opened desk drawers, pulling out boxes of ammunition. "None of us will tell if you do one more thing for me."

"What are you going to do?" Something small and hard congealed in his stomach. He did not ask why. He knew already that neither Kalm nor Kylene would ever explain that to him.

"Never you mind me. You point a man out to me tomorrow, and I'll do the rest. It won't be long, just another couple of watches. Kylene says you'll get away and have a nice long life."

"What did she tell you?"

The Algheran stared at him. "I could do something useful or I could rot. She didn't care which."

The Algheran was happy, Dieytl realized with horror as he turned away.

As he mounted the Ironwearer's gun on a small stand and stared through the sights, Kalm ha'Nyjuc pursed his lips and blew air through them as Timmial lan Haarper had often done.

A man from another era might have caught an echo of the "Colonel Bogie March."

# CHAPTER TWENTY-NINE

*The coach arrived at last.*

Still sprawling at his table, Harper listened with faint interest, waiting for the tavern to empty. He dropped a two-mina coin beside the untouched glass on the table, watched it clatter until it stopped, then went slowly to the doorway.

Kylene was the first to appear at the door of the coach, her almond eyes squinting at the unaccustomed light. From this distance, she seemed both older than Harper remembered and younger.

He held back, waiting to be noticed. The people he had noticed earlier outside the tavern were not so reticent. "Molminda lin Chantiel," a spokesman began. "On behalf of the association of parents . . ."

Harper chortled. Kylene murmured a denial and scurried across the pavement to him as an enormously large woman pushed and pulled herself through the coach door.

"Tayem, aren't you going to notice me?"

*Getting squeezed here*, Harper noticed. He chuckled for an answer, then surrendered to Kylene's wishes and hugged her in return, rubbing his cheek on the top of her head. "Hasn't been that long, girl. Ummm, you smell nice."

"In the wordth of our gloriouth Thovereign Majethy, and my namethake, Queen Molminda the Third, mothe fortunate and honored, dethpite the mothe threnuouth circumthan-

395

theth—" A schoolmarmly elbow bent; the woman wiped her ample brow.

Harper grinned, looking down. "What are 'threnuouth circumthantheth,' kid? Putting up with you?"

"No." Kylene rubbed her cheek against him. "Lightning or something hit one of the stations just before we got to it. There was an explosion. A man was killed."

"Ugh!" The big man grimaced.

"Does that mean you appreciate me?"

He hugged her tightly. "Yeth, I apprethiathe you, little Myth Kylene. I really do."

"Good. I appreciate you, too."


Far away, alone, another Kylene wept.


Here ends Book Three of *The Destiny Makers*.
The tale will conclude in Book Four,
*The Last Reckoning*.

SOLDIER OF ANOTHER FORTUNE

## ABOUT THE AUTHOR

Mike Shupp is an aerospace engineer living in Los Angeles. This is his third novel.